"Gestating?"
Stacey stared at him.

He nodded.

"I appreciate your coming out in the middle of the night, Dr. Halliday, but my dog simply cannot be pregnant."

He tossed his stethoscope onto the counter. "If you'd like a second opinion, there's a veterinary clinic out by the interstate. You can stay the night at a place right off the square in town. I'll show you the way."

She tugged at her bottom lip, and he couldn't help but notice how full and rosy her mouth was. Despite all the warning signs she exhibited, she'd caught his interest.

At last, she said, "Thank you. But you've done enough. Just give me directions and I'm sure I can find the motel. You must want to get back to your family."

"My family?" Michael hadn't mentioned anything personal.

"The gas station attendant said how understanding your family was, but I'm sure your wife must miss you when you go out on calls in the middle of the night."

That fussy line had disappeared from her mouth. She seemed softer. Something clenched in Michael's gut. Slowly, he fixed his eyes on hers and said, "I don't have a wife."

Other Avon Contemporary Romances by
Hailey North

PILLOW TALK
PERFECT MATCH
DEAR LOVE DOCTOR

HAILEY NORTH

Tangled Up In Love

AVON BOOKS

An Imprint of HarperCollinsPublishers

This is a work of fiction. Names, characters, places, and incidents are products of the author's imagination or are used fictitiously and are not to be construed as real. Any resemblance to actual events, locales, organizations, or persons, living or dead, is entirely coincidental.

AVON BOOKS
An Imprint of HarperCollins*Publishers*
10 East 53rd Street
New York, New York 10022-5299

Copyright © 2002 by Nancy Wagner
ISBN: 0-380-82069-2
www.avonromance.com

First Avon Books paperback printing: June 2002

Avon Trademark Reg. U.S. Pat. Off. and in Other Countries, Marca Registrada, Hecho en U.S.A.
HarperCollins ® is a registered trademark of HarperCollins Publishers Inc.

Printed in the U.S.A.

10 9 8 7 6 5 4 3 2 1

This book is dedicated to Leonard Keith Wagner,
the best brother any sister ever had!

With special appreciation to Lori Schega, D.V.M.,
and Scott Abadie, D.V.M.,
and all the wonderful staff of
Abadie Veterinary Hospital
in Harahan, Louisiana.

And, of course, loving thanks go to Snickers,
Fresno, Pumpkin, Puff, Missy . . . what's that?
Why do the cats get named first?
Well, *c* comes before *d* . . .
Don't worry, Sugar, Max, Dodger Dog,
Spike, Abbie, and Lexie,
you all hold a most special place in my heart.

The world would be a much lonelier place
without animals to watch over us.

6/02

Chapter 1

"The man you need is Dr. Mike."

Stacey St. Cyr stared at the attendant of the all-night gas station, hoping this overgrown child of a man with his bulging blue eyes could provide the answer to her prayers.

He chose that moment to aim a shot of his chewing tobacco at the Pennzoil can tilting just to the right of Stacey's Ferragamo pumps.

She refused to blink. "Where can I find this Dr. Mike?"

"Yep." The man leaned back against a display of Red Man and crossed his arms. "Had me a cow once. For milk. Then she went dry and I thought I was gonna have me a whole lotta steaks!" The man went off on a run of laughter that ended with a hacking cough and another shot at the oil can.

Stacey glared at him, but her irritation was really intended for her best friend and business partner Donna Bell. Just wait till she got back to New Orleans! It was

Donna who'd insisted Stacey take a vacation in the backwoods of Arkansas when she ought to be home in New Orleans doing what she did best—running St. Cyr & Bell Advertising and Public Relations.

"Lucky for me, and the cow, too, now that you mention it," the man said, "that was right about the time Dr. Mike came to town."

"How nice," Stacey said. "Do you have his phone number?"

The man's only answer was a rhythmic massaging of his gums.

"I need a vet," Stacey said, "and I need him—or her—now." She tapped the toe of one pump on the concrete floor.

"Well, like I said, Dr. Mike's the man you need. He came out to my place, took one look at Bossy, and greased her teats with Vaseline. Next day, she was giving milk like nothing had happened!" He slapped the knee of his overall-covered legs and beamed.

"How nice," Stacey repeated. All she needed was some hick country vet working on True Blue. True was a purebred bearded collie and even though some dog show purists didn't countenance the breed, Stacey knew there was no smarter, sharper, loving dog than a bearded collie.

Normally True loved to go for a ride, seeming to delight in hanging her head out the window and tasting the wind. But on the long drive north from New Orleans, Stacey's beloved collie hadn't once lifted her head to look out the window. Then she'd started whimpering, and thirty minutes ago she'd thrown up in the front seat of the otherwise immaculate interior of Stacey's Lexus.

Only her concern for True could have possessed her to stop after midnight in Doolittle, Arkansas, population apparently next-to-nothing. The shiny clinic just off the interstate had appeared state-of-the-art, but Stacey hadn't spotted an after-hours emergency number. That had led her into town in search of aid. She'd found two places open; she chose Gas 'N Go over the country-western biker bar.

"The number," she said, reaching for the telephone on the counter.

The man turned toward a mirror decorated with fishing lures, yellowing news clips, and an array of business cards tucked into the edges of the frame. As he chewed and searched, Stacey caught sight of herself in the mirror.

Instinctively, she lowered her shoulders and straightened her spine. She smoothed a stray strand of her long dark brown hair back over her shoulder. Her mother had raised her to look her best no matter the circumstances. She couldn't do much for the slight shadows beginning to show under her eyes, but as the attendant pulled one of the cards from the mirror, Stacey reached into her purse, found her lipstick, and applied it.

"Looking good, there," the man said.

Stacey snapped her purse shut. She read the number on the card upside down, and closing her mind against the grime coating the old-fashioned telephone, she lifted the receiver and dialed. No point in running up her cell phone bill's roaming charges.

"Don't know how Dr. Mike does it," the man said. "If he didn't have such an understanding family, you'd be out of luck."

Stacey nodded. She was sorry to wrest any man out of a sound sleep, but as the daughter of two doctors, she knew medical professionals had this happen to them all the time.

The phone rang and rang and rang some more. Glancing out the window toward her car, where True lay huddled in the front seat, Stacey asked herself again why she'd taken a week's vacation.

Because you had no choice, she reminded herself.

"Hello," a sleepy and very husky male voice answered.

"I'm sorry to bother you," Stacey said, "but my dog is very ill and Mr.—uh"—she peered at the name embroidered over the attendant's shirt pocket—"Tim—"

"Tim's my brother," the attendant corrected. "I'm Billy."

"You're at Gas 'N Go?" The question came over the phone line, the man sounding slightly more awake.

"Yes, but how did—"

"Tell Billy to give you directions to my office. Or do you need me to come over there and get the dog?" Some of the huskiness had disappeared, but the man's voice was still soothingly deep and calming.

"Thanks. The directions will do," Stacey answered, impressed by the considerate question.

"Meet you in twenty minutes." Click.

Twenty minutes. Stacey normally waited longer than that for her hairstylist—with an appointment. "He said he'd meet me there."

Billy stared at her as if she'd said something pretty stupid. "Course he did. That's Dr. Mike. Just follow the road on into town. You can't miss his office. He's right smack on the square." This last bit was followed by a nod of approval.

She thanked him and raced to her car. True lifted her nose and whimpered. "Poor little one," Stacey said as she pulled onto the road. "Hang in there. We'll get you fixed up." Stacey hoped it was true, but, a city girl at heart, she hadn't much faith that a man who effected bovine cures with Vaseline would know what to do for her precious pup.

The attendant was right about one thing. Downtown Doolittle was easy to find. She drew up in front of a central square, site of a stately courthouse and no doubt during the day also home to a flock of pigeons and a gaggle of old men in overalls lounging on the picturesque benches dotting the lawn.

But all was deserted. At this hour of the night, no one but Stacey surveyed the scene. No other cars circled the square. Despite her anxiety over True and her discomfort at having her schedule interrupted, Stacey felt some of the serenity of the place seeping into her. Of course, had she not insisted on squeezing in that business meeting in Alexandria, she'd already be relaxing in Hot Springs.

She followed the street around to her right, checking the storefronts for the veterinary practice. A wooden boardwalk fronted all the shops, and from the low lights left on, Stacey identified the wares: handmade baskets, antiques, hand-forged iron pieces, wildflower designs, donuts. If only she had more time in her life, it was the kind of place she'd like to explore. But once True was tended to, she would be under way.

Stacey circled the square. Can't miss it, the attendant had said. On her second time around, she spotted the animal hospital, wedged between Harolene's Craft & Hobby and an antique shop. Two lights flickered on, illuminating the front door, and Stacey pulled into the angled parking that fronted the two-story building.

All the square's shops sported carved wooden signs. She made out the name, HALLIDAY ANIMAL HOSPITAL. Silly, but she'd been looking for DR. MIKE'S.

A man appeared in the doorway, framed by the lights. Stacey stroked her beardie's head, then got out of her car. The man crossed the broad, raised walkway that ran along the front of the shops, similar to the banquettes in New Orleans' Jackson Square.

He wore jeans and a T-shirt that wasn't quite tucked in. And cowboy boots. His hair could use a good trimming, or maybe it was just rumpled from his pillow. That flash of a thought warmed Stacey.

He didn't look like any of the vets she'd visited. Stacey hesitated even as he reached her side.

"Dr. Halliday," he said, his voice in person even deeper than over the phone. "Let's check the patient."

Stacey glanced down at the hand she'd automatically extended in greeting. Parking it in the pocket of her suit jacket, she said, "That's why I'm here."

He nodded and headed for the passenger side. "It's best if you open the door," he said, pointing as he snapped out what might be advice but Stacey read clearly as an order.

But of course he was right. True wouldn't go to any stranger without Stacey's consent. Annoyed with the man for being correct, Stacey turned her back on him, opened the door, and called to her dog. "Come on out, True Blue."

Her loyal and normally obedient dog hunkered down on the seat, her nose attached firmly to her front paws.

"Let me," the vet said, easing Stacey to the side.

She watched, partially irritated, but mainly impressed, as Dr. Halliday lowered his body gracefully until his head was level with that of her dog's. "Hi, girl," he murmured. "I heard you weren't feeling so good. Let's take a look at you and see if we can't get you patched up."

"Wuf!" For the first time since Stacey had been an hour out of New Orleans, True lifted her head and looked around. Then she let the veterinarian pick her up, all sixty-four pounds of her, and march toward the entrance of the animal hospital.

"Get the door, will you?" was all he said.

Stacey slammed her car door shut, hurried past the vet toward the door of the clinic, and jerked it open. Even if the man was abrupt—bordering on downright rude—he did have a way with True. And that, Stacey reminded herself, was all that mattered.

Still, she noticed how the fabric of his jeans outlined the well-honed lines of his thighs and hips. And he'd hoisted True as if she weighed no more than a cream puff. Strength, Stacey thought. And—

Whatever other attributes she might have listed in his favor fizzled as he commanded, "Wait here." And then he disappeared through a swinging door.

"Oh, no, you don't," Stacey said, following the pair of them before the door had completed one full swing back and forth. "That's my baby, and where she goes, I go."

Arms full of dog, the man shrugged.

He deposited True on an examination table in a small room whose walls were covered with pictures of dogs. Greyhounds, Labradors, poodles, you name it, their photos plastered the walls. Yet what held Stacey's attention was the way Dr. Halliday's T-shirt had come untucked from his jeans the rest of the way. He looked rumpled and sleepy and appealing in an oddly charming way.

"Does she have her shots?"

"Of course."

He looked at Stacey then, straight on, his brown eyes studying her in a way she didn't quite like. Or perhaps she liked it more than she should.

"She's not wearing her tags."

"I take them off in the car."

He grunted.

"Well, I don't like to wear heavy necklaces. Why should True?"

He shook his head slightly, his hands on the dog's abdomen, tracing a slow route up and down.

True whimpered slightly, then, as if to apologize, licked the vet's arm.

"I think she's eaten something that disagreed with her, but I can't imagine what." Stacey began to pace. She hated to sit still when things around her were uncertain. Action soothed her.

The man said nothing, simply continuing his examination.

"But I don't know what she could have gotten into. I feed her the best food, give her chew toys only when she's supervised." Pausing, Stacey reflected on the past several days. She actually hadn't been home much. But in the past year she'd spent so little time away from work. "My neighbor's daughter takes her for her daily walks."

"You don't?" He seemed mildly disapproving.

Stacey paused in front of a poster illuminating the life cycle of a heartworm. "I have a very busy schedule."

The man's gaze sharpened. Stacey felt him cataloguing her business suit, her pumps, her sensible blouse, her simple hairdo. For a moment, she found herself wishing she wore something softer, something sexy. But then, that just wasn't her style.

"I see," he said, turning his attention back to the dog.

"She's quite dependable. And reliable."

"She seems like a good-natured animal."

"I was referring to my dog walker," Stacey said.

He stretched his arms over his head and yawned mightily. The movement caused that darn shirt of his to expose an enticing view of a flat stomach and a tapering trail of dark hair. A shiver of curiosity to see more stole over Stacey. This man was a complete stranger to her, but perhaps that very fact freed her to feel desire—an emotion she'd denied herself ever since Robert had wrecked her carefully laid plans for life and love.

She reached out one hand and stroked True behind the right ear—her favorite spot. And all the while she was wondering what he looked like beneath the rest of his clothing.

He must have caught her staring. Flashing a look that she read as annoyance, he tugged at the short tail of his shirt and stuffed it into his jeans. Then a smile, the first real one she'd seen from him, warmed his face and lit his eyes. "My daughter Jessica wanted to help with the laundry this week. I'm afraid none of my shirts fit anymore."

Pride. Stacey heard it clear and strong in his voice.

Pausing just before settling his stethoscope at his ears, he grinned and said, "Next time we'll work on dryer heat settings."

"What a lucky child," Stacey murmured.

He shook his head and pointed to the earpieces of the scope. Stacey knew he hadn't been able to hear her words, but she'd said them more for her own benefit. If she had done that to either her mother's or her father's wardrobes as a child, she'd still be hearing about it. Of course, each would have blamed the other for not having taught her any better during her time with the joint-custodial parent. Stacey sighed. What a lucky child.

Down came the stethoscope. "Her age?"

"She turned one last month." Didn't a child imply a mother?

"I'll check her urine to start."

"Do you think she has an infection?" And didn't that imply this gorgeous though rather enigmatic man was married?

The vet looked at her, rather oddly, she thought, but simply turned and opened a neatly labeled cabinet, retrieved a plastic cup with a lid, and quickly retrieved a sample via gentle pressure on True's bladder.

"Useful technique," Stacey said. Oh, well, she'd only been indulging her fantasies.

"Yes, but it's only one test. I'm also looking for other things." He shifted True onto her side, and being the friendly dog that she was, True offered her belly for a rub. The doctor seemed to study her for a long moment and stroked her gently. Just watching the way his hands drifted across True's furry tummy started a quiver of sensation deep within Stacey.

"What brings you to Doolittle?" The vet had moved to a side counter and had his back half turned from Stacey. Next to him on the wall hung the one decoration not featuring dogs. A crystalline blue lake rimmed by wooded hillsides appeared on the photo. Beneath the appealing scene ran a banner, LAKE DOOLITTLE—YOUR RETIREMENT HAVEN.

"I'm on a driving trip," she said, still studying the calendar. Better that than the curve of his hips and butt. She had a thing for men's butts. Tight and firm and lean beneath worn jeans. She'd dated Robert for six years, handpicked him as the one man so like her there would be no way marriage between them could fail. They were both in advertising and public relations. They were both offspring of professionals. They were both New Orleanians. But now that she considered the issue honestly, a year after he'd left her for a twenty-year-old equestrian, Stacey realized she'd never liked Robert's derriere.

She should have trusted her instincts, not her carefully constructed rules.

"Driving anywhere in particular?" He'd turned around and now leaned against the counter, arms crossed over his chest.

True sat trustingly on the exam table, much more alert, apparently over the horrible discomfort that had led Stacey to Doolittle.

"Why do you ask?" She suddenly felt quite reluctant to explain she was on her way to a spa in Hot Springs—

all by herself, with only her dog for companionship. Donna had known she wouldn't go without True and had even made arrangements for a dogsitting kennel near the hotel. No, Stacy didn't want to explain that this vacation had been forced on her as a cure for her workaholic tendencies. Okay, maybe *tendencies* wasn't a strong enough word.

He tipped his head sideways, not quite a shrug but giving the impression that if she didn't want to tell him, he wasn't going to press. "You may want to board your dog if you plan to spend a lot of time in your car."

"She looks fine now," Stacey said. "What do you think was wrong with her?"

"Nothing a little time won't cure. If you'd mentioned she was gestating, I would have known immediately what was happening."

"Gestating?" Stacey stared at the man. "You're saying True is pregnant?"

He nodded. "One good look at her mammary glands gave me the answer." Then he seemed to realize her surprise. "You didn't know?"

"She can't be. I haven't mated her yet. She's a bearded collie from the top stable in the country. She has papers. I have commitments to the owners of her sire for her first pups!"

True looked over at her and woofed softly. For a crazy moment, Stacey thought her dog was smiling.

Dr. Halliday certainly was. As a matter of fact, he was laughing.

"This is not funny," Stacey said.

Michael Halliday stifled his rather unprofessional outburst and regarded the woman who'd roused him from the first good night of sleep he'd had in the two weeks since his daughter Kristen had broken her right arm during soccer practice.

The woman glared at him, her nose in the air, her posture as stiff as a general conducting troop inspection. And a pretty nose it was. Too bad the full lips beneath it weren't curving upward. He was willing to bet the woman had a pretty smile.

When her schedule allowed her to produce it. He frowned. No matter how deprived he might be of feminine companionship, there was no point in inviting attention from a woman too busy to walk her own dog.

Or too important. Oh, yeah, she had the executive look down to a T. The suit, the pumps, the leather bag with its outer pocket cradling a cell phone. He pictured her back in the city—because of course she was from a city—rushing from meeting to meeting. Managing portfolios? Arranging corporate buyouts? Another look at the suit and he had it pinned—another lawyer. Another bossy lawyer, too busy to walk her own dog, much the way his ex-wife had been far too occupied to be bothered with their daughters—or their marriage.

Michael no longer felt like laughing.

The woman was speaking. He forced his attention back to the job at hand. The dog was his patient. He had a responsibility to the animal, which meant it was his duty to inform and educate the owner.

"I said I think you're wrong."

"Excuse me?" Michael thought for sure he'd heard her incorrectly.

Her lips were set in a stubborn line, but even given

her expression, he couldn't help but notice how full and rosy her mouth was.

"I appreciate your coming out in the middle of the night, but True simply cannot be pregnant."

"Because it's not penciled in on your Day-Timer?"

"How do you know I use a Day-Timer?"

He tossed his stethoscope onto the back counter. "Lady, it's written all over you. If you'd like a second opinion, there's a clinic out by the interstate."

She tugged at her bottom lip, apparently weighing his statement, and possibly her own obstinate behavior. That was hopeful thinking on his part, Michael realized, but he wanted her, for whatever reason, not to be as stuck on herself and her view of the world as she appeared to be. He was the one who wanted a second opinion—of a stranger who'd wrested him from bed, then insulted him. Despite all the warning signs she exhibited, she'd caught his interest.

"Get a life," he muttered, mostly to himself.

She looked at him sharply. That made him smile as he realized she thought he'd been speaking to her.

"To get another consultation, I'd have to spend the night in town," she said slowly. "That other clinic was closed."

Michael leaned forward and stroked the collie's head, refraining from adding, *So was I.* The dog was calm now, all symptoms of distress vanished. She gazed at him, big brown eyes trusting and warm, and thumped her tail gently against the examination table. "She seems to like it here," he said. "It's unusual, but the pregnancy could have led to motion sickness. Just getting out of the car could have helped, but you're welcome to board her and let me observe her. You can stay at a place right off the square called the Schoolhouse Inn. I'll show you the way."

At last, she said, "Thank you. But you've done enough. Just give me directions and I'm sure I can find the motel. You must want to get back to your family."

"My family?" Michael hadn't mentioned anything personal.

"The gas station attendant said how understanding your family was, but I'm sure your wife must miss you when you go out on calls in the middle of the night."

That fussy line had disappeared from her mouth. She seemed softer, genuinely concerned for disrupting his life. And as she spoke, she was lightly rubbing one hand over True's belly.

Something clenched in Michael's gut. He swallowed hard, watching her gentle strokes, picturing her hands on his own body. Nuts. He had no business fantasizing over this woman. Too many lonely years in this godforsaken village of a town had finally gotten to him. Slowly, his eyes fixed on hers, he said, "I don't have a wife."

Chapter 2

"Oh," Stacey said, "I'm sorry."

He laughed, but without a smile. "Don't be."

So who was his family that was so understanding? Stacey studied the man lounging against the counter, arms gracefully crossed across his broad chest. The V of his T-shirt revealed glimpses of wiry chest hair. Dark brown hair, tousled from sleep, brown eyes bright despite the hour of the night—or rather morning.

Eyes that gleamed with a simmering spark that set Stacey to wondering just what lay beneath that appealing surface.

And just how can a gorgeous guy like you not have a wife? Are the women in Doolittle blind?

Not that any of this mattered to Stacey. She'd had her shot at marriage. Robert had possessed every quality she considered essential in order to guarantee a relationship that weathered all storms. After what she'd endured as a child, she'd taken her time, chosen carefully, and tested every possible potential problem before she'd agreed to marry Robert.

Robert—who'd jilted her after a year-long engagement for a woman as opposite Stacey as any God could have created.

She'd rather live her life on her own than risk facing that awful hurt all over again.

Alone.

But alone didn't mean she had to be lonely all the time.

True sighed and sank her nose farther down on her paws.

Stacey dragged her mind back to the moment. The doctor was watching her, a questioning, curious, almost empathetic look in his eyes. Before she could think of what to say to cover the silence, he said, "So what business brings you to Doolittle?"

"What makes you think I'm here working? Don't I seem like I'm on vacation?"

His brows lifted. "By business, I simply meant purpose," he said gently.

She blushed, embarrassed by her own sensitivity, which no doubt came from Donna's insistence that Stacey worked too much. Well, given that overreaction, perhaps Donna knew what she was talking about.

"I'm on vacation." She sounded stubborn. But who was she trying to convince? This man whom she'd just met—or herself?

Meanwhile, he'd joined her at the exam table where True lay. He was stroking the dog's head with long, sensitive fingers, the nails trim and neat. Surgeon's hands, just like her father's. Stacey touched the back of True's neck, careful to avoid contact with the vet, but unconsciously or not, her fingertips brushed his. The unexpected heat of his flesh startled her and she snatched her hand away, still staring at where their skin had made contact.

"Surely Doolittle wasn't your destination?" His voice carried a hint of irony.

Stacey forced her gaze away, fixing it on the calendar on the wall just over the vet's shoulder. LAKE DOOLITTLE— YOUR RETIREMENT HAVEN read the banner below a scenic mountain lake photograph. She'd seen a billboard just prior to turning off the interstate in search of a vet. Choice golf course lots still available, the sign had proclaimed.

In a flash, she made up her mind. "Actually, I'm on my way to Hot Springs, but along the way I'm researching retirement property."

He shot her an amused look. "You don't look ready to be settling down with the social security set."

"Oh, no, it's for . . . my parents." Wouldn't they laugh! Dr. Louis St. Cyr and Dr. Joanne St. Cyr would work until they collapsed.

He smiled then, and Stacey was ever so glad she'd told that whopper.

"You might check out Lake Doolittle while True is resting. I hear it's quite the place." He made a small face when he said it, though, and Stacey wondered why.

"But not your cup of tea?"

He shook his head. "Not that there's a lot to do in Doolittle, but at least you can walk out your front door and go somewhere that offers some variety. The library, the coffee shop, the bowling alley. Out there, it's your home, the golf course, or the clubhouse."

"Are you from here?" Stacey's curiosity got the better of her, and as long as he kept stroking True's head in that rhythmic fashion and talking in that low, deep, reassuring voice of his, her need for sleep seemed to be held far at bay.

"Nope," he said, and just as abruptly as he answered, he pushed back. "Time to get her in the kennel."

So much for talking all night. But Stacey nodded. The guy had gotten out of bed to rescue her dog. Of course he wanted to get back home.

Yet he hesitated. "You must be close to your parents," he said.

She nodded. As long as her mother and father weren't in the same room at the same time, that was true.

"That's nice," he said. "My parents taught us you can never have enough time with your family."

"Ah," Stacey said, because she didn't know what else to say.

"When are they joining you?"

"Joining me?" She stared, then quickly averted her gaze. The tile on the floor was a rather fascinating honeycomb pattern. And she had a clump of dog hair on her otherwise spotless pump, she noticed.

"Or are they just going to let you make their decision for them?"

That was when she should have retreated, said she was conducting only a scouting mission. Stacey didn't understand what got into her otherwise normally functioning, rather intelligent brain, but she heard her own voice say, "Oh, no, they'll be up later this week. Maybe not here," she added hastily, "but to whatever place looks the best."

He nodded and reached for True's collar. "Well, Lake Doolittle is the only retirement complex south of Hot Springs Village, so if you like it, you'd better hope they do."

She choked then, but quickly covered her reaction. But darn it, this man had made her say those things. Or was it simply the first whopper she'd told inevitably leading to the second? She stared at his hands, at the strong arms topped with a dusting of golden brown hair, and admitted that Stacey St. Cyr, businesswoman extraordinaire, was acting out of character. Her entire Day-Timer was booked, her appointments in Hot Springs neatly printed in place. Even the facial, mineral bath, and massage had been penciled in. Stacey left nothing to chance.

"So I guess you may be boarding True more than one day?"

"It looks that way," she said slowly, wondering whether she should bundle the collie into the car and make a getaway. But one look at True's trusting and now-calm eyes stopped her in her tracks. "Where's the kennel?"

"In the back. I'll take her," he said.

She could still change her mind. Or get some rest and leave first thing in the morning. Relieved by her escape plan, she said, "Yes, please."

His smile appeared briefly, then vanished. Had she imagined it? Then he nodded and said, "Sure, follow me."

True hopped from the table and followed amiably.

They moved into a hallway, past more chrome tables and tiled floors. Dim lights, one buzzing slightly, hovered overhead. From the back came the raspy barking of an unhappy dog, quickly followed by a canine chorus as the vet led Stacey and True into the boarding section of the hospital.

"I don't keep a lot of animals here," he said, "but any new one always seems to wake up the others."

That was for sure. True barked, adding to the volume, then stopped, her paws planted on the concrete floor. She looked for all the world like someone who'd formed a sit-in. Clearly she wasn't budging.

"True, come," Stacey said in her best dog obedience training voice.

The dog lowered her full body onto the floor, a low whimper coming from her throat.

"She seems intimidated," the vet said. "This happens sometimes." He moved ahead, opening the door of a large kennel, and moved about, filling the water and food container.

True held her own. Several of the dogs subsided and soon only one, a particularly determined chow, refused to calm itself. Stacey watched as Dr. Halliday approached the dog's kennel, speaking in a low, reassuring voice. Soon, that dog joined the others in a peaceable silence. That voice, Stacey realized with a start, was the same deep, calm tone he'd used with her on the phone.

A woman could grow quite fond of a voice like that, not to mention the curves of his butt.

"True, time to hop into bed," the vet said, again in that magical voice. This time her dog stood and Stacey followed with the lead held loosely in her hand. She let go as True bounded into the kennel. The vet unhooked the leash and, after patting the dog's head gently, locked her in.

True sniffed her way around the kennel, then settled down, her nose resting on the bars.

"Be good, baby," Stacey said, stroking her nose. She turned to find the doctor watching her, no longer curious or questioning, but she knew, in an instinctive way, that he enjoyed the view. Pleased, yet concerned about True, in a whisper she said, "I think she'll be okay, don't you?"

He nodded and motioned toward the door. They left the animals behind. In the brighter light coming from the examination room, the doctor appeared quite matter-of-fact. Stacey kicked herself for letting her imagination go wild. It helped in the public relations business, but she needed to remember, guys were guys. Michael Halliday was just a guy. And she was a woman who made her own way in the world.

"She'll be fine," he said. "Now let's get you to the Schoolhouse Inn so you can get some rest, too."

"I'm sure if you give me directions I can find it."

"I'm sure you could," he said, leading the way through the reception area toward the front door. "But I'd feel better knowing you're there safe and sound."

"You would?" Stacey warmed at his concern, a sentiment that somewhat ameliorated his bossiness.

He shrugged. "It's the responsible thing to do."

"Right." Nothing personal there. He'd probably do the same thing for a stray dog or cat.

He opened the front door, then switched off the light. Darkness filled the area that earlier had been a pool of light. Stacey stepped outside, breathing in the crisp night air. Hints of a flower she couldn't place drifted to her senses.

The doctor locked the front door, then joined her. He stood there, silent, watching the square.

"It's nice out here," Stacey said, whispering so as not to disturb the peace of the scene.

"Doolittle isn't such a bad place," he said, also softly.

Stacey wondered whether he was trying to convince himself of that fact.

"There was definitely more energy and intellectual stimulation when I lived in Boston, but there's always the Internet to turn to."

Stacey wondered whether he was trying to convince her or himself, when he continued, "For better or worse, everyone knows their neighbor. The courthouse is used more for records storage than criminal trials. My girls can ride their bikes down the street without me worrying about what might happen to them."

Stacey lifted her head, watching his face. When he mentioned his daughters, he smiled in a gentle, doting sort of way. Perhaps his children were his reason for being in Doolittle.

So where was their mother?

"Where's the inn?" She let her voice rise. She had no need to speculate on the doctor's personal life. Across the street, in the cluster of trees planted along the walk leading to the courthouse, a lone bird squawked.

He pointed to the right. "A few blocks. Why don't you follow me? I'm in the back. Watch for the pickup to come around." Without waiting, he moved toward her car and she did the same, thanking him as he opened her door for her. With no directions, she had no choice but wait and follow his truck. Either that or head back to the interstate to the cardboard motels that dotted the exit ramps.

The interior of her car smelled of True's lost battle with her queasiness. Stacey wrinkled her nose at the aroma. First thing tomorrow she'd have her car detailed. Out of habit, she began a mental to-do list but paused when she realized that after taking care of her auto and visiting True, there was nothing on her list.

Nothing she *had* to do.

Nothing to take her mind off a very good-looking, intelligent, gentle guy who had children but more than likely an ex-wife, based on the way he'd chased off her offer of sympathy. Surely a widower wouldn't have spoken as he had.

Stacey's own stomach rumbled at the thought of a divorced guy. Anyone who'd lived through the hell of her childhood would react the same, she thought. And then, as she realized her hands were clenched on the steering wheel, she made herself sit back and laugh at her own silliness. She was making up stories about a man who out of professional courtesy had come out in the night to aid her sick pet.

Too much imagination.

A soft beep of a horn disturbed her mental wanderings. Stacey started her car and backed from the parking space. "Good night, True," she said softly.

The doctor drove one of those he-man pickup trucks she'd seen in car commercials where the guys were always sweaty and out rousting cattle or digging holes for fence posts. It looked big enough to cart a bull around, and she smiled at the memory of the cow smeared with Vaseline by the good vet.

Well, he'd cured her, so maybe he was right about True.

That reminded her of the third item for her to-do list. Second opinion.

Funny how that had slipped her mind.

The truck braked and turned right, leaving the square behind. Within two blocks, houses replaced the commercial buildings. Two more blocks, and the truck slowed and pulled in front of a square clapboard building topped by a large bell. Shrubs and flower beds decorated the front lawn that rose slightly as it reached toward the steps leading to a broad porch and the double front doors.

Only one light shone in a front window. Otherwise, all was quiet here, too.

Michael watched her headlamps in his rearview mirror. It was the decent thing to do, to escort her to the hotel. He would have done the same for any woman, or man, for that matter, in the middle of the night in a strange town.

With Stacey St. Cyr, though, he knew he'd offered with mixed motives. Half of him hoped she'd slip off into the night; the other half wanted to make darn sure she didn't.

"You never should have let yourself get to this point of deprivation," he muttered as he parked and climbed out of his truck. When he was panting over a woman so much like his ex-wife, he definitely needed his head examined.

She'd stopped, too, and was already opening her trunk. He crossed over, knowing her things would be neatly arranged.

Sure enough. The trunk light glowed, revealing one small overnight case, a larger suitcase, and what looked like a laptop computer bag. A pair of running shoes were tucked into the side well.

"You take your computer on vacation?" Michael said, sounding a bit more harsh than he should. He'd wanted to ask about the shoes. He ran almost every day. Would she want to join him? Nah, she'd be too busy attending to the catch-up work she'd probably carted along on her trip.

She swung around. "Hey! I didn't hear you come up."

"Sorry," he said.

"I take my laptop everywhere," she said, rather primly and with the light of battle in her eyes.

"Sure, me, too," he said, producing a grin, despite the confirmation of his assumption. She was as sensitive about working too much as he was about his rescuing tendencies.

"You do not."

"Do, too."

Then she laughed and her whole face opened up. He laughed with her, then said, "Come on. Let's get you inside. What do you need to take?"

She pointed to the small case. "Just this, but I can—"

He reached for the overnight bag, cutting off her protest. She shut the trunk and fell into step beside him. Progress, Michael thought, amused and unaccountably pleased.

They strolled up the broad sidewalk. "This used to be where the children lined up after recess," he said.

"So it really was a school!"

"Doolittle's original."

"Did you . . ." Her voice trailed off, as if she'd answered her own question, which she probably had pieced together from his earlier reference to Boston.

His own grade school had nothing in common with this quaint shoe box. Boston Public was a world unto itself. He rang the night bell. Stacey was standing close enough to him that the sweet fragrance tinting the night air could be her perfume, or it might be the flowers the Schoolhouse Sisters planted everywhere they could dig or set a pot or planter.

"Will someone be awake?" she asked, glancing at her watch as they waited.

"You do that a lot, don't you?"

"Do what?"

"Check your watch."

She bristled. "Do not."

"Do, too."

"Hey—" and again she laughed.

He joined her just as the door opened, and that's how Sweet Martha, as most everyone called the coproprietress of the Schoolhouse Inn, found them.

"Good evening, Sweet Martha," Michael said, pleased it was she and not her sister Abbie, whose nickname Crabby was equally accurate, though not nearly as flattering.

"Goodness gracious, Dr. Mike, it's not evening. It's the middle of the night. But to you it may as well be noontime, the way you're always out and about." She paused for breath and peered at his companion, her bushy gray brows rising to meet the nightcap plopped atop her silvery locks. "And who's this? All dressed up, too!"

"I'm Stacey—"

"One of my clients," Michael said, cutting her off, realizing that would drive her crazy but secure her a room for the night in the Schoolhouse Inn.

Stacey shot him a look that said she could have handled the situation on her own. He smiled, knowing better.

"Oh, well, then," Martha said, opening the door wide and beckoning them inside. "But you can understand we don't let just anyone in. When the city closed our precious school and my sister and I decided to run the inn, we promised ourselves no matter how much someone wanted to pay, they had to be good people." She tugged at her floral wrapper. "After all, we have our own rooms upstairs. But one of Dr. Mike's people, well, of course."

"Of course," Stacey echoed.

"Now, what was that name again? We don't hear it too much around here." She frowned and the two hair curlers at the sides of her cheeks wiggled.

"Polly and Chuck's daughter is a Stacey," Michael said.

Stacey rolled her eyes and he flashed her a quick grin. She'd have to survive Sweet Martha's own brand of interrogation, if she didn't want to sleep at Motel 6.

Of course, she'd been planning to do just that.

And he hadn't let her go.

"Third Grade is open," Martha was saying as she led

them into the parlor. "It's a very cheery room. It's done in apple green and pink."

Stacey nodded and murmured, "Lovely."

Michael sensed from her low-key response she wanted nothing more than to sink into sleep.

The mantel clock chimed three times. No wonder! He shouldn't be feeling at all wide awake, but somehow from the moment this woman had entered his clinic all sleepiness had fled.

Along with most of his hard-earned common sense.

"Will you be with us long, dear?"

Stacey glanced from her pumps to her watch, then smiled. At last she glanced over toward him, somewhat shyly, he thought. "That depends on the doctor," she said.

Michael would have sworn his heart leapt in his chest. He grinned like a fool.

"You see, my dog is ill, and Dr. Halliday's the one who can say when she will be well enough to travel," she continued.

Splat! So much for his short-lived elation.

Sweet Martha nodded. "You just do whatever Dr. Mike says. He saved my own little Hemingway's life. Now scoot home with you, Dr. Mike," she said, "and let me show this young lady to Third Grade."

He knew when he'd been dismissed. "You may visit True anytime after nine," he said.

"Why, she won't be up and about by then," Martha said. "Though breakfast ends at ten and you wouldn't want to miss Abbie's biscuits."

"Thank you, Dr. Halliday," Stacey said, offering him her hand. "I appreciate your assistance tonight."

Michael grinned. Sweet Martha wasn't the only one present who knew how to convey "get lost now." But rather than let her get away with the brisk handshake he knew she'd intended, he folded Stacey's hand into his much larger one, holding it longer than necessary. The look she gave him then was one of pure challenge.

"Until tomorrow," he said, releasing her hand.

"I'm sure I won't need to trouble you again," she responded.

"Oh, Dr. Mike likes to be helpful," Martha insisted. "Life hasn't been the same since he's come to Doolittle."

Michael smiled at the Schoolhouse Sister and at Stacey, who seemed to be having difficulty finding the words she was seeking. He winked at her, then turned and left. Behind him, he heard Stacey say to Sweet Martha, "I'm sure Doolittle doesn't know what hit it."

Chapter 3

Sunlight streamed in, something she recognized even though Stacey had her eyes closed. Birds sang. Awakening slowly, Stacey moved her feet around. Funny, but she didn't make contact with True, who, despite it not being the best of habits, always slept at the foot of Stacey's bed.

She opened her eyes. Ruffles, eyelet, green and pink floral chintz met her gaze. Gone was the serenity of her pale yellow room, a color she'd chosen because it brought gentle sunshine inside her home.

And then she remembered.

She was back in Third Grade.

Sitting up against the bed pillows, Stacey smiled. She hadn't dreamed Miss Martha.

Which meant she hadn't imagined Dr. Michael Halliday into living, breathing, and, darn it—appealing though awfully take-charge, three-dimensional existence.

Downright bossy. He'd been most high-handed in

arranging her accommodations. Not that Stacey could complain about the results. Now that her eyes had adjusted to the light, she welcomed the sunshine dappling the carpet and beckoning her to rise and check the view from the windows.

But the bed was far too comfortable to leave. She snuggled under the apple-green comforter. As a rule, Stacey never slept well in strange beds. Had she chosen a roadside motel, the drone of the traffic would have had her tossing and turning all night.

Yet here she'd slept like a baby. Or perhaps she should say like a third-grader.

Stacey smiled. Perhaps the domineering doctor knew a thing or two.

Even if he had insisted her dog was pregnant. Why, True was little more than an overgrown puppy, too young to be bearing a litter of her own.

"Especially with some mutt for a father," she said, frowning. She'd been unreasonable to protest the vet's diagnosis. Her frustration and annoyance were more properly directed at the teenager whose job it was to walk True every afternoon. What she should do was get the girl on the phone and ask her just how closely she'd monitored True on her daily jaunts around the neighborhood.

Tap-tap-tap-a-tap-a-tappa!

Stacey jumped and almost dropped her purse. She'd been reaching for it to use her cell phone to dial her dog walker.

Again, the brisk, rather musical knock sounded at the door of her room.

"Yes?" Stacey called. "Who is it?"

"Mrs. Clark," sang a voice.

She certainly didn't know a Mrs. Clark. "Of course you don't," Stacey muttered to herself. "You don't know anyone in this town and no one knows you."

Except for the doctor.

"Take your time, dear," Mrs. Clark called, her voice lilting on the endearment. "I'll enjoy a cup of coffee with Sweet Martha."

Stacey threw the covers back, grabbed the silky robe she'd packed, and stalked to the door. Her nose next to the jamb, she said through the wood, "I don't believe I know you."

"No problem, dear," she said. "Dr. Mike sent me."

Stacey yanked open the door. One hand on her hip, the other on the knob, she surveyed the woman. Her brain registered "round." Round face, with rosy red cheeks and a dimple in her chin, her soft brown hair swept into a bun. She wore a bright blue suit and tennis shoes with white socks. Stacey blinked. The woman couldn't be taller than five feet, because even barefoot, Stacey had to look down to stare. At last, she said, "And just why did Dr. Mike send you?"

The woman produced a business card. "Mrs. Clark, real estate agent extraordinaire, at your service, Ms. St. Cyr."

Stacey studied the card. "Thank you, but I really don't need an agent."

Mrs. Clark nodded. "Dr. Mike said you would say that. Now, why don't you pop into something that won't leave you catching cold, and I'll be downstairs and ready to roll when you are?" She repeated her nod, patted Stacey on the shoulder, and whisked off in the direction of the front parlor.

Stacey slammed the door shut.

"Dr. Mike said you would say that," she mimicked. Of all the meddling men she'd ever had the displeasure to meet, Dr. Michael Halliday took the cake.

She tore off her robe and reached for her suitcase. "Bossy! Domineering! Interfering!" She ran out of adjectives just as she remembered she had to step across the hall to the bathroom shared with First Grade.

Stacey dragged the robe back on, tightening the sash with an emphatic tug. If there was one constant in her life these days, it was that she was the leader, the one who took charge. Donna was a terrific partner and sounding board, but it was Stacey who'd built their company. And she hadn't accomplished that by letting others take charge.

She yanked the handle, then stepped into the hall. The bathroom sparkled with light from the high window. The fixtures gleamed. Fresh flowers adorned the wood washstand, which held crisp white hand towels and a bowl of cherry-red soaps.

And she could have been at Motel 6.

So maybe the doctor wasn't so bad after all.

What was wrong with accepting a bit of country hospitality? Back home in New Orleans, she would have steered out-of-town clients to the better hotels, or to the more picturesque bed and breakfasts. Certainly she wouldn't have put them at a dreary motel bordered by the airport and a frontage road.

"Loosen up, Stacey," she said. Just because one guy

had stolen her trust and broken her heart didn't mean that every attractive member of the opposite sex skulked about with ulterior motives.

Not simply attractive.

Gorgeous.

She sighed and washed her hands in the porcelain bowl painted with a floral motif. Feeling much more in charity with "Dr. Mike," she crossed back to her room. She dressed and made her way toward the front parlor.

As soon as she heard the trilling voice of Mrs. Clark, she halted. Every pleasant thought of the doctor evaporated.

"I understand her parents are moving here," she overheard as she approached the second of the double parlors.

"Then surely she'll visit, if she doesn't join them. Ooh, this will be very interesting."

That had to be Martha's voice. Stacey squared her shoulders and swept into the room. She was starving and she'd be darned if these two gossips would deprive her of her tea and crumpets, or whatever breakfast consisted of at the Schoolhouse Inn.

"If only those children—"

Stacey's entrance cut off whatever dire warning the real estate agent had in mind. "Good morning," Stacey said, checking her watch to make sure she hadn't slept into the afternoon.

Martha rose and motioned toward a buffet loaded with a silver tea tray and coffeepot, plus platters of heart-shaped muffins and biscuits. A bowl overflowing with apples, oranges, and bananas occupied one corner.

"Just help yourself and sit right down with us," Martha said. "The other guests have come and gone."

"And then we can be on our way," Mrs. Clark chimed in.

Stacey nodded politely, all the while wondering how best to rid herself of the real estate agent's proffered services. She filled her plate and poured out a cup of watery Folger's coffee that looked more like tea than the pungent brew she was used to in New Orleans. Perhaps she'd find a decent espresso in the town square.

Mrs. Clark pulled out a chair for her, and Stacey, with a funny feeling that her life had ceased to be under her own control, settled into it.

Just as Stacey popped a delicious bite of muffin into her mouth, Martha asked, "Tell us about your parents. What do they do?"

Around the mouthful, Stacey said, "Doctor." Her manners were going to the dogs. The less she had to say, the more comfortable she'd be with this farce. Why, oh, why had she ever said she was scouting retirement property?

"We could use a doctor's wife in our garden club," Martha was saying. "Dr. Edgard's Sally was always so good with roses." She sighed and added, "But now she's only pushing them up with her toes."

Stacey choked on her heart-shaped muffin. She refrained from correcting the assumption that only her dad was a doctor. But wouldn't her mother have a fit! She'd probably throw her scalpel across the town square.

"It's refreshing to meet a young lady so willing to

help her parents," Mrs. Clark said. "Tell me about their needs. Are they looking for the golf course, planned community lifestyle, or a simple home in the country?"

"Why, Patty Clark, you know there's no such thing!" Martha shuddered. "Simple home in the country, my foot. It's up with the chickens to milk the cows and slop the hogs and then all day long breaking your back over the vegetable garden. And then when you do get to sit down, you've got a lap full of peas to shell or beans to snap."

"Well," exclaimed Mrs. Clark, "I never knew you felt so strongly. I'm from Little Rock originally, so I don't know firsthand about country life, but it always seems so idyllic."

Stacey finished her muffin, thankful the two of them had found something other than her parents to dissect. As soon as she could slip out unnoticed, she'd bolt.

"Idyllic, yes, from a magazine cover," Martha said. She turned to Stacey, and said, "Make Patty drive you straight to Lake Doolittle Retirement Haven. That's where any woman would love to live out her retirement years."

"Are you regretting your decision to run the inn?" Mrs. Clark was quick, Stacey had to admit. The agent was probably pricing out the listing in her head, marshaling buyers, and crafting an ad.

"Not at all. But to retire in luxury with the man who's been your lifelong love—well, it's enough to make anyone teary-eyed."

Stacey choked again, this time spewing the weak coffee onto her napkin. Her parents had entirely different means of inducing tears!

Martha hopped up and patted her on the back with

light fluttery strokes that Heimlich never would have recognized. But her heart was in the right place, so Stacey thanked her and used the disruption to excuse herself and flee to her room.

Funny how quickly Third Grade had become a haven.

Well, too bad, because she was checking out. She tossed her robe into her overnight bag and grabbed her purse. Halfway to the door, she halted. What was she thinking?

She hadn't paid her bill.

Darn and double darn.

And with that meddling doctor arranging everything the night before, she'd had no chance to ask the cost, which ruled out simply leaving a check on the pillow and hightailing it past the parlor.

Of course, she hadn't paid her vet expenses, either, but that was different because she had to collect True. She'd settle up, then scoot out of town.

If True was well enough to leave.

Stacey released her grip on the suitcase and set it back on the gleaming wood floor next to an apple-shaped rug. What would it hurt to spend one more night? It was a pretty room and she'd slept better than she had in months.

In the hallway, Stacey met Mrs. Clark bearing down on her. "Ready?"

Oh, no. Just because she was staying in town didn't mean she had to continue this real estate farce.

"Mrs. Clark, there's something I really must—"

"Of course there is," she said, taking Stacey gently by the elbow and leading her toward the front door. "Dr. Mike said you'd never agree to look at listings until you'd visited your dog. He said to drive you straight over to the animal clinic."

Stacey, mouth opening and then closing, found herself propelled out onto the porch of the Schoolhouse Inn. Was there anything Dr. Mike didn't manage?

Ready to fume, Stacey found herself blinking against the bright sun. As her eyes adjusted, she watched a squirrel scamper across the front lawn. A fat cat on the porch blinked and stretched out a paw. Only a few clouds drifted across the vivid blue sky.

Looking around, taking in the tranquillity, Stacey realized back home the sky was probably just as blue, but she was rarely outside in the daylight to enjoy it. Perhaps a vacation wasn't such a bad idea after all.

"My car is right here," Mrs. Clark said, pointing the remote opener at a cream-colored Cadillac.

"Oh, I can drive myself," Stacey said.

"Tut-tut-tut," her realtor said. "What would people say about me if I let a client do that?"

That you respected my wishes? Stacey kept her thoughts to herself and took a seat inside the spacious car.

The town square was only a few blocks away. Mrs. Clark chatted about property values and retirement considerations, but Stacey only nodded and let the words flow musically around her ears.

Saturday morning in the square was quite a contrast to the night before. Every parking spot appeared full. Vendors crowded the courthouse lawn.

"We have a Farmer's Market every Saturday," Mrs. Clark said, pride in her voice. "Your parents will love Doolittle. There's always so much to do."

Stacey glanced sideways, remembering Dr. Halliday's laconic words. Evidently his idea of activities worth pursuing varied greatly with those of the agent. And she was pretty sure she'd agree with the doc on this point.

A mud-splattered pickup truck pulled out from the parking spot Stacey had occupied last night and Mrs. Clark glided her Caddy smoothly into the coveted slot. "I have to pop in down the street. I'll meet you back here in, say, thirty minutes?"

Stacey nodded and for the second time made her way into "Dr. Mike's" domain.

He was standing behind the counter, leaning forward, intent on something he was saying to a gray-haired woman clutching a wriggling scrap of poodle to her chest.

The woman nodded and gazed at the doctor, soaking up every word. "Oh, yes, I'll be sure to do that, twice a day," she said.

Did everyone in this town dance to his tune?

Well, she didn't. But as soon as she heard her own internal voice, Stacey knew it was sheer stubbornness on her part. Of course the woman should do what the vet was telling her to do for her pet.

"I don't know what we'd do without you, Dr. Mike," the woman said.

He smiled and glanced past the patient and straight at Stacey. He smiled, quiet and confident, and Stacey regretted her immediate response to his look. Because of course she smiled back.

He tipped his head, just enough that she knew he might be speaking to the poodle's owner, but the words were intended for Stacey. "Well, don't worry, Mrs. Pinkerton, I'm not going anywhere."

And he kept his gaze on Stacey, far too long for her own comfort. Fortunately, a young lady in a smock printed with sketches of cat and dog faces joined him behind the counter and handed a receipt and three bottles of pills to Mrs. Pinkerton.

Dr. Halliday stepped to the side, then disappeared.

Relieved yet a tad disappointed that the doctor hadn't approached her, Stacey moved forward, waiting her turn to ask the girl about True.

The door to the back examination area opened.

She turned.

Dr. Halliday stepped out, covered the two square feet between them in one easy stride. "Stacey," he said, offering her his hand.

She accepted. His skin was between warm and cool, his fingers scrubbed and slightly roughened. The hands of a doctor, hands that healed.

"And how was your night at the inn?"

Stacey withdrew her hand. "Very nice," she said, meaning it and at the same time noting that the circles under his eyes had darkened. "I don't think I thanked you properly last night." Yeah, because she'd been too occupied vacillating between annoyance at his attitude and admiration of his physical attributes.

"No problem." He kept standing there, despite the several patients waiting out front. He was too close, really. Behind him, Mrs. Pinkerton was stuffing the medicines in her purse. The poodle yipped. What was Michael waiting for?

"How is True?" Stacey asked to snap him back to action.

"Good." He crossed his arms across his white jacket. "Much better."

"May I see her?"

"Of course." He shifted his hands to his hips but made no move toward the back of the clinic.

"Is something wrong?"

"Oh, no," he said softly, his eyes never moving from hers, "things haven't been this right in quite some time."

Was he referring to her presence? Nah, impossible.

"Thank you," Mrs. Pinkerton called over yet another poodle yap.

At that, Dr. Halliday turned to wave good-bye. When he swung back around, he seemed once more a matter-of-fact veterinarian conversing with a client.

"True rested well," he said, the intense expression in his eyes retreating.

Stacey blinked. Had she imagined his behavior? Invented it because she wanted him to look at her in some special way? Nah, that would be nuts.

"I'll take you back. If it's okay with you, we can run an ultrasound on Monday."

"Why do you need to do that?"

"I know you don't believe that True is pregnant." He grinned. "The ultrasound, as the saying goes, is worth a thousand words."

Chapter 4

Michael watched Stacey form the words of protest, grinned as she started to sputter, "But, but, but—"

But she hadn't believed him. He'd read her correctly. Just a country doc with no skills.

Even knowing that's what she'd thought, he'd spent a sleepless night dreaming up ways to keep her around town long enough to learn what lay beneath her Ms.-In-Control surface.

Now he waited to see how she'd react. Would she acknowledge the truth or opt for a polite disclaimer? She seemed to be forming words in her mind, choosing, discarding. An adorable look of consternation had settled on her face. She wore the same skirt as the night before, but she'd left off the jacket. The sleeveless silk top showed her body to advantage and softened her tough lady executive look.

Her arms were slim and toned. She might not have time to walk her dog, but she apparently made time for exercise.

"You're right."

"Excuse me?" Michael's inventory of Stacey was cut off abruptly as she waved a hand in front of his face.

"I just said you are right that I didn't believe you." She parked her hands on her hips, drawing his attention to that shapely curve. "But you don't have to do the ultrasound unless there's a medical reason to do so."

"No?"

She shook her head. "I was simply shocked last night. And it reflected poorly on my puppy parenting skills." She laughed and Michael began to smile as he watched her face light up. "Who doesn't hate admitting to imperfections?"

He grinned and opened the door that led to the back of the clinic. "You can visit with True in the exercise area out back."

One of his teenage assistants popped out of the cat room just then. "Evan, please take Ms. St. Cyr to see the bearded collie that came in last night."

"Sure thing, Dr. Mike." The teenager smiled shyly at Stacey, revealing a mouthful of braces and a look of instant adoration in his eyes.

Yeah, Michael understood that expression. Longing for the unattainable. "I'll stop by after I see this patient," he said, indicating the cat room.

"Thanks," Stacey said, following Evan and looking all around her as she walked down the hall. Michael liked her curiosity, her awareness of her surroundings.

Damn, he liked her, period.

Abruptly, he turned and pushed open the door to the cat exam room.

His mind more on the woman now back by the kennels than on the pampered Persian lolling on the exam table, Michael greeted both Queen Victoria and her owner, Mrs. Guinness. Queen Victoria, it seemed, had swallowed Mrs. Guinness's grandson's 1910 Indian Head penny.

"And," the portly retired banker continued as Michael's thoughts strayed, "that just happens to be the most valuable penny in his collection. And that little darling threatened to choke it out of my precious cat!" She harrumphed and Michael wondered whether Stacey would stay in the back long enough with True to allow him to escape to speak with her again.

"I told my daughter-in-law when she decided to work part-time instead of staying home with her children that I would wash my hands of the consequences, and now look what's happened!"

Michael nodded. The Persian looked supremely content. Mrs. Guinness brought Queen Victoria in far more frequently than was necessary and he knew the cat was in perfect health. The grandson was in his daughter Kristen's class and Michael thought him a good kid. High-spirited, but nothing wrong with that. There wasn't a mean bone in his body and he doubted the boy had meant any harm at all to the cat at any point. What Mrs. Guinness needed, he reflected, was a second Mr. Guinness.

And what he needed . . .

Last night Stacey St. Cyr had intrigued him. And irritated him. Not to mention made it darn hard for him to get back to sleep.

This morning, seeing a softer side of her shining through, he could honestly say that he liked what he saw.

"So you will x-ray my poor, brave kitty, won't you?"

"Has she had a bowel movement since she swallowed the penny?" From some distant point, Michael forced his attention to the immediate issue.

"Why, I don't know." She stroked her cat and cooed, "Have you, precious?"

Michael restrained himself from rolling his eyes. He'd seen a lot as a vet since opening his practice in Doolittle. And most of his experiences had little in common with the theoretical world he'd inhabited as he had trodden the path of academia. A professorship in a prestigious veterinary school didn't require hand-holding the Mrs. Guinnesses of the world.

Yet here he stood on a beautiful spring morning, in the forgotten town of Doolittle, Arkansas, doing just that.

Stacey could well be his salvation.

Not a quick fix.

But a woman to bring him out of the slump he'd suffered for the past several years.

A woman with the energy of the city, the brains, the beauty, the intensity that he hadn't experienced since his first few months with Pauline.

Those few golden weeks when they'd found so much in one another that fascinated them. Those days in which they'd cast all care and precautions to the wind.

Those fateful moments in which Kristen had been conceived.

"Why do you ask about whether she's visited her pan, Doctor?"

Pregnancy had chased all thrills offstage. Pauline had hated gaining weight. She'd refused any intimacy. If he hadn't rushed them to the courthouse to marry within the first trimester, no doubt she would have insisted on becoming a single mother or, worse yet, gotten her way and had an abortion.

"Doctor?"

Michael started. "Sorry," he said. "I was, er, reviewing the possibilities in my mind." Possibilities. Yes, what had been infatuation, what might be called puppy love between Pauline and him had led to their marriage, to the first of their children being born, and eventually to their divorce. They'd had no foundation, no common interests. He'd vowed never to repeat that mistake.

But he was so tired of being alone, away from people to whom he could truly relate.

And into his world strode Stacey St. Cyr.

He couldn't turn his back. A golden ring came around only once, sometimes never. He'd grab for it. And if he lost, well, then he would have given it his best. And if he won . . . well, damn, but that was so much scarier than losing that he couldn't even contemplate that outcome. Despite her tough exterior, he glimpsed a lovable lady lurking beneath the surface, just waiting to be coaxed into showing herself to the world. He'd be willing to bet her "I don't need any help" attitude was a stance acquired after suffering a major hurt, and one she would slowly let go of. If he was wrong—well, as gamblers were fond of saying, if you didn't buy a lottery ticket, you stood no chance at winning the jackpot.

He cleared his throat and folded his arms across his chest, fingering his stethoscope. "Chances are the penny will pass through in the stools. Rather than doing anything now, we can wait. You can go home and check her litter pan."

"No need for that." Mrs. Guinness whipped out her cell phone. "My grandson is at my house for the entire"—she gritted her teeth on the adjective—"weekend. I'll instruct him to check things out." She punched in the numbers. "And that will teach that young man to count his coins where I most specifically told him not to."

Michael suppressed a grin. If her grandson wanted the penny back badly enough, combing through a litter box should prove no deterrent.

When someone wanted something badly enough, what was an obstacle or two? Or an entire obstacle course, for that matter?

And what did he want badly enough to plow through dreck?

To stay with his children.

Absolutely.

He'd never doubted that decision.

What else?

Mrs. Guinness was still talking on the phone, no doubt giving her grandson specific instructions along with an additional piece of her mind.

A knock sounded on the door.

A winsome face, all big eyes and gap-toothed smile, that he loved so fiercely, peered around the edge of the door. "Hi, Daddy," his eight-year-old said. "May I come in?"

He'd taught his daughters always to ask before entering an exam room. There were things he never wanted them to see. With a glance at Mrs. Guinness, who stopped her telephone tirade long enough to wave and smile at Jessica, Michael nodded. He was pleased but surprised to see Jessica, her mother having insisted that she start ballet on Saturday mornings rather than "hang out with those smelly animals."

She skipped over to his side and hugged him. He returned the hug. A sweet emotion he was always at a loss to describe swept over him. Oh, yes, he'd done what he had to do for his children's sake, as well as for his own. But when, if ever, would he have the opportunity to focus on his own needs that operated apart from his children?

Mrs. Guinness snapped her phone shut. "He found it!" She planted a kiss on her cat's nose. "And now my precious Queen Victoria won't have to have nasty X rays. You are a genius, Dr. Mike!" She straightened, and for a moment Michael thought she was going to kiss him, too.

She patted Jessica on the head, evoking a grimace from her. "I'll go help in the back and get the kittens ready," Jessica said.

"Okay," he said, before thinking.

In the back.

Where Stacey was visiting her dog.

Well, why not? If Michael had his way and persuaded the fascinating Ms. St. Cyr to spend more time in town, they were going to meet sometime.

Why not? Michael suppressed a shudder as he thought of the pranks his girls had played on the other two women he'd dated since his move to Doolittle.

"Now, don't you think Queen Victoria is shedding just a trifle too much?"

He bent his head back to the patient, his mind on quite another female.

* * *

True looked every bit her normal perky puppy self. Watching her frisk around the dog run, Stacey had trouble believing how sick her dog had been last night.

"Pretty!"

At the sound of a girl's voice, Stacey turned around. A pint-sized brunette was clinging to the door handles and holding on as if the door were a swing. She gave herself a push with one foot and grinned, obviously pleased with her improvised amusement.

Stacey couldn't help but grin in response. True was a beauty. "She is, isn't she? True's a bearded collie."

The girl giggled. "Not the dog. You."

"Oh." Stacey glanced around. "Why, thank you," she said, surprised. She studied the girl more closely and the light bulb went off in her head.

Same dark hair. Same brown eyes. The grin was different, a puckish look she couldn't imagine on Dr. Michael Halliday's more serious face. But perhaps it was the two missing front teeth that altered her expression. Just to check her conclusion—not that Stacey was at all curious, she assured herself—she called True to heel and, as the dog responded, walked toward the child.

"What's your name?" she asked, stroking True on the head.

The girl continued swinging on the door. "Daddy says I'm not to answer that question unless I know you. So who are you?"

Smart, yet sad that children had to operate with such defenses. "I'm Stacey," she said, "and this is True. The doctor here took care of her last night."

The girl nodded. "That's why he got home in the

middle of the night last night." She jumped down from the door and patted True. "I'm Jessica. Want to help me with the kittens for the square?"

"Well, I . . ." Stacey trailed off as she watched the happy glow on the girl's face begin to fade.

Under her voice, Jessica said, "Grown-ups never have time. They always have something else to do. 'I have to go to work. I have to see a client.'" When Jessica sighed and fixed those big brown eyes on her, Stacey knew she couldn't say no. Hadn't her parents always said those very same things to her?

"I have to ask the doctor about True first. What do you do with the kittens?"

"We take them across the street so people can see them and give them homes." She reached out and took Stacey's hand. "Come on. I'll show you where they are."

She headed back through the door. Stacey quickly clipped True's leash back on her collar and let Jessica lead both of them back into the clinic. Mrs. Clark would have to be disappointed. Kittens were immensely preferable to retirement property.

Michael had just ushered Mrs. Guinness to the front reception area and turned, intending to go in search of Stacey and Jessica, when Scotty, his able and trusted assistant and jack-of-all-trades, cleared his throat in that way he had of indicating Michael had best pay attention.

Michael quirked his brows, knowing Scotty would read the inquiry in the nonverbal signal.

Sure enough, Scotty tilted his head slightly in the direction of the door and the now-departing Mrs. Guinness.

As silent as Queen Victoria's owner was vocal was the man standing just inside the clinic doors. At his feet sat a mottled black and white coon dog, her nose on her paws, one of which was bandaged with a splint, a device Michael had gingerly built around a paw he'd reconstructed from what was left of the mean jaws of a trap.

"Mr. Washington is wanting to speak to you," Scotty said in a low voice.

"Of course." The dog wasn't due for a follow-up appointment until the next week. Knowing the man had little money, Michael had charged him only the barest of costs for the delicate operation. His unwillingness to make the sort of profits the shiny clinic on the outskirts of town thought nothing of banking was a constant source of irritation to his ex-wife Pauline. She complained on a regular basis, to anyone who would listen, how much better off their children would be if he were only able to suck up and act like a real businessman.

Something her second husband knew a whole hell of a lot about.

Michael turned around, leaving the door to the back of the reception area ajar. "Mr. Washington, how are you?" he asked, extending a hand.

The old man, who made his living off the land, from what Michael could figure out, wiped a hand on his overalls and shook with a grip far stronger than his wizened body led Michael to expect. "Can't complain," he said.

The coon dog stirred and rose, sniffing at Michael's knees.

"Then things can't be too bad," Michael said, studying the splint with a careful eye. Mr. Washington wouldn't want to run up his bill any higher than it already was, but Michael wasn't one to let an animal suffer due to human pride, error, or stupidity. "Coon's looking pretty good." Coon was the only name the old man called the dog, something the city-bred Michael had trouble comprehending, though he'd run across this matter-of-fact approach to hunting and working animals more times than he could count since relocating to the hills of south-central Arkansas.

Mr. Washington nodded. "I was in town for the market. Got some things to unload for you."

Things. Michael nodded, knowing in accepting whatever goods the man had brought he was saving his client's pride. But he'd draw the line if the man tried to dump a pig on him. One of his first patients had done that and Michael had been too dumbfounded, one month out of his beloved professorship at Tufts Veterinary School, to refuse the tribute.

The pig, along with Jessica and Kristen's assemblage of cats, dogs, and birds, still lived at his house on the edge of Doolittle. He didn't have the heart to turn him into bacon.

"Be right back," the older man said. "Stay, Coon."

The dog settled onto the floor, not quite on his feet, but close enough for Michael to tell she took comfort from his presence. Michael remained out front to see what "things" were coming his way. The waiting room was empty now, but he had patients in the back to tend to. And no doubt there'd be the usual rush after twelve when people realized closing time was at two and they'd better hurry over or wait until Monday.

Funny how predictable some people were.

Not everyone, though. His own daughters—now,

they were two of the most unpredictable creatures. Just when he thought he understood what mattered most to Kristen, she'd switch up on him. Or take Jessica, agreeing to go to ballet instead of hanging out at the clinic on Saturdays, and then showing up here anyway.

But perhaps she'd consented to the ballet lessons only to silence her mother.

Michael sighed. He'd sure been guilty enough of that.

The bell on the door clanged and Mr. Washington stepped through, a bushel basket balanced on one shoulder.

Coon rose, her nose sniffing.

Mr. Washington lowered the oversized container to the floor. To his relief, Michael saw a mound of gleaming dark red apples. He'd feared worse, possibly homemade jerky from some of the animals trapped by the man and his dog.

He heard a shuffling noise behind him and figured Scotty was watching from the counter. Scotty kept a straight face, no matter what. Hell, there could have been a family of squirrels in that basket and Scotty would have maintained that stoic expression of his.

"From the cellar," Mr. Washington said, lifting one from the pile and handing it to Michael.

He took it and, knowing he was under scrutiny, bit into it. Juice trickled down his chin. He chewed and nodded and around the mouthful, said, "Tastes great." And it did. He'd probably never had one apple in all his years in Boston that tasted quite so fresh.

"Your family can use these?"

Michael nodded.

"If you had a wife, she could put up some applesauce

for you." He said it somewhat forlornly, as if truly sorry for Michael.

"True," Michael said, thinking that the one wife he'd had would have laughed uproariously, probably right in front of this kind-hearted old man, for his old-fashioned statement.

"Mind if I check Coon's leg as long as you're here?"

"Didn't come in for that."

Michael bit another chunk of the apple, smiling around the mouthful. He wisely said nothing. While he let the man consider his offer, he turned slightly, thinking of asking Scotty if he wanted an apple.

But Scotty wasn't behind the counter.

Stacey and Jessica were.

Stacey was watching him, and he wondered just how long she'd been standing there. She was smiling at him in a way she hadn't even once the night before. And Jessica, his little angel who could also be quite a pistol, was smiling up at Stacey as if she'd found a new best friend.

"We're just looking for a Magic Marker," Jessica said quickly.

At least his daughter had remembered she wasn't allowed behind the counter.

But he didn't have the heart to call her to task for it. Not when he was standing there in front of a patient, staring like an idiot. What struck him most was how alike Stacey and Jessica looked. Long dark hair, slender bodies, but built, as the saying went around Doolittle, "with Ford toughness." All night he'd been haunted by Stacey's eyes, so dark, large and innocent a man could lose himself there.

Michael finally finished the bite he'd taken. When he

turned back to Mr. Washington, he saw the old man watching him with what looked suspiciously like a twinkle in his eye. "Reckon that would be okay."

The man reached for Coon's leash, which Michael was pretty sure the dog wore only inside the clinic, per Michael's rules. Michael bent and hefted the basket and led the way to the exam room, the sound of Jessica's melodic chattering and Stacey's occasional replies drifting his way.

He hoisted Coon to the table. "That was the best apple I've ever had in my life," he said as he began to unwrap the bandage around the splint.

Mr. Washington crossed his arms over his chest and leaned back against the wall. "Reckon you might get yourself some applesauce out of that batch after all."

Chapter 5

Mrs. Clark didn't take no easily. Ignoring the yapping poodle and the mewing cat waiting their turn in the clinic reception area, she surged forward on her toes and fastened an earnest hand on Stacey's forearm.

"You don't have children of your own, do you, dear?"

Stacey shook her head, knowing it was fatal to agree with anything the persistent realtor said. But she couldn't very well say she had children when she did not. Implying her parents were still married was enough of a whopper!

"They have to learn that adults have matters that have to be attended to. You must be firm. Firm." Her grip tightened and Stacey winced. And then she pulled her hand free. She wasn't going to be bullied by this woman!

Jessica popped through the door leading from the back of the clinic and raced over to Stacey. "Come on," she said.

"Forgetting your manners?" At the sound of Michael's

voice, Stacey turned. He must have followed his daughter.

Jessica made a face, but said sweetly enough, if rather automatically, "Hello, Mrs. Clark. How are you today? Now can we please leave?"

Michael pressed a finger against his lips. "That decision is entirely up to Ms. St. Cyr. She did have plans and she may or may not change them."

Three pairs of eyes fixed on Stacey.

Mrs. Clark—expectant, demanding.

Jessica—pleading, hopeful.

Michael—warm, assessing.

"Surely," Mrs. Clark said, "your parents are expecting a report from you. Won't they want to see what you've found for them?"

Stacey thought she detected a smile on Michael's face. Easy for him to be amused by Mrs. Clark's pushy sales techniques when he was the one who'd set the realtor on to Stacey.

"A busy career woman like you," Mrs. Clark went on. "Why, you can't afford much time away from work. Someone might steal a client or a project." She fanned herself with a road map she'd been highlighting when Stacey came to tell her she wasn't going house hunting.

"I can stay away as long as I choose," Stacey said, reacting strongly, if not accurately, to Mrs. Clark. In a flash of temper, she forgot all about being forced out of the office by her concerned business partner.

"Of course, dear. And when are your parents joining you?"

"If we don't leave now, it'll be Tuesday before we get homes for those kittens!" Jessica tugged at Stacey's hand.

"Tuesday," Stacey said, following Jessica's unwitting lead. Stilling the girl's small hand in her own, she continued. "So we can look at retirement homes tomorrow." Flashing a smile, she turned to leave with Jessica.

"Tomorrow is Sunday."

Stacey waited.

"We have church in the morning and I'm expected at my mother-in-law's house for dinner. We won't be able to start out until at least three P.M."

Michael held out a hand. "Let me borrow the map, Mrs. Clark, and I'll take Stacey on the initial scouting trip. Then you can show her the places she thinks the best on Monday."

Mrs. Clark brightened. "Dr. Mike, you are always thinking!" She pressed the map into his hand, no doubt relieved that an agent with a more forgiving mother-in-law wouldn't be called into action.

"Happy to help," Michael said, a smile lighting his eyes as he turned toward Stacey.

Help? Stacey certainly needed some! What was she thinking? One fib led to another. But with Dr. Michael Halliday looking at her the way he was, she quit thinking and savored the moment. After all, she was on vacation.

Yeah, vacation from the truth.

"Are you ready?" Jessica was dancing around like a Spanish flea. Nodding, Stacey realized she could use some breathing room. Being too close to Michael rattled her mind. Not to mention her body.

Turning toward the back of the clinic, he brushed her shoulder just then. "I'll walk over with you."

"Dad, I can do it myself," Jessica said, her small hands firmly planted on her hips.

Stacey watched in amusement as the girl's father mimicked her body posture and the determined expression. "I know you can," he said, "but I'm offering to help."

"That's okay," Jessica said, surprising Stacey by reaching for her hand. "My friend Stacey is going with me."

"I see." The grin Michael flashed at her would have melted a less resistant heart. But despite her physical attraction to this hunk of man, Stacey knew she had no business responding to him. She was simply passing through Doolittle and his charm made the trip more enjoyable. Of course, his take-charge attitude had also cost her more time than she'd ever dreamed of spending there. "So Stacey is your friend," he said.

Jessica nodded. "Besides, you're always teaching me the importance of independence." The eight-year-old stumbled slightly over the last word, but got it out.

"Have I ever told you that you argue far too well for a child your age?" He smiled as he said it and Jessica beamed back, obviously pleased by what she took rightly as praise.

Something tugged at Jessica's heart as she watched father and daughter. The two of them were joined in a circle of love and as she stood outside that special bond, she couldn't help but wonder wistfully if she would ever live that feeling.

"I'll drop by after my last patient." Holding the door to the back open for them, he said, "True should be up to some fresh air, if she won't object to keeping company with kittens."

"She looks perfectly recovered to me," Stacey said. "Do I need to bring her back after we're done?" She paused, curiously waiting to see if he'd cook up an excuse. She was fairly sure he was doing his best to extend her stay.

"Oh, as long as you don't take her out on the road for long periods of time, she should be fine."

"I see." And just how was she supposed to get back home to New Orleans without doing exactly that? Jessica skipped in an impatient circle and Stacey left that question unasked. For the moment, she was oddly content to remain in Doolittle.

Twenty minutes later she and Jessica had the cleverly designed "cat house"—a wood and wire cage with plenty of room for the eight kittens and one adult cat to romp, sleep, and eat—in place among the other vendors spread out on the courthouse lawn. The cat house had been built atop a large red wagon. When asked about its origin, Jessica said with a surprising lack of emotion in her tone, "My sister and dad built it, but Kristen never comes to help anymore." Her voice may have been flat, but the scowl on her pretty face warned away any further questions.

Which naturally made Stacey all the more curious about Jessica's sister. She had also wondered whether Michael would have allowed Jessica, no matter how "independent" she was, to go work at the town market on her own, but it didn't take her long to understand why Michael was comfortable doing so.

When they pulled up with the cat house, they were greeted by an older woman selling homemade pickles, apple butter, and blueberry preserves. But rather than hello, she barked, "Two more minutes and I was coming to look for you, young lady."

A black man in overalls carving a duck out of a block of wood looked up to inspect Stacey. She smiled at him, and he nodded. "We all keep an eye on Dr. Mike's girls," he said. "What with her dad being so busy and her mother always gallivanting around town with Cecil Gardner, somebody's got to help him out."

Jessica turned her back on the adults and bent her attention to one solid black kitten busy poking its front paws out of the cage. True followed her over, looking all around, eyes bright and tail thumping contentedly.

Stacey surveyed the scene also. The vendors ranged around the lower edge of the grassy knoll that rose to the front steps of the courthouse, a building designed in the sturdy style of the Works Progress Administration, meaning it had been guarding the square since the time of the Great Depression.

The economy of Doolittle seemed bustling enough today. Women strolled by, an occasional man in reluctant tow, while the benches dotting the courthouse lawn were occupied by local guys. The vendors came in all sizes, shapes, and gender. Their wares were even more varied, from what Stacey could see glancing to her left and right. Truck gardeners with fruits and vegetables, herb stands, and baskets hand-woven from local oak (so said the sign; Stacey couldn't have told whether they were native to Arkansas or yet another foreign import). For someone who made her living creating clever ways to help people sell their products, she spent little time out and about watching consumers exercise their choices. She mulled over that thought just as Miss Martha appeared, along with a taller, thinner version of herself walking at her side.

"Miss Martha, want to take a kitten home?" Jessica smiled up at her with such an angelic expression Stacey expected the bed and breakfast co-owner to melt, open the string bag looped over her arm, and pop in a kitten.

Instead, her reaction was a quick and rather nervous glance toward her sister. "Jessica, if I've told you once, I've told you a million times that we can't have another pet."

"I should hope not," the other sparer of the sisters said with a grimace. "That one fat cat you keep threatens to eat us out of house and home. I found that beast with his nose in my meringue this morning. The next time that happens will be that animal's tenth life."

Sweet Martha sniffed. "Well, Abbie, that's no way to talk, especially as it was Jessica's daddy who saved Hemingway's life. But never mind that. You were busy this morning and didn't get to meet Stacey St. Cyr. She's the guest staying in Third Grade."

"I'm in third grade, too," Jessica said, squaring her shoulders and jutting out her chin. "And even I know that cats don't mess up houses. People do. So why can't you give a home to another kitty?"

"Nice to meet you," Stacey murmured, pretty certain that neither one of the Schoolhouse Sisters planned to answer the girl's question. Just then True chose to take exception to the oversized straw bag hanging from Abbie's arm. It was pretty ugly, but that was no reason for True to start barking wildly. Only by a quick and strategic tug at her leash did Stacey prevent her dog from launching herself on the target.

"Wild beast!" Abbie's face flushed red. "You see, Jessica Halliday, what comes of treating animals like people."

Her sister fluttered her hands. "Well, really, Abbie, it's

not fair to blame the dog. If you didn't insist on buying those nasty rabbits, that sweet puppy wouldn't have made a beeline for your bag."

Jessica made a face. "Life isn't fair. When grown-ups argue, nobody says anything. When kids argue, someone always gets sent to their room."

Martha shrugged, possibly in apology, possibly in despair. For better or worse, her fate seemed joined to that of her grumpy sister, compatible or not.

"We'll see you this evening," Miss Martha said, moving off with Abbie, who was defending both her anti-pet position and her award-winning recipe for rabbit stew.

Stacey made a quick decision to avoid dinner at the Schoolhouse Inn. The salad bar at Shoney's off the interstate was far preferable to baked bunny.

Looking pleased with herself, True sat back on her haunches.

"You'd better not take your dog to their hotel," Jessica said, lifting the frisky black kitten out of the cage and cradling it in her arms. "Miss Abbie's likely to poison her. Kristen says everyone calls her Crabby Abbie."

A teenage girl and boy approached, arms wrapped tightly around one another's waists. They appeared lost to the world. Stacey envied them their self-absorption. To her surprise, the boy slowed his pace, brought the couple to a halt in front of Jessica and said in a sulky voice, "I don't like black cats."

Jessica placed her body around the kitten and snarled as mightily as any mother cat would have. "Only ignorant people think black cats are bad luck."

"Who are you calling ignorant, punk?" The boy

turned to his girlfriend. "Let's adopt this animal and show her just what bad luck black cats can be."

"Forget it," Jessica said.

"Aren't these cats looking for homes?" The boy looked even uglier.

Stacey had let things go far enough. She loosened her hold on True's leash and said, "Keep walking."

The girl bristled. "You can't tell my guy what to do."

"I'm the adult here," Stacey said, pretty sure she had never before used those words. "Your boyfriend is disturbing a child in my care and if the two of you don't move on, I'll call the police."

The girl sneered but plucked at the boy's sleeve. "Come on, Dirk, let's blow this scene and go to the lake."

He shrugged and started to turn away. Then he halted and said to Jessica, "Hey, aren't you Kristen's kid sister?"

"What's it to you?"

He laughed. "You're one weird family," he said, grabbing his girlfriend around the neck and stalking off.

Jessica stroked the kitten's nose. "We are not weird," she said softly.

Stacey got the feeling Jessica had been called that more than once. "How long have you lived in Doolittle?"

Jessica kept her attention on the kitten. Stacey wondered if she'd pushed too much by asking. She knew too well what it felt like to be asked personal questions one wasn't ready to answer. Bandied between her own father and mother's adult domains, as a child Stacey had hated the times the grown-ups had asked her stupid questions, all in the name of pretending to be interested in her. And even as a child, Stacey could tell the difference between the people who were her parents' friends and the ones who wanted to use them to get ahead. She'd learned early on just how murky the political maneuverings at a teaching hospital could be.

So was Stacey asking Jessica because she wanted to know more about the girl's father?

Jessica returned the black kitten to the cat house. "My parents got divorced when I was five and we lived in Boston. I started first grade there but had to come here after Christmas."

Stacey closed her eyes for the briefest of moments, hearing in the girl's voice the pain of her own childhood spent as the frayed rope in a tug-of-war between her divorced parents. She clenched one fist. Slowly, she relaxed her hand and glanced over at Jessica, prepared to squelch her own memories and offer comfort.

She expected Jessica to look as angry as she herself was feeling. Instead, the girl's face had brightened and she was waving energetically, beckoning someone over.

Not just any someone.

Michael.

He waved back, approaching with an easy stride. His progress was interrupted several times by people calling to him. Head bent, he paused to listen to a vegetable vendor.

At the same time, two middle-aged women paused in front of the cat house and ogled a pair of tussling kittens.

"They have all their shots," Jessica said, hope in her voice.

Stacey shared the sentiment. So far they'd not placed one animal.

The two women conferred, then asked to hold one each. As Jessica reached in, the mother cat placed one paw over the kitten closest to her.

"Poor mama," said one woman.

"She needs a home, too," Jessica said.

"What will happen to the ones you don't place?" The woman bussed the kitten with her nose as she asked the question.

Jessica sighed and shook her head. "There's not enough room in the shelter for the cats already there."

The woman's eyes widened. Clearly, she didn't want to ask a child as young as Jessica what they were all thinking.

"My dad won't put them to sleep. But other doctors might," she said. "And they would at the county shelter, if no one takes them home after five days."

The matter-of-fact way she relayed the harsh facts of life for homeless animals tugged at Stacey's heart. The child stood there stoically while both the other women and Stacey were dabbing at the corners of their eyes. In many ways, Jessica was eight going on eighty.

"How many of the kittens are hers?"

"The four black ones."

"Four. I don't know . . ."

"How can you break up a family?" the other countered.

Stacey felt Michael's presence before she saw him. He'd approached as she had been concentrating on the fate of the cat family. Ignoring her dad, Jessica reached inside for the other two black kittens. "You should only take them if you can take care of all of them," she said.

Michael nodded, looking pleased with his daughter. He shifted his stance and the next thing Stacey knew, the two of them were standing shoulder to shoulder, the cotton of his polo shirt brushing her bare arm. He remained quiet, allowing his daughter to transact her business.

What a wonderful man.

The thought came unbidden. Stacey savored the moment. She felt an odd sense of being in the right place at the perfect instant in time.

"We'll take the mother and the four kittens," one of the women said. Her friend nodded. "But we'll need to come back for them."

Stacey glanced sideways at Michael. Most of the guys she knew would have jumped in at this point, issuing directions, explaining the procedure. He kept silent, not moving except to give Stacey a satisfied smile.

"Great," Jessica exclaimed, putting the kittens back in the cat house. She reached into the bottom of the wagon, pulled out a folder, and took a page from it. "Here's what you need to know about what they eat and where to pick them up."

They accepted the paper. One woman said, "You're a very efficient young lady."

Jessica nodded. "I know."

Her dad cleared his throat.

"Oh, right. Thank you," she added. Glancing back toward her dad, she said, "This is my dad. He's the doctor who doesn't put animals to sleep. Unless, of course, they're very sick."

"Thank you, sweetie," Michael said. To the women, he said, "Dr. Halliday. If the animals need anything, just call my office. The number is on the sheet."

"Oh, you're Dr. Mike!"

"Yes." He looked slightly uncomfortable at the note of recognition.

"Doolittle is lucky to have someone like you."

Stacey smothered a smile. How had Michael Halliday escaped the women of Doolittle to remain single? In three years, surely the entire eligible female population had been after him.

"Doolittle would be even luckier," Michael said, "if this city banded together and built a new animal shelter."

"That's a good idea," one of the women said. The other one played with one of the kittens through the cage. "Let us know if we can help with that."

Michael nodded and thanked them and then they moved off.

Jessica, a frown on her pretty face, said, "Kittens shouldn't have to die because people don't care enough to take care of them."

"Oh, sweetie," Michael said, putting an arm around his daughter, "you have enough cares without taking on the animal population. Leave that to us types with tougher hides, okay?"

Jessica shook her head. "Sometimes it takes a kid to make things happen."

"Why doesn't Doolittle have a decent shelter?" Stacey belonged to the local Society for Prevention of Cruelty to Animals group in New Orleans. Her company donated advertising services to the annual black-tie fund-raiser and in the past two years, as her income had grown and she'd been able to afford the expense, she'd purchased a table and invited some of her favorite animal-loving clients.

Michael glanced around at the clusters of people dotting the courthouse lawn. He seemed to be weighing his response. He smoothed one hand over Jessica's long hair but fixed his dark and definitely unreadable eyes on Stacey. "How about I answer that question over dinner tonight?"

Was he asking her out? As in a date? Stacey was still considering the implications of his invitation when Jessica looked up at her dad.

"I don't know why you have to wait to answer the question, but it'll be fun to have Stacey over for dinner."

Michael made a slight choking noise.

Ah, so he was asking her out.

Stacey smiled at him, amused at his consternation.

"She can bring True over so Crabby Abbie won't hurt her," Jessica added, reaching over to pet the dog who'd been sitting quietly yet observing all that was going on around her.

She was sure she heard him sigh. "Jessica, it's not polite to use that nickname."

She placed her hands on her hips and said, "It's not very nice to threaten animals."

He tossed up his hands. "I'll fire up the grill," he said. "Pick you up at six?"

Stacey grinned. An eight-year-old as duenna wasn't a bad idea. If she spent too much more time around this man, she just might need a chaperone.

Chapter 6

Perhaps it was best having Stacey out to the house rather than one-on-one at a candlelit table at the Verandah, Doolittle's one aspiration to a fine dining establishment.

Including his daughters from the beginning might be the key to preventing the disasters he'd encountered with Kristen and Jessica the few other times he'd dated in Doolittle. The thought brought him up short. This woman was in town for two, maybe three more days. But if her parents retired nearby, didn't that mean she'd be back? Michael reflected with another sideways glance at Stacey. If he could get a word out of her, he'd explore that line of inquiry.

On the short drive from the Schoolhouse Inn out to his house, Stacey had been quiet, as quiet as he'd ever seen her.

In what little time he'd known her.

Not that time mattered to Michael.

He liked what he saw of Stacey St. Cyr. She'd lowered the window and the light breeze ruffled her hair. She had her chin tipped up slightly, as if she were tasting the air as she breathed it in. Michael grinned and glanced in the rearview mirror at True, fastened with a safety harness in the back of his truck. Stacey's dog was also leaning into the wind, a look of sheer doggie pleasure on her face.

The ride in the truck wasn't bothering her pregnant dog. Stacey seemed content to stay, for the moment, anyway. Now, if only the evening didn't chase her back to New Orleans.

She stirred, turned her head, and smiled at him. When she moved, the stretchy fabric of her red blouse clung to every curve. He tightened his grip on the steering wheel. Along with that enticing shirt, she wore white slacks and sandals. Fire-engine-red polish decorated the toes that peeked from beneath her slacks.

Yeah, he wanted a peek.

That demure look of hers, tinged as it was with the hint of a devil beneath the angelic surface, sent Michael's blood teasing his body in a way he didn't need just before he arrived at his house.

After dinner, though . . .

She gave him a soft smile, then turned her head back toward the window, apparently absorbed by the sight of the wood frame houses, dogwood trees, and the occasional swing set decorating the front yards along the peaceful road that led toward his house.

He stretched out an arm along the back of the seat. "You're quiet tonight," he said softly, wondering what she'd do if he stroked the back of her neck where the thick weight of her hair had parted just enough to hint at the soft skin calling to him.

What the hell.

Why wonder?

Find out.

He reached his fingers out, eager like a high school kid for that first touch, just as she shifted sideways in her seat, facing him with an earnest expression.

He caught his free-falling hand and parked his arm back on the seat again.

"I've been thinking," she said.

"Ah." He turned right on Peony Lane, the road that ended at his house. He wished he lived on a street with a more guy kind of name, but the house, tucked away at the end of the road on half an acre, was perfect.

"About the animal shelter problem."

"You're thinking about the shelter." He'd been lusting after her while she was ruminating on one of Doolittle's problems. He nodded, very thoughtfully, he hoped. "And . . . ?"

"You need money. Therefore, you need a fund-raising campaign. It's not enough for people to be fuzzily aware of a problem. They have to have it drawn out for them in 3-D."

"So just mentioning the need to people isn't enough." He could still admire her breasts while concentrating on the topic, he discovered.

"Oh, no." She shook her head and Michael continued his dual concentration experiment. A long lock of her hair fell forward over her shoulder and nestled in her cleavage.

Michael hit the brake, a little harder than he'd intended, and pulled into his driveway. "We're here," he said. "Can we talk more about your ideas after dinner?" That was good. He'd have a real reason for more time alone with her.

"You mean when your children aren't listening?" She smiled. "Of course."

Michael did a double-take. He hadn't been thinking of protecting his girls from the realities of animal homelessness. Jessica and Kristen were more likely to lead a campaign than to bury their heads in their pillows. But he nodded. Then he caught himself. Honesty mattered more than any other trait. If he and Pauline had managed one ounce of honesty, his life wouldn't be in the mess it was at present.

Stacey was reaching for the door handle.

"Wait," he said.

She paused, a question in her eyes.

"There's nothing Jessica and Kristen haven't seen or heard when it comes to the shelter problem."

"Oh." That questioning look grew.

He touched the back of her hair, the same spot where he'd wanted to stroke her neck. "But I'd still like to talk about it with you. After dinner. I know a quiet place we can go."

"Ah," she said.

It wasn't a yes, but it wasn't a no. He could work with that. And it was a good thing because at that moment three of his dogs spotted True in the truck and dashed straight toward them, followed by Jessica, wearing no shoes and crying.

Stacey stared at the approaching menagerie and at the girl who'd gone from the self-possessed child of earlier in the day to the very picture of a little one in distress. But Michael didn't look all that worried as he climbed out of the truck, walked around, and before she knew it, opened the door for her.

"Dad!" Jessica called.

The dogs barked. True answered with a volley of her own.

And from closer to the house came a high-pitched wail. "You little brat. I'm going to kill you!"

"Welcome to my home," Michael said, a rueful grin on his face.

Stacey stepped down from the truck cab as Jessica launched herself around Michael's legs. "She started it," she cried, pointing back toward the house.

Another brown-haired girl, by looks that awkward age between child and teenager, stalked toward them from the front porch of the two-story house. One arm was encased in a cast, Stacey noted, and the girl's face was set in an intense frown. So this was Kristen.

One of the three dogs turned around and headed toward her in a choppy, hop-skip of a gait, which Stacey soon realized was the result of having only three legs.

"What's up?" Michael said, tugging Jessica gently free of his leg as he told the dogs to sit.

Stacey calmed True, loosening the safety harness while maintaining a firm grip on her leash as she leapt from the pickup to check out the other dogs.

"She's a brat, that's what's up," Kristen said, drawing up to them and giving Stacey a bold once-over before hunching her shoulder and turning on her dad.

Stacey blinked. She'd never been rude, not even once in her life, that she could recall, so this girl's behavior startled her. The St. Cyrs might have fought each other over who had the highest claim to Stacey's affections, but they always agreed on enforcing proper behavior. If Miss Manners ever retired, either parent could write her column.

"She thinks she's so special 'cause she gets away with things I could never have done," Kristen continued, building a hysterical pitch to her voice. "*I* had to take ballet. *I* had to parade around on those stupid beauty pageant stages like some sort of freak! But does *she* have to?" She jabbed a finger in her younger sister's direction and Stacey flinched, as did the younger daughter.

Stacey stole a glance toward Michael. He was standing, his arms at his sides, a look far more sad than mad on his face. She had to fight the urge to walk over to him, to offer comfort.

This scene had nothing to do with her.

She was a guest, apparently arrived at a most inconvenient time.

The best thing to do was for her to slip away or take True for a quiet walk.

"Michael, I'll just—" She must have made some gesture, because he reached out and caught her gently by the forearm.

"Please, don't go." He released her, but she could still feel his touch on her skin. "Kristen. Jessica. We'll address these issues later. We have company tonight and why don't we start right now by remembering a few of our manners?"

Jessica wiped her tear-stained cheeks and smiled up at Stacey. "Hi, again," she said.

That was all it took to reignite her sister's fury. "Oh, you've already met the company, have you?" She raked a glance over Stacey, shrugged, and said, "So Dad's back to trying to replace our mother, is he?"

Stacey gasped in unison with Jessica.

Michael strode forward and took his older daughter by the shoulder. "To your room with you," he said, his voice stern. "I'll be up before dinner and if you've found your manners under your bed or stuffed away in the back of the closet, maybe you can join the rest of us."

"What did I do?" Kristen jerked her arm away and stalked off, her head high.

Michael stood there, head tipped up toward the softening early evening sky.

Stacey felt his sigh in the tips of her toes.

But she felt Kristen's pain, too. She'd been there. Oh, yes, she'd been there. *So Dad's back to trying to replace our mother, is he?* How many times had she thought the same thing, through all the years she'd been exposed to her father's girlfriends and two additional ex-wives?

She wished she could go to Kristen and explain it wasn't like that at all. But why should the girl listen to her? Stacey wouldn't have believed any of the females who'd sought after her rich, successful doctor dad, or been pursued by him.

It was Jessica who went to her sister. The tears of a few minutes earlier might never have occurred, as she skipped over to Kristen and said in a voice clearly heard over the barking one of the dogs had started, "Oh, she's not one of them. Dad invited her and her dog because she's my friend."

"Boy, are you stupid," Kristen said, and marched toward the house.

Jessica turned around, tears right back in place.

"Come on inside, Stacey," Michael said, slipping an arm around his younger daughter and giving her a quick hug. "Unless you've changed your mind and want to escape?"

Jessica slid one small hand into her dad's and the other into Stacey's, gazing up at Stacey with an expression so trusting, Stacey couldn't have let her down even if she had a plane to catch. Stacey flashed father and daughter a quick smile and shook her head. True looked up at her, as if checking out the possibility of slipping free to chase the other animals.

Michael dabbed at Jessica's cheek with the back of one thumb, in a comforting and reassuring gesture. Stacey almost wished she were the one crying, just to feel that touch.

Silly, she told herself, as they moved toward the house.

"Why don't you run ahead and put the dogs in the back yard?" Michael said to Jessica.

"They don't like being shut up."

"I don't like shaving, but I do it anyway," Michael said in a gentle but firm voice.

"Oh, okay." She let go of their hands and called the dogs. They ambled after her, turning the corner of the house.

True watched them, every muscle in her body alert. "I don't think it's group playtime," Stacey said, keeping a firm hand on her dog's leash.

"They're pretty tame," Michael said, "but I wouldn't recommend unsupervised visitations. Sir Walter can get pretty worked up. He's the three-legged marvel."

"What happened to his leg?"

They had reached the porch and Michael paused with one foot on the bottom step. A flash of pain crossed his face; then, as quickly as it had appeared, it vanished. Stacey wondered if she had imagined it, but as soon as he spoke, she knew the image had been real.

"Some idiot shot him. When I found him, his leg was mangled and infected beyond saving. I put him up for adoption, but no one wanted him. Country dogs don't normally get by on less than four legs, it seems." He glanced off into the distance, then faced her again. "He'd been at the clinic for two weeks. He learned how to open his cage and when I'd go in in the mornings, there he'd be, strolling around in the back as if he owned the place."

"And you couldn't bear to part with him?"

He shook his head, then smiled. "You get used to a lot of things in this business, but sometimes an animal gets under your skin and you just can't give up on it."

"So you brought him home?"

"So I did."

"And the others?"

He smiled. "Kristen rescued the standard poodle when someone moved away and left him. Jessica wanted to keep the shepherd after he showed up at the house in a rainstorm. And the Heinz 57, the lovable mixed mutt, is the housekeeper's dog, and that's another story. That's enough for now."

True barked, once, then twice.

Stacey and Michael laughed and smiled at each other. "It's almost as if she knows what I said," he said, reaching down to pat the bearded collie on her head. "Come on. If I don't start that grill, we'll be driving into town to the Sonic."

"As long as they don't serve rabbit, that's fine by me."

About to stride up the stairs to the porch, Michael halted. "Rabbit?"

"You know, bunny."

"As in the Easter bunny?" He made a face, thinking she was probably joking.

"Miss Abbie had a package of rabbit in her bag today. She said she was making stew out of it. I figured it was some sort of local specialty."

Michael made an even more pronounced face of disapproval. "The people around Doolittle will eat anything they trap. There had been a rabbit-processing plant here for some time, but it went out of business very recently. Jessica has a rabbit hutch in the back yard. The idea of munching down on bunny bones just does not appeal to me."

"So what's on the menu for tonight?"

"We keep talking like this and it'll be grilled vegetables." He held out a hand and was pleased when she slid her own into his. "Let me get you settled and then I need to talk to Kristen."

She left her hand in his for only a moment, pulling free as he opened the front door. "So you're not really leaving her in her room until dinner?"

"No, Stacey, I'm not." One hand on the door, he studied her. "Did I sound too harsh?" He hadn't meant to, but sometimes the kids pushed buttons in him he didn't know he had.

True barked again, then looked around expectantly.

"Not harsh," Stacey said slowly. "But it's so hard to be that age and so . . ."

He waited, wondering what adjective she would pick. The other two women he'd dated—or attempted to date—in Doolittle had had little sympathy for Kristen. Everyone adored Jessica; she was an angel of a child. Even Kristen's mother could take her only in small doses. But she was his daughter, his brilliant, if somewhat too easily tormented child, and he loved her, faults and all, and brooked no criticism of her from others.

"So vulnerable," she said softly.

For that description alone Michael could have kissed her. Not to mention the way she'd turned all soft and contemplative. She was running one hand over the bearded collie's ears, fingering them gently as she stood there, so close to him.

Yet so far away.

Kiss her.

Yeah, dammit, kiss her now.

Her lips parted, as if she'd read his mind.

Michael let go of the door and turned to her.

She looked up, a dreamy expression on her face, her hold on True's leash slackening slightly.

"Stacey," he said, taking in a short breath, all he could manage as he inhaled her scent, a hybrid of pure woman and a heady perfume that had to carry a hundred-dollar-an-ounce price tag.

"Yes, Michael?" She wet her lips with the tip of her tongue.

"You're very . . ." he hesitated. Dammit, he didn't know her well enough to kiss her. She'd probably leap in his truck and demand to be driven back to town. And he didn't want her to go.

"Yes?" He could have sworn she was breathing pretty quickly herself.

"Sensitive," he said, lowering his head to her now-tipped-up face.

"Dogs all locked up," Jessica called, careening into the front yard and attacking the front steps in a run.

Michael swore, not too softly, and stepped back.

"So near and yet so far," Stacey murmured.

Or at least he thought that was what she said. But then she turned to his daughter, one hand outstretched, and, seemingly unaffected or possibly even unaware that he'd been about to kiss her, said, "Want to walk True with me?"

And Michael had to keep from putting his hands on his head and pulling out his hair.

Chapter 7

But Jessica, it seemed, had other plans. "Come inside and I'll show you my room."

"Why don't you go upstairs first and make sure it's presentable?" Michael said, seizing the opportunity to recapture the moment with Stacey.

"You already made me clean it up."

Michael opened the door, held it, and pointed. "Go. Now."

Jessica went.

And Stacey stepped inside, too, leading True.

"We did straighten up a bit in honor of your visit," he said, taking one quick glance around the entry hall. That was all it took to show him his efforts had already been destroyed. In the short time it had taken him to collect Stacey at the Schoolhouse Inn, Kristen's in-line skates, tennis shoes, socks, and portable CD player had landed in the hall.

Along with Jessica's hula hoop.

"Careful," he said, and caught Stacey by the arm just

as she was about to trip on the purple plastic hoop. "You're entering a land mine."

She glanced down at her bare arm where his hand rested. "Yes, I can see it's fraught with danger." And then she smiled at him and he knew she wanted him to kiss her.

And there he stood with a hula hoop in one hand.

He must look ridiculous. He dropped her arm, turned, and thrust the toy outside the front door, where it clattered onto the boards of the porch. When he swung back around, Stacey had moved into the hall and was gazing into the living room that opened off to the right.

You should have kissed her, dummy. Michael shook his head and led Stacey into the living room. The area served as den, family room, and homework central. At any given time, including this moment, there were books everywhere, his laptop up and running, two game consoles, and a stack of videotapes that brought to mind the Leaning Tower of Pisa. Tonight yet another pair of Kristen's shoes added their own flair to the decor.

"How homey," Stacey said, pausing by the battered upright piano Michael had bought secondhand when Kristen started lessons.

Michael grimaced. Visions of a suave bachelor pad danced in his mind, a place done all in black leather and chrome. He closed his eyes for a moment and added to the scene a waterbed with satin sheets. But when he looked again, there he was smack in the center of Middle American fatherhood.

He must have made a face, because Stacey said, "I meant that as a compliment."

"Ah," he said, not sure he believed her. He'd be willing to bet she was the leather sofa type. Or antiques, the real thing, not look-alikes made in the back room of some French Quarter tourist trade furniture store.

"A home should look like a home, not a museum." She sighed and ran one hand lightly over the keys. The notes rang sweetly, dispelling the gloom that had threatened to settle over Michael.

"That it should," he said, stepping beside her and picking out what little he remembered of the "chopsticks" duet.

Stacey let go of True's leash and joined him.

"You do that really well," he said, following her lead and picking up the tempo.

She smiled and nodded. Her hair fell forward over her shoulder and Michael lifted a hand from the keyboard to tuck the silky strands behind her ear. She continued playing. He left his hand on her hair, smoothing it softly.

Stacey forced herself to concentrate on the keys. She built the tempo, skipping almost recklessly as the feel of Michael's hand on her head created a funny sensation of longing mixed with a healthy dose of panic.

What was she doing here in this man's house, savoring his touch? She'd only just met him. She'd dated Robert for three months before she'd let him do more than kiss her good night. She was Stacey St. Cyr, and she believed in caution, in doing one's research, in making slow careful choices because the very idea of a relationship with a guy sent her into scared mode.

He moved his hand to the back of her neck. The gentle circling of his thumb on her bare skin sent shivers through her. Stacey ended the piece in a crescendo and then paused, her hands hovering over the ivories.

His mouth against her hair, Michael whispered, "Play something slow."

She nodded. Her mouth was dry, her fingers clammy. And deep within her, heat and moisture demanded attention, clamored for satisfaction.

Stacey didn't know a lot of pieces from memory. Chopsticks didn't count because everyone knew that. Years ago, haunted by the tragedy of love gone bad, she'd memorized the theme from *The Godfather*. She began playing the poignant notes composed by Nino Rota.

Michael's hands continued their magic. Stacey sighed, in a good way, and abruptly lifted her hands from the keys.

"It's too sad," she said.

He moved one hand to the side of her cheek and bent his head, his eyes dark and intense with desire. Stacey breathed in the scent of him. She closed her eyes, knowing he was about to kiss her. Then she quickly opened them. She didn't want to close her eyes. She wanted to experience every moment as fully as possible.

He brushed the outline of her upper lip with his thumb. "So pretty," he said softly.

"Thank you," Stacey said, amazed at just how badly she wanted him to hurry up and kiss her.

She turned slightly so that her body brushed against his.

He cupped her chin.

"Dad!"

Stacey jerked back.

True barked and rose from where she'd been sitting.

Michael swore under his breath and turned toward the doorway. Jessica was just skipping into the entranceway. She paused, hands on her hips. Stacey wasn't sure whether she'd seen them about to kiss or not.

"What is it, Jessica?" Michael sounded fairly matter-of-fact, but Stacey saw the way his chest was moving in and out and knew that he was as disappointed at being interrupted as she was—if not more so.

Jessica pointed to Stacey. "I cleaned my room, so can Stacey come upstairs now?"

Michael looked as relieved as Stacey felt. "Sure, if it's okay with her."

Stacey smiled and touched a finger to her lips. The appreciative grin she got from Michael lit her up in a way she had no business feeling. What was she doing, practically promising him they'd start up again from where they were interrupted?

"I'll take True outside and fire up the grill," Michael said. "What's a bit more heat?"

Stacey laughed and Jessica looked at her as if she were a nutty adult as she took her by the hand and led her up the stairs.

A colorful computer-printed sign announced that the room to the left of the stairs was Jessica's. Feeling a bit like a trespasser, Stacey followed the child into her room, a charming mix of white princess furniture and a stuffed animal collection to rival any F.A.O. Schwarz window display.

Over Jessica's introductions of the animals, two of which turned out to be fat and lazy cats of the live variety, Stacey heard Michael's steps on the hall stairs. Her sense of anticipation surprised her as she waited for him to join them.

"This is my veterinarian Barbie," Jessica said, holding up the perfect plastic babe dressed in a white smock over green scrubs. "Mrs. Beebe made her for me."

"Very nice," Jessica said, half turning her head, only to realize Michael had gone the other way at the top of the stairs.

Kristen. He was checking on Kristen. The muffled bass that had been providing background stopped and then Stacey heard father and daughter, chatting happily, head back downstairs.

A wave of emotion hit her then and she realized it was admiration for this man she barely knew. No wonder she wanted to kiss him. Here was a guy who took wonderful care of his family as a single parent, not to mention the townspeople and their pets.

You want to kiss him because he's sexy and you're starved for a man.

Stacey blinked.

"Yeah, this one's pretty cool," Jessica said, apparently taking Stacey's reaction as praise for her biker Barbie. "Scottie made this one. He says the helmet is just like his."

"You certainly have a range of unusual Barbies," Stacey said. "I only had the normal ones when I was a kid."

Jessica patted the floor next to where she was hunched over her dolls. "Sit down. I've got lots more to show you."

"And I'm sure you can be showing her those after dinner," said a softly accented female voice from behind

Stacey. She jumped and swung around, not expecting another woman in Michael's house.

Gray eyes met hers, assessing but kind, under a mass of graying brown hair. The woman could have been their grandmother, Stacey guessed, but probably wasn't. Jessica didn't leap up to greet her but didn't ignore her exactly.

"I'm Eleanor Beebe," the woman said.

"Stacey St. Cyr."

"She's my new friend," Jessica said, pulling out a Barbie dressed in buckskin, complete with fringe. Where she'd found the high-heeled moccasins, Stacey couldn't imagine.

"I heard you were a-coming out for dinner, so I turned back around and headed straight here."

Stacey knew her puzzlement showed on her face.

"They told me at the market Michael had been there and mentioned he was a-having company. Well, that wouldn't do if I weren't here, says I." She rolled up the sleeves of a pink cotton blouse that was tucked into the plump waist of a flowered skirt. "Dr. Mike thinks he can do it all, but he needs to let some of the rest of us help, too."

Jessica nodded. "Dad does do it all," she said.

"Well, not as a-long as I have breath left in my body," Mrs. Beebe said. "He helped me when I needed it and unlike some of the other less-than-grateful people in this town, I'm a-here to help him, too." She folded her hands together and smiled. "Now, Miss Jessica, why don't you bring one of those dolls down to the kitchen and make yourself useful with supper?"

Jessica looked as if she were about to object, but after a quick glance at Mrs. Beebe's sweet, soulful expression, she plucked trapper Barbie from the pile and jumped up.

Disappointing Mrs. Beebe was not something the sensitive Jessica was about to do, Stacey thought as she followed them downstairs to the kitchen, a cheery room done in sunshine-yellow and white. A greenhouse window jutted out from the sink and counter area, leading the eye past several beautiful African violets to the back lawn beyond.

There Michael was tossing a ball to Kristen, who seemed quite adept at catching it while at the same time keeping the arm laden with the cast safely tucked by her side. Two other dogs had joined True and the trio chased back and forth as the ball moved from father to daughter.

Stacey had to force her attention back to the kitchen, away from the sight of Michael relaxed and happy, his shirt pulled loose from his jeans at the waist, showing a tantalizing glimpse of smooth, bare skin.

Jessica propped her doll on the butcher-block table situated between the sink and the refrigerator. Stacey immediately recognized it as a Boos, the only kind a serious chef would own. Eyeing the basket of fresh green beans and obviously sensing the work ahead, Jessica said, "Maybe I should go see if Dad needs help."

"All right, lovey," Mrs. Beebe said with a fond smile. "But take that munchkin lady with you."

Jessica giggled. "That's a Barbie, not a munchkin. The munchkins live in Oz."

Her smile fading somewhat, Mrs. Beebe said under

her breath as Jessica slipped out, doll in hand, "Well, a frog would be more welcome on my table than that doll."

"Not a Barbie fan?" Stacey asked.

Mrs. Beebe scowled, a surprisingly harsh contrast to her earlier soft expressions. "Those dolls teach girls the wrong lessons. There's more to life than being some man's plaything."

"Of course," Stacey said, "but . . ." She trailed off, realizing she'd been about to say how nice it would be to be the right man's object of desire.

Mrs. Beebe glanced at her with shrewd eyes. "Aye, there's a place for it, but most men are too dense to know how to do right by a woman. Now, Dr. Mike, it's a miracle to me his wife up and left him. Any female who would do that has to be crazy."

Stacey hoped her curiosity didn't show too avidly. "Do you know his ex-wife?" She crossed her fingers, hoping for confirmation of that status.

Mrs. Beebe pulled a bag of carrots and a head of cabbage from the refrigerator and studied it. "I'm thinking a big dish of coleslaw would be just right with the grilled chicken. And biscuits, of course. And I think I'll whip up an apple pie."

"Sounds great," Stacey said.

"Why don't you wash your hands and scrape these carrots?"

The only carrots Stacey knew came from the market in plastic bags, already washed and cleaned and arranged in neat sticks, but she took the vegetables and the peeler Mrs. Beebe handed to her and set to work removing the outer surface. Mrs. Beebe began whistling softly and dumping flour into a large mixing bowl.

When she could stand it no longer, Stacey said, "So you were saying the ex-Mrs. Halliday lives in Doolittle?"

"Oh, was I?" She nodded and tossed some baking powder into the bowl. "It's not Christian to gossip, but seeing that you are new to town, I s'pose there's no harm in letting you know some of Dr. Mike's history."

She sighed and stirred the ingredients with a large wooden spoon. "If it weren't for Dr. Mike, I'd probably be six feet under. Or still wishing I was, near 'bouts."

Stacey clasped a carrot and stared at the woman. Was there no end to Michael Halliday's rescue feats? As curious as she was about the former wife, she was far more interested in Michael, though of course none of it really mattered, she reminded herself. She'd be back in New Orleans and this jaunt to another time and a far different world would be nothing but a vacation memory. Still, she put down the peeler, leaned against the sink, and prepared to listen. Somehow, she didn't think Mrs. Beebe needed any prompting.

"The Lord works in mysterious ways," the older woman said, raising and then lowering the Morton's salt with an emphatic thump. "I never knew that I was meant to be a bride. I had a-been working as a house-keeper and happy I was to do so."

She stirred the mixture in the bowl as shouts of laughter filtered in from the back yard. Stacey itched to turn around and share the scene out the window, but now was not the moment.

"Then along came Pastor Beebe and asked to marry me, his wife having died giving birth to their fifth little one. That was more than twenty years ago." Mrs. Beebe jerked the spoon out of the bowl. "You seem like a smart young thing, so I guess I don't need to say this to you, but it's a wise woman who gets to know a man before she walks to the altar, and not after."

"That's for sure," Stacey said with feeling, thinking of Robert. Perhaps he'd done her a favor jilting her. "So was Mr. Beebe looking for a wet nurse for his children?"

Mrs. Beebe shook her head. "Oh, but I knew that and that was fine by me. I raised that baby and the older kids, too, as if they'd passed through my own loins. The children were never a problem. Mr. Beebe was."

"Oh," Stacey said, unsure of what to add. She wasn't sure what this had to do with Michael.

Mrs. Beebe scattered a handful of flour over a large sheet of wax paper and dumped the contents of the bowl out onto it. Stacey admired the glistening biscuit dough and gave thanks she'd escaped the Shoney's buffet and the baked rabbit for Mrs. Beebe's culinary creations.

"You see, Miss Stacey," the housekeeper said with a shake of her head, "what Mr. Beebe really wanted was a punching bag."

"He beat you?" Her voice rose. Stacey hadn't been expecting this sort of revelation.

"Aye, he started like all the monsters do, in little ways, and then worked up to the big ones. He waited, mostly, until the children were off at school or having their sleepovers at friends' houses." She waved a rolling pin and said, "And I just let him do it."

Stacey felt sick to her stomach. "How long did it go on?"

Mrs. Beebe flattened the ball of dough in one swift

surge of the rolling pin. "Oh, I a-married him when I was just past thirty, and Colleen—that was the baby—is twenty now and in school in Fayetteville. Mr. Beebe got worse after Colleen went to college. That's when people started to notice and talk. But they only talked amongst themselves and whispered at church when I'd be wearing long sleeves and a high collar and foundation as thick as syrup to cover up the bruises."

Stacey clutched the carrot peeler, watching as Mrs. Beebe, her mouth only slightly downturned despite the sorrow of her tale, paused to rummage in a drawer and then moved back to the Boos table with a biscuit cutter in hand. "But it was Dr. Mike who helped me."

Stacey nodded. Of course Michael Halliday would speak out. A lump formed in her throat as admiration for him flooded through her.

"Mr. Beebe preached a fine sermon—his last in the pulpit in this town, if he'd only known it then—then came home, drank a big old bottle of strong spirits, and threw the jug at my dog." She slapped the cut-out biscuits onto a baking pan, showing more fire than she had to that point. "Now, you can hurt me, but don't hurt my animals. He like to broke my poor Sparky's back and I snatched that jug up and hit Mr. Beebe upside the head. The Bible doesn't allow for violence, but it does speak for justice. Mr. Beebe beat me pretty bad before I left out of there with Sparky to get him to the doctor."

"And you went to Dr. Mike."

Mrs. Beebe nodded. The tray was now full of biscuits ready to be baked. She glanced around, blinked, and said, "My, oh, my, my, what am I a-doing? Talking on like this. Forgive me. You don't want to hear all these old ghost stories." She dusted flour from her hands and said, "How's that coleslaw coming?"

Stacey gaped at the woman. She couldn't stop the story now, not when she'd gotten to the part about Michael. Stacey wanted to know more about him. Admit it, she told herself, loosening her death grip on the vegetable peeler and picking up one of her abandoned carrots, Stacy St. Cyr wants to know everything there is to know about the amazing Dr. Michael Halliday. "Coleslaw is almost done," she said, forgetting she hadn't yet chopped the cabbage, let alone finished the carrots. "So what happened when you took your dog to the vet?"

Mrs. Beebe plopped a bowl of green apples onto the butcher-block table. "He took one look at the dog, said Sparky would need X rays. He sent him off with one of his assistants, then asked me what happened to my eye. I was so hurt for my little dog that I broke down and told him Mr. Beebe beat us both."

Broke down? Stacey marveled at the woman's description. Why hadn't she asked for help so much earlier? But she knew better than to ask that question. No one who'd been in such an abusive situation ever needed her own judgment questioned. Stacey might as well ask herself why she'd spent six years of her life trusting the skunk who'd lied to her and left her at the altar. For some things there were no answers.

Stacey watched the apple peel disappear at the speed of light under Mrs. Beebe's efficient fingers as she waited for the rest of the story. After a long pause, the other woman shook her head and said, "You can be sure as the night is long that as soon as I told him the truth I could have bitten off my tongue."

"Why? I can't imagine Michael—Dr. Halliday—being anything but understanding."

"That's true, but he was all a-ready to charge in and have Mr. Beebe arrested and, well, you see, my dear, I was afraid. As horrible as it was, I'd started thinking I deserved all those bad things."

"No one deserves to be abused." Stacey tossed down the peeler and abandoned all pretense of progress on the coleslaw. She couldn't stand to see people or animals hurt.

Mrs. Beebe shrugged. "The mind is a funny thing." She began slicing the peeled green apples. "But there's no stopping Dr. Mike once he has a cause under his craw, as they say."

Stacey wasn't familiar with the expression, but she knew exactly what Mrs. Beebe meant. "So he took matters into his own hands." It was a statement, no question implied. Of course Michael Halliday had acted.

"He took me to the Schoolhouse Inn that night and the next day I moved in here. He made his ex-wife— she's a lawyer, did you know—work out a divorce and then he saw to it that Mr. Beebe's congregation voted him out. How he did that I'll never know. Those same people had looked the other way for years and years." She sighed, but then her face softened. "But I can't blame them. I did the same thing. His children never knew. I told them we divorced, and bless their hearts, they still a-visit me. Oh, yes, Dr. Mike saved me in spite of my own self."

Stacey blinked and wiped at her eyes with a quick sweep of her hand. "What happened to Sparky?"

Mrs. Beebe walked over to where Stacey stood by the

window and inclined her chin as she leaned over the sink to wash her hands. "That's him, out there sunning himself next to the lilac bush."

Sure enough, a little Heinz 57 dog lay curled, his nose on his paws, sleeping blissfully, oblivious to the game of Frisbee being played by two girls, three other dogs, and one very special man.

Chapter 8

Being a single dad had its good moments, but it sure had its rough ones, too. Michael loved the evenings when everything went smoothly—and cherished them, because they were so rare. Tonight, with Stacey sitting between Jessica and Kristen, and Mrs. Beebe doling out another panful of hot biscuits, Michael took a moment to count his blessings.

He took an even longer moment to admire Stacey. Stacey stumbling into his life topped his list of 1,001 things for which to be thankful. At the moment, she sat at the dinner table with her head bent toward Jessica, listening to his younger daughter relating how and why she'd been given her trapper Barbie outfit.

Michael couldn't swear to it, but he thought Stacey's beautiful eyes pooled with tears as Jessica described the injured pet the country trapper, cousin to the man who'd been in today with his hunting dog, had lost. Jessica had been there in the clinic that Saturday, far too young, in Michael's opinion, to watch a dog bleeding to death from buckshot. But she'd insisted on staying and had held the hand of the country guy's son, as the dog died, too far gone for Michael to do anything to save him.

Just then Stacey lifted her head and looked over at Michael. Her eyes were misty and she gave him a thousand-watt smile that lit him through and through.

At that moment in time, he would have thrown himself in front of a train to keep her there in town.

Heck, at any moment, he'd do so.

"Animals are just too much trouble," Kristen said, breaking the moment with her tough pronouncement.

But Michael wasn't fooled. He understood why Kristen no longer helped in the clinic. Some people were too gentle to take the pain of suffering and helplessness, and for all her bravado, his older daughter was as sensitive as they came.

Kristen took another biscuit and crammed it into her mouth.

Mrs. Beebe sighed, in that soft, slightly manipulative way of hers, showing her disappointment with Kristen's manners. Kristen glared at her. So much for their productive and positive talk before dinner, Michael thought.

The phone rang. Kristen leapt up, knocking her chair backward with a crash.

"Sit," Michael said.

"But it might be for me," Kristen said, a few crumbs of biscuit sprinkling her blouse.

"You know the rules," Michael said, rising and reaching for the portable phone he'd left on a side table. He received so many emergency calls on his home number he kept the phone within range, as well as the pager he carried. But he guarded his family from interruptions as much as he could.

He halted in surprise as Kristen dashed past him, grabbed the phone, and began talking rapidly as she headed toward the door to the kitchen.

"No phone fun during food time," Jessica said. Michael grimaced as her sweet, yet prim voice reminded him that he had to face this disciplinary situation. Kristen was going through a difficult time, but that meant a sense of order and structure was even more essential.

"Tell whoever it is you'll call them back after dinner," Michael said.

"But it's Amanda and I need to talk to her now," she answered, and went right back to chattering.

"Kristen's being very bad," Jessica said to the table in general.

Michael glanced over his shoulder. Stacey was forking up a bite of coleslaw, listening politely to something Mrs. Beebe had just said, even though Michael was positive she was paying avid attention to Kristen's antics.

"Kristen," Michael said.

Her voice rolled on, reaching the peaks of treble excitement that indicated boy talk. Michael sighed. Only twelve years old and she endured the angst he'd been spared till his later teen years. He worried, a lot, about his girls growing up too fast.

"Time's up," he said, crossing to her side and removing the phone from her grasp. To her friend, he said, "Kristen has to go now."

"Dad!" Kristen's voice rose to a wail. "How embarrassing. She'll think I'm a child."

"Well, you are," Jessica said. "You're only four years older than I am, and if I'm a child, you are, too."

"That was no more embarrassing than your own behavior," Michael said, reseating himself and pointing to Kristen's spot at the table.

She slumped into her chair and glowered at him.

"We had a family meeting. You agreed to our rules. Now follow them."

Jessica said under her breath, "Kristen got in trouble. Kristen got in trouble."

"And Jessica is going to if she doesn't mind her mouth," Michael said.

Jessica flashed him a grin. He shook his head and glanced over at Stacey, thinking with longing of the quiet candlelit restaurant where they could have been spending the evening. Great first date. Yeah, the kind that never got a second chance.

Only Stacey didn't appear too horrified. And she hadn't hightailed it out of the house. She was studying Kristen with a sympathetic look in her eyes and Michael couldn't help but wonder if she knew just how much he appreciated her quiet yet supportive presence.

"No one in this family cares what happens to me," Kristen said.

From her seat between the two girls, Stacey caught Michael's pleading look and flashed him a smile in response. He'd invited her over at full risk of self-revelation. With two children as chaperones, there was no call for first-date pretensions. Kids were too out there, and by that fact showed their parents' true colors.

"We care," Michael said, pouring more iced tea into his glass. "Would you care to share the crisis you and Amanda were discussing?"

Jessica made a silly face and Kristen rolled her eyes, but Stacey noticed her trembling lip.

"You wouldn't understand anyway," she said.

Michael reached over and smoothed one hand over her shoulder. "Try me, sweetheart."

Kristen sniffled and patted her dad on the hand.

Stacey had to glance down at her plate. If he touched her that gently, she'd blurt out all her troubles. She was finding it hard to remember how annoying he could be. No wonder the town was ga-ga over him. So why was this sensitive, sexy man no longer with his wife? She hated to search for hidden flaws, but she couldn't help it. Six years and every form of due diligence she'd followed during her engagement, and still she'd gotten burned.

"Well," Kristen said, dragging the one word out to three-plus syllables, "there's this guy."

"You are so boy-crazy," Jessica said, posing her trapper Barbie in a split that would have made her the envy of any gymnastics team.

"What do you know?"

"I know Bobby Peters doesn't like you anymore."

"That's not true!" Kristen turned to Stacey and caught her arm. "See what I have to put up with? I wish I were an only child!"

Stacey wasn't sure how to respond, but before she

knew it, she said, "I was an only child and I always wanted a sister."

"Well, be careful what you ask for," Kristen said, but then she glanced over at Jessica and, rather than giving her grief, produced a grin for her little sister.

Michael smiled at Stacey, warming her more than she cared to admit.

"So, anyway," Kristen said, "Bobby does like me, but Amanda says that's why he won't do this project with me, but we have to have a partner or we don't get credit, but if he did it with me, then the other kids would think he liked me, so he had to pick Caitlin, but now I don't have a partner and Caitlin thinks Bobby likes . . ."

She kept going, all one long sentence, told in a single breath. Stacey dissected the flow of words and reached the essence of the message—Kristen was the only kid in the class without a partner. Kristen, still the new kid in town, was the one left standing outside the circle.

"How many kids are in your class?" Michael asked the question.

"Twenty-one." Kristen looked at him as if she couldn't understand why he'd interrupted to ask such an irrelevant question.

"Simple solution," Michael said, obviously reaching the same conclusion Stacey had. "Tell the teacher. She can't assign an impossible task."

"Dad, I can't do that. Besides, if Bobby really liked me, he wouldn't have asked Caitlin. Would he?"

Mrs. Beebe leaned over and patted Kristen's hand. "There's no accounting for behavior sometimes, child."

Michael frowned, but the expression vanished as soon as it appeared. "Nor for impossible assignments."

"It's not really impossible," Stacey said slowly.

Kristen and Michael both stared at her. Together they said, "Why not?"

"*Partner* doesn't necessarily mean one plus one."

"But she said . . ." Kristen trailed off.

Michael glanced from his daughter over to Stacey, who'd steepled her fingers together. "Three can be a partnership, as well as two, or five, or four."

"But then it's a group," Kristen said.

"I'll just get that apple pie," Mrs. Beebe said, rising from her seat.

As she did, the phone rang.

Everyone looked at everyone else. Kristen half rose from her seat, then lowered her body. Michael rose, then sat back down. The phone continued to shrill.

All eyes turned to Stacey. The ringing was coming from her purse, which she'd hung from the back of her chair.

She reached inside and glanced at the caller ID.

"No phone fun at dinnertime," Jessica said.

Stacey recognized her father's number.

"It's my dad," she said, flipping open the phone.

"How come she can answer the phone?" Kristen asked, glaring at her dad.

Stacey's father's voice boomed in her ear. "Do you know a Mrs. Clark?"

"Mrs. who?" Surely she hadn't heard correctly. The agent couldn't have tracked down her dad in New Orleans. But even as the thought crossed her mind, Stacey knew the agent most certainly could and obviously had.

She groaned, remembering that she'd mentioned over biscuits that her father was a doctor in New Orleans. She easily could have located her dad.

"Clark."

Even without looking directly, she felt Jessica and Kristen staring at her.

"Can I call you later?"

"I've got a date," her three-times-married-and-divorced dad said, sounding pleased with himself. Stacey cupped her hand more closely around the cell phone. Her dad was supposed to be married—to her mother.

"Well, I guess the rules don't apply to grown-ups," Kristen said in a sulky voice, her good humor evaporating all that quickly.

"Kristen, Stacey is a guest," Michael said. "Now finish your dinner."

"When I'm a guest at Amanda's I have to follow their rules."

"This Mrs. Clark seems to think I'm buying property in godforsaken Arkansas. She e-mailed me photos of retirement condos. I would have ignored her as just another form of spam mail, but she insists you are involved."

Michael was watching her, not blatantly, but clearly curious. After all, she'd led him to believe her parents were coming to town, so he'd expect nothing more than a confirmation of plans. If only she hadn't announced it was her dad, she could have fibbed her way out of the situation. Yeah, Stacey, just what you need to do. Tell one more itsy-bitsy story to go with all your other ones!

"I am." She took a deep breath. She was known for telling her public relations clients that if any disaster befell them, always act completely in control. "You and

Mother are still flying into the airport in El Dorado on Tuesday, aren't you?"

"Stacey, have you been drinking?"

She glanced at her iced tea, the sides of the tall glass glistening with condensation. "No, Dad. It's that situation we discussed. I can't really go into it right now, but if you can't make it, I'm sure Mother will be glad to do it by herself."

"Bobby likes Caitlin," Jessica said all of a sudden, dancing her trapper Barbie onto the table.

"Stupid. You don't know anything."

"There's nothing your mother can do that I can't do better." Her father had only momentarily been caught off guard. "I don't know what nonsense you're up to, but if you're in trouble, you know I'll be there."

"Caitlin's sister is in my class." Jessica sat back, satisfied with the blow she'd delivered.

Stacey sneaked a peek over at Michael. He was running one hand through his hair as he followed his daughters' game of verbal insults. "It's not exactly trouble," she said slowly, "but things are kind of tangled up."

"It's not nice to be a-calling your little sister stupid." Mrs. Beebe gathered her plate. "Now let's clear the table and taste that apple pie."

"You can explain it when I get there. And don't bother your mother. I can handle whatever needs to be done without that wom—your mother, interfering. Call my office for me, will you, sweetpea, and have them clear my appointments on Tuesday and tell them where I am to meet you."

"I'm at the Schoolhouse Inn in Doolittle, Arkansas,

but I'll call your office. And, Daddy, I need you Wednesday, too, okay?"

"Two days? All right, but I have to be back for the opera Wednesday night." Her father paused, and he said in a softer voice, "You're going to like Larissa."

"Right. Well, thanks," Stacey said. Right. As much as she'd liked any of his other girlfriends or follow-up wives. She must have made a face because Jessica giggled. " 'Bye, Dad. Have a nice da—" Stacey slapped her phone shut. She'd almost said *have a nice date*.

"Everything okay at home?" Michael asked, stacking cutlery on his plate.

Stacey nodded. "Just like always." Yeah, her dad out with a new chick probably younger than Stacey.

"It must be nice to have parents," Kristen said. "You always wanted a sister, but there are some things that are better than a sister." She pushed her chair back. "May I be excused? I don't want any pie."

Michael nodded, sorrow in his eyes.

"We have parents," Jessica said.

"Yeah, right," Kristen said. "I meant ones who live in the same house." With that she snatched the portable phone from the side table and stalked out of the room.

Mrs. Beebe shook her head. "Jessica, help me with these dishes." Her face somber, the younger girl picked up the coleslaw bowl and followed the housekeeper to the kitchen.

Michael dropped his face in his hands, just for a moment, then looked over at her. "It is so hard to watch her suffering," he said.

Stacey nodded. She wanted to go to him, to put her

arms around him and offer the comfort he so desperately needed. A part of her rose from the chair, yet another whispered that it wasn't her place, that she barely knew this man, that he was a man and would therefore reject what might appear to be tenderness.

From what she had learned from Robert, men preferred desire to empathy. She'd been the model of companionship and he'd chosen an airhead sexpot who had not a clue in her head about his business concerns. And look at her dad. He'd been lucky enough to be married to a brilliant doctor and he'd left her for a nurse's assistant. Not even an RN!

She knew her thinking was all confused. Go to him. Hug him.

"I never wanted her to be hurt," Michael said. "Kristen took the divorce hard. Jessica sees the good in everything and I think she appreciates the lack of tension. But Kristen— What am I doing, boring you with all this stuff?" He pushed his chair back. "You don't want to hear this."

"You're not boring me." Stacey rose. Slowly, still worrying over whether she should or not, she stretched her hand out toward him. Before dinner, when he'd almost kissed her, she'd been all nerves and anticipation. Now her own fears of intimacy pushed away other feelings. Her fingers brushed his and he clasped her hand.

She looked into his eyes, seeking not only to offer comfort, but also to find the reassurance her support would be accepted as such and not misinterpreted.

"Let's go outside," he said.

Without letting go of her hand, he led the way from

the dining room to the front hallway, then out onto the porch. He paused in front of the porch swing, where he let go and gestured toward the swing.

Stacey settled onto the green and white ivy-patterned cushion. Michael joined her, leaving a careful six or so inches between their bodies.

"It's very hard to lose one's family," Stacey said, thinking of her own childhood.

"Tell me about it," he said. "You think you're doing the right thing and then one day, bam, the truth jumps out and smacks you on the side of the head and you realize you've gotten it all wrong." A shadow of a smile flitted across his lips. "Except for the kids. That part is right, even with the aches and pains."

Funny, but his perspective was that of the dad losing his family. Stacey realized how different that was from her own hold on the past. Well, if she wanted to know more about Michael, she might as well be brave enough to ask a few questions. And she did want to know more about this man. She watched as his chest rose and fell, the cadence mirroring the rhythm of the swing he was creating with the barest movement of one strong leg. "Have you been divorced long?"

He had his hands clasped in his lap. He loosened his fingers and cracked his knuckles. "Almost three years. Kristen was nine and Jessica five."

Stacey nodded, unsure what to say next. Perhaps words weren't needed.

"Have you ever been married?"

She shook her head, then added, "Engaged, but not married."

"Ah." He half turned and put his arm along the back of the swing. "Want to tell me about it?"

"We're talking about you," she said.

"Right. Me." He left his arm there, and Stacey was pleased by the knowledge of it near her. If she tipped her head back just the slightest bit, her hair would brush his hand. "Pauline and I married too young." He cleared his throat. "No excuses here, but she was pregnant and I still believe it was the right thing to do."

Stacey forgot about analyzing how Michael might react to her touch. Impulsively, she placed a hand on his thigh and said, "What other choice did you have?"

"Well, Pauline wanted to have an abortion, but I wouldn't stand for it." He laughed somewhat dryly. "She's not the mothering sort."

"But it was your baby," Stacey said, her hand still on his thigh.

He nodded. "Kristen. And no matter how much grief I go through with her, I thank God every day I made the choice I did."

Stacey blinked. For someone who prided herself on being pretty much in emotional control, she was feeling a rush of emotion.

"Yes, she was our baby. And silly me, but I thought it would help to have a second child. But that only accentuated our problems." He placed his other hand on top of hers. "You're sweet to listen to all of this. I don't normally dump my entire life history on someone on a first date."

First date.

First implied second.

Stacey wet her lips. "Oh," she said.

Duh. Why, oh, why couldn't she be more clever? No

wonder she'd only been serious with one man in her entire adult life. She could never think of the right thing to say, or she spent so much time analyzing what move to make she made none at all.

"So, um, what happened?"

"Short version? I followed the professorship track in veterinary school, completed a doctorate, was tenure track at Tufts. Pauline finished law school, landed a job with a top Boston firm. We had child care around the clock."

"Babysitters." Stacey hated that word. As the daughter of two doctors, she'd known some of her babysitters better than her own parents.

"Yep." Michael toyed with her fingers and Stacey thought she'd died and gone to heaven. His touch just felt so darn good. Emboldened by that realization, she tipped her head back ever so slightly and let her hair brush against his forearm. She couldn't be sure, but she thought she heard him catch his breath.

He went on. "I came home one night and found Kristen crying in her room. Both Pauline and I had missed her Christmas pageant at school. Pauline was out of town at a conference and I had gotten called into emergency surgery. All the other kids' parents were there. I realized I couldn't go on like that. It wasn't fair to the girls. So when Pauline came home, I said we had to have a serious talk."

Stacey let her head go the rest of the way back and leaned against his hand. It was so strong and reassuring. "Then what happened?"

"She broke down and told me she'd been having an affair with another lawyer, whom she'd just seen at the supposed conference she'd been to, and that she wanted a divorce."

"Whoa!" Stacey sat up. "What an awful shock!"

He nodded. "I can't say I wasn't in some part of my heart relieved. We'd been living a sham life for some time. Pauline and I were two people who never would have gone on more than a few dates if we hadn't let our hormones run away with us and I hadn't used a condom I'd been carrying around in my wallet since Noah beached the ark."

Stacey laughed, despite the pain embedded in his story. "Timing is everything, isn't it?"

"You can say that again," Michael said, his voice suddenly huskier.

And that's when Stacey knew he was going to kiss her—really kiss her.

Chapter 9

"You're very easy to talk to," Michael said, fingering the soft fall of her hair and listening with one ear for the sound of his daughters' voices.

"Thank you," Stacey said. "So are you."

He dropped his hand onto her bare shoulder. "Your skin is so delicate."

She laughed slightly, a breathless sort of giggle, enough to let him know she wanted him to kiss her as much as he wanted to do it. "I guess I should say thank you again."

"Later," he said, teasing her arm with light strokes of his fingertips. He wanted her shivering with anticipation and desire. He'd observed how tightly wrapped she was, and he wanted to watch as she melted with need. He was willing to bet she rarely faltered in her self-control. Even a kiss—especially this first kiss—had to pack a wallop. It was just as well Jessica had interrupted them at the piano before dinner; they hadn't had nearly enough lead time and his own desire for her had rushed his usual patient style.

Michael settled lower on the swing, shifting their bodies so that they just touched. "We've talked a lot about me, but not much about you," he said.

She wriggled around on the swing and tipped her face so that she looked directly up at him. When she did, her knee brushed his thigh and he almost forgot all about whetting her appetite. "Michael Halliday," she said, catching him by the shoulders and taking him completely off guard, "if you don't kiss me, I'm going to scream."

He laughed. And so did she. Then, holding her gaze, he brushed one thumb over her lower lip. "It's nice to know," he said as he explored the outline of her mouth, "that we're on the same chapter, same verse." He pressed ever so lightly on the line of her lips. She sighed, drew his finger inward, and tasted it with her tongue.

"Delicious," she murmured, her breathy voice enveloping his hand.

That did him in. He wanted to drive her crazy with desire, yet he was the one being tortured here. A simple kiss wouldn't satisfy the cravings racing through his body and heating his blood. What was it about this woman? He'd met her . . . hell, less than twenty-four hours ago. He'd clearly been wandering in the desert far too long.

But logic didn't matter to him. Not at the moment. He slipped his thumb away from her warm lips and tipped her face up to meet his own hungry kiss. Her lips moved, began to part, and then he sensed her hesitation.

He wasn't going to lose her now. Cupping her head

in one hand, he pressed her toward him. Parted her lips. Suckled her tongue. She gasped and writhed against him and he knew she was giving herself to him.

With a moan, she lifted one hand, as if drugged, and pulled his face even closer to her own. Michael smiled and gentled his siege of her sensual defenses. Planting a feathery kiss on her lips, he whispered, "I've been wanting to do that all day."

He kept his hand on her hair, smoothing it, sifting the weight of it through his fingers, enjoying the way she smiled up at him. And then he lowered his mouth to hers again. He forgot his surroundings, forgot his responsibilities, forgot the bleak reality of the existence to which he'd pledged himself for the sake of his children.

He knew only the feel of her flesh, the fragrance of her scent, and the heat of her tongue dancing against his.

"Oh, God," he groaned, knowing he should slow down. The miracle of it was that she didn't sit up and primly adjust that enticing red blouse that skimmed her body. His fingers itched to explore beneath the slinky fabric that outlined her excited nipples. For her willingness, he was damn grateful. And pleased. And even more excited.

Stacey didn't recognize herself. Wanton and wild, she pressed her body against Michael's, drawing him to her, tasting his mouth, and giving herself up to him in a passionate dance she could have sworn she didn't know the steps to. Not that she wasn't experienced, because of course she and Robert had been intimate during the six years of their courtship.

But never had she felt this surge of passion.

Never had she wanted to climb down a man's throat and drown in his greedy, demanding kisses.

Never before had she had the need to change to dry panties from one simple kiss.

Hah! There was nothing simple about this kiss.

And then he broke away, his lips merely brushing hers. She moaned, shamelessly deprived by the loss of his claiming kiss. "God, that was even better than the last time," he said, and Stacey knew she was a lost soul.

As self-contained and self-controlled as she was, she wanted to be lost to all sanity. Never had she experienced this desire as fantasy-turned-reality; never had she believed she could spiral out of control the way Michael's kiss promised was possible.

And then he took her mouth yet again. Her breasts strained against the silky fabric of her bra. She thought she heard a button pop, but couldn't be sure. Didn't want to know.

She kissed him back, returning the ardor. Slowly, though, ever so slowly, a dim, shuffling sound, almost a warning bell, began to toll in her mind. She tried to ignore it; she didn't want to be sensible and sober and pragmatic. She wanted to be swept away by Michael.

The noise sounded again, and suddenly Stacey realized she was hearing footsteps. She pulled swiftly away from Michael, one hand to her swollen, heated lips. He groaned and reached for her.

She stilled him with a quick hand to his chin.

He blinked and must have realized she was trying to signal to him.

"Daddy?"

Stacey heard Jessica's little-girl voice and thanked the heavens she'd pulled away from Michael before his daughter pushed open the screen door to the porch. *You'll like Larissa,* she heard her father saying, and Stacey straightened and scooted a few inches clear of Michael. Stacey knew too well what it felt like for a child to be surprised by the sight of her father in the arms of a woman not her own mother.

That was a heartache Stacey had vowed she'd never ever bring to anyone.

"Jessica." Michael straightened and ran one hand through his hair. He jerked his arm free of Stacey's shoulders and turned toward his daughter. "Are you looking for me?"

"I was," she said slowly, not stepping onto the porch. "But I think maybe you're busy."

Uh-oh. How much had she seen? There was no reason Michael couldn't be kissing her. He was free to date, to meet a new woman, to find someone to love and to cherish. Or just someone passing through town to kiss on a Saturday night. Stacey realized she preferred the former thought to the latter. But now wasn't the time to think of herself. There were children to consider.

Jessica was only eight. And she was vulnerable. And what if Kristen, who exhibited the yo-yo of emotions perfectly natural to a twelve-year-old, had walked in on them?

Stacey shook her head at her own wayward behavior. "We're not busy," she said. "Why don't you come out and swing in the swing?"

"I don't think so," she said. "Mrs. Beebe says it's time

for dessert. She asked me to tell you." And with that, she turned back into the house.

"Jesus." Michael blew out a breath. "Give me strength." He dropped his head into his hands, breathing quickly.

"I'd guess she saw or heard us," Stacey said.

"I am an idiot," Michael said, dropping one word at a time, like a shoe falling. "Forgive me. I just had to kiss you." He grinned, a flash of an expression that lit his features, then disappeared. "I'm glad I did, too, and I think you are as well, but I must be out of my mind. Protecting my kids comes before whatever it is I want."

He reached out and stroked the back of her neck as he finished his sentence. "So what do you say we take up again on the ride back to the inn?"

Stacey let out the breath she'd been holding. "I'm not sure that's a good idea," she said, quickly before she lost her resolve. The last thing Stacey wanted was to inflict harm on Michael's girls. "Maybe I should call a cab."

"This isn't exactly Manhattan," he said dryly, studying her more closely than she wanted him to. "I'll take you home. Give me the word and I'll keep my hands to myself."

She touched his knee then returned her hand to the safety of her own lap. "It's not that I didn't enjoy every minute."

He rose from the swing, grinning.

Stacey did, too, wishing she could tell him about her father and his girlfriends. No time like the present. "Michael, there's something—"

Kristen hurled out the door, beaming. "Hey, Amanda and Bobby and Torie and Caitlin and I are going to be partners!" She danced over, the portable phone clutched like a trophy overhead.

Stacey smiled, happy she'd helped out. She exchanged glances with Michael.

"And Bobby thought it was pretty cool of me to think up this solution," she said.

"Kristen, you know that was Stacey's suggestion," Michael said.

She hugged him then danced off. "Oh, I know, and thank you, Stacey, but they don't care about that. They don't even know you. Besides, if you hire a consultant and she saves your business, no one ever knows it was that person and not you, right?"

Stacey nodded. "Good logic. That's sort of what I do professionally, too."

"See, Dad, I told you. Oh, yeah, Mrs. Beebe says the ice cream is melting off the pie."

"We're coming." Michael opened the door and Stacey preceded him inside, her moment of truth-telling come and gone.

Stacey didn't stay much longer than it took to sample the tart and juicy apple pie. It was hard to appreciate Mrs. Beebe's efforts watching Jessica cling to her dad. Her earlier friendly approach toward Stacey had evaporated. She regarded Stacey with dark, silent eyes.

Understanding all too well what Jessica was experiencing, Stacey kept her interaction open and cheerful. She wanted to reassure her she was no threat to the cocoon of Jessica's life and chose to talk about her work in New Orleans as a means of communicating that her stay in Doolittle was the briefest of sojourns.

Jessica relaxed a bit, but insisted on riding with

Michael and Stacey back to the inn. She sat between them in the pickup. True stayed behind at the house. Stacey had hesitated over that, knowing it meant she was further indebted to Michael's generosity—and that she'd have to return to collect her dog.

Jessica's self-imposed role as chaperone was both frustrating and convenient, Stacey thought as Michael and his daughter walked her to the door of the Schoolhouse Inn.

Of course, he didn't kiss her, so she didn't have to experience that out-of-control, roller-coaster feeling that his lips on hers created.

So why, when she shook his proffered hand as she would have any client she met with, did she feel an aching for more?

"Shall we meet at ten to view those properties Mrs. Clark mentioned?" Michael asked, one arm around Jessica.

Stacey started. All she could feel was the lack of his lips on hers. Darn it. That wouldn't do. "Ten. Right. That would be fine."

"But Dad . . ." Jessica said, then trailed off, a most disconsolate look on her face.

"Yes, Jessica, tomorrow is the day you go to church with your mother and Cecil."

A mulish expression took over the little girl's features and Stacey couldn't help but sympathize. And realize, too, that that meant Michael was free to show her around—to view properties she cared nothing about seeing.

"I don't like their church," Jessica said, stubbing her toe against the floorboards of the porch.

"God visits all churches," Michael said.

"That is beautiful," Stacey said, quite spontaneously.

He shrugged. "He also doesn't mind stopping by a rowboat on the lake on a Sunday morning."

Stacey smiled. "Now that's a theology I can get behind."

"So why do I have to go to church with them?" Jessica said.

"Because your mother wants you to, and she . . ." He hesitated, then said with a firm voice, "And she wants what is best for you."

"Then she could have stayed married to you."

Michael glanced at some point over Stacey's shoulder, his expression grim.

Impulsively, Stacey reached out and touched Jessica's shoulder. "Adults don't always know what's right," she said softly. "Growing up doesn't bring any guarantee of answers."

Jessica regarded her, quite serious, but not so stonily. After a long pause, she said, "So why bother growing up?"

"That is a good question," Stacey said. "All I can say is that life is a process and sometimes we reach where we are supposed to be."

Jessica wrinkled her nose. "That's awfully hard to understand."

"And so is growing up," Stacey said.

Jessica nodded and slowly snaked one hand into Stacey's. "You're okay," she said.

Stacey clasped the child's hand, her own heart in her throat. It was all she could do to make herself meet

Michael's expression. What she saw there sent a chill, of the warmest sort, down her neck, through her arms, and into her fingertips.

"Tomorrow," he said softly, his eyes devouring her.

She nodded, not sure if she'd be there or not. Some emotions were just too strong for her to handle.

Dr. Louis St. Cyr sat on one of the barstools in the darkened rim of St. Charles Avenue's Red Room and drummed his manicured fingertips on the side of his glistening martini glass. Ten minutes, and Larissa still hadn't reemerged from the ladies' room. How the hell could someone spend that much time taking care of business?

He'd been dating her for three weeks now. He'd decided tonight was the night to take her to bed. They'd already been to dinner, at Emeril's, and on impulse he'd pulled over at the Red Room. As much as he desired his newest affair of the heart, he wasn't quite ready for the action of the bedroom.

Face it, Louis, he told himself, you're not the young animal you used to be. He watched as a twenty-something *GQ* cover model wanna-be led a woman vaguely familiar to him out onto the dance floor. He should have settled down a long time ago, but the demands of his practice and the yawning mouths of three ex-wives— well, to be grudgingly fair, all except his first, Joanne, Stacey's mother, who did just as well for herself as he did—dictated that he maintain the furious pace he did at the hospital.

A ticking set off in his brain as he studied the woman. He knew her, but from where?

He peered across the wafting cigar smoke. Couldn't be. No way.

Just then the music stopped and the couple drifted by. Dammit to hell.

It was Joanne, looking twenty years younger than she had a right to.

He must have caught her eye, because she motioned to her dance partner and he paused, looking as uncertain as any deer caught in the headlights of an oncoming truck would have.

"Louis," she purred, one silken-draped hip thrust before the other in a walk she'd learned he knew not where. Certainly when the two of them had been man and wife—for those few disastrous years—she'd never moved like that.

His normally well-controlled jaw dropped. Literally. Words failed him.

Her brows lifted, the merest movement, but enough to telegraph to him that she knew just how dumbfounded he felt. Some things didn't change; they'd always been able to read one another.

"I'd like you to meet Brandon," she said, indicating the puppy hovering at her side.

At that moment Larissa glided up, every beautiful blond hair in place, pouty lips perfectly glazed, eyes bluer than blue, her breasts rising proudly above the neckline of her sleek black dress. Up until that moment, Louis had thought her the loveliest woman in the place—hell, in the entire city.

Next to Joanne, she looked like a high school senior about to be sent back to her room to change before being allowed out to the prom.

"And this is Larissa," he said, shaking hands with Joanne's date.

"Hello," Larissa said, surveying Brandon with interest and Joanne not at all.

For a ludicrous moment, Louis thought of urging the children to run along and play. He had to press a hand to his cheek to keep from laughing at the absurdity of the idea.

"Isn't this lovely," Joanne said, then turned to her date. "Darling, I've an urge to tango."

"Then I do, too," he said, casting one last appreciative glance at Larissa before excusing them and leading Joanne toward the dance floor.

"Well, I'll be damned," Louis said, regaining his barstool and his grip on his martini glass. Larissa stood there for a moment, then turned and rubbed up next to him.

"Weady to go?"

He grimaced. He'd never minded her habit of baby talk. Not until now. "Have a seat," he said. "I haven't finished my drink."

"Okay," she said. The tall barstool did wonders for the slit in her dress, revealing enough leg to beckon even a man with no imagination straight to her side.

He caught several of the hovering men noticing. Normally he liked having other guys envy him for having caught the babe of the month. It made him feel . . . younger. He tightened his hand around the stem of his glass. He'd always sworn he wouldn't fall prey to that, but here he was, nearing sixty and acting like a fool.

Joanne, several years his junior, looked closer to forty than fifty as she sashayed on the dance floor.

"I heard that BoyznGirls are coming to the arena," Larissa said, circling one finger on his knee.

"BoyznGirls?" He finished his drink and signaled the bartender. "Don't you want anything?"

She shook her head. "No, thank you, Louis. You know I only have wine with dinner."

He nodded. "As a doctor, I have to admire your moderation. As a man"—he watched as the bartender began the ritual of preparing the perfect martini—"well, it's more fun to have someone to share things with."

She puckered up her lips and for a moment he thought she was going to lean over and kiss him. Instead, she said, "I'm going to cry. You've never said one mean thing to me before tonight."

"Babydoll, that wasn't mean." He laughed despite himself. "You should see how I treat the residents."

"Well, it was a trifle critical. And you know I'd do anything in the world to please you."

"Yes, I do know that." Louis smiled and tipped her chin upward. "You are lovely," he said. "What did you say your degree was in?"

"Political science."

"And I suppose you're going to go to law school and sue lots of doctors?"

"I'd rather just marry one." She giggled.

"Lawyer or doctor?"

"Why, Dr. St. Cyr, how can you ask that question?"

He shook his head. "Just testing," he said. He craned his neck and checked around the bar, spotting at least two prominent attorneys, guys he knew from a local duck-hunting group. Fortunately they weren't medical malpractice sharks. "Want to meet some friends of mine?"

"Oh, yes," she said.

He tossed some bills on the bar, took his drink, and slid off the barstool. He led Larissa over to where Bill and Jeff were in heated discussion, no doubt about which singles resort in Cancún was the hottest place to spend the weekend. Surely they couldn't be talking law with that much enthusiasm.

"Hey, guys," Louis said.

They broke off and looked up. A round of greetings followed, with appreciative looks at Larissa. Louis and Larissa were invited to join them, and soon the two guys were falling over each other to see who received more eyelash flutters and cooing responses to their witty lines.

Louis sat back and studied the dance floor. Joanne and her escort were back on the floor. She shimmied and shook along with the twenty-somethings all around her.

What in the hell had happened to her?

And what was happening to him? Other than the brief moment in time when the two of them had leapt into the sack together, they had never, ever been compatible. If she said tomato, he screamed eggplant. If she said vacation in Paris, he bought tickets for Rio. When she'd said let's name the baby Genevieve, he'd scrawled Stacey on the birth certificate form.

"Louis, are you feeling okay?" Larissa stopped entertaining the guys long enough to touch his sleeve solicitously.

"Sure, sure." He downed the rest of the martini. "Ready to go?"

She pouted. "But I'm having fun."

"Guys, one of you see Larissa safely home?" He turned to her. "If that's okay with you? I am feeling a little under the weather."

Bill and Jeff nodded and in unison said, "I'll do that."

"You really don't mind?" Larissa smiled at all three of them.

Louis rose, kissed her on the top of her beautiful silken head, and thanked the stars for rescuing him from his own blind stupidity as he made his way through the throng to the exit.

Maybe it was a good thing he was going to Arkansas. Hell, maybe he'd go on up in the morning. He had no idea why Stacey needed him there, but he'd always had a blind spot when it came to his little girl. If she wanted his assistance, that was all that it took to bring him running. He sighed, admitting to himself that the ages-long competition he'd conducted with Joanne was the other reason he so spoiled Stacey.

It was almost a shame Joanne wouldn't be there. After seeing her tonight, Louis could think of many worse things to do than get reacquainted with his first wife. That thought lodged in his mind. The last time the topic had arisen, Stacey had told him Joanne still lived in her Warehouse District condo. He drove a few more blocks toward his lakefront home, and then turned the car around and headed in the opposite direction.

Chapter 10

Stacey had just shut the front door of the Schoolhouse Inn when her cell phone rang for the second time that evening. She grabbed it quickly, without glancing at the caller ID, as she didn't want to awaken any other guests. Nor did she want to bring either one of the sisters out to ask her how her evening with Dr. Mike had been.

"Hello," she said.

"Oh-mi-god, you're alive!" The voice was most certainly that of her business partner, Donna Bell, but the tone was foreign to her. She'd never once seen Donna flustered, not even when, nine months pregnant with her fifth child, her water had broken during a presentation before a major client.

"Of course I'm alive," Stacey said, slipping back outside to the porch swing to hold what would no doubt prove to be a lengthy conversation. Settling onto the swing made her feel closer to Michael, which was of course a ridiculous thought to have flit across her mind.

"When the Arlington told me you hadn't checked in,

I hate to admit it, but I feared the worst. You were so worn out when you left I had visions of you falling asleep behind the wheel."

The Arlington. She hadn't canceled her reservation! "Donna, I am so sorry you were worried. It never crossed my mind to call you." Yeah, because her mind had been possessed by Michael Halliday.

"Well, where are you? Did you take my advice and hop a plane to Paris?"

Stacey laughed. "Not exactly. I'm in Doolittle."

"I'm guessing that's not in France."

"Arkansas."

"What's the attraction?"

Stacey hesitated, a trifle too long for her own good.

"Is it a guy?"

"Not exactly."

"It is a guy!" Donna's voice rang out in a triumphant note that Stacey didn't trust. "Stacey, that is fabulous. Who is he and what's his sign?"

"Oh, it's nothing like that," she said, ignoring both queries. "True got sick—actually, it turns out she is going to have puppies, can you believe it? So the vet said he wanted to check her overnight. I guess he's right, but honestly Donna, he's the most annoyingly bossy man. Everyone I've met in this town does everything he tells them to do—"

"Stop," Donna said, laughing. "You, Ms. Needs-to-Be-in-Control-Always, are calling someone else bossy? Do you realize that means you've met the man of your dreams?"

"It means no such thing," Stacey said, half cross despite how well she liked Donna. "I'm simply spending another night or two here because driving disagreed with True."

"Uh-huh," Donna said. "So what's he look like, this bossy animal doctor?"

"Tall, dark, and handsome," Stacey said, "but that's got nothing to do with the price of tea in China."

"That's true," her friend said. "After all, that description matches your useless ex-boyfriend. What do his eyes look like when he's smiling?"

"His face lights up," Stacey said, responding without thinking. "Hey, wait a minute. Don't get me off track here."

Donna laughed. "You sound happier than you have in ages."

"I hate to admit it," Stacey said, "but you were right about me needing a vacation. I already feel much more relaxed. I haven't thought about work since . . ." Stacey trailed off, unwilling to confess she'd deviated from the standard New Orleans to Hot Springs route in order to call on two potential clients in Alexandria, in northern Louisiana.

"Since last night?" Donna said dryly. "There was a message on voice mail this morning from Alexandria Home Health, singing your praises. But if one day away makes you feel this good, I can't wait to see what results a week in Doolittle brings."

Stacey held her protests. It would do little good to insist she wasn't remaining in the burg of Doolittle for the remainder of her vacation. But she would have to call about her reservation. It was very unlike her to forget about that sort of detail. Then she realized Donna hadn't said why she'd phoned the hotel looking for her. "Is everything okay in New Orleans?"

"Ah, not exactly." Her partner's tone of voice had lost its lighthearted note.

The porch cat strolled by, tail swishing. Evidently it hadn't gotten in Crabby Abbie's way that evening. In the darkness surrounding the porch, crickets chirped and a lone bird, up past the usual bedtime, sang out. In Doolittle all was well. But in New Orleans? Stacey knew it had to be a work emergency that precipitated Donna's call. Donna's personal life ran a pleasantly steady course, a state Stacey envied, though she was pleased for her friend, naturally. "What's broken?"

"Now that you ask," Donna said, "it's Key Financial. The comptroller has turned up missing, along with a substantial portion of the company's supposed investment profits. Kyle Key wants us to put out the fires public-relations-wise and he wants the plan by tomorrow and out to the press by first thing Monday."

Stacey groaned. The cat jumped to the porch railing and regarded her without much curiosity. "Just another silly human," Stacey muttered.

"What was that?"

"For once in my life I don't feel like working," Stacey said, testing the words as she said them. She pushed against the porch and rocked the swing gently.

"But you have to," Donna said. "You're the one who knows the account inside and out. And he's paying premium. And we've got that new lease on the building and the company cars and two new employees."

"Oh, I know all that," Stacey said. "Indulge me in

my rare moment of weakness before I plunge into an all-nighter."

"Right now I'm feeling sort of silly I insisted you not take your laptop," Donna said. "If there's a twenty-four-hour Kinko's or some such I can send you the files you need . . ."

"Oh, don't worry about that," Stacey said. "My computer is safe in my trunk."

"You little skunk!" Donna laughed, but she sounded relieved. "You know I'd prepare this package if I had the background on it. If you rough it out and get it to me via e-mail by tomorrow afternoon, I'll make sure it's ready to show to the Key people Monday for distribution to his biggest clients. He's worried they'll get nervous and jump ship. So he needs history, security measures, profitability. You know the stuff, charts and bells and whistles, to dazzle the doubtful."

"Oh, yes," Stacey said. Something moved across the grass and the cat dove off the railing, laziness transformed into a killing machine. A tiny squeal erupted, then broke off.

"I guess I'd better get to it. Will you be home tomorrow?"

"Oh, of course. It's Petey's birthday. He's having ten other eight-year-olds over. I've rented extra game stations and piled in enough hot dogs and sodas to stock a city under siege."

Petey's birthday. Stacey wondered, for a fleeting moment, if that event had anything to do with Donna needing Stacey to pull together the Key presentation. Even as the thought flitted across her mind, she dismissed it. Stacey was invaluable, she was the one who knew Key backward and forward. She'd simply have to work through the night—or skip her appointment tomorrow with Michael Halliday.

When she'd left him tonight, she'd been tempted to scamper off and avoid the emotions he stirred up in her. Escaping, after all, might be easier. And that was one thing, she'd realized sitting here, that she wasn't going to do. The feelings Michael generated in her scared her, but they were also the sweetest thing she'd ever known. Though she shouldn't allow those sensations to blur reality. Michael had three strikes against him: He was too used to being the guy in charge, he was divorced with kids, and yeah, did she mention he lived almost a thousand miles from her home?

"I guess I'd better get to it," Stacey said, at last, not at all happy to have to do so. Yet, once she got started, it would be fine. Work, after all, was what she did best.

"Thanks," Donna responded. "And you know I wouldn't call you on vacation if this weren't an emergency. And I can't wait to hear all about your doctor friend when you get home."

"There's nothing to tell," Stacey said, but she knew Donna wasn't buying that as they said good-bye.

She gave herself a few more minutes in the swing, inhaling the pungent fragrance of whatever plant was climbing the edges of the railing. The cat had returned to its post, evidently unsuccessful in its attempt to end the life of the creature it had pounced upon.

There was one other chore she wanted to get out of the way before she set to work on the Key project. It was funny to think of phoning her mother as a chore, but Stacey could phrase it no other way. She and her mother had a friendly, almost collegial relationship. Joanne, as Stacey had addressed her for years, treated her daughter the way she'd treat a younger doctor in her practice. She bossed, she instructed, and she solicited her input. Nothing wrong with any of that, Stacey believed, but sometimes she wished for a mom who would simply hold out her arms, hug her close, and whisper everything's going to be okay, no matter what you do.

With Joanne, there was always some element of assessment. Launching into her own public relations firm had been a move Joanne supported, even funneling money into the start-up costs, with an expected rate of return on the investment. Her dad, on the other hand, had written out a check, kissed her cheek, and waved her on her way.

Lately, though, her mother had been acting differently. She'd seemed worried, then suddenly, as if someone had waved a wand over her, she'd metamorphosed into a woman trying out for the cover of *Maxim* magazine for men. Her mother, just past fifty, was experiencing a midlife crisis.

She groaned and the cat pricked its ears. "No, I'm not some creature for you to gobble up," she said, pushing herself out of the swing. "I'll be lucky if Joanne doesn't show up here with some gigolo in tow," she muttered, striding to the car, retrieving her laptop, and making her way to her room.

It was late, but Joanne never went to bed before midnight. She devoured medical journals the way Stacey did mystery novels. Not for nothing was Dr. Joanne St. Cyr the dermatologist of choice in New Orleans.

Stacey kicked her shoes off, climbed on top of the four-poster bed, and punched in the speed-dial code for her mother's number. It was eleven-thirty on a Saturday night and if all things were running true to form, Joanne should be propped up in bed reading.

The phone rang. It was picked up but no one answered.

"Hi, it's Stacey."

"Just a minute," a male voice mumbled.

Stacey stared at her cell phone. She must have hit the wrong button. But then her mother's voice, clear as day, said, "Hello, Stacey. What an inconvenient time for a telephone conversation."

"Uh, sorry," she said, unsure whether to hang up or plunge ahead. "I thought you'd be reading."

"Stacey, it's Saturday night."

"I know that."

"You need to get out more."

"As a matter of fact, I was out. Earlier tonight."

"Good. Why are you calling?" Her mother maintained her usual businesslike tone, then stifled what Stacey swore was a giggle.

"I think I'd better call back tomorrow," Stacey said.

"I won't be home. I'm going to Jazzland."

She'd dialed the wrong number. The woman on the other end of the phone was definitely not her mother. "You hate amusement parks."

"Whether I do or I don't, it's an experience I've decided to encounter. Now, Stacey, I really must know the purpose of this call. As you've no doubt deduced, I have company."

Her mother had never remarried. She'd hardly ever dated, at least not that Stacey had known about. "It's about Dad," she said.

"You're calling about your father?" Something shifted in her mother's tone of voice. "What about him?"

The strategy it would take to get both her parents to Arkansas on Tuesday wasn't something Stacey had exactly figured out. Sometimes she let her intuition guide her, and now was one of those times she needed the winged goddess of gut instincts propped on her shoulder. It would be a lot simpler to tell Michael the truth. Yet some corner of her mind and heart drove her to pursue a means of luring her parents to Doolittle. She knew it had to do with the ridiculous, long-lived dream of them reconciling. Perhaps once outside their usual environs, they'd see life—and one another—in a different light.

"I'm worried about him."

"You call me up at eleven thirty-seven on a Saturday night to tell me that? There's nothing to worry about. I saw him tonight. He was in fine form, with a young thing on his arm at least half—oh, well, to be accurate, three-quarters—your age. What's to worry about?"

"He's talking about retiring," Stacey said, knowing from his comments about his latest girlfriend, Larissa, that her mother was telling the truth.

"Ridiculous," Joanne said.

"But he's coming up here on Tuesday to look at retirement property."

"Where is 'up here'?"

"Arkansas."

"What in the world are you doing in that godfor-saken state?"

"I told you I was going on vacation."

"Oh, yes, you did and I suggested Paris over Hot Springs. If you'd invested as I'd suggested, a week in Paris would have been well within your means."

Stacey gripped her phone. This conversation was tak-ing far longer than she'd intended. Her mother wanted it over with. But she couldn't give up. Not yet. She hated to bring in the big guns, but she knew, as any child did, how to push her parent's buttons. "Daddy's actually coming to help me out of a bit of a bind. And he said the last thing I should do was bother you with it."

"Is that so?"

"It's just that True got sick and I had to stop in this small town of Doolittle. I'm staying at this quaint little place called the Schoolhouse Inn and I happened to say I was looking for retirement property for my parents, which of course was a fib."

Stacey took a deep breath, knowing she was risking her mother leaving her to her own devices, but perhaps if Joanne now had a new man in her life, she'd be sym-pathetic. "Well, there's this hunk of a guy involved in the story and I didn't want him to think all I did was work, work, work—"

"So you told him you were looking for retirement property for one of your parents. Naturally he'll think you're a sweet little homebody and it won't be until the first time you cancel a date to handle a client emergency that he'll figure out you're not at all what you've repre-sented yourself to be." Joanne sighed and Stacey could picture her shaking her head. "That's no way to start a relationship," she said. "On the other hand, you certainly don't need your father to rescue you. And it's just like that man to tell you not to bother me. This situation calls for a mother's touch. Call my secretary with the details and have her arrange for me to be there."

"Thank you," Stacey said meekly. "You can fly into El Dorado and drive from there. I'm sorry I interrupted your evening."

"Of course you did the right thing. The very idea of your father insisting he should handle this . . ." Joanne rang off without saying good-bye.

Stacey allowed herself a weak smile of momentary victory.

The real battle would come when the two of them showed up and she had to break the news to them that they were to portray a happy, loving couple about to sail into the sunset of their retirement years together.

"Ha," she muttered as she plugged the power cord into the wall and arranged her laptop on the bed. Last night she'd been able to withstand the bowl of Hershey's almond kisses decorating the table in front of the window. She carried that over to the bed, positioned herself cross-legged in front of the computer, and pulled up her files on Key Financial.

She'd rather think about work than what her mother was doing right now.

She'd also rather think about investment failures and absconding comptrollers than dwell on the nugget of truth in Joanne's comment about pretending to be someone you weren't.

Stacey was willing to bet she was the only woman in Doolittle planning to work through the night.

The next morning, Michael rolled over, hit his snooze button, and groaned. He had to get the kids ready for Pauline's, but with only two hours of sleep, he didn't feel like moving.

Mrs. Beebe's neighbor's horse had foaled during the night. What should have been routine went wrong. Michael wasn't a large-animal specialist; hell, he wasn't even a large-animal novice. But the phone had rung around two A.M. and he had responded.

After two hours of struggle and finally turning the breech foal, he and the farmer had managed to deliver the colt. And when Michael had driven off, bleary-eyed but satisfied, both mare and foal were doing fine.

Which was more than he could say for himself.

A knock sounded on his bedroom door. "Come in," he called. Jessica skipped across the floor and landed with a thud on the bed. She wore her pajamas with the panda bears rollicking across the top. Her long hair was wildly tangled and he knew it would take forever to work the brush through it. With a sigh, he pushed up against the pillows and said, "Ready for breakfast?"

She shook her head. "I'm sick," she announced.

Michael recognized the routine. Every time she was supposed to go to Pauline and Cecil's, Jessica diagnosed herself as ill. Michael couldn't really blame his daughter; Cecil pretty much turned his stomach, too. But Pauline was her mother. And Pauline, in her own way, loved her children. That fact alone kept Michael determined to maintain the role of peacekeeper and enforcer of custody visits as necessary. Otherwise, he'd be just as happy for Jessica and Kristen to stay with him 24/7.

"Cecil eats his boogers," Jessica said out of the blue.

"What did you say?" Michael stared at his younger daughter. She was the picture of innocence, eyes wide, her knees tucked to her chest, her arms wrapped around her pajama legs.

"Cecil—"

"He's Mr. Gardner to you."

"Mother says we should call him Cecil. She said that makes him more comfortable with us."

Michael nodded. "All right, but it isn't nice to say someone eats his boogers."

Jessica wrinkled her nose. "But we're supposed to tell the truth."

"Yes." He couldn't handle this discussion, not on a few hours of sleep. How could one explain the relativity of truth to an eight-year-old? "But you don't always have to announce everything you know."

Jessica nodded. "Does that mean I shouldn't tell Mother that you were kissing Miss Stacey?"

Michael choked. He started coughing. His ever-helpful daughter jumped up and pounded him on the back.

Kristen, in a sleepy daze, her cast gleaming white against her dark blue pajamas, joined them. "It's too early to be having so much fun," she said. "Who was kissing who?"

"No one," Michael said.

"Daddy kissed Stacey," Jessica said, obviously willing to align with her older sister on some issues.

"How would you know?" Kristen said.

"Last night. On the porch." Jessica sat back on her heels, her head tipped to one side. "I saw."

Michael felt like an innocent man forced to stand in a lineup for a crime he hadn't committed.

"Well, like, who cares?" his older daughter said with a world-weary shrug. "We know she's only passing through town. It's not like those other dates he's had."

Jessica giggled. "You mean the teacher we chased with the frogs?"

Kristen sat on the bed. "Or the lady from the bank."

Michael had never known why the bank manager, one of the only eligible women in Doolittle smart enough and pretty enough to interest him, had dropped him like a hot potato. "What did you two pull on her?"

Kristen and Jessica exchanged glances. "Secret weapon," they said in unison, then burst into a rolling fit of giggling that no protests from Michael could quell. He let them laugh. And he resolved that his next date with Stacey would be as far away from his house as possible.

Stacey.

He checked the clock. Some impression he'd make on two hours of sleep. Running a hand across the stubble thick on his chin, he considered begging off. Stacey no more wanted to look at property than he wanted to show her. Of course, she'd been polite, stuck in this dump of a town, with her dog practically held hostage. He had to be out of his mind thinking he could interest her in a small-town vet who delivered horses instead of getting a decent night's rest.

And then he remembered what her lips had felt like,

parting beneath his, opening to him, inviting him to taste her mouth.

He'd be crazy to let her slip away.

"Hup-ho," he said, throwing the covers back and wrapping them both in the comforter and lifting them off the bed, careful not to disturb Kristen's cast. Mindful of his parenting responsibilities, he always slept in his T-shirt and an old pair of workout shorts. Carrying his daughters to the door, he kissed the tops of their heads and said, "Time for breakfast, girls!"

Chapter 11

The knocking on her door would not stop. "Go away," Stacey said, but her voice came out more of a sleepy croak than a command. Visions of the realtor hounding her as she'd done yesterday morning—had that been only yesterday morning? No way! Stacey sat bolt upright.

The little metallic balls of kiss wrappers flew like ducks disturbed by golfers in City Park. The motion also started her screen saver out of sleep mode. The last piece she'd written—a press release designed to deflect the flack over the investment losses—stared at her from the monitor of her laptop.

The knocking persisted. Stacey sighed, both unwilling and unable to face either of the Schoolhouse Sisters. "I don't want any breakfast," she called.

That brought silence. Her lids drooped. She remembered watching the clock slide past four A.M. That must have been when she'd cleaned the last chocolate from the dish. She'd sneak out to a grocery and refill the bowl.

The knock sounded again. Impulsively, she hurled one of her pillows at the door. The apple-shaped bell wrapped in wildflowers hanging from the doorknob clanged. Immediately shocked at her own rude behavior, she leapt from the bed and padded over to the door to apologize to whichever sister was so determined to rouse her.

Stacey opened the door and rather than the plump bosom of Martha or the spare form of Abbie, she stared smack into the broad chest of Dr. Michael Halliday.

It was silly to say she recognized his chest without first glancing upward to confirm his identity, but silly or not, Stacey knew. Something about the way the dark blue cotton smoothed across his chest, lifting almost imperceptibly with the beating of his heart, whispered to her. She put one hand to her incredibly disheveled hair and tipped her head back.

"Hey, sleepyhead," Michael said, the corners of his eyes crinkling as he smiled at her.

Stacey shut the door.

Or tried to.

One boot-clad foot stood between her and privacy.

"What are you doing at my door?" she asked, deciding to discuss his presence rather than amputate his foot. "This is a private hotel."

"Yes, and the people in the room next door are probably trying to sleep."

"Not after all the knocking you were doing." But Stacey inched the door open. It wasn't as if she weren't decent, having worked through the night and fallen asleep fully clothed. But she looked a fright!

"Martha asked me to collect you for breakfast. She

says Abbie gets edgy when the guests don't eat the food she prepares."

Stacey said thoughtfully, "She's wrapped so tight she's almost scary."

"It's a good thing I'm here to protect you, then," he said.

Stacey laughed. "I'm not the helpless creature type." She'd relaxed, letting go of the door, and stepped back into her room a bit. Michael, without seeming to make an effort, now stood inside the doorjamb rather than in the hallway.

He regarded her for a moment, then reached out and fingered the ends of her hair where it had fallen forward on one shoulder. "Do you always look this good in the morning?"

Stacey shook her head. All she could think of was the way she could feel his touch from the tips of her hair to the tips of her toes. It shouldn't be possible, but it was.

"I'm a wreck," she said, wetting her lips with her tongue.

"And I'm a mongoose," he said, shutting the door. He lifted a handful of hair and inhaled. "Vanilla? No, almond."

She swallowed. "It's the conditioner. It's almond-scented."

"Good choice," he murmured. "I didn't realize your hair was this curly."

"It's from thinking," Stacey said. "I twist it around my fingers to help me think." She lifted one hand to demonstrate and brushed against Michael's wrist. Quickly she dropped her hand.

Michael shifted and let go of her hair. Leaning against the wall, now completely inside Third Grade, he said, "And what are you thinking about this bright Sunday morning?"

Stacey cast a covert look at her bed and stifled a groan. First she'd concocted the retirement property story to cover her workaholic tendencies and now she was pretty much caught outright. Maybe she could edge him around and he wouldn't see the bed. She wasn't sure why it mattered so much to her, but she desperately wanted to appear to be a balanced, fairly normal woman who actually had a life outside of her work.

Admit it, she thought. You want Michael to like you.

He must have followed the direction of her gaze. He narrowed his eyes, as if focusing.

Stacey stood on tiptoe and smoothed the side of his hair. Feeling very much like the risk-taker she was not, she said, "I just wanted to see what your hair felt like." It was a goofy line, but perhaps it would distract him from the bed, where her laptop hummed away.

"Help yourself," he said. "The picnic will wait."

"Picnic?" She ran one finger, then two, through the thick hair above his ears.

"I thought while we were scouting property we could enjoy an encore of coleslaw, biscuits, and chicken. Mrs. Beebe packed a basket before she left for church. Unless, of course, you're one of those people who don't do leftovers."

Stacey moved her hand to the back of his neck, inching him away from the wall. With a subtle movement, she had him now facing partially away from the bed. "I love leftovers," she said. "But I haven't even had breakfast yet. Is it really lunchtime?"

"No, but it's good to plan ahead." He put his arms around her and drew her into an embrace that had more in common with two people about to twirl around the dance floor than with a man about to kiss a woman.

Stacey sighed and moved with him.

He led her in a pirouette, then into a waltz step. Their bodies floated as one. Fred and Ginger could have taken pointers from their perfect timing. So caught up was she in the feel of his arms around her, Stacey forgot about shielding the bed from Michael.

His rather matter-of-fact voice intruded on her vision. "Aren't these the same clothes you were wearing last night?"

Stacey stumbled and landed on one of his insteps. She saw him wince and then he lifted her up and off him. They were right at the foot of her bed. She turned so that her back was to the high mattress and he followed suit. "You're very observant," she said.

He cocked his head sideways, toward the length of the four-poster bed. "Thank you. I've also noticed that you're keeping me away from the bed. Are you attempting to preserve our reputation or is there something you're hiding?"

A little too observant.

"I'm guessing it's not another man."

"How did you get to my room?" She was more curious than concerned.

He'd draped his arm across the back of her shoulders

and was again sifting her hair through his fingers. He grinned. "I had to charm Miss Martha in order to bypass the parlor. Anyone less trustworthy than yours truly would not have been given the pass-go card. You were going to miss breakfast. I said I'd rouse you."

Stacey smiled. "Well, you're good at that."

He pulled her closer. His breath warmed her ear and his touch stirred desire in her she logically shouldn't be experiencing. She'd only just met this man. Last night she'd kissed him like a wild woman. And now . . . Stacey knew she was ready to do the same again.

Michael moved so their bodies were inches apart. The collar of his polo shirt tickled her throat. "Want to show me what's on the bed?"

"It's my laptop," she said.

He scooped her up and tipped her onto the mattress. He was tall enough that he didn't need the aid of the small stepstool to mount the four-poster bed. But instead of joining her, he leaned forward onto the mattress and patted the top of the covers between where she now sat and her computer.

"You work a lot, don't you?" he asked.

"What makes you think I was working?" Of course, she said it far too hastily.

"You don't look like someone who plays Freecell just to pass the time," he said, his voice dry but his eyes regarding her intensely. "There's nothing wrong with taking your work seriously."

"I did have an emergency to take care of," she said.

"Me, too." He ran a hand over his eyes, then smiled at her. "Rough night last night. I was out on a difficult equine delivery until just before dawn."

"You were?" Stacey leaned back on her elbows. "Tell me about it."

He shook his head and yawned. "How about later? The important thing is both mare and foal are doing fine."

Stacey glanced at her computer. Saving face for Key Financial seemed so trivial next to helping a horse give birth. "You worked most of the night, didn't you?"

He nodded.

"So did I." She plucked at the fabric of her slacks. "You're right. These are the clothes I wore to dinner. I fell asleep in the middle of a sentence, I think. I was just embarrassed to admit it."

He cupped his hands on her knees. The warmth of his touch seared through the light cotton. "I'm the last person in the world you need to pretend for, especially if the topic is working too much." He smoothed his hands around her knees. "I let myself be used by the town of Doolittle, for my own reasons, I suppose. Maybe you're like that, for reasons of your own, with your clients. The question is, do you enjoy your life as structured?"

Stacey regarded the man fondling her body and making such good sense to her mind. How had she been so lucky as to stumble across someone so wonderful?

Now was the time to come clean.

He leaned over, lifted her laptop, and set it on the floor. Then, before Stacey could say, *There's something I want to tell you,* he'd joined her on the bed.

They were on top of the covers, but they might as well have been naked on a desert island. The way he was devouring her with eyes as hungry as her own raw need opened her to him. Rumpled slacks, tousled hair, flaky mascara, no lipstick . . . none of it mattered. Not to Michael, and certainly not to Stacey.

He leaned over her and she parted her lips.

Closed her eyes.

And waited.

And waited.

No kiss came.

Stacey peeked out from half-closed eyelids to check what was keeping Michael from kissing her.

Darn it, she liked it when he kissed her. It kept her from thinking too much about what she was doing. It felt so good, all she could feel was his touch.

"You have beautiful ankles," he said, lifting one foot and feathering a kiss on the inside of her ankle.

"Th-thank you," she said, astounded. No one had ever kissed her leg before. Certainly not Robert.

"These slacks highlight your ankles," he said, as if considering whether that was a good thing or not.

"They're capris," Stacey said, wishing they were shorts or a miniskirt so Michael could place another kiss and then another higher up her leg.

"Ah, capris. Of course," he murmured, his mouth against the curve of her calf where it disappeared beneath the cloth. "A clothing form designed to drive a man crazy."

Stacey giggled. "Kissing my ankle is crazy, but I like it."

He suddenly let go of her leg and straightened. Towering over her, he said, "Time to go."

She stared up at him. She didn't feel at all like going anywhere. And as she studied him and she saw with a start his arousal jutting against the fabric of his pants, she realized he didn't want to leave, either.

Her gaze must have remained on the object of her fascination, because Michael grinned and rested one hand on his belt buckle.

With a demure glance, she raised her hand, to cup the warm hard heat beneath his buckle. "Go where?"

He sucked in his breath and she smiled as he pushed into her palm. "Yeah, like it or not, time to head out of here."

"Oh." Stacey wrinkled her forehead, considering the situation. She certainly didn't consider herself a fast woman. Goodness, she'd only had sex with two other boyfriends before being engaged to Robert for six years! But surely one or two more of those marvelous kisses wouldn't hurt. And she wasn't thinking of his lips against her leg. "Well, all right," she said, leaning back and wriggling against the covers, her arms thrown over her head. "It's just that I'm so-o-o sleepy."

"You make it hard for a guy to do the right thing," Michael said, still standing.

"I can see that," Stacey said, amazed at her own boldness.

He reached out a hand. She lifted hers and he grasped it and pulled her to a sitting position at the edge of the bed. Then, before she could pucker up, he'd wedged his legs between her knees, reached around her body, and pulled her tight against him. Her breasts crushed against his midsection. Breathing quickly, he said, "Walking out of this room is the last thing I want to do right now."

Stacey squirmed. His groin was hot and demanding, pushing into her. She was on fire in a way she didn't recognize. Work, not passion, was Stacey's strong suit.

Michael tipped her chin upward. His eyes blazing, he said, "We could have sex here. Now. I could rip those pants off you and take you, explode inside you like I'm dying to. And that would be that. You'd scurry back to the city and no matter how great the sex, you wouldn't come back for more."

Stacey started to shake her head. Why, she wasn't sure, except she wanted to say, *But I wasn't asking for just sex,* but then of course that was not exactly true. "Why do you say I'd run away?"

He lifted his brows and then smoothed her hair gently from her forehead. Holding her less tightly, he said, "Male intuition?"

She smiled. "I thought there wasn't any such thing."

He nodded somberly. "And there's no such thing as love at first sight, either."

His kisses didn't frighten her, but that comment did. Stacey edged back on the bed. Michael slowly let go and stepped back from the bed. "I'd like to get to know you," he said.

She clasped one of the bed pillows to her chest, holding on as if it were an airline seat cushion being used for flotation. She regarded him, letting her own breathing return to normal. Finally, she nodded. "Me, too."

"Great. So how about that picnic? Or do you have to work?"

"I'm finished for the moment," Stacey said. "But I need a shower and my hair is a mess. . . ." He was looking at her as if she'd gone bonkers.

"You're beautiful," he said. "How about you toss on some shorts and grab a swim suit and we'll head to the lake?"

"Well, all right," she said, but reluctantly. Even the thought of ducking her head underwater in a bathtub caused her to shudder. She didn't even own a bathing suit. No need to mention that now. "I like to be ready to face the day, but since it's just the two of us and you've already seen me at my worst, I suppose that's okay." Then a thought struck her and she said, "Is it just the two of us?"

Michael nodded. "Kristen and Jessica are at church with their mother and Cecil."

"That's right. The church Jessica didn't want to attend."

He sighed. "That child is far better suited to Buddhism than to the Baptist church."

"I don't suppose her mother agrees?"

He looked surprised. "That comment is right to the point. Perhaps if it had been her idea . . ."

"Joint custody is a nightmare, isn't it?" Stacey rose from the bed and stretched. Had she packed any shorts? Surely Donna had said something about the hotel in Hot Springs being casual.

"Sometimes I think it would be far simpler for me to have sole custody," Michael said, moving over to the table in front of the window and sitting down. "Pauline has never enjoyed being a mother. For her it's more like playacting. And now she's using the girls to help Cecil's political ambitions."

"How's that?"

"He and his family have run Doolittle and the county for ages. He's now planning to go for a state senate seat. Having a wife and two photogenic children makes him far more attractive than being a single, middle-aged man."

"I see." Stacey sat back on her heels beside her overnight case. "So when they're not needed, they stay with you."

"You got it."

"Perhaps that's easier on them than two weeks here, two weeks there, or every other weekend. They'd probably go to church anyway, right, whether it means much to them or not? So this way they go to church, Sunday dinner, and get to come home."

Michael was studying her, no doubt exercising more of that male intuition he'd referred to. But Stacey didn't feel like talking about her own miserable experiences with being the child rope in the tug-of-war of divorced parents. "Where's the lake?"

"About five miles out of town. Actually, there are several, including Lake Doolittle, the one the retirement community is built around. We can drive by there on the way back, if you'd like."

She got up. "I need the other suitcase out of my trunk or I'll have to spend the rest of the day in these clothes."

"Toss me your keys and I'll get it for you," Michael said, rising from the chair. "And then I'll wait for you in the parlor."

She handed him her car keys. Their hands touched. "Thank you," she said.

He smiled and kissed her, a sweet promise of more to come. "I'll save a muffin for you," he said, "and fix you some coffee to go. How do you take it?"

"That's sweet of you," Stacey said. "Just cream, thanks."

"You know me," Michael said, opening the door, "always taking care of people."

He shut the door behind him and Stacey stood there, touching her fingers to her lips. Always taking care of people.

Always taking charge, he might as well have said.

Yet, being taken care of by Michael Halliday felt awfully good.

But she shouldn't let how yummy he made her body feel make her forget how he'd handled this situation, barging into her room, making her salivate with desire, then having the nerve to insinuate she couldn't handle a little bit of passion.

She was no 'fraidy cat!

Let him kiss her. Let him knock her socks off. Let him bring on his best sweet smile that sent shivers of wanton need up and down her spine.

A slow smile formed on Stacey's lips.

He thought she'd flee, did he?

What would *he* do if she drove him to distraction with desire?

Chapter 12

"I love the water," Michael said, pausing with his toes curled over the edge of the creaking wooden dock that bobbed in the water a bit too freely for Stacey's comfort.

"It's nice," she said, wishing there were a railing to hold on to. When Michael had pulled into the picnic area adjoining the lake, she'd expected him to set the hamper onto one of the cluster of tables shaded by the branches of the pine trees.

Instead he'd led the way to the dock and plopped the hamper into one of the frail-looking boats tied to one side of the wooden structure, then stepped out to the end.

"Nice?" He glanced at her and then said, "Of course, you're used to the magnificence of the Mississippi and the Gulf. Maybe it's because I grew up on the Atlantic, but the lake keeps me grounded." He grinned. "As ironic as that expression may be in this circumstance."

"It's the earth that does that for me," Stacey said, inching back toward the shore.

"Ready for our picnic?" He turned, and darn it if he didn't catch her standing there nibbling nervously on her lip and staring at the tiny boat she was sure he planned for them to climb into.

"I am hungry."

He stepped beside her and tipped her chin upward. "What's wrong?"

"Oh, nothing."

"Hmm." Michael tapped the side of his head. "I live in a household of females. If there's one expression I've learned to be leery of, it's that one."

"Why don't we have our picnic over there?" She turned and pointed toward the towering pine trees.

"Stacey, are you afraid of the water?"

"I'm not afraid of anything," she said, glaring at him, both upset and relieved he'd guessed correctly. Now she wouldn't have to go out on that boat.

"I'm not sure you've proven that point," he said, "but let's not argue it. Can you swim?"

She quit chewing on her lip. It was always so embarrassing to admit to a deficiency. She shook her head.

"You never learned to swim?" His amazement was a bit too strong.

"And what's wrong with that?"

He shrugged. "If it doesn't matter to you, it's one thing, but I'm willing to bet it bothers the heck out of you."

"Does not."

"Does, too."

"Does not!" Stacey had made it to the point where the dock joined the land. She stepped onto solid ground.

Michael joined her. He loomed beside her, a determined expression she wasn't sure she appreciated fixed on his face. "Have you ever tried to learn how to swim?"

"Not exactly. Well, sort of."

"Tell me about it."

She stood there, hearing his commands but realizing he asked because he cared. Slowly, she began picking her way through her explanation.

"My mother swims like a fish, but my father isn't a water person at all. They never agreed on my swimming lessons and somehow it was all wrapped up in my mind with the tension. So I avoided the water and then in high school they made us swim." She smiled wryly. "I don't know if you can imagine how traumatic it is to be the only girl in the class left on the side of the pool when everyone else jumps in."

"No wonder you identified with Kristen's anguish at being the only one left out of the class project."

She smiled at him, rather shyly. "Some things feel like they happened yesterday."

"And I'm guessing those swim lessons were a nightmare."

"Oh, yes. You know how some people have dreams about having to take a test and they've never been to class or they can't find the room?"

He nodded. He noted that she'd unclenched her hands. Pleased that she was relaxing with him, he said, "With me it's an English essay I've never finished."

"Because you were always good at math and science, right?"

"Yep. But I've never met a sentence I couldn't mangle."

"I find that hard to believe," Stacey said. "You can't tell it from listening to you."

He shrugged. "Just don't put a pen in my hand. It becomes a dangerous weapon."

She laughed.

Michael joined her, happy the vision of her recurring nightmare had receded. He was certain it had to do with swimming. "If you ever want a one-on-one lesson, guaranteed to be gentle, let me know."

"Oh, that's okay," she said rather hastily. "So what's in the basket?"

"Maybe it would be a good idea," he said. "It's better to face one's fears, you know. You said you feel safe with me."

She nodded, possibly considering it. He grinned as she lifted a long strand of hair and twisted it around her index finger. She really did use her hair as a thinking aid.

He could think of many other things to do with her hair. For starters, he'd love to see her wearing nothing but the thick dark cascade of hair falling over her shoulders just teasing the tips of her puckered nipples. He must have made a sound, because through his imagined vision, he heard her voice.

"Not today," she said.

"No time like the present."

"Later."

"Nah." Michael studied the stubborn slant of her chin. He'd taught Kristen and Jessica how to swim when they were toddlers. He'd already kicked his shoes off; he wore shorts and a T-shirt and his watch was waterproof. Facing Stacey, his back to the lake, he began walking into the water.

"What are you doing?"

He kept moving.

"Are you nuts?"

Waist-high now, he let himself drop, shifting easily into float position.

"If you drown, I can't save you," Stacey called.

He tipped his head up. She had edged closer to the water. Her toes were almost getting lapped by the wave motion he'd set up. It was a quiet day, with most of the townspeople still at church or sleeping in. Soon there'd be other swimmers and boaters dotting the area. He needed to persuade her to join him now.

He started thrashing his arms.

"Crazy fool!"

"Come on in, the water's fine," he called.

She stood there.

He swam toward her. Knee-deep, he held a hand out to her. Gently, he said, "I'll help you, Stacey. I won't let go of you. I won't duck you under. The first moment you say stop, I'll do so."

Stacey tipped her head sideways, tempted by his offer. He did seem to be enjoying the water. She'd also hated her fear of swimming but had never taken the time or courage to overcome it. "I'd like to," she said at last, "but I don't have a swimsuit on under my clothes."

He grinned. "Neither do I. Get rid of those sandals and wade on in."

She plucked at her white T-shirt. "I don't know. . . ." But despite her words, she removed her shoes. Eyes crunched tight, she tiptoed in. She felt his hand cover hers and she waded in. When the cool water reached her waist, she shivered and opened her eyes. Her T-shirt rode up from the wave motion and then, completely drenched, it clung to her body. She caught Michael staring at her breasts.

"Michael!"

"Hey, it's better than a bikini," he said. He winked and said, "All we're going to do today is practice floating, okay?"

"If you say so."

He let go of her hand and she clutched at his shoulders.

"Easy," he murmured. "Water is buoyant. Water is your friend. Say that to yourself and then lay back across my arms. Arch your back, but just slightly. Watch me, first." He demonstrated a move Stacey knew from past experience and failures she couldn't duplicate.

"That never works for me," she said.

Michael puffed his cheeks out and puckered up his lips, then said, "Pretend you're a fish."

"I bet this is how you taught your daughters to swim."

"Yep."

"Did it work?"

He nodded and held his arms out in front of him. "Come on, Stacey-fish, give me your best float effort."

She didn't know how, but she eased her feet up, letting go of the safety of the soft soil of the lake bottom. Arching backward, easing her head onto the water, she felt Michael's strong arms beneath her and slowly forced herself to relax. "I am a fish," she said.

"Red fish. Blue fish. Brave fish," Michael said.

She grinned at the Dr. Suess reference. As she did, she relaxed more. She wiggled her arms in the water and kicked her feet timidly. She kept doing that until she was actually getting a feel for the ballast of the water beneath her.

Michael was gazing down at her with a look as warm as the sun overhead in the sky. "Brave Stacey," he said.

And that's when she realized he'd slipped his hands out from beneath her. She started to flail. "You can do it on your own," he said.

Forcing herself to breathe, she kept moving, kept her body from bending at the waist and her feet from seeking the lake bottom.

"That's it," he said, his commanding voice steadying her.

"Michael," she said in awe, "I'm actually floating."

"Yep. Like I said, no time like the present."

She bravely lifted one hand and splashed him. He returned the favor; then, as she started to lose her concentration, he caught her and guided her back to her feet and toward the shore.

Stacey was elated that she hadn't floundered the way she always had before. She pulled her wet hair back from her face and plucked at her T-shirt. "Thank you for the lesson," she said.

"No problem," Michael said, staring at her as if he were hungry for something far more satisfying than what was in the picnic hamper Mrs. Beebe had packed. "Now that we've conquered floating, want to brave the rowboat? We can dry out while we drift in the sun."

"What the heck," Stacey said. "What's one more challenge?"

He grinned, then swooped down and kissed her quickly. The move was so swift she thought she'd imagined it as he loped toward the boat where he'd left the hamper.

Once they were out in the middle of the lake, it took Stacey some time to relax. But the warmth from the sun and the gentle rocking of the boat, combined with Michael's calm, quiet presence, began to work on her. And as she relaxed, she remembered she'd planned to drive Michael to distraction. Eyeing him where he sat only a foot or so from her, head tipped back, eyes closed, his lean, tanned legs stretched toward her, she began rolling the bottom of her T-shirt upward.

Sure enough, she caught him peering from beneath one lid. Good. Too bad she didn't have the nerve to discreetly remove her bra. Or did she? Normally she wouldn't have done it. But there, in the middle of the lake, her wet clothes pretty uncomfortable, she bent forward, unhooked the undergarment, and, slipping it off one arm, then the other, she tucked it behind her on the seat.

Michael almost tipped the boat when he shot upright.

Stacey let out a muffled cry as the boat rocked.

"It's okay," he said. "Forgive me. But darn it, you ought to warn a man when you're about to strip." Michael was staring at her. Well, heck, to be specific he was staring at her nipples through the T-shirt.

She had to admit Michael's reaction was pretty darn satisfying. Robert had gotten so that he barely looked at her, and they'd been about to be married. He liked leaving one dim light on when they made love, but then he'd close his eyes most of the time.

Stacey hadn't been able to figure that out. Not that it mattered anymore. But Michael made her so very aware that she was a woman.

"It's easier to dry without an extra layer of clothing," Stacey said.

"Clothing just plain gets in the way, doesn't it?" Michael said.

She'd bet he left all the lights on. A rush of warmth, not at all induced by the springtime sun, stole across her body. And he wouldn't close his eyes, either.

She had no business thinking these thoughts. Still, she treated herself to a survey of his lean, muscular legs dusted with light brown hair. He wore shorts that were loose-fitting like swim trunks but tight enough to reveal how well-built a man he was. Remembering how he'd felt pressing between her thighs heated Stacey even more.

She noticed a scar on the side of his knee and focused on that white line. It was more ladylike than picturing what he'd look like freed from his shorts. "What happened to your knee?"

He lifted his cap and grinned. "You disappoint me, Stacey."

She blushed. "You've been watching me watch you!"

He nodded. "Look all you wish."

She folded her hands on her lap. "Did you have an accident?"

He shook his head. "Knee surgery."

"Meniscus?"

He looked surprised. "Yes."

"It's a little more noticeable than one would expect."

"And you're pretty knowledgeable."

"You mean for someone who isn't a doctor?" Stacey heard the bristle in her voice.

"Whoa. Don't take me wrong, please." He'd pushed his cap back on his head. "I meant it as a compliment."

"Sorry."

"Let me guess. There's some more personal history involved here." He leaned forward. "Want to share it with me?"

"I'm the daughter of two doctors. I was pre-med, doing great. But I hated it." Stacey paused, reflecting. "No, I didn't hate it. But it wasn't what I wanted to do."

"Your heart wasn't in it?"

"That's right. I mean, I could do it. I would have been a competent doctor. But I didn't want to repeat . . ." She trailed off.

"Repeat . . . ?"

"My parents' lives," she added. She'd been about to say *my parents' mistakes.* But that would get into the mess of their wrecked marriage. "I wanted to be me. Whatever that meant, wherever it took me."

He nodded. "That makes perfect sense to me."

"Did you always want to be a veterinarian?" She was curious. He was so good at it, but he just didn't seem like a man born to the life he was living. He no doubt could have been the world-famous surgeon her dad had always wanted her to be.

"Yes and no." He looked off across the lake as if seeking a vision there or perhaps watching the replay of his life, something Stacey could appreciate. "I knew I wanted to be an animal doctor rather than a people doctor. Talk about not pleasing one's parents. Neither my father nor my mother is an animal lover. It used to drive them crazy when I'd bring home strays and tend to the wounded birds in the neighborhood."

"But they thought you'd grow out if it, right?"

"Yep. And turn into a proper research scientist."

"Following in their footsteps?" Stacey spoke sympathetically.

"My father is a chemist. My mother is a mom."

"You mean a Donna Reed stay-at-home mother?" Stacey was amazed. She knew so few of those.

"Well, yes, I guess you could say that." He laughed. "Though I wouldn't give a penny for your skin if my mom caught you calling her that. She raised all seven of us kids and ran the neighborhood. And I'm not sure she even owns a strand of pearls."

"Then you should get her some for Christmas," Stacey said. "So you went to vet school. Why animals and not people?"

Michael trailed a hand over the edge of the boat, letting the water ripple around his fingers. "Animals are more of a challenge. They can't tell you what hurts or how long they've been experiencing a symptom. You have to listen with all your heart and mind to an animal patient. And not everyone can do that."

"It's a special calling, isn't it?" Stacey had never thought of it in terms of being harder than dealing with humans. She smiled slightly, wondering what her parents' reactions would be to that statement. She'd have to remember to ask them. And she'd have the chance all too soon.

"I suppose that's true," Michael said, "but what I

wanted to do was research and teach. And I was well on my way to that. I'd been promoted to assistant professor the week Pauline broke the news she was in love with someone else and wanted to move to Arkansas—with the girls."

"Oh, my."

"Yep." He splashed a hand against the pretty display of ripples and broke the rhythmic pattern. "Things don't always work out the way we want them to." He looked at her across the small space that separated them and smiled. "But you know the old saying, don't you?"

"Which one would that be?"

"When life burns your toast, make diamonds from the carbon."

"Did you make that up?"

He shrugged. "I couldn't stay in Boston and visit Kristen and Jessica a few times a year. And Pauline, who rarely has time or emotional energy to spare for our daughters, wouldn't listen to reason and leave them with me. Though she is their mother and I had to consider what was best for everyone." He stared across the horizon, his expression stoic. He'd done what was best for everyone involved—but at what cost to himself?

"Well, that's a sad tale, isn't it?" He stretched out again, leaning his head against the back of the boat. "I don't know how I got off on that tangent, but thanks for listening."

"You're welcome," Stacey said. "Thanks for sharing. I think it's wonderful that you have such a close relationship with your children. But it must have been very hard for you to give up what you loved doing."

He nodded, then chuckled. "And you should have

seen the first time this city slicker got called out to deliver a breech calf! I didn't think to wear rubber boots
and I got my shoes stuck in the mud and manure and
sucked right off my feet. Saved the calf and the cow,
though. And the next day the farmer delivered a pair of
Arkansas Reeboks to my clinic."

Stacey smiled. "I know just the boots you mean, only
we call them Louisiana Reeboks. The shrimpers wear
them."

"Well, I was darn thankful to have that nice new pair.
Had to throw out that pair of Cole-Haan loafers and I'd
paid a pretty penny for them back in Boston." He
smiled at her, and Stacey returned the smile, savoring
the intimate exchange. "Arkansas isn't so very far from
Louisiana, is it?"

"Next-door neighbors." Her heart was beating more
quickly than it should for simply sitting beside a man.

"Close enough to visit often?"

"Oh, sure," she said, her voice rattling on as quickly
as her heartbeat. "A hop, skip, and a jump and you're in
the middle of the French Quarter."

"Is that where you live?"

"No. I live uptown."

He cocked his brows. "I've only been to New Orleans twice, both times for conferences. Fill me in on
the geography?"

"Ooh, explaining New Orleans to a nonnative—
now, that's a challenge. Most tourists visit the French
Quarter. That's probably where you were, right?"

"Yes."

"So if you take the St. Charles streetcar and head out

of the Quarter, you're going toward uptown. I live near Tulane University, near Audubon Park."

"Gotcha. I've done that ride. It's a nice area." He sighed. "Not exactly Doolittle, is it?"

"No, but Doolittle has its charms."

Michael nodded. "You know, that's true. A year ago I was still fighting it, but now I've come to appreciate some of the small-town virtues."

"And the town has adopted you with open arms."

"What do you mean?"

"Everyone loves you. They call you Dr. Mike. That gas station attendant knew he could call you in the middle of the night and you'd come out and rescue me."

Michael grinned somewhat ruefully. "I guess I've been filling in the empty spots of my life every way I can."

Stacey wished she could reach over and touch his hand. He needed someone to comfort him, the way he did for others. And to her pleased surprise, she realized she wanted to be the person to offer that healing, warming touch. She'd thought earlier what she felt for him was pure sensual attraction, but now she felt something much deeper and closer crowding around the desire.

Impulsively she scooted forward. The boat rocked and she dropped to her knees beside the hamper, clutching the sides with both hands. "Oops."

"If you'd like to move closer," Michael said, "which would be nice, just ease on over." He placed his hands on either side of the boat. "We won't tip over."

Stacey hung there, bending forward, wanting to move, but afraid of revealing too much of herself. But it was such a short distance that separated her from Michael.

"One foot forward," Michael said.

She edged her toes out from beneath her knees.

"That's it. Just skirt the hamper."

"Um, if it's not too ungraceful, how about I just crawl on my hands and knees?"

"That'll work."

"I feel kind of silly," Stacey said, easing past the lunch basket and pulling herself up against Michael's sturdy knees. "For someone who's used to being in charge of things, it's pretty unnerving to be afraid to move."

He placed his hands over hers. "It's okay to feel vulnerable."

She started to shake her head, to disagree emphatically, and then as he smoothed his palms over her hands and smiled into her eyes, and she began to feel what she could only describe as safe despite her unreasonable fear of drowning, she decided an argument wasn't necessary.

He spread his legs and pulled her in close, so that her breasts brushed against his belly. Then he leaned down and captured her lips with his. One hand cupped around the back of her head, he devoured her mouth, crushing her to him.

She couldn't breathe.

But who needed oxygen?

She mated her tongue with his. The earth revolved around her as the only reality she felt was his mouth, his lips, his tongue, his heated intake of breath swallowing her very essence. Light-headed, Stacy clung to Michael, offering herself to him, wanting the moment never to end.

But slowly, very slowly, he pulled his face away, his

breathing harsh and rapid, his dark eyes huge in his face. But he kept her pinned between his legs.

His arousal, hot and wanting, pressed against her belly. She glanced down and saw her breasts straining through the thin cotton top. And Stacey, proper and prim in so many ways, just plain didn't care. Another second locked in that kiss, and she would have gladly pulled the shirt over her head.

Michael brushed the pad of his thumb across one swollen nipple. She trembled and started to lift her mouth for another kiss.

And then she paused. She wanted to kiss more than his lips. Leaning forward, she scooted the tail of his shirt free from his shorts. The sight of his taut stomach had been teasing her and she could withstand the temptation no more.

She lapped at his skin, suckling gently, then shifted lower, easing one hand beneath the elastic of his shorts. He groaned and placed his hands on the back of her hair. The heat of his erection seared her palm. She tightened her grip, thrilled by the rush of sensation. She'd done that to him! And how she wanted to do more.

"I don't know how much of that I can take," Michael said, his voice roughened with desire.

Stacy lifted her head. "Just a little bit more?" She moistened her lips with the tip of her tongue.

"You're going to push me over the edge," he said, his hands still clasped around her head.

"I'd like to," she said. "Let me?" She was shameless. Stacey really didn't recognize herself, but she felt freer than she could ever remember feeling.

He groaned again. Ever so slowly, he pulled her up

against him and held her tight. His heart pounded against hers. But instead of kissing her, Michael shook his head.

She leaned away, her question clear in her eyes.

He traced the line of her lips with one finger. "I chose this rowboat for a reason," he said. He smoothed her hair with a gentle touch. "I figured I'd be forced to keep my hands to myself. You do something to me, Stacey. The chemistry . . . well, it's incredible. But I've fallen victim to chemistry before and vowed not to make the same mistake twice. Add to that that I'm a starving male and, well, I'm trying to do the sensible thing here."

"Oh." Stacey tipped her head sideways and reached for a strand of her hair. Twisting it around her fingers, she said, "So it's as if you haven't had ice cream for months and months, and when you reach the market, any kind will make your mouth water. It doesn't have to be Häagen-Dazs or Ben & Jerry's or BlueBell—just plain ol' generic vanilla and you want to eat the entire carton. Only, once before, you did that and ended up puking, so you've decided not to have any ice cream no matter what?"

He laughed and reached out and stilled her fingers. "Close. Except for the no matter what." His voice roughened around the edges. "I'm just trying to take things a step at a time. But you taste better than any ice cream I've ever tried."

She nodded. "Well, you're safe with me."

"What do you mean?"

"Tasting is okay because that's as far as it will go. I'm

not a woman cut out for more than a casual date or two." She tried to sound nonchalant and sophisticated and hoped like the devil she'd carried it off. Darn this man! He affected her far more than she was comfortable with.

"Hmm."

"Hmm, what?"

"Have you ever been married?"

"No." Stacey hesitated to say more. She despised her tale of woe, playing the role of the woman left at the altar. But he'd been honest with her, sharing the story of his marriage and divorce. And he hadn't been jilted before the wedding—his wife had left him for another man. "My fiancé called off our wedding the night of the rehearsal dinner. He'd been seeing someone else and just hadn't known how to tell me. Well, she—the new girlfriend—found out and drove him to my office and waited until he delivered the news."

"What a schmuck." Michael hugged her close and then gently eased her around so that she was leaning back against his legs. "I'd have to call that good riddance to bad rubbish," he said.

"Yeah, well, it hurt."

"Of course it did." He kneaded her shoulders. She'd tensed up thinking of Robert.

"But the pain goes away. And you live again."

Yeah, right. Stacey kept quiet. It had been almost a year. Living through her parents' divorce had already made her cautious; Robert's behavior had merely been the icing on the cake that convinced her marriage was a miserable thing and not meant for her.

He leaned closer and said softly, "The hurt will ease, Stacey."

She sighed. "Let's just drift awhile, okay?"

"Fair enough," Michael said.

Chapter 13

Michael had no objections to drifting—or to letting the topic go. Despite the undertone of tension in her voice, Stacey seemed content to lean against him and he was more than pleased to have her there. Idly he stroked her hair and began to braid the silky strands. Her presence soothed him.

Yeah, when she wasn't arousing him beyond all reason! The clingy fabric of her damp T-shirt begged his eyes to stray downward. He forced his eyes from the visual feast and tugged the cap over his brow. Dammit. He really had come out on the lake with the best of intentions. To spend some time getting to know Stacey was his priority of the day. No doubt about it, he liked what he'd seen so far, at least once she'd gotten over being quite so prissy.

It wasn't every night Ms. Corporate Executive strode into a mixed animal practice in the middle of nowhere Arkansas. The look of incredulity on her face when he'd told her her dog was pregnant flashed in his memory and he chuckled.

"What's so funny?" She murmured the question. Her head had tipped slightly to the side. Poor thing. She had worked most of the night.

He started to say, *Oh, nothing.* This was definitely a no-win situation. If he answered honestly, she'd no doubt swell up like an indignant peacock, just when she'd started to soften like ice cream left to warm on the kitchen counter. If he made up something, she'd probably see through any impromptu fabrication.

Could she laugh at herself? When all was said and done, there was so much pain in life, it was pretty darn valuable to be able to sit back and howl.

He'd reach the end of the braid. Draping the thick length of silky hair over her shoulder, he leaned forward and said, "Just thinking about Friday night."

Sure enough, her shoulders stiffened. But she said easily enough, "Anything in particular?"

"True's pregnancy diagnosis."

"What about it?" She was definitely sitting up straighter now.

The view of her breasts was even more enticing. Michael wished he'd kept his mouth shut. "Please understand I wasn't laughing at you, but the look on your face was pretty amusing."

"You mean when I refused to believe you."

"Yep."

"That was pretty bad of me." She tipped her head around and smiled at him. "I can be a know-it-all."

He grinned. "Me, too."

Stacey swung her head back around and settled

against Michael's knees once more. She had been pretty outrageous. "The worst of it, even more than that I had no idea True had been near another dog, was that I refused to believe you 'cause I thought you were some know-nothing. And here you are a vet school professor." She sighed and said, "I really should learn not to rush to judgment based on assumptions."

"Having children helps that," Michael said.

"How is that?" She felt a pang as she considered that given her determination not to pursue marriage she'd also charted her course in life to ensure that she would miss out on the mysteries of parenthood.

"They see the world without the preconceptions most of us have acquired. It always amazes me how I can take something for granted and then either Kristen or Jessica will pop up with something completely off the wall."

He chuckled again. Stacey liked the way his chest moved when he laughed.

"The first time Jessica saw a pregnant woman, she asked me how many babies were in a mommy litter."

Stacey smiled. "Cute. They probably spend more time with animals than humans."

"Just about true." His voice shifted and she detected a shading of concern as he said, "Kristen doesn't come around the clinic much anymore, but we certainly have enough animals at the house." He glanced at his watch. "Speaking of Kristen, we'd better head back. What do you say we have our picnic on shore?"

"Lovely," Stacey said, though she didn't mind being out on the water now. She was happy to remain where she was, safe with Michael. She shifted forward so he could reach the oars and set the boat in motion toward the shore.

Before she knew it, Michael was helping her out of the boat. He turned and hauled the hamper from the boat, along with her discarded bra. That he tucked under his arm. "I think I'll keep this," he said.

"Oh, no. There are a lot of people around," Stacey said, suddenly self-conscious of her clinging top.

Michael glanced around. "Well, I see Rusty the boat-keeper," he said, "and oh, yes, there's a young couple setting out a picnic and, if I'm on target, about to shed a few pieces of their own wardrobes. No, I think this garment shall be my spoils of war."

Stacey wrinkled her brow and pretended to pout. "What war?"

He wiggled a brow at her. "The war between the sexes, or haven't you heard of that one?"

She stepped farther onto the grassy edge of the water, putting a bit more distance between herself and the lapping waters of the edge of the lake. "I'm not engaged in that war."

"Ah, but of course you are. You said you weren't a person who could be coaxed into more than a date or two. Now, if that isn't some tactical hit-and-run strategy designed to lure the enemy, tell me what it is."

Stacey laughed and then immediately said, "I take that back."

"You can't take back laughter." Michael looked up from where he was tying the rowboat to a dock that Stacey realized matched the number on the side of the craft.

She wrinkled her brow. "Well, I'm not trying to lure anyone. I've just had enough situations in life to convince me that a relationship between a man and a woman is one sure recipe for disaster."

"Hmm," Michael said, walking toward her, gently swinging her bra from side to side. "Perhaps you simply haven't met the proper chef."

She smiled, but realized it was a rather prim attempt. "I spent six years of my life making darn sure that I'd selected the appropriate man designed to fit every specification for the perfect husband for me. I considered age, weight, IQ, academic background, career choice, career progress, family, upbringing, background—"

"Were you falling in love or buying a dog to haul to American Kennel Club shows?" He said it jokingly, but it didn't take much for Stacey to realize she'd really put him off.

"I was seeking a husband who would last a lifetime," she said, backing up until she reached the edge of the picnic table she'd spotted as she climbed from the boat. She plopped down, with as controlled a gesture as she could muster given that a sliver of wood had wedged itself into the back of her knee upon first contact. "Ow!"

"What's wrong?" Michael stepped quickly to her side, lowering the hamper and her lingerie to the table.

"Nothing," she said from behind gritted teeth. She didn't want or need to be rescued. She'd simply reach down and pluck the offending splinter from her leg.

"Well," he said in a voice she found frustratingly mild, "for nothing you sure are making an awfully funny face."

"I believe I have a splinter in the back of my knee," she said, mustering a tone of quiet dignity.

"I'm a doctor," he said. "Turn around and bend over and I'll check it out."

"I don't need any help."

He lifted his brows. "Okay. I'll set the table while you operate on yourself."

"Thank you," Stacey said, raising her leg and feeling behind her knee. Her finger bumped against the sliver of picnic table and she flinched as it drove farther into her flesh.

"Mrs. Beebe packed this in blue ice so the coleslaw is nice and fresh," he said, apparently intent on ignoring her dilemma and allowing her to solve the problem herself. "And she included a thermos of iced tea. I hope you don't mind sweetened."

"That's fine," Stacey said, furrowing her brow as she attempted to wriggle the splinter from the flesh just above the bend in the back of her knee. It bit into her and she whimpered. "Sweetened is okay, though I normally prefer the poison blue stuff—but when you're going to die from tetanus that really doesn't matter, does it?"

"Let me help you." Michael put down the packet of chicken. "Don't be silly."

That did it. If only he hadn't added that last phrase. "I don't need any help. I like taking care of myself. I don't need a husband, and I don't need a doctor." Stacey leapt up from the bench, her cheeks flaming as she realized she'd lost control. She never, ever let go of her emotional reactions. She'd learned as a child and later on, while balancing her business with all of the social obligations Robert committed them to, often without remembering to consult her schedule, that remaining calm and in control was always the best option in any situation.

But now she was shouting.

And darn it, it felt good.

Michael was regarding her with a look that Stacey could only describe as a mix of compassion, admiration, and bemusement. "I'm only offering to help remove the splinter," he said. "Nothing more, nothing less."

"Oh." Stacey plunked back onto the bench. "All right," she said, none too graciously.

He rose. "Okay, hop up, turn around, lean on the table, and stick your leg and buttocks up in the air a bit."

"What?"

He gestured her around, guided her so that her head was bent low over the surface of the table not covered by the spread of their picnic lunch, and adjusted her lower body so that her derriere was practically waving in the breeze. "I'm trying to get to your knee," he said, obviously reading her mind.

"Okay. Just get the darn thing out."

She felt him prod the back of her knee, gently and then more precisely. She pictured his tapered fingers and broke into a sweat. It had to be from the pain, she told herself. Lost to the sensation of Michael's hands on the back of her leg, she realized from somewhere within the fog of sensation he'd created that a vehicle had screeched to a halt beside the boat dock, sending a shower of gravel into the air.

A car door slammed and Stacey heard familiar voices cry out, "Daddy! Daddy!"

She jerked her head toward the parking area. Not ten feet away, Kristen and Jessica were climbing out of a Suburban, followed by a woman from the front passenger seat. All three stopped in their tracks and stared at Stacey and Michael.

What a sight it must have been! Stacey dropped onto the seat of the bench, her face red. "Whatever will they think?"

Michael straightened. Calmly enough, he said, "They will understand that I'm removing a splinter from your leg."

"Right," Stacey muttered, noting the avid curiosity firing the expression of the approaching adult female.

"Daddy!" Jessica flung herself against her father. She spared not a glance for Stacey. At a slightly more sedate pace, Kristen approached, holding her cast-sheathed arm at an awkward angle. Bringing up the rear was the woman who had to be their mother.

She and Kristen could easily have been taken for sisters, Stacey thought. Kristen was tall for her age; her mother stood around five-foot-four and she had on high heels, along with a vivid coral suit. Her hair and makeup were flawless.

"So this is how you amuse yourself while I'm taking the children to church," the woman said as she walked up to Michael. She cast a look designed to shrivel what was left of Stacey's composure, sizing up the long hair beginning to loose from Michael's informal braid, the short shorts and damp T-shirt clinging to her breasts.

The passenger door opened and closed and a middle-aged man with almost no hair on the front and top of his head walked slowly toward them.

"Daddy, Cecil is horrible!" Jessica hadn't let go of her dad.

"I told you not to speak ill of your stepfather," her mother said. "Cecil has a right to his opinions."

"And so do we," Kristen said, her voice mutinous. "Why should he be able to veto something I want to do? Even Jessica agreed with me."

Jessica snuffled against Michael's chest. Stacey noticed that Kristen might be dry-eyed, but she was shaking. Whatever had happened?

"I'd like to know what is going on," Michael said, "but first let me introduce Stacey to you, Pauline. Pauline, Stacey."

Stacey said hello. Pauline nodded. The driver of the Suburban had just reached her side. "As long as we're pausing for a garden party, this is Cecil, my husband."

He reached out and shook Stacey's hand. Grateful for the more human reaction, she responded with a brief smile. Kristen rolled her eyes and cradled her broken arm.

"So what is going on?"

"It's a good thing we saw your car—"

"The dog was hurt—"

"You've allowed these children to become absolutely selfish—"

Only Cecil maintained his silence.

"One at a time." Michael held up a hand. "Pauline?"

"Honey," Cecil interrupted, "why don't you just leave the kids here with their dad and let them explain? We're going to be late to the luncheon as it is and you know how I hate to be late for a political meeting."

She gave him a saccharine smile and patted his hand. "You don't mind, do you, Michael? These kids have been impossible. They can't manage to treat Cecil with one ounce of respect. Their behavior before, during, and after church was embarrassing."

"Why don't you just shut up?" Kristen ground out the words. "How would you like to be left on the side of the road bleeding?"

"That's enough!" Pauline snapped at her daughter and took Cecil by the arm. "If you don't mind your manners, you won't be going to that summer camp in Fayetteville you've got your heart set on."

"Will, too," Kristen said.

Jessica sobbed harder.

Stacey cast her eyes down at the ground. Her tummy cringed with tension just from watching the scene. And she was an outsider. She stole a glance at Michael and saw a muscle in his jaw working side to side. He stroked Jessica's hair, much the same way he'd soothed Stacey earlier.

"Why don't you two go on and I'll straighten this out?" Michael's expression appeared carefully controlled. "I'm sure the girls won't mind missing out on whatever luncheon you were headed to."

"Politics," Kristen said, her voice full of scorn. "I should go into politics just to tell people not to vote for Cecil."

"Michael, if you can't make her behave, I am going to have to take stronger measures."

"Pauline, will you please shut up?"

"Well!" His ex-wife looked surprised.

Stacey was willing to bet Michael, in order to keep strife from affecting his girls, rarely told her where to get off. Perhaps he should do it more often, she thought, as Pauline clamped her mouth shut and clung to Cecil's arm.

"We agreed that you would not unilaterally threaten

punishment. Telling Kristen she can't go to camp violates that guideline. If you'd like to discuss our family arrangements, you may come see me one-on-one."

"We are going to be late," Cecil said.

"Sorry, darling," Pauline said. "Give Mother a kiss," she said.

Stacey wondered just whom she was addressing, her daughter who'd turned her back to her or the younger one with her head buried against her father's chest. But to her amazement, Jessica turned around, marched to her mother's side, and kissed her cheek. Kristen, belligerence in her expression, refused to follow suit.

"Until next Sunday," Pauline said. "And don't be late for church again, please." She spared one more glance for Stacey, then strode back to the car with her husband.

"I hate my mother," Kristen said, bursting into tears.

Chapter 14

The uproar had been caused by a dog. More specifically, by a dog Kristen had spotted limping beside the road. She'd wanted to stop and rescue it; Cecil had refused to let her load the muddy animal into his Suburban.

Pauline had supported Cecil, while maligning their father for "warping" them. According to Kristen's report, her mother believed that normal girls were interested in boys and dolls, not disgusting canines full of fleas and bulging with pregnancy.

"And that's what did it for me," Kristen said as Michael drove slowly along the road back to town. "As soon as Mom said it was pregnant, I couldn't let those pups be born in some drainage ditch."

"Can we keep them?" Jessica was squeezed into the small bench behind the seats of the pickup, her little face excited and tear-streaked. She still eyed Stacey with reserve, but the hunt for the dog seemed to have taken her mind off the scene she'd encountered at the boat landing.

For her part, Stacey was holding up admirably, Michael thought. She'd flinched but calmly withstood Pauline's offensive behavior. He'd have to remember to warn her about Cecil, as she'd appeared all too willing to accept his open-handed friendliness as sincere. Michael knew better. Cecil was running for state legislature and in an election year everyone was Cecil's friend.

But Michael was pretty sure that any man who wouldn't stop to help an injured dog wouldn't remain on Stacey's good list.

"We don't even know that the dog is pregnant," Michael said, finally remembering to answer the last question posed.

From her post between Stacey and himself, Kristen pointed her nose toward the front window. "I realize it is only a hypothetical situation, but I still don't understand how Cecil can be so mean. If I were as important as Cecil, I'd make sure this town at least had a decent animal shelter. But now he's too busy eating lunch and shaking hands to help one starving animal."

Stacey turned from where she was scanning out the passenger window. "Why doesn't he support a new shelter?"

Kristen shrugged, one arm around her cast. "Because he's selfish."

"It's not as simple as that," Michael said. "But if Cecil and his family threw their weight behind the campaign, it just might get built."

"So there is a shelter but you need a new one, is that right?" Stacey said.

"Someplace animals can go when they don't have a

home," Jessica said. "We can't take them all in, at least that's what Daddy says."

Michael offered a one-handed hug to his daughter from across the back of the seat. "We help the ones we can. And if we find Kristen's dog, I'll let it stay with us, providing it passes its checkup."

"Not like Baby Dog," Jessica said.

"What happened to that one?" Stacey asked the question in a low voice.

"Heartworms. It followed Jessica home from school several days in a row, but we couldn't bring it back from the clinic."

"It's not fair to the other animals," Kristen said, surprising Michael with her support. He was surprised, too, that she was the one who had insisted on retracing the route from church in an attempt to locate the dog scorned by Cecil. Since her break with the clinic, she hadn't exhibited much interest in animals at all.

"Did you hurt your arm again?" Stacey was speaking to Kristen.

His older daughter shrugged and said, "It's nothing."

"You're holding it differently than you did yesterday," Stacey said.

"Hey, if I need a second lousy mother I'll order one on-line, okay?"

"Kristen!" Michael pulled the pickup to a screeching halt on the side of the road. "Watch your mouth. We're searching for this dog for you, and the least you can do is refrain from insulting behavior. Apologize to Stacey."

Without looking away from the front window, Kristen said, "I apologize."

Michael blew out a breath and said, "That won't get

you any points for sincerity. What did you do to your arm?"

Kristen's lips formed a line as solid as the cast on her arm.

From the back of the seat came Jessica's whispered, "She hit Cecil with it."

"I did not!"

"I'm not moving this truck until I get the truth from you," Michael said. So much for his wonderful day alone with Stacey. He'd planned to bob on the water, talk, and eat their picnic. But he'd also intended to have some time alone with her at his house, and talking wasn't uppermost in his mind when he thought of Stacey in his bedroom. Mrs. Beebe had every Sunday off and the kids hadn't been due home until after Sunday church and the luncheon event Cecil and Pauline had scurried off to attend.

"I took my seat belt off and tried to grab the wheel," Kristen said.

"Did Cecil hit you?" Michael heard the steel in his question and knew Stacey did, too. She was watching him, eyes wide.

Kristen shook her head. "No, he just pushed me away from the steering wheel."

The words, *I'll kill the bastard*, rode right up to the tip of Michael's tongue and then he clamped his mouth shut. The kids didn't need to hear him talking like that. Instead, he pulled onto the road. "We'll drive this stretch once more," he said, "and then I'm taking you to Dr. Heller. And you, too, Stacey, for that splinter."

Kristen glared not at him, but at Stacey. No doubt Stacey was in the figurative doghouse for pointing out how Kristen had been hugging the casted arm. Michael was grateful to Stacey and would tell her so, just as soon as the two of them were alone.

"There she is!" Kristen pointed to the opposite side of the road.

Along with the others, Stacey turned her head in that direction. The truck slowed, but before Michael could make a U-turn, a large truck and trailer loaded with narrow logs swung around the curve, heading in their direction. The dog chose that moment to lift its head and begin to climb out of the culvert on the side of the road where it had been crouching.

"It's going to be killed!" Kristen screamed, and Jessica covered her ears. Kristen flung herself against Stacey's chest and said, "I can't look." The dog paused, sniffing the air, and the truck barreled past.

"You can open your eyes now," Jessica said. She reached forward and patted her older sister on the back.

Stacey smiled at her, and for a moment she thought Jessica would return the expression. But with a grave air, she shifted toward her dad, who had maneuvered the pickup through a U-turn and was parking well off the side of the road in front of where the dog stood.

So Jessica wasn't ready to consider resuming friendly relations. The rejection affected Stacey; she knew better than to pretend otherwise. She ached for the child's position, knowing only too well the experience of being usurped by Dad's new lady friend. But from the other side of the interaction, she had no knowledge of how to ease the fears her very presence stirred up within the child. If only she could tell her she was just a pal and that Jessica had no need to worry.

But sometimes when Michael looked at her with that marvelous light in his eyes, or when she caught him gazing at her as if she were a chocolate truffle, it worried Stacey, too.

Kristen was reaching across Stacey for the door handle when Michael placed a hand gently but firmly on his daughter's shoulder. "You wait here."

She made a face, but relented. "All right," she said with a sigh. "Thanks for coming back to look for her."

Michael smiled and cupped one hand briefly against Kristen's cheek. "Let me see what we're dealing with here. Stacey, do you mind staying put?"

"That's fine," she said, unsure of whether she'd rather face a possibly feral and/or injured dog or the relentlessly stolid Jessica and the volatile Kristen.

They watched as Michael approached the dog.

"It's a cocker spaniel," Kristen said.

"No, it's not," her sister said. "It's a springer."

"You think you know so much. You're only eight."

Jessica stuck her tongue out.

Stacey wasn't sure whether to be amused or not. "How can you tell what breed it is?"

They both stared at her. "You just can," Jessica said.

"Yeah, it's like knowing your right hand from your left," Kristen said. "Only it is not a springer spaniel."

"Maybe English," Jessica offered.

To Stacey, the dog met the description of bedraggled mutt. It let Michael walk up to it, shying only a bit when he leaned close to examine the animal's front leg.

"I know it's broken," Kristen said, her voice sorrowful. "After this, I'm never taking care of another animal. It's just too damn painful."

"You're not supposed to swear."

"Wait till you're twelve. You will, too."

Stacey smothered a smile. She certainly related to that world-weary pronouncement.

"I don't think I want to be twelve," Jessica said. "I think I'll skip ahead to twenty-two."

"Why is that?" Stacey asked before she remembered that Jessica was pretty much not speaking to her.

Jessica shrugged. "Teenagers are silly."

"So why not just wish to be twenty?" It was Kristen, eyes glued to the scene of Michael lifting the dog in his arms, who asked the question. But she didn't sound as if she cared about her sister's answer.

"There's just so much fuss about change," Jessica said. "I'd be through all that at twenty-two."

"And then what would you do?" Stacey wondered whether she should hop out of the truck and help Michael, but decided to wait. She didn't want to startle the dog while it lay peaceably in Michael's strong grasp.

Jessica looked at her as if she'd asked the stupidest question in the whole world. "I'm going to be a veterinarian."

"Right," Kristen muttered. "You'll be sick of watching animals suffer and die by then."

"You only see the bad things," Jessica said, sounding almost like the twenty-two she'd wished to be.

"Let me out of here," Kristen said, jerking open the driver's door and tumbling out onto the side of the road.

Michael shouted something and the dog barked and flailed against Michael's chest. Stacey eased from her side of the truck and walked slowly to the bed of the truck, finding and lifting the safety harness she knew from transporting True was hooked to the base of the pickup.

While Kristen fretted at his side, Michael deposited the dog in the truck and, with a grateful glance at Stacey, took the harness and fastened it over the dog's head. One front paw hung at a lifeless angle and was covered in blood. Michael's shirt bore smears of red.

"Get back in the truck, Kristen," Michael said, his voice stern.

"I just wanted—"

"Get in the truck this second."

Kristen turned and did as she was told.

Michael stood there, wiping sweat from his forehead and dirt and blood from his hands. The dog cowered in the back of the truck, whimpering. Michael let loose with a low torrent of swear words, then looked up and said, "Sorry, but some things just plain upset me. This poor bitch was probably turned out in the local form of dog birth control and then hit by a car."

"Birth control?"

He gave a bitter laugh. "Yeah, the dog ends up expecting puppies and the owner drops it off alongside the road somewhere, hoping it won't find its way back and not caring if someone kills it."

"So she is pregnant?" Stacey peered at the dog and realized its belly was far more distended than True's.

"Oh, yeah. She'll probably whelp within the week." He straightened from wiping his hands on the knees of his jeans. "Do you mind driving? I'm going to ride in the back with her."

"I can drive."

"It's a stick."

Stacey grinned. "I'm a driving fool."

He nodded, a ghost of a grin on his face, too. He walked her to the left-hand side of the truck, opened the door, and said, "Stacey's getting behind the wheel. We're going to the clinic to check out the dog. Kristen and Jessica, I want to commend both of you for caring enough to insist this dog be rescued."

Both girls nodded, faces serious. Kristen asked, "Is she going to be okay?"

"We'll know soon."

Her face puckered up. "Well, if she's not, I'm never stopping for another dog. I just can't take it."

Michael leaned in and put his arms around her. "Go ahead and cry. It's hard to watch anyone suffer."

She sniffled and then raised her head. "I refuse to cry," she said, crossing her arms. "Crying is for weak people."

Michael sighed and stepped back from the truck door. "I know where you learned that," he said, "but let's discuss that particular sentiment later. We've got a dog to take care of."

Stacey climbed behind the wheel. He closed the door and stood there, watching her and his daughters, then moved slowly to the back and joined the injured dog, squatting down beside her.

In the rearview mirror, Stacey watched as he spoke in gentle tones and smoothed his hands over the dog's ears. She couldn't help but remember how wonderful his strong and caring hands had felt when he'd soothed her in almost the same way. Michael Halliday was a man it was proving hard not to want to get to know.

* * *

Louis St. Cyr hated to admit when he was wrong. He could recall only two times in his life when he'd done so. The first was during his senior year in high school. It was a minor matter when all was said and done, but he'd incorrectly identified a fellow classmate in his exclusive Catholic boys' school as one of two culprits involved in a cheating scandal. When he realized his error, he'd marched himself into the headmaster's office to clear the wronged boy. Instead of thanks, the boy had given Louis two black eyes. It seemed his short period of being the accused had raised his stock among his peers and he was less appreciative of Louis's retraction.

The second time . . . well, as he stood in the courtyard leading to Joanne's condominium, Louis considered the second time. He'd been young, much too young to have been a father as well as a doctor, not to mention a husband. The only job he'd done well was his professional one. Joanne had been coping as well as she could with her college finals and a pregnancy that left her sick and exhausted by the afternoon of each day. The baby was due in less than a month. Joanne had vomited twice, the second time producing blood. He'd rushed her to the hospital, damn the final exams.

Stacey had been born three and a half weeks premature. That night he'd confessed to a sedated Joanne that he never should have gotten married.

Now, thirty years later, he pressed the bell to her front door and straightened his tie. Come what may, he'd decided to approach Joanne. For once in his life, he was prepared to set aside his personal differences and seek Joanne's cooperation.

He'd hate to submit to a lie detector test on the question of his motives in doing so. Sure, he was curious as to why Stacey wanted him in Arkansas. But if it had been truly serious trouble, she would have told him so.

Admit it, Louis, he told himself as he rang the bell a second time. You're standing here because Joanne looked too damn good to ignore.

He buzzed again, annoyed at the wait. Finally he heard footsteps and the door swung open. He opened his mouth, his speech well prepared.

And then he stopped. He'd been poised to respond to a range of objections.

But he hadn't been prepared for someone other than Joanne to answer the door, not at this time on a Sunday morning.

Chapter 15

Michael knew his decision would be unpopular with everyone involved. The courthouse square was pretty much deserted, this being Sunday. When Stacey pulled into the spot right in front of the clinic door, both cab doors swung open and the three of them spilled out.

The dog cowered and whimpered as the noise volume escalated. In a low voice, Michael said, "Stacey, can you take Kristen and Jessica home for me while I tend to the dog?"

"Dad!" Jessica balled her fists on her hips. "We're not leaving you here. We're going to help."

Kristen glanced nervously at the back of the truck. "Yeah, we don't cut out halfway through a job."

"Good for you," he said, "but this is my job to finish. You and Jessica did your part." Fortunately, Stacey moved closer to the truck and he said only to her, "Kristen's too sensitive. I don't want her inside when I set this leg and I don't want her there when I test for heartworms."

Stacey nodded. "You mean the dog might not make it."

"That outcome has to be considered."

"I am going to be a veterinarian." Jessica was still intent on objecting.

"Yes, you are, sweetie," Michael called, "and when you are, you may stay and help. But not today. Someone has to go home and take care of Wolf and Whistle and Sir Walter, and what about True?"

"Oh."

"So you and Kristen are going back to our house with Stacey." He looked at Stacey, standing there so competent and caring, and he felt a rush of admiration almost as strong as the desire he'd experienced earlier. "If that's okay. I'm sorry to impose, but Mrs. Beebe's off and Pauline's useless—"

"Of course I don't mind," Stacey said cheerfully, though she looked slightly unsure. "If your daughters don't."

Kristen had sidled closer and was peering at the dog. "Don't let her die, okay, cause I'd have to hate Cecil forever."

Michael groaned. He'd have a few choice words with that schmuck later. "Kristen, I need you and Jessica and Stacey to load up. Now. And while I'm working to save this dog, I want your word—and yours, too, Jessica—that you'll behave yourselves with Stacey."

Jessica crossed her arms and regarded her dad steadily. She spared not a glance at Stacey.

"Okay," Kristen said. "Just don't try to mother us."

Stacey nodded. "How about we concentrate on the

animals? I know True's missing her walk and I'm sure the other dogs are, too."

Kristen stole another look at the injured dog, then said, "I don't know why you're wasting time. Jessica, into the truck."

Michael sketched a salute. "Do you mind letting the back down?"

Stacey rounded the end of the truck, fiddled with the handle mechanism, and then lowered the gate. He edged forward, carrying the dog. "The keys to the clinic are on the key chain," he said.

She rushed ahead and had the door open for him as he reached it. "I can take it from here. And Stacey, thank you. I'll make up the afternoon to you another day."

She brushed his hair from where it had fallen down over his forehead. "It's okay," she said. "I'd rather be useful than goof off anyway."

He grinned. "And I'd like to be the guy who helps you learn to goof off."

The dog struggled against him, and Michael said, "But that's a lesson for another day. I may be a couple of hours, but I'll call the house."

And then he disappeared into the clinic, leaving Stacey standing beside the door with a bemused expression on her face. Bemused, and if he was any judge of the female mind, very much interested in Michael Halliday, despite the way the afternoon had turned out.

He settled the dog onto the exam table, reached for the phone, and paged Scotty. He'd need some assistance, but he'd not been anywhere near to letting his eight-year-old play vet tech in this situation. As he began to clean the leg, he whistled softly.

All things considered, this Sunday was turning out to be one of the best he could recall in a long, long time.

Stacey turned the key in the ignition and placed both hands on the wheel. Taking a deep breath, she pictured the brochure of the Arlington Hotel and Spa in Hot Springs. Had her plans gone according to Donna's master scheme, Stacey would either be soaking in a tub or enjoying the services of a masseuse at this very moment.

Instead, she sat behind the wheel of a pickup truck, hoping for inspiration to guide her through the afternoon until Michael's return.

"Ready?" she asked, feeling rather inane.

Jessica had retreated to the space behind the seats. Kristen stared moodily out the window. Stacey's stomach grumbled. "Anyone hungry? Mrs. Beebe sent a picnic basket with your dad."

"Picnics are for babies," Kristen said. "Let's go to Sonic."

"Sonic stinks," Jessica said. "I want Dairy Queen."

"Dairy Queen. Gross me out. Do you have any idea what they put in that plastic ice cream?"

"Where do you think Sonic gets their burgers?"

Stacey felt a bit like a spectator at a ping-pong match.

"They probably grind up stupid kid sisters," Kristen said. "They do the world a favor."

"Hey!" Stacey couldn't take it anymore. "Give me a break here, okay? I'm an only child and I'm not used to this sort of verbal warfare."

Both Jessica and Kristen broke out giggling.

"Verbal warfare." Kristen looked impressed. "Nice phrase, Stacey-o."

Surprised but relieved at their cease-fire, Stacey backed the truck out of the parking slot and drove around the square. "Nothing is open here," she observed.

"Of course not. It's Sunday."

"Does everyone in Doolittle go to church on Sunday?"

"Don't you?" That was Jessica, engaging in conversation, even if the question did carry an implied criticism.

"I usually do," Stacey said. "But I didn't go today. Or yesterday."

"Yesterday?" Kristen swung her head around from her study of the passing street. "You go to church on Saturday?"

"I'm Catholic," Stacey said. "We can go to mass from four o'clock on Saturday up until Sunday evening."

"That's funny," Kristen said. "We used to be Catholic, but I never knew that. We always went on Sunday."

"We're not Catholic anymore," Jessica said. "I think it's because Cecil said Catholics don't vote as often as Baptists."

Amused by that statement coming from an eight-year-old, Stacey glanced in the rearview mirror at the young fount of wisdom. "So Cecil is involved in politics?" She'd rounded the square and couldn't remember which direction led toward Michael's house. She hated to interrupt their first real conversation, so she simply picked one of the four roads leading away from the courthouse.

"He wants to be in the state legislature," Kristen said. "But he'll never get my vote. Not after today."

"You can't vote. You're only twelve."

"Well, I'll be eighteen before you are."

Jessica stuck her tongue out. Stacey smiled. She'd have to remember that tactic when stumped by an irrefutable truth. Right now she was going to take a teeny advantage and find out something about Michael. "So is your dad still a Catholic?"

Kristen shrugged her shoulders in an "I'm not sure of the answer" gesture. Jessica said, "We go to church with our mother. So I don't know what Daddy does." Then she frowned. "Except today he went out with you. And that's not the same as going to church."

"True," Stacey said, though she couldn't help but think that the moments of peace shared with Michael earlier on the lake provided as much spiritual nourishment as many of the hours she'd spent in church. And judging from his kisses, sex with Michael would be pretty much a religious experience. Her thoughts surprised her and she swept her attention back to her surroundings.

"There's a Steak 'n Shake," she said. "Any objections to that?"

"Yuck," Jessica said.

"I'd rather eat dirt," Kristen said.

Stacey drove on by. She passed a Kmart and a feed store.

"Hey, where are we going?" Kristen pointed to the interstate sign. "We don't live this way."

"We're being kidnapped!" Jessica let out a howl. "Daddy!"

Stacey pulled to the edge of the road. "I am not kidnapping you. Jessica, please, calm down. I am simply lost."

"Right," Kristen said. "Doolittle's way too small for

anyone to get lost. Boston, maybe, but not this dump." She grabbed at the door handle. "Quick, Jessica, I'll save us."

Stacey slapped the auto-lock before Kristen could tumble out.

"Will you both calm down and give me directions either to some restaurant that doesn't serve objectionable food or to your house?"

"We can always escape when we stop for food," Kristen said. "Turn around, go back the way we came, go past the high school."

Stacey did as instructed, halting only when Jessica screamed, "DQ!"

Rather than mediate what she was pretty sure would be a healthy argument, she stopped for Jessica to indulge in a Blizzard complete with blue M&M's, then motored to Sonic for Kristen's double cheese with curly fries. So as not to pick sides, she then made a trip through the Steak 'n Shake for her own fast-food treat, an oversized burger she normally would have avoided at all costs. Their hunger and preferences satisfied, neither Kristen nor Jessica attempted to escape their so-called kidnapper.

For a few minutes, chewing on her burger, she appreciated why her own parents had substituted a poodle for the baby sister Stacey had repeatedly requested.

Walking the dogs proved only slightly less contentious than choosing a lunch place. It took quite some time for Kristen and Jessica to argue over who got to walk Wolf, the shepherd, and who got Whistle, a rambunctious standard poodle. They did agree that Stacey could handle both True and Sir Walter, the three-legged Lab who lived to sniff every scent along the way.

Stacey was a little surprised they hadn't yet heard from Michael. She hoped the rescued dog would be okay. Breaking bad news to Kristen and Jessica would be terribly hard to do. Even though they hadn't mentioned the injured dog during all their squabbling, Stacey was pretty sure the animal was very much on their minds. Every so often she'd notice Kristen sighing, a sad look in her eyes. And Jessica had hugged the large shepherd with special affection, whispering something that sounded like, "Every dog should be as loved as you."

They made it around several blocks of the neighborhood in fairly peaceable fashion. And then Jessica said, "Bet you haven't finished your homework yet."

"That's none of your business," Kristen replied.

"You were talking on the phone the other day instead of doing it. Daddy knows, too."

Kristen tossed her head. "There are some things you are just too young to understand."

Surely Michael would make it home before evening. Or perhaps Mrs. Beebe would be there to handle this new wrinkle. As Kristen had informed her, Stacey's role didn't include "mothering," which definitely included helping with homework.

Stacey paused as Sir Walter lunged back from a bee that buzzed past his nose. True stopped, too, her tongue lolling. Stacey rubbed her dog's head. "Good girl," she said. "Your puppies are going to be very loved."

"Every puppy should be loved," Kristen said, her voice mutinous. "Life sucks." She stalked off, Wolf cantering beside her.

Stacey sighed. "Come on, Walter, let's get moving."

"She'll be okay with Wolf," Jessica said. "She needs to

cry. Kristen wouldn't hurt so much inside if she cried more."

Stacey stared at the child. "You know, you are very wise."

Jessica shrugged. "I learned it from my dad."

"Your dad says it's good to cry?" Not exactly your macho male perspective, but then Michael wasn't your run-of-the-mill guy.

"I've watched him," Jessica said. "Sometimes he cries when he plays music. When the coon hound died, he cried. So did I. That was when the man gave me the trapper Barbie." She stroked Whistle's back. "But Kristen doesn't know how to wash the sadness away. That's what I heard Daddy say one time to Mrs. Beebe." Jessica looked down the street at Kristen's retreating back. "Maybe I'd feel better about you kissing Daddy if I cried."

"Oh, Jessica, I'm sorry, I didn't mean to upset you." Stacey knelt down in front of the girl. "I would never do anything to hurt you, or your sister. Your dad and I were just—well . . ." she trailed off. How to explain to an eight-year-old they were carried away by just how fabulous their kisses made them feel?

A tear welled in Jessica's eye. "Cecil kisses my mother when he thinks we don't see. Maybe it's better to watch, like when you know an animal is hurting, and you can pay attention and understand."

Stacey cast a look down the street. Kristen had stopped, her back turned to them. Feeling a bit like a woman stretched in two directions and about to be snapped in two, she said to Jessica, "Your dad and I aren't going to do anything to make you cry."

"Promise?"

Stacey nodded. Jessica was a precious child, a child who adored her dad. The last thing Stacey wanted to do was come between that relationship. She sighed and rose to her feet. "Let's catch up with your sister," she said.

They finished the walk in silence. Upon their return to the house, they made sure the dogs drank water. Stacey fed True one of her favorite treats and did the same for the other animals. Kristen disappeared into the house, and returned to the back porch to announce she'd checked the answering machine.

"Three messages," she said. "One was Dad, and the other two were for me."

Stacey and Jessica were just finishing their animal care. They headed into the house as Kristen collected the portable phone, obviously on her way upstairs to indulge in her favorite phone pastime.

"Mind sharing what your dad had to say?" Stacey asked.

"Oh. Right. The dog is going to be okay, but it's taking longer than he expected."

Stacey checked her watch. All the fast-food visits and the dog walking had taken far longer than she would have dreamed. It was after four o'clock.

"Ooh, I don't feel so good," Jessica said, her face turning a funny shade of white. "I think I'm going to—" She dashed out of the kitchen. Judging by the wretching noises coming from the downstairs hallway, she didn't make it to the powder room.

Kristen paused in the doorway. "I told you DQ wasn't fit for human consumption. Gee, I wonder if her throw-up is blue and green and orange."

"Why don't you go see?" Stacey said. "You can help her clean it up."

"Oh, no. I'm a kid and that's a job for a grown-up." Kristen bounded out the door and Stacey heard her take the stairs two at a time. "Oh, yeah," she called, "Dad said he'd be home no later than six."

Six! The day would practically be over by then. With a shock, Stacey realized she'd fallen asleep early that morning before sending her work to Donna via e-mail. Donna would be standing on her head! She'd probably tried to call several times once her son's birthday party had ended.

Where was her cell phone?

Stacey didn't know.

And, amazingly, she didn't care.

Feeling like a woman out on parole, she hurried to the hall to check on Jessica, which was pretty funny, because she was a lot better suited to doctoring press releases than dealing with an eight-year-old's tummy turmoil.

Fortunately for Stacey, Jessica was already cleaning up after herself. She had one of the embroidered hand towels from the downstairs guest bathroom and was mopping up the floor. "I'm feeling much better now," she confided. "But Dairy Queen is still better than Sonic any day."

Armed with a bottle of 409 she'd found in the kitchen, along with a few paper towels, Stacey knelt to assist Jessica. When she did, the splinter she'd almost forgotten about pricked her mercilessly. She let out a strongly voiced "Ouch!" and dropped back on her heels.

Jessica looked at her quizzically.

"It's nothing. Just a splinter in the back of my knee. Your dad was trying to fix it when you and your sister and . . ." Stacey shut up. She didn't want to bring the scene to mind any more than she just had.

"Is that really what he was doing?" Jessica regarded her steadily. Hunched as she was over the floor, powder-blue towel in hand, she appeared incongruously mature. But she was still very much a child, Stacey reminded herself as she answered with a gentle, "Yes, he was trying to remove the splinter I'd gotten from backing into the picnic table."

"Well," Jessica said, hopping up and abandoning the towel, "I can do that. Show me where it is, and I'll have it out in no time."

Stacey stared at her. She started to object, but snapped her mouth shut just in time. Jessica wasn't your average child. If she said she could do something, Stacey believed she could. Besides, the only harm that could come from letting her try was a bit of discomfort, and that Stacey already had from the stupid sliver of wood wedged beneath her tender skin.

"I'll have to disinfect the tweezers. And a needle. Now, where's the Neosporin?" Jessica tapped one long finger against the side of her head and Stacey realized she had her father's tapered, delicate fingers, fingers so like those of her own father's. Jessica did indeed have the hands of a surgeon.

"Why don't you go in the front room and lie down and I'll be right in?" Jessica said.

"Why don't I do that?" Stacey nodded, collected the messy towel and other cleaning gear, and headed into the kitchen. She'd rather have Jessica operating on her than staring so silently and soulfully as she'd been doing earlier.

She gave a passing thought to where it was she'd left her purse and cell phone. It must have been inside the cab of the truck. Yes, that was it. She started to go out, but when she heard Jessica pattering toward the front of the house, she decided to wait. When the doctor was ready, after all, the patient should be at her post.

Stacey stretched out on the sofa on her tummy. As Jessica was getting her things arranged on the coffee table, Stacey asked, "You're sure you're not going to be a people doctor?"

"I think animals make more interesting patients," Jessica said.

"Hmm." Michael had said something very similar earlier that day. Gosh, but their time at the lake seemed as if it had taken place days ago. "My parents are doctors," Stacey said.

"Both of them?" Jessica sounded interested.

Stacey flinched as Jessica swabbed the back of her knee with something cold.

"Yes. My mother's a dermatologist and my father is an orthopedic surgeon."

"You're going to feel a prick now," Jessica said. "I wish my mother was a doctor, too."

"Rather than a lawyer?"

"How did you know that?" Jessica said, probing.

"Owee!" Stacey bit on her thumb. "That hurts. Your dad mentioned it."

"Oh. Sorry," Jessica said. "Almost there. It's buried deep."

"Hey, guess what?" Kristen skidded into the room. "Oh, no, you're not letting her play doctor on you, are you?"

Stacey groaned. "And why shouldn't I?"

"The way she was puking, she should be in the hospital ward herself. You are weird, little sister," Kristen said, while wielding the portable phone and dancing in circles around the room.

"Good news from your friends?" Stacey asked, trying to keep her mind from the probing going on behind her knee.

"Are you kidding? They're brain-dead." She dropped onto the floor beside the coffee table. "This whole group assignment thing is buzzing my head. We're supposed to agree on a community interest project and implement it, but we can't even come up with something interesting, let alone a project we all agree is important and useful. And our idea has to be turned in tomorrow!"

"I see," Stacey said. "Maybe when your dad comes home he'll help you."

"Dad?" Kristen groaned and batted her head with the phone. "All he ever thinks about is animals."

"And what's wrong with that?" Jessica jabbed a trifle indignantly with the tweezers.

"Watch it, there," Stacey said. "Argue after the operation is successful, if you please."

Kristen giggled. "You sure talk funny."

Stacey wasn't sure whether she was pleased to be so amusing. "Thank you," she murmured. "You know, you could do worse than concentrate on animals."

"What do you mean?" Kristen hovered somewhat in the range of Stacey's vision, hampered as it was by her prone position on the sofa.

"Think of the dog you rescued this afternoon. What would have happened to her if you hadn't cared enough to stop and your dad didn't care enough to take her to the clinic?"

Kristen clapped a hand to her mouth.

Jessica rooted in Stacey's leg, gently but with purpose.

"I've got it!" They both cried out at the same moment.

"Got what?" Michael asked as he entered the room, amazed and unaccountably pleased at the scene before his eyes.

Chapter 16

"Got what?" Michael repeated his question, relieved to see his daughters and Stacey apparently getting along just fine.

No one answered. Instead, all three of them said, "How's the dog?"

Michael crossed the threshold and settled on the end of the sofa where Stacey lay. Jessica was holding up a serious-sized splinter and eyeing it critically.

"Not just one anymore," he said.

Kristen dropped the phone. "She had her pups! I wanted to watch."

Stacey had half scooted around and was watching him closely. He wondered if she could read the exhaustion that racked not just his body, but his soul. Two of the pups hadn't lived, one had been born dead, but three of them were tucked beside the mother dog in a kennel in his clinic.

"How many?" Jessica asked, applying antibiotic ointment to Stacey's leg.

"Three."

"Only three?" Jessica capped the tube, and then glanced over her shoulder at her sister. "Three's a good number," she said.

Kristen, not one to pay too much attention to detail, might not realize how small a litter that was. "Can we go see them?"

Michael shook his head. "They were born a bit premature, so they need extra rest right now."

"Well, as soon as they're old enough, I'd like to take a picture," Kristen said. "I've decided what to do for our team project."

"Team project?" Michael knew he should know what that meant, but right now he couldn't place it.

Stacey murmured her thanks to Jessica and sat up. Kristen plopped onto the sofa and threw her hands up in a dramatic gesture. "Dad, you have to know what I'm talking about."

He ran a hand over his eyes.

Stacey said in a soothing voice, "Want some iced tea?"

He brightened. "Mrs. Beebe always leaves a pitcher on Sundays."

Stacey smiled. "I took a wild guess she might do that." She rose and slipped from the room.

Michael watched her go. An odd feeling flitted through his gut and he grasped to identify it, but was interrupted by Jessica jumping onto his lap. "I threw up," she announced, reverting from doctor to patient.

"It's the partner thing that I didn't have a partner for until Stacey-o said we should be a team."

"Stacey-o?"

"That's what Kristen calls Stacey," Jessica said.

"Ah." He hoped the name had been dubbed in a spirit of affection, but knowing Kristen as he did, she was just as likely to have hurled it during one of the low points of her behavior. And she was capable of using it or any other nickname as a positive or negative, given the waxing and waning of her moods.

"And then I got my team, but every idea they came up with was, like, really stupid." Kristen sighed. "It's hard being the smartest kid in the class."

Michael nodded. "It's a blessing and a curse," he said gently.

"Oh, I know that." Kristen leapt up and spun around. "Anyway, for the project we have to do something that's good for the community. Like Doolittle can be called a community." She rolled her eyes.

"It's our home now," Michael said, stroking Jessica's hair.

"Yeah, well, thanks a lot," Kristen said. "It would have been so much cooler to grow up in Boston."

"You wouldn't have met Bobby," Jessica said in a sleepy voice.

Sleepy but not too far gone to direct a home hit. Michael had to suppress a smile.

Stacey walked back in, carrying a pitcher and four plastic tumblers. She paused in the doorway.

Michael knew his exhaustion was affecting his normally rational mind, but he thought at that moment that Stacey looked like an angel. Never mind the harps and wings, Stacey in her shorts and top bearing iced tea was the sweetest sight he'd seen in a long time—at least since earlier that day when he'd been peering around her shoulder at her perfectly rounded breasts outlined in the seductive drape of her soaking-wet T-shirt.

He slipped Jessica from his lap and settled her on the couch. Then he rose and crossed the room, meeting Stacey halfway. Taking the tray from her, he noted the clink of the ice in the pitcher as their fingers brushed, and Michael knew she felt the contact as strongly as he did. Eyes dark and wide, she watched him, a little too seriously for his comfort, and then walked beside him as he carried the refreshments to the coffee table that also held Jessica's surgical supplies.

"So you operated on Stacey?" Michael set out the cups.

"Yep." Jessica, wide awake now, was sitting up on the couch.

"And did the patient behave?"

Jessica giggled. "I'd give her a B-minus."

"A what?" Stacey placed her hands on her hips. "I didn't even wiggle."

"But you said, 'Owee.' "

" 'Owee'?" Michael imitated the sound in a high-pitched voice. "Definitely a B-minus."

"Hey," Kristen said loudly, "does anyone in this family care about my team project idea?"

Jessica kept on giggling. "Maybe even a C-plus."

"You always grade your patients?" Stacey poured tea into all the glasses.

Michael nodded.

Kristen quit her spinning around in the room and threw herself onto the sofa next to her sister. "I am an unappreciated genius," she said soulfully, accepting the glass from Stacey and swallowing most of it in one long gulp.

"You are a young lady with rather poor table manners," Michael said, but in a very mild voice.

"Ha, but I'm not at the table, am I!" Kristen smacked her glass down on the coffee table and leapt up again. "I'm about to announce my idea. I do hope you'll listen."

"We're all ears," Michael said, pleased to see her having gone from the despair of no partner to the epitome of excitement over whatever idea she'd sprouted. With Kristen, one never knew. Her last big thing had involved soccer. But she couldn't just play on the local team. She had to be in charge of fundraising for new uniforms. When they'd raised only enough money for half the shorts and tops, she'd gone out to play in a fury of frustration and had ended up breaking her arm.

It was both a blessing and a curse, he reflected, scooting Jessica over and making room for Stacey on the sofa right next to him on the other side. Still standing by the coffee table, she hesitated. He patted the space beside him, and after a long moment she moved over and sat beside him, both hands wrapped around her iced tea glass. Well, even if her body language was oddly closed off, at least she was near, her leg brushing his, his body registering her presence with the warmth she always brought to him.

Always.

What was he thinking? He'd met her Friday night. Hell, it had been almost Saturday morning when he'd answered her emergency call.

No matter.

"Dad, are you paying attention?"

He smiled. "Absolutely."

"Okay, here goes," Kristen said. "Our project is going to be a new animal shelter for Doolittle."

Jessica clapped her hands together. "I like it. I can help, too."

"No, you can't. This is for our class project, for a grade, dummy."

"Don't call your sister a dummy." Michael said it automatically, the way he always did when they name-called.

"Well, how could she help?"

"Tell us what you're planning," Stacey said. "I think it sounds marvelous."

"Thank you," Kristen said. "At least Stacey-o is listening. Daddy always says the shelter over in Heritage is a dump. It turns away more animals than it can take and we know the ones that end up there pretty much get put to sleep. They don't do anything to help."

Michael nodded. "That's true."

"And Daddy takes in all he can," Jessica said. "And the cat house can't handle much more than it already does."

"What's the cat house?" Stacey had relaxed her grip on the tea glass, Michael noted.

"Martha and George White are seventy-year-old cat lovers who turned their house into a kennel. I go over there every so often and treat the animals," Michael said. "People are always dumping new strays in their yard, or maybe the cats just have a feline network that spreads the word. But they're old and it's getting hard for them to take care of them."

"How many cats do they have?"

"At any given time, between fifteen and twenty."

"It's not a solution," Kristen said, sounding very much like the businesswoman Michael was pretty sure she'd turn out to be. If not a politician. He smiled at the thought of his daughter running against her stepdad and trouncing him in an election. But he wanted far more for Kristen than to stick around Doolittle, Arkansas.

Stacey leaned forward and set her cup on the tray. When she moved back onto the sofa, her body fit perfectly against his, warming not only his flesh but his soul. Michael knew he could sit there all night, surrounded by his family.

The thought zinged in his head and he realized what he'd been trying to identify earlier. He enjoyed on a regular basis the warmth of love, the give and take of family life, including Kristen and Jessica's good-natured squabbling. But missing was the completion of the circle, the gap that Stacey, nestled against him on the sofa, filled so well.

"The town needs to come together for the homeless animals," Kristen said, pulling Michael away from his reverie. "People need to quit dumping animals or closing their eyes or just hoping someone else takes care of the problem."

"A new shelter properly staffed and funded will take a lot of money," Michael said.

"I know that. But my idea will work because I'll get the kids in my class involved and then they'll get their parents and pretty soon the money will all be there." Kristen joined them on the sofa. "It just has to happen."

Michael feared Kristen was going to run into another wall of heartache. His own efforts to interest residents in improving shelter services had made little headway, mainly because no one cared enough to appropriate the necessary public funds or donate private monies. Still, he would be the last person to discourage Kristen from trying.

Just then Stacey leaned forward, set down her iced tea glass, and steepled her fingers. A look of concentration on her face, she said slowly, "How about a marketing plan?"

"What's that?" Kristen sounded interested.

"Great ideas need structure to bring them to fruition. I've done plans for fund-raising events fairly frequently. A plan involves goal-setting, charting the means to the end. You identify your donor targets, levels of giving, rewards." Interestingly enough, Stacey's body language and tenor of speech had shifted. Michael realized he was seeing Stacey in creative work mode, something that fascinated him.

He appreciated the difference. He, too, shifted into a different energy state when he was on duty. Pauline never had. She'd been the same day and night, or so it had seemed to Michael. Stacey out by the lake had been a different personality than the woman engaging in Kristen's idea.

"Shouldn't helping animals be its own reward?" That was Jessica asking the question in her sweetly innocent fashion.

Stacey shook her head. "It's human nature to want a thank-you, even if it's as simple as your name in the paper. Most campaigns give rewards or prizes in graduated order depending on the level of money or pledges one makes."

"Hmm," Kristen said. "Do you think my teacher will be upset if our team gets you to help us?"

"Oops, that's a good question." Stacey leaned back. "I was getting ahead of myself there." She grinned somewhat shyly, looking adorable. "I do that when I hear a project that excites me. I just jump on in head first."

"I'll meet with the group," Kristen said. "Make sure they agree, but since their ideas are way stupid, of course we'll do this one."

"If you do your own homework," Michael said, thinking aloud, "couldn't part of your project be to hire a marketing consultant? Then you hire Stacey's company and calculate the cost of that into the amount you need to raise."

"Way to work around an obstacle, Dad." Kristen raised her hand for a high-five.

"And I could donate my services," Stacey said. "I did that once before, for a battered women's shelter."

"Mrs. Beebe would like to know that," Kristen said. "She was married to the meanest man in town and still would be if my dad hadn't run him off."

"I didn't know you knew that story," Michael said.

"Mrs. Beebe tells everyone you saved her life."

"I simply helped her when no one else would."

Stacey leaned back on the sofa. That line was a recurrent one in Michael's life. Glancing over at him, she smiled. She liked the way it felt sitting close to him. Perhaps because the four of them were there, and Kristen was the focus of the conversation, Jessica didn't seem to mind her proximity to Michael.

It was funny, in a way, sitting here as if she belonged in their family circle. She was a guest, but she felt at home, more at home than she often did in her own lovely New Orleans house she'd restored in the hopes that she and Robert would live there together the rest of their lives.

At least she'd held title to the house in her name alone.

Stacey sighed and Michael looked questioningly at her. "Mrs. Beebe and a lot of other people have many reasons to be glad you came to Doolittle," she said.

"The animals, too," Jessica said. "But I don't see how your idea is going to help get a shelter, Kristen."

"What do you mean?" Kristen stood up. "Money always helps."

"But how are you going to get it? Bake cookies?" Jessica made a gagging sound. "Nobody would buy anything you made."

"Jessica, be nice," Michael said.

Stacey suppressed a smile. Maybe she should have tried that line that afternoon when the sisters were arguing over fast-food destinations.

"Okay," she said. "Dearest sister, nobody would eat anything you cooked."

Well, maybe not. It was comforting to realize the two of them carried on like this routinely, not just when she'd been the afternoon's chauffeur. How did people ever get through parenting? Perhaps she'd been too hard on her own stepmothers. Surely no one could do this impossible job well.

Why was she thinking about that? Stacey shook her head and decided to focus on the animal shelter idea. It was a heck of a lot safer than mulling over stepmothering, which had nothing to do with her life.

Publicity and marketing—now, that she understood.

"You need a gimmick," Stacey said.

"Like a prize?" Jessica said, scooting over so she sat between Michael's knees. "Will you braid my hair, Daddy? It always helps me think."

"Sure, sweetie." Michael began finger-combing her long curly hair and as he did he looked over at Stacey and smiled. Something warm and tender unfurled within her as she realized he was picturing the same image she was of him braiding her hair out on the lake.

He nodded and his glance held a promise Stacey wasn't sure she could handle. His look was intimate and searching and spoke of coming close and not letting go.

She suppressed a tremble she couldn't explain and concentrated on gimmicks that might work. "Let's brainstorm," she said.

"Is that when you have thunder inside your head?" Jessica giggled.

"Well said," Stacey said.

"What would you use for a gimmick, Stacey-o?" Kristen had sprawled on the carpeted floor and was tapping one finger against her nose.

"We had a contest in my class last year for who could read the most books," Jessica said, "and the winner got a Harry Potter poster."

"Posters are good," Stacey said, "especially for participation prizes, as in you gave twenty-five dollars, thank you."

"What goes on the posters?" That was Kristen, still tapping her finger, evidently her thinking pose. Stacey raised one hand to her hair and began twisting her finger around and around.

"Us," Jessica said. "Mother always says I'm a poster

child for someone who's too smart for her own good. So why can't I be on the poster? And you, too, Kristen, since this is your project."

"That's very generous of you, baby sister." Kristen sat up. "Not us, stupid! The puppies! The ones who were born today! And we'll call them pound posters or puppy posters and they'll be our mascots."

"That's brilliant," Stacey said. "And why not use you and Jessica along with the puppies? After all, you rescued them."

"Won't that make every kid in my class who doesn't like me pea-green with envy?" Kristen grinned from ear to ear.

"Not exactly the most admirable motivation," Michael commented, "but all for a good cause."

"That's a great first step for a donation reward," Stacey said. "And what about we build up to an event—say, a dog show—and each person pays so much to enter, and if you enter a dog you've adopted or rescued, you get a discounted admission. And we make it the social event of Doolittle and people come all dressed up and pay a fee to get in?" She was really warming to the idea, generously copied from an event she'd assisted with in New Orleans. But they wouldn't mind; it was all, as Michael said, for a good cause.

"You can make the posters your school project," Michael said, "and the rest of us can help pull the show together."

Kristen chortled. "And you know who'll have to eat crow?"

"Who's that?" Michael asked as he finished the last tuck to Jessica's braid.

Stacey admired his handiwork and longed to have those gentle hands moving over her hair.

Face it, not just your hair, Stacey St. Cyr. You'd love to feel them on your face, your lips, your throat, your neck, your breasts. . . . She took a deep breath. What was she doing, fantasizing along these lines? It would do her no good. As wonderful as it was sitting here pretending to belong, she knew she didn't. And she never would.

"Cecil."

"That's interesting," Michael said. "Why?"

"Because he and Mother won't be able to stand not being part of the event of the year. He'll want to take it over and hog credit and those puppies will tell the truth."

Jessica said, "Yeah, they'll bite him in the butt."

"Jessica!"

"Sorry, Daddy, but he deserves it."

"Punishment isn't ours to mete out," Michael said slowly. "However, I do have an idea that would prove pretty satisfying."

Stacey could tell by the glint in his eyes that this was going to be good. She loved watching Michael's range of expressions.

"He's running for office. He can't afford to ignore a political bandwagon. Let's make this a big enough deal that he'll have to support public funding. We can always tell him no one will know the story about how he left the dog to fend for itself on the road—with a broken leg and puppies about to be born—if he gets the city, county, and state behind the project."

Kristen jumped up and curtsied in her dad's direction. "I bow to genius," she said. "I truly am your daughter."

And Stacey, without thinking, threw her arms around Michael and hugged him.

Chapter 17

Michael pulled up in front of the Schoolhouse Inn. His truck was starting to know its own way to the parking spots arrayed in front of the sisters' flower beds.

One glance at the unusually quiet Stacey confirmed she had fallen asleep, her head nestled against the passenger window of the truck. The poor darling had drifted off on the couch after the impromptu dinner Michael had thrown together, a dinner that resembled the picnic the two of them had never had a chance to sample.

When Mrs. Beebe returned, promptly at nine as she did every Sunday evening, Michael had shepherded Stacey to his truck and headed back.

Not that he wanted to take her back to the inn.

He wanted her to stay.

A hint of moonlight touched her face and Michael studied the curve of her cheek, the way her nose rounded a bit at the tip, the peaceful relaxed state of her sweet face. How could he have just met someone and feel this comfortable? And it wasn't only that feeling that surprised him. Stacey stirred softly and Michael knew some of what he felt was a desire to protect and to cherish this woman who was such a funny mixture of prickly "hey I don't need anyone's help" attitude and vulnerability.

That dickhead who'd tossed her out the day before their wedding had hurt her badly. But, as Kristen would say, it was both a blessing and a curse. Clearly she was so much better off without the jerk, but why she would have drawn the conclusion she would never pair off with anyone else Michael couldn't understand.

Not that he was in the pairing-off phase of his life. The kids took precedence.

Stacey's lashes fluttered. Michael knew he was being selfish, sitting here in the truck watching her, but it was a picture he didn't want to disturb until he had to. Because the next scene was one he wouldn't like at all. He'd walk her to the door, give her a properly restrained good-night kiss, and return to his truck, lonely, horny, and not at all consoled by having done the right thing.

He'd far rather have her beneath him in his bed, naked and wet and pulling him down to her. He could see her hair streaming across his pillow, or maybe he'd flip her over and take her from behind and it would be hanging like the veil of a harem girl over her shoulders. She'd be panting and calling his name, over and over as he entered and claimed her.

A bead of sweat trickled down the back of his shirt. Michael shifted and tipped his head against the back of the seat. What a picture, a picture just waiting to be turned into reality.

He could have her, too.

But dammit, what would he do about it once he'd tasted her?

Yeah, once wouldn't be enough with Stacey St. Cyr. Once would only whet his appetite.

He groaned. His jeans had tightened around him. He'd better wake Stacey up. A few more minutes and he wouldn't be able to walk her to the front door.

Stacey knew she was dreaming. She had to be, because she was swimming and everyone acquainted with her would laugh at the very idea. Stacey was afraid of water, fearful of being pushed beneath even the placid blue water of a backyard pool and not being able to touch her feet to the solid surface that assured her she was not in danger.

Yet now she darted and flowed like a dolphin, master of the sea. And, like any self-respecting dolphin, Stacey wore no clothing.

She stirred and a murmur of excitement escaped her lips. Naked and swimming! She snuggled against her unaccountably firm pillow and held on to the incredible sensation. But even as she did so, she heard a sound very much like the gurgling of water being drained from a bath and she fought against being swallowed by the vortex.

Stacey landed a punch or two in her struggle, the second of which resulted in a whoof of air being expelled. She opened her eyes and to her vast relief found herself not about to drown in a bathtub.

Instead, she was cradled tight against Michael's chest, his arms wrapped around her, his hands soothing her head, his gentle voice telling her, "It was only a dream. You're safe with me."

"I was going down the drain," she said, realizing even as she spoke the words just how silly they sounded.

"There's no drain in this truck," Michael said, reasonably enough.

Stacey laughed, if somewhat shakily. "I don't know what happened. I guess after not sleeping much last night I conked out. And I was having a beautiful dream—at first, anyway."

"Tell me about it." He hadn't let go, though she was clearly calm now. Instead, he held her closer, his body more in the center of the seat than behind the steering wheel. And his hands! They were all over her head and shoulders and neck, but moving so slowly and sinuously they didn't feel at all invasive. Quite the opposite, actually, Stacey thought, snuggling her chin into his chest with a sigh.

"I was a dolphin, and swimming, both silly concepts, but it felt . . . well, you know, it felt right." And then she paused. "No, I wasn't a dolphin, only I was swimming like one, and—oh, I was naked."

"Nice," he murmured, lowering one hand to her back and tracing slow, lazy circles along the base of her neck.

"It was," she agreed, and then immediately blushed. "I mean, I felt really free."

"Free is beautiful," he said, his hand drifting lower until it reached the spot where her shorts gapped away from the curve of her buttocks. His hand left the cover of her blouse behind and seared her flesh as it slipped beneath her shorts.

Stacey inhaled sharply.

His hand stilled.

She cuddled against him. "Don't stop," she said. "I like being free."

"So how did the dolphin get into the bathtub?"

She shook her head, moving against his chest as she did. "I don't know."

Gently he tipped her face up toward his. "Don't put limitations on yourself you don't need," he said. "I'd suggest the dolphin was you fencing yourself in, attempting to escape from certain fears. So you retreated to the known—that is, the normalcy of the bath as opposed to a large body of water—only to discover that path led to your sure drowning."

"Do they teach psychological dream interpretation in vet school?"

He tapped her on the cheek. "I take it that means I hit the nail on the head?"

She met his searching gaze. "Yes."

He nodded. "I want to kiss you," he said.

"Please," Stacey whispered. "Please, yes."

With the one hand already behind her, he cupped her closer, drawing her almost onto his lap. His warm fingers spread across the cheeks of her derriere and Stacey shivered with desire and excitement.

She offered her lips to him.

She expected his touch to be gentle, an exploration, a tasting, an assessment of what they'd first shared the night before on his porch.

The hungry way he took her mouth shook her to the core. He didn't taste; he devoured her. Pulling her to him, he parted her lips and suckled her tongue, kissing her like a man starved, and a man who could wait no more for what he'd been desiring.

Stacey gasped and he swallowed even the sounds she made. And then, rather than being shocked at the way his hands and mouth were everywhere over her, within her, possessing her, Stacey let the reins she held on her own behavior slip.

She pressed her breasts against his chest, marveling at the heat the gesture ignited. She tipped her head backward, encouraging him to explore further.

Michael's breath was coming in harsh gasps. She knew by the way he'd pinned her lower body against his heated arousal that he wanted nothing more than to be free of the restraint of their clothing and to plunge inside her.

And with the wild abandonment she was feeling, she did nothing to discourage him. She cupped one hand against the front of his jeans and kissed him with a tongue that danced in a rhythm she'd learned from him only moments before.

More daring than she'd ever been, she let her fingers tug at the metal buttons of his jeans. She met a stiff resistance; then, when the first one slipped free, the lower fastenings slipped free all at once. He groaned and traced one hand, the one not still igniting fire where he played with the tantalized skin of her buttocks, inside her blouse. He followed the line of her bikini top and then pushed it below her breasts.

Leaning forward, he tugged at the fabric of her blouse until her nipple was exposed to the night air—and to his hot mouth. She let out a moan when he moved his lips from hers, and then an even more excited moan, more of a low growl, really, as he suckled her breast, tugging gently on her swollen nipple until she panted against him.

Almost falling back against the door of the truck, she reached out with two hands and captured his arousal through the white cotton of his underwear. "Sexy," she said. "I like a man in briefs."

"Minx," he said, his mouth moving against her breast as he spoke. The feel of his breath against her naked skin sent prickles across her flesh. He licked her goose bumps and grinned.

Leaving one hand at his groin, she moved the other to his head. So intense were the feelings, she wanted to tear him away from her breasts; yet she wanted to hold on so that he never quit kissing them. She shuddered as a wave of passion built within her. She'd read of women having orgasms from kissing alone, but Stacey had never believed such a thing happened in real life.

Right about now, though, she was beginning to be a believer.

Head thrown back, she dragged her fingers through his hair as she cupped him more firmly. If making out in a parked truck felt this good, what would it be like to go to bed with Michael? "Divine," she murmured.

He let out a ragged breath. "Inspirational."

And suddenly he lifted his head, abandoning her breasts. He cocked his head to the right, then the left.

"What is it?" Stacey didn't want him to leave any open space between her body and his lips.

"Thought I heard a car."

Stacey giggled. "It's kind of like being teenagers, waiting to get caught."

He nodded and lowered his mouth to hers. But instead of the ravenous bruising kisses of earlier, he brushed his lips softly over hers, hovering, and then trailing a path down her throat. "So much for restrained behavior," he said, but didn't sound too unhappy with himself.

"I understand the principle," Stacey said, smoothing the tangles she'd made in his hair with her wild fingers. "But for some reason it's even more important to you. Want to tell me about that?" Asking a guy a question during heavy petting was definitely a no-no, Stacey figured, but since he'd slowed down and seemed to be alert to outside interruptions, it seemed as good a time as any. Besides, she not only wanted to kiss this man, she wanted to understand him.

At first he didn't reply. Stacey waited, watching his face for a clue to his feelings. His chest rose and fell steadily, calmer now that their glaze of passion had tempered itself.

"I told you Pauline was pregnant when we married." He shifted away from her, tugging his jeans back in place, though not fastening them. He sat upright, and then, to Stacey's pleasure, reached out and eased her against the curve of his chest and shoulder.

She couldn't see his face from that embrace without twisting her head around, but she didn't mind too much, as the way he held her made her feel special. Fitting her back to his chest with a contented sigh, she said, "I'm assuming you had determined not to let the same thing happen with someone else."

Michael tucked his arms around Stacey's waist and reflected on her choice of words. He was pleased she hadn't said *make the same mistake again*. He stroked the soft skin of her hand. "That's true, but it goes beyond just not getting someone pregnant by accident."

He hesitated. She felt so incredible wrapped in his arms. Words were almost a waste. But she'd brought up the topic and it made sense to explore it—together. "Guys are supposed to be horny bastards who run away from the *r* word and the *c* word," he said, thinking out loud.

"Let's see. That would be *relationship* and *commitment*."

"Yep. Well, I managed the *c* part. I got married, then there was the pregnancy, the bar exam for her during that time, the diapers, and no sleep. Then it was all work." He quit moving his fingers across her hand and clasped it tight. "My work. Her work. Day care for Kristen."

"So you had commitment but no relationship?"

"We had our role as parents, but it was more of a partnership. Everything was a negotiation of her interests versus mine." He sighed. "I don't know why I'm telling you this crap."

She stirred against him and returned the pressure on his hand. "Maybe because you don't want to make the same mistake again?"

"*Mistake* is the right word in this context." He sighed.

"You were awfully lonely, weren't you?"

Stacey had whispered those words and Michael almost didn't catch them. When he realized what she'd said, the truth of her statement hit him. "Very wise observation," he said dryly. "How'd you get so smart?"

"My own brand of torment," she said lightly. "But you stayed married and you even had a second child. So . . ."

He heard the question. If things were so bad, why had he done that? He could waffle on that answer, but Michael preferred truth to falsehood. He liked Stacey. She seemed to like him. Being truthful at the beginning of a relationship—aha, there was that *r* word—set the tone. "Kristen was almost four. Our marriage was pretty much in name only. My parents wanted us to go away for a long weekend, so they babysat. Pauline and I went to the Poconos." Michael shook his head, remembering. "We had nothing to say to each other. We had sex, once, and she spent the time at the pool. I played golf. At the end of the weekend I knew we were in serious trouble. Talk about stupid behavior."

"And that's when Jessica was conceived."

"Yep."

"You know, I don't want to talk about this anymore," Michael said. "Just remembering makes me sick. But to wrap it up, Pauline threw a fit, but in the end she had the baby. We stuck it out until she told me she'd met someone else and wanted out."

"If she hadn't done that, would you have stayed married?"

"I don't know. I used to agonize over that question. You hear so much about how divorce is hard on children. I've read the statistics and the studies that say kids of divorced parents have trouble achieving their own happy relationships. My parents were pretty upset."

Stacey sure had gotten still, almost as if she were

holding her breath. She was probably thinking he was an idiot, getting his wife pregnant twice without meaning to, and then wrecking his kids' lives by not being able to work out a relationship with his attractive, intelligent wife. "Anyway," he said, "I know Pauline is happier. I'm happier. The kids seem to handle the situation fairly well. I'm still lonely, but"— he lifted her hand and kissed her palm—"not nearly so lonely now."

Stacey twisted around to face him. She wanted so badly to share her feelings, to tell him how afraid she was of trusting any man, of how watching her parents' battles had convinced her marriage was a field of land mines approached only with the greatest of caution.

And even that method had blown up in her face when Robert had betrayed her.

But how could she share these fears? With two daughters, the last thing Michael wanted to hear were these insecurities caused by divorce.

So instead she clasped her hands around his neck and buried her breasts against his chest. Reassurance could come in many ways. She tipped her mouth to his and whispered, "Kiss me. Kiss me so hard I can't think."

Strong arms wrapped around her body and pulled her even closer. He clearly needed no other invitation as he slanted his mouth over hers and then parted her lips with his tongue. Stacey, feeling brave and racy and more desirable than she could ever recall feeling, wrapped her tongue around his. She was rewarded by a growling noise deep within his throat as he joined her in the tantalizing dance.

Stacey let one hand trail to Michael's waist and then lower as she slipped her hand into the front of his jeans and cradled his erection. He groaned and tugged down the fabric of her blouse and brushed his tongue across her nipple. She gave herself up to the sweet, spiraling sensations building within her.

Swept away by those feelings, Stacey was stunned when Michael pushed her hand away from his groin, pulled up her blouse, and said, "Shhh. Stacey, stop."

"What?"

And then she heard it, a rapping sound on the window of the truck. Still dazed with passion, she blinked and realized someone was tapping on the fogged-up windows.

She fumbled with her clothing and hair and Michael did the same. Then he wiped at the glass with the back of his hand, clearing the view.

A man stood there, a rather tall man with silver hair, wearing a suit and carrying a briefcase.

"Oh, no," Stacey said.

"Well, he doesn't look like a Doolittle resident, but he doesn't appear dangerous," Michael said. He turned the key in the ignition and lowered the window.

"Evening, sir," Michael said.

The man nodded. "Good evening to you, too. Hello, Stacey."

Stacey grasped the front of her blouse, hoping it wasn't gaping open. She shot a sideways glance at Michael and said, somewhat weakly, "Hello, Daddy."

Chapter 18

"That's your father?" Michael swiveled his head from the distinguished gentleman back to the woman he'd just been kissing senseless.

Stacey was nodding, not exactly leaning close to face her parent through the window of the truck.

Michael felt like a kid caught with his hand in the candy jar, or, more accurately, down his girlfriend's blouse. "I was just dropping Stacey off," he said.

"Daddy, this is Michael, er, Dr. Halliday. Michael, my father, Dr. Louis St. Cyr."

"Dr. Halliday, is it?" The silver-haired man regarded him with slightly less disfavor. "Well, I'm sure we can exchange credentials at some other, more appropriate time. I'm looking for the Schoolhouse Inn, and you, young lady, have a lot of explaining to do."

She was a grown woman. Michael didn't think that tone was called for. "I'll walk you inside," he said to Stacey.

"Good. No, not good." Her face got all scrunched up

for a minute. She was thinking, and it seemed likely she was deciding whether or not it was better to leave him sitting in the truck.

"Is your wife with you?" Michael looked around but saw only the man and the Lincoln that had pulled up alongside them while they'd been lip-locked.

"My wife?" Dr. St. Cyr regarded him with amusement. "I work fast, but not that fast."

"Er, Daddy means he's here alone." Stacey scooted to the passenger door. "Thank you for a beautiful day, but I'd better be going now."

A duo of brilliant floodlights came to life, bathing the truck and all three players in what was turning out to be a rather strange scene with a light worthy of an Arkansas noon. From the porch, the sisters called in unison, "Who's there?"

Michael poked his head out the window and said, "Don't shoot. It's me, Michael. And Stacey."

"And who else?" That was Abbie's grim voice. Michael grinned but wiped it from his face quickly. Knowing Abbie, she was carting a shotgun or at least a .22, and if she suspected the man was up to no good, she'd probably use it, to no poor effect.

"I, my dear woman, am Dr. St. Cyr, of New Orleans, Stacey Suellen's father."

"Your middle name is Suellen?"

Stacey nodded. "From *Gone with the Wind,* only I would far rather have been named after Scarlett. It's all one word and I hate it when it's spelled wrong, so I never use it."

He grinned again. "I've never read the book, but I have a fair idea from the movie why you say you'd rather be Scarlett." He placed one hand on the door of the truck. "I'm definitely coming inside with you and your pappy. Who knows what other tidbits I might glean?"

He was sure he heard her groan. Well, he'd decided at some point far too early in their time together that he wanted to know everything there was to know about this woman. She was such a funny blend of starch and sugar. So whatever it was she didn't want him to know—and it didn't take much of a diagnostician to figure that one out—he planned to tag along and learn.

"Goodness me," Miss Martha said, bustling over to the truck, "whatever are you all doing out here instead of coming inside like civilized folks?"

Stacey blushed and Michael quirked one brow at her. Well, if the sisters couldn't figure that one out for themselves, he wasn't about to fill in the blanks. He stepped out of the truck, shook hands with Stacey's father, and moved around to open the door for her.

If he hadn't, he had the feeling she might have remained inside. Her father removed a garment bag and overnight case from the trunk of the Lincoln while Stacey swung her legs to the side of the cab and tugged at a long strand of her hair.

"Oh, dear," she said, "I just wasn't ready for my father. I thought he was coming on Tuesday." But at least she accepted his outstretched hand and joined him on the path beside the vehicle.

"Tomorrow's Monday," Michael said. "It's really only a day early." He glanced at his watch. "How did it get to be so late?"

Stacey glanced over toward where her father was

shutting the trunk. "Kissing, when done as well as you do it, can consume quite a bit of time."

He smiled. "You have a very sweet way of wording a compliment. I'd like to take up where we left off—another day. I promised the girls I'd be home to tuck them in and I just realized it's after ten."

"Of course," Stacey said, looking a little more relieved than he would have liked. "Daddy, Michael has to go."

Her father nodded. "Nice to meet you. Next time, though, I recommend you two get a room, preferably in a hotel with a decent Michelin rating. Stacey was raised better than to be making out in a pickup truck."

"Yes, sir," Michael said. He waved at the sisters ogling them from the porch, and kissed Stacey on the cheek before he turned and jumped behind the wheel of his truck.

At least her father hadn't suggested there be no next time.

Stacey recovered enough from the shock of her father's unexpected arrival to give him a quick hug before they headed to the porch. "Thanks for coming, Daddy."

"Yes, I can see you've been left to your own devices too long," he said, dryly. "Who are the formidable dragons awaiting us on the porch?"

"Sweet Martha and Crabbie Abbie," Stacey whispered. "They run the Schoolhouse Inn. They'll probably put you in Eighth Grade."

"Is that the nomenclature for the hotel rooms?"

Stacy nodded.

Her father sighed. "It's a shame there's not a Ritz-Carlton in every corner of the globe."

"It's quite charming, actually. And breakfast comes with."

Her father jabbed at his waistline with the side of his overnight case. "It will no doubt be wasted on me. I'm on a strict diet."

"You?" Stacey stared at her dad. Something was up. He'd grumbled about coming to Arkansas and leaving his chick of the day behind and he'd never been or needed to be on a diet in his life, and here he'd shown up ahead of schedule.

He shrugged. "One can't be too careful with one's health."

"Oh, of course."

"Now, don't try and derail the subject," he said, sounding very much like the distinguished professor of orthopedic medicine that he was.

"What subject was that?" Thank goodness they'd reached the steps to the porch. She didn't want to talk about Michael right this moment. She was still too jumbled up from the emotion and passion to sort it all out.

The sisters came to her rescue. Both of them stared at her dad as if they were seeing Cary Grant in the flesh.

"Oh, my," Miss Martha said, "will you be staying with us long?"

Her father opened his mouth and Stacey threw him a "be nice" glance. "That depends," he said. "It's a factor of the quality of the accommodations and the circumstances that led to my daughter asking me to arrive on your doorstep."

"Oh, my, you sound very educated," Martha said. Abbie nodded, but didn't look nearly as impressed.

Stacey was pretty sure Abbie had a lot less use for men than did her more bubbly and talkative sister.

"Right now I'm simply tired. My needs are simple.

I'd like a king-sized bed, a private bath, cable television with at least two premium channels, and a glass of sherry before I retire."

Martha blinked. "Eighth Grade," she said, and opened the front door.

Stacey smiled. "Only the best for my dad." It was always like that. He had a way of commanding attention and of getting people to want to please him. Stacey had never figured out how he did it. It was certainly a useful technique to have in one's repertoire. She, on the other hand, was pretty certain she came off as just plain bossy or possibly even bitchy when she was making a request in such situations.

"We don't have cable," Abbie said, stopping in the hallway to hang her shawl on the row of pegs decorated with paintings of wildflowers. "They have it over in El Dorado but we never had it installed."

Her father blinked. "Well, then, how will I get to sleep?"

Abbie tipped her head to one side. "You might just try shutting your eyes once your head is on your pillow."

"Why don't I pour you a nice glass of sherry?" Martha had him leave the garment bag and case in the hall and led them into the front parlor, where she settled Dr. St. Cyr in the best chair beside the hearth. "Is Stacey's mother joining you tomorrow?"

"You'd have to ask Stacey the answer to that question."

"Tuesday," Stacey said. "You remember, Daddy, she had those other things she had to take care of first."

He stared at her. He knew something was up, but would he play along? As much as she missed Michael's presence, Stacey was thankful he wasn't party to this charade. She really needed to find a moment to explain to him the truth about her parents.

Her father scowled and said, "Yes, Joanne always has something on her plate."

"Well," Martha said brightly, "I think maybe I'll take a little sip of sherry, too. Stacey?"

She didn't care for sherry, but she nodded. There was no way she was leaving her father alone with the sisters.

"We're hoping your mother will get involved with our garden club," Martha said, handing tiny glasses of sweet brown liqueur around.

"Well, if she does," her father said, "she'll be staying longer than I plan to. I've got five cases on Thursday."

"And the opera on Wednesday night," Stacey added, remembering how emphatic he'd been about having to be back to escort Larissa.

He scowled, this time even more fiercely. "I don't think I'm going this week."

Stacey put two and two together and definitely came up with four. Or so she thought. So Larissa hadn't lasted, had she? Well, she couldn't say she was sorry. It would be just too embarrassing to have a second step-mother younger than she was. Stacey had been through it only two years ago and she didn't want to do it again. Or maybe her dad was getting smarter and he'd broken it off. Now, there was an encouraging thought.

The phone rang and Abbie left the room. Martha chatted about types of sherry with Stacey's father and Stacey tried to sit back and relax. Abbie came back into the room. "That was a woman calling herself Dr. St. Cyr. I told her I didn't see how she could be Dr. St. Cyr when he was a he and he was sitting in the front parlor. I'm afraid she said some rather unpleasant words, so I had no choice but to hang up on her."

Stacey dropped her face in her hands. What a nightmare. Immediately her cell phone began ringing in her purse, which she'd dropped by her feet. She considered ignoring it, but that would only make things worse.

It was, of course, her mother.

"Is your father in Arkansas with you?"

No *hello, how are you?*

"Why do you ask?"

"That means yes."

Stacey faked a smile for Miss Martha, hovering too close for comfort, but accepted a refill on her sherry. "It's rather late, Mother, and I still have work to do. Can we talk tomorrow?"

"Work? I thought you were on vacation." Her voice softened. "If there's one thing I've finally learned, too much work is not the answer to life's mysteries."

"Wow," Stacey said. This was her mother speaking? Her role model in workaholism? After Robert's desertion, Stacey had concluded she'd be like her mother. Everyone knew Dr. Joanne St. Cyr kept the longest hours at the hospital, booked more surgical cases than any other dermatologist in the city, plus had developed her own line of cosmetics.

"But that we can discuss in the morning. Put your father on the phone."

"But . . ."

To her surprise, Stacey glanced up to see her father crossing the room, hand stretched out. Without a word, she passed the cell phone to him. She'd better get to her room and finish that emergency public relations project. She'd need the consulting fee just to cover her cell phone bill.

"There's no need for you to come rushing up here," her father said.

"What excellent sherry," Stacey said to the sisters, in a voice loud enough to blur whatever words were about to be exchanged between her parents. Even conversations that started out in a civil fashion escalated to shouting matches. "Where did you find it?"

"The liquor store at the county line," Abbie said.

Martha said hastily, "So did you and Dr. Mike have a nice day together today?"

"Oh, yes," Stacey said. "We went to the lake and had a picnic, or were about to when we had to stop to rescue a dog."

"Darn animals," Abbie said. "Some beast got loose in my canna bed and rooted up my shoots. Gives a whole different meaning to the word *shoots*, let me tell you."

"It might have been a possum," Martha said.

"You what?" That was her father, working up in volume, almost shouting into the cell phone.

"Or a raccoon," she added.

Had she gone to Hot Springs, Stacey reflected, about this time on a Sunday evening she would have been curled up in her hotel bed alone except for the television and the latest Kinsey Milhone escapade. "Maybe it was one of those rabbits," she said, keeping her face perfectly straight.

"No," Abbie said, "I can say for a certainty it wasn't any rabbit."

"You're where?" There, he'd achieved a full roar.

He thrust the phone toward Stacey. "You may as well give your mother directions to this establishment."

"Oh, I'll do that," Martha said.

Stacey let her. To her dad, she said, "Where is Mother now?"

He swirled the sherry in his glass and lifted it toward the light. Then he downed it in one swallow. Even Miss Abbie seemed impressed enough to scurry to his service so his glass was promptly refilled. "It would appear she is at the only service station still open at this hour of the evening and it is attended by a not-too-bright young man named Billy Bob or Bob White or some such appellation."

"That would be the Gas 'N Go." Stacey grinned at the thought of her mother conversing with Billy. She'd probably insist he correct his name tag if he was still wearing his brother's shirt.

Martha handed the phone to Stacey. To her relief, the connection had ended. "Your mother is one lively lady."

"You can say that again," her father said.

"I hope she likes Eighth Grade," Martha said. "It's a very masculine room."

"I should hope so," her father said. "That's my room. I can do without the cable for a night or two, but I will not be surrounded by little lace crochets and fluffy pink pillows." He shuddered. "I endured that once, for about two months."

"Oh, uh," Stacey began, unsure of how to phrase what had to be stated but intent on derailing him from the recollections of the woman who'd come close to being her first stepmother, a wispy ex-deb already twice divorced at thirty-five. Daddy had gravitated to Missy because she was the opposite of Joanne, but thankfully her penchant for pink had driven him away. "My parents don't . . . well, they need separate rooms."

"But that will cost twice as much," Martha said, dismay for the expense clear in her voice.

"And that means we'll earn twice as much," Abbie said, frowning sharply at her too-helpful sister. "Give the customers what they want, remember?"

"Oh, of course." Martha smiled and looked around the room. She tugged at the scarf that was doing a none-too-adequate job of covering her hair curlers. "Now, where did I leave my sherry?"

From his vantage point outside the parlor windows, and just around to the right side of the front porch, Michael paused and checked the occupants of the room. Still a full complement of the Schoolhouse Sisters, Stacey, and her father. Well, he might as well step onto the porch and knock on the front door, then. He'd been hoping to avoid a group scene.

He wanted to see Stacey, and Stacey alone.

After their nighttime ritual of reading a selection of Jessica's and of Kristen's from the *Golden Treasury of Poetry*, Michael had tucked in his daughters, informed Mrs. Beebe he had to check on the newly delivered puppies, and then raced back to the Schoolhouse Inn. He'd hoped to find the parlor dark, the parties dispersed to their rooms. That being the case, he would have tiptoed around the building and tossed pebbles at the window of the Third Grade room.

He couldn't say in words why he had to see her

tonight, but he knew in his gut it was true. Her father's appearance on the scene had reminded him that Stacey was only passing through Doolittle.

True could handle the drive back to New Orleans as long as Stacey stopped frequently and let her walk around.

She could see property with Mrs. Clark on Monday while he was in the clinic, and be off with her dad that night.

He wasn't ready for her to leave.

"Stop where you are or I'll make you sorry you were born."

Michael froze. The voice was female, well spoken in a rather soft and lilting way, but very, very menacing.

Slowly he lifted his hands over his head and turned from the window.

At least she was wielding a flashlight and not a handgun. At least not that he could see. But the arc of the beam half blinded him.

"That's it. Step out of those bushes and around in front of the porch."

Michael did as she instructed. "You're probably thinking I'm a prowler, but I'm not."

"And I'm the Queen of England."

"You could be, but you sound much younger."

She laughed. "Fairly witty, for a housebreaker."

"Honest," he said, dropping his hands and extending his right. "Michael—"

"Uh-uh," she said. "Keep your hands up while I decide what to do with you."

"You might ring the doorbell," Michael said, "and tell them Dr. Mike's in the bushes."

"You're a doctor?" She cast the flashlight toward the ground, at least taking the full brunt of the light out of his eyes.

He nodded. Blinked. Let his eyes adjust to the darkness. Thankfully, the sisters had turned off the floodlights. The woman holding him at bay had dark rich hair, swept up in a French knot. She was probably in her forties or possibly older. Her posture was perfectly erect, her suit of navy linen impeccably cut, her matching leather pumps gleaming.

"So what would you do with a number sixty-four Beaver blade?"

Michael grinned as he recognized the name of the scalpel. "Slice and dice with it?" And then his grin broadened. He pictured Stacey the night he met her. This intrepid female was no doubt the woman who'd given birth to Stacey.

"Define parthenogenesis."

"Dr. St. Cyr, your daughter and husband are inside. I really am not a prowler. I was simply peeking in the window to see if Stacey was still there." That sounded slightly more civilized than saying he wanted to know whether Stacey was alone in her room.

"My daughter may be inside," his captor said, "but my husband certainly is not."

"Ah," Michael said, as the front door opened and Stacey's father stepped out onto the porch. "I suppose that man is the King of England?"

Chapter 19

Stacey edged out onto the porch to say good night to her father, her steps shadowed by the sisters. She was brought up short by the sight of not only her mother but Michael, heading her way.

"The next time you decide to run into trouble," Stacey's mother said as she approached the porch, "will you please do so nearer to civilization?" Her mother, brandishing a sturdy flashlight, surged forward, matched step by step by Michael. "I had to stop twice for directions—and that's with a GPS in my Cadillac. I don't know what ordinary people do."

"Ordinary people stay home," her father said. He chose that moment to flip up the top of his Zippo in a practiced motion. He took his time coaxing a flame from his cigar, then clicked the lighter shut.

Stacy sighed. After a night of almost no sleep and the emotionally charged day, the last thing she was up for was round nine thousand nine hundred and ninety-nine of the ongoing war between her parents.

On the porch now, Stacey's mother presented her cheek. Stacey distributed a dutiful kiss.

"I see you're still trying to kill yourself," she said to her ex-husband.

Miss Abbie smiled. Her sister blanched and said almost gingerly, "Welcome to the Schoolhouse Inn."

Joanne nodded, still glaring at the glowing end of Louis's cigar.

Michael skirted her dueling parents and stopped near enough to her that his arm brushed hers. She smiled gratefully at him. He winked and said in a low voice, "I came back to tuck you in, too."

He slipped an arm around her and Stacey let her body relax slightly against his. From her protected stance, she watched her parents debate who should be in Arkansas rescuing Stacey from whatever contretemps had overcome her and who should have remained in New Orleans. With Michael by her side, the volume of their argument seemed to have faded. She observed them almost as if from a distance, the pleasant spell broken only when Michael said, "Correct me if I'm wrong, but I thought Stacey was in Doolittle because the two of you wanted her to locate retirement property for you."

Oh-oh.

But Stacey was saved from providing an explanation by the simultaneous laughter of her mother and her father. The two of them exchanged amused glances.

"No offense to your town or your state," her father said, "but this is the last place I'd ever retire."

"And the same is true for me," her mother said.

Then her dad, his gaze unusually friendly, said to her mom, "Remember what we used to say we'd do when we were old and gray?"

Her mother smiled and her face suddenly looked much younger.

Miss Martha clasped her hands together and sighed romantically. At least she and Miss Abbie seemed to be enjoying the show taking place on their front porch.

Then her mother said, in a tone softer than Stacey could remember her using toward her father, "Grey Island. We were going to make buckets of money and buy our very own island off the South Carolina coast and set up our own little world." And then her expression went from nostalgic to bleak. "But we couldn't agree on who would be president of our country and who would be veep."

"We could have shared power," her dad said, somewhat pensively.

"You? Share control?" Her mother laughed and the sound wasn't at all musical. "The way you let me share in the decision of what to name our only child?"

He clamped his cigar between his teeth and said, "You supplied the middle name." But he sounded a trifle defensive.

"Suellen? Suellen?" Her mother's voice rose. "I told you Scarlett, but you wrote it down wrong."

He shrugged. "They both start with *S*. What difference does it make?"

Stacey stared. "I've never heard this gem of family history before. So I really was supposed to be named Stacey Scarlett." She tasted the sound of the name on her tongue. It was an awkward combination, typical of her parents' warring tastes.

Her father studied the buildup of ash on his cigar with a critical eye. "I think I already apologized for that peccadillo."

"Apologized?" Her mother crossed her arms over her chest. "Never has such a thing happened."

"Well, I do know how to admit when I'm wrong, and it was bullheaded and wrong of me not to have double-checked the name before I filled in the birth certificate form."

Miss Martha's head was whipping back and forth as she followed the raging argument. "My, but this is more entertaining than *The Young and the Restless*."

"I don't know why you waste electricity on that pap," Abbie said. "Seems to me you people ought to get to bed and gather your strength so you can argue some more in the morning." And with those words of advice, she clomped into the inn.

"Let's follow her cue," Michael said in Stacey's ear, guiding her toward the front door.

Miss Martha's jaw dropped as she watched Michael, for all intents and purposes heading to Stacey's room. "I'll just see her to her door," he said, casting one of his engaging smiles at her.

"Oh, of course, Dr. Mike," she said. "It's just that we have a reputation."

"I think," Michael said, speaking gently but clearly with authority, "that the St. Cyrs would like to get settled in their rooms. I'll see myself out."

Martha's mouth moved, but in the end all she did

was nod. As Stacey moved inside, she heard the older woman offer to show her mother to her room.

And then Stacey, with one strong arm around her shoulder, thought of nothing but being tucked into the four-poster bed with Michael beside her.

She picked up the key to the room from where it hung on a wooden peg beside the front parlor, grabbed her purse, and walked midway down the hall to the door stenciled with THIRD GRADE.

At the door, she fumbled with the key, very much aware of Michael's presence, remembering their intimacies in the cab of his truck. Had they been alone in her room then, would he have found the will to exercise restraint? Stacey blushed as she admitted to herself that restraint was the last thing she desired from Michael Halliday.

He took the key from her, unlocked the door, and led her inside. Shutting the door firmly behind them, he said in a voice loaded with intensity, "I walked out of this very room this morning determined to do the right thing. Michael Halliday always does what's best for everyone else, but tonight I'm doing what I want—for me." He advanced on her, and Stacey trembled with anticipation.

He no more wanted restraint than she did.

Despite craving him as badly as she did, she took a step backward and bumped against one of the posts of the four-poster bed. Without hesitation, he closed the distance between them. He removed her purse from her hands and dropped it on the floor with a thunk, then kicked it aside.

"Stacey, you make me crazy," he said, gazing into her

eyes, then taking in her body from head to toe. "You're sexy, you're sweet, you're clever, you're fearful." He traced the line of her chin and lifted her mouth to his.

He tasted, he conquered, he reduced her to a quivering shell of her normally contained self.

"Michael, oh, Michael," she managed to say when he at last lifted his mouth from hers.

He grinned. "You don't know what to do when heart overwhelms mind, do you?"

Stacey furrowed her brow. "Of course I do," she said, then broke off. Was that why being with Michael confused her so? Because she barely knew him, because her mind told her not to do what her body wanted so badly to indulge in? "Well, maybe not usually," she said, "but I do tonight," she said, reaching for the buckle of his jeans.

He nodded, but stilled her hand. "Tonight, then, put aside everything except how you feel." He brushed a fingertip across her forehead. "Lovely Stacey, who works so hard and does everything so competently. Tonight you're not in charge of anything."

Her heart was racing far too fast. "What do you mean?" She knew what he wanted. He wanted sex, which in her experience meant he wanted her to fill her mouth with him, then open her body and give herself to him.

He smiled, more satyr than saint. "I think you're used to being in charge at the expense of your own pleasure," he said. "And I think it's about time you realized just how different things can be."

Stacey puckered her lips. Her nipples had swollen and her breasts strained against her bra. She realized wetness had slicked her thighs. "D-different?"

Michael nodded and with nimble fingers unfastened

her top and slipped it from her shoulders. It fell to the floor.

Recognizing her cue, Stacey again reached for Michael's belt. His arousal was straining wildly against the front of his jeans and she wanted to free him from the prison of the fabric.

"Uh-uh," Michael said, capturing her wrist and lifting it back and up against the bedpost. Then he did the same with her other arm, a wicked grin on his face. "You keep those there."

"But . . ." Stacey trailed off in a blush of confusion.

"I want you screaming," he said. "I want you writhing against me. I want to know no man has touched you the way I'm about to touch you."

"But if I don't use my hands," she said, feeling incredibly open and vulnerable in the way her breasts jutted upward and her body was offered to his gaze, his touch, his every means of pleasure, "how can I . . . I mean, how can I . . . ?"

"No need to finish that sentence," Michael said, stripping her shorts from her legs and tossing them across the room. "You are so beautiful."

He rocked back on his heels and gazed up at her. Stacey started to lower her arms and he shook his head. "Not until I say so."

She trembled but left her arms raised over her head, wrapped around the cool wood of the bed. "I've never felt like this in my life."

He nodded, obviously quite pleased. "Good," he said, shifting her legs farther apart and running his hand in a sensuous line up her thigh just to the edge of her panties. He circled one finger along the line where fabric met skin, then rose and, his eyes fixed on hers, slowly unclasped her bra and tossed it aside.

He sucked in a breath. Cupping her breasts, he lowered his mouth to first one, then the other. Stacey thought she'd pop out of her skin the way she'd practically fallen out of her bra. Without thinking, she lowered her hands and pressed his head even closer. Almost panting, she said, "Aren't you going to take your clothes off?"

He flicked his tongue across her nipples. Already rose-colored and swollen with desire, they almost ached from his touch. Stacey groaned and writhed against him.

Against her breast, he whispered, "I tried to stay away from you. I went home. I put my kids to bed. But I had to come back."

"I'm glad you did."

"And I'm going to make you even more glad," he said, lifting his head. "Arms back," he said, giving her a searing look. "Fair is fair. I promise you can have your way with me—whatever you say, I'll do—but this time, let me take you out of your mind."

She hesitated. It sounded so good, but she was afraid it wasn't possible. "I always think too much during sex," she said.

"Uh-huh," he said, kneeling before her and easing the crotch of her panties to the side. "You might start by not talking so much."

She started to say that was pretty much impossible, but as he dipped his tongue into the hot, craving lips between her thighs just at the moment, she cried out but no words followed.

He didn't even pull the panties off, she realized through a haze as he tasted and suckled and began a demanding, rhythmic motion that called to a primitive side of herself Stacey hadn't even known existed. He glanced up at her as she was looking down, amazed at the sight of Michael between her legs, coaxing her to pleasure she hadn't known she could taste.

Then he slipped a finger inside her and began to call to her body in a tempo that was building a liquid fire. She gasped, and one hand let go of the post. She cradled it around her breast and urged herself to answer the call Michael was sending to her body.

"Let me drink you," he was saying, Stacey realized through her haze of desire and wanton need. "Spill yourself against my lips and let me taste all of you," he said.

Stacey had quit thinking. She'd quit worrying about taking care of Michael and satisfying his needs. He wanted her to explode. She wanted to do so. She rocked her hips and he moved with her, one hand cupping her derriere, the other echoing the rhythm of his tongue and lips as they devoured her very essence.

"Oh, oh," she cried, and, amazed at the sensation, catapulted over the sensual edge he'd created within her, her body quivering, her soft sensitive lips pulsing against Michael's mouth.

She fell against him and he caught her up and lay her on the bed. She sprawled before him, quivering still, her mouth and eyes wide open. Her hair splayed over the comforter and she stripped her panties from her legs.

Michael watched her, his own body aching for the release he'd just brought to her. Swelling even harder, he considered the knowledge that he'd brought to her a pleasure she had never known before. He could tell that, and he was thrilled to be the one who'd shown her how incredible she could feel.

He wanted her always to feel that wonderful.

In one swift move, he hauled the computer from the bed where Stacey had left it that morning, then stripped off his clothing. As much as he'd wanted to gift Stacey with her own pleasure, now he wanted his.

She was watching him as he stepped free of his pants, her eyes wide and curious. He stood before her, letting her look her fill, at the same time savoring the taste of her still on his lips. "Thank you for trusting me," he said.

She nodded and then blushed slightly. "You have a beautiful body," she said.

He joined her on the bed, positioning himself by her side. He took one of her hands and clasped it around his shaft. "It's all yours to play with."

A gleam of mischief sparked in her eyes. "You did say I could have my way with you."

He lifted a strand of her hair that had fallen across her face and moved against the wonderful warm pressure of her hand. He should have pulled out the protection he'd stuffed into his jeans pocket when leaving his house before settling on the bed. Lying beside Stacey like this, it felt too good to move. In a voice that came out sounding almost drugged, he said, "I did say that."

Her other hand joined the first. She enveloped his arousal, her hands moving in a tempo that echoed the blood pounding in him. Or maybe it was the other way around. He gasped and took her mouth with his, his tongue plundering harder and deeper with every driving sensation of those incredible hands.

"Stacey," he said, breaking off the kiss at last. "Slow down, or I won't make it."

Her beautiful eyes all innocence, she said in a saucy voice, "I think you're making it pretty well."

"I want to be inside you," he said. "Another minute of those hands and that'll never happen." He cocked an eye at her.

She smiled, somewhat shyly considering her hands were still tucked around his throbbing arousal. "I read an article in *Redbook* on how to give your husband a hand job. I guess I got it right?"

He laughed. "You minx. And I thought *Redbook* was about hair and recipes." He grabbed his jeans from the floor and tore open the condom packet.

Stacey pushed back on her elbows, lifting her head and shoulders to better view the sight of Michael naked and aroused and about to join his body with hers. She quivered in anticipation, the heat and sensations he'd brought to life within her still pulsing, still begging for more.

Yes, she wanted him inside her, deep and thrusting and demanding. She glanced over at the bedpost as Michael worked the condom on and smiled, then leaned forward. "Let me," she said, and guided the sheath on, placing kisses along the way as she did.

He groaned, and that made her smile even more. "That's a beautiful sound," she said, feeling naughty and a little bit wicked knowing she'd brought it on.

"Oh, yeah," he said, tumbling her back onto the bed.

Stacey opened her legs.

But instead of hovering over her and then pressing into her, he shook his head and motioned with his hand. "Turn over," he said, his voice roughened with need.

She wasn't sure what he had in mind. Robert had been a very one-dimensional lover. But after the joyful release Michael had brought to her while she'd been practically pinned against the column of the bedpost, Stacey wasn't asking any doubting questions.

She rolled over and he pulled her up so that she was on her hands and knees. Talk about naughty! She was beyond sensation as Michael placed a pillow beneath her chest and spread her legs farther apart.

He was stroking her derriere and hips and reaching around to slide first one finger, then a second inside her. Stacey gasped, and then he pushed into her and she forgot all reality except the explosive sense of being possessed, of Michael filling and taking and slowly easing outward, then moving, moving, moving inside her, touching places she'd never known existed, setting fires that had never burned within her.

"Michael, Michael," she cried out; then, in a distant part of her mind, she recalled she was in a house where her parents slept, as did two fussy old ladies.

But Stacey didn't care. She didn't care how much noise she made as Michael, his hands in her hair and on her back pressing her downward even more, driving into her, shouted out her name and shuddered his release deep within, filling not only her body, but her mind and her soul.

Chapter 20

Later, Michael could have kicked himself. He should have predicted her flight from intimacy. But at that moment, lying beside Stacey in a satiated tangle of limbs, he was far from thinking.

He was only feeling.

And feeling awfully darn great.

He ran one finger down the line of her jaw, along the column of her throat, and around her lush breast. She stirred against him and he tightened the leg thrown across her lower body in a simulation of a hug.

She sighed and smiled and stroked him lightly on his back.

"So good," she murmured.

He hadn't even exerted himself to remove the condom. He really should, but the effort to disentangle himself seemed too great. "For two people who just had sex together for the first time," he said, speaking out loud without really thinking, "we sure move well."

She nodded, her hair tickling his chest with the movement of her head. "My body could sense you," she said, almost in awe. She blushed and said, "I guess I haven't lived much."

He drew her close and kissed her brow. "Good. I'll show you everything you ever need to know."

That was when she grew quiet, but Michael, drifting off himself, didn't really pay attention to what should have been a red flag. Holding her close, his breathing slowing, he sank into a sweet slumber.

Stacey clung to Michael, memorizing the feel of his flesh under her touch. She stroked his back lightly, careful not to wake him, and smoothed his hair. He'd softened and drawn away from her body, the condom glistening against his skin. Tenderly, she pulled it free and tossed it into the wastebasket beside the bed. When she moved to do so, he stirred, and she shushed him.

His head dropped back to the side, and Stacy snuggled her backside against his body, fitting her derriere into the curve of his groin, relishing the way he'd made her feel when he'd so dominated her from behind. Just then he stirred and draped one arm around her rib cage. She swallowed, hard, and wondered how she'd live without being able to savor more and more of Michael Halliday.

But live without him she would.

He'd gotten under her skin in a way she never would have predicted. In just a few short days, she'd experienced a range of emotions she hadn't known herself capable of feeling.

He meant too much to her.

And sticking around Doolittle, spending more time with him, especially more time in his arms, would only leave her open to hurt when the inevitable occurred.

Relationships weren't meant to last. Part of her brain acknowledged that truth, while another screamed out against it, naming it a falsehood. But she only knew she couldn't take the pain of losing Michael the way she'd had her life ruptured by Robert's betrayal. If Michael already meant this much to her, how much greater would the agony be?

She placed a kiss on the back of his hand and clung to him as if her life depended on it.

On the porch of the Schoolhouse Inn, Louis looked up in surprise as the front door opened and Joanne slipped out. She'd gone in earlier, in what was for her a rather mellow fashion, following the proprietress to her room. Louis had stayed behind. The cigar he'd chosen was a Churchill, with his favorite ring gauge. Louis hated to rush a good cigar and considered it a crime to hurry a great one.

He'd done that with Joanne, he realized, studying her as she approached. Wooed her, married her, gotten her pregnant, and then rushed off, eager to see what else the world had to offer a young doctor with every trapping of success his for the choosing.

But now Joanne was in her prime, as was he. Or had he seen the most he would make of his days? Brilliant doctor, everyone agreed. Top-flight surgeon. Not a bad golf handicap, either.

In the husband and father category, he knew how he

rated. Indulgent dad; lousy spouse; technically proficient lover. Funny thing about that last category, but no one had ever excited him the way his first wife had. He used to blame her for that, cursing her for the spell she wove over him. And then, determined to break it once and for all, he had cheated on her repeatedly until she discovered him and kicked his ass out of paradise.

"This place is a step back in time," Joanne said, leaning against the porch railing.

No hello. No, that wouldn't be Joanie. He grinned. She hated it when he called her that.

"That it is," he said, eyeing the end of his cigar. "I'm done with this if you'd like to join me on the swing."

She wrinkled her pretty little nose but took a seat beside him. Not too close, not too far.

"What do you know about this doctor?" Joanne asked the question without looking directly at him. Louis turned sideways in the swing. He wanted to make it really difficult for her to avoid his line of vision. Ever since Joanne's front door had swung shut on that baby-faced wonder who probably called himself an actor but earned his living as a waiter in the Quarter, Louis had wanted one thing and one thing alone.

And what Louis wanted, he normally got.

Except when it came to Joanne.

"Seems harmless enough. Intelligent fellow, it would appear, if he's taken to Stacey."

"Robert," Joanne said deliberately, "was intelligent. He was also a prick."

"No accounting for taste, is there?" Louis had let his cigar die out and now he placed the butt on the porch.

He'd probably get detention from those sisters for doing so, but he wanted to have his hands free. Just in case.

"I don't want to see Stacey hurt," Joanne went on. "There had to be something going on if she called you and me to come up here."

"I did find that a bit unusual," Louis said. "But people in love do funny things."

"In love?" Her voice rose. "When did she meet this man?"

He shrugged. "I don't think time matters in these situations."

She was quiet. He watched her, all poise and polish, as unruffled as ever. And that's when he saw it, the pulse that fluttered in her throat. And that's when he wondered if her thoughts were running along the same path as his.

"No," he repeated, rising from the swing and catching himself before he made the mistake of reaching for her hand, "time doesn't matter at all." He stepped toward the door. "I'll see you in the morning."

Michael awoke with a start. Stacey was curled on her side, her back to him. He lifted his arm from around her waist slowly, easing himself away from her and off the bed. Poor darling needed her sleep. Gazing down at her, her face so peaceful, her lips curved upward, he decided not to wake her.

He had to go home, of course.

He had to be there when the girls woke in the morning. Otherwise he wouldn't move from Stacey's side. He forced one leg, then the other into his underwear and jeans, and then stuffed his feet into his shoes, not bothering with his socks. At last he retrieved his shirt from the floor.

Lord, but he hated to leave.

It wasn't just the sex, though his body felt better than it had in a long, lonely time. He felt purified, released from some sentence imposed from both without and within.

Yet he'd found his pleasure at her expense.

Michael frowned. What had he been thinking? He, Mr. Responsible, determined to do the right thing, especially what was best for Stacey, and he'd come back tonight knowing he'd bed her.

After he'd spent the day resisting every temptation to do so.

What had gotten into him?

One glance at Stacey's beautiful body answered that question.

"Idiot," he muttered.

It didn't matter that he wanted her. He knew she was vulnerable. How would she feel in the morning when she woke up? Stacey wasn't a one-night stand type of woman and he couldn't offer her anything beyond that.

He had his family.

They came first.

She had her company, her life in New Orleans.

He ran a hand over his eyes. Here he was, stuck in a town where he didn't belong. For an instant, he longed to be free, wondered what it must have been like to have been as selfish and demanding as Pauline. What would she do if he announced he was relocating to New Orleans?

Would she insist Cecil disrupt his life and the two of

them troop off to Louisiana in order to keep the kids near both parents?

Michael felt cold and lonely as he crossed the room and picked up an afghan from one of the chairs. He walked slowly back to the bed and gazed down at Stacey. Her chest rose and fell in a fluid, peaceful rhythm. She had one hand curled against her cheek. He tucked the crocheted afghan around her. She stirred, but her eyelids didn't even flutter.

The depth of her sleep and magnitude of his own selfish actions reinforced his decision to go home without waking her.

He turned and slipped from the room, knowing as he did that he was leaving behind the most precious woman he'd ever met. Unless, of course, he could convince her to stay.

The knock on Stacey's door the next morning was one she vaguely recognized. It wasn't the irritating tapping of Mrs. Clark or the manly and demanding contact Michael had made.

This sound reminded her of Sundays growing up when she'd been very, very young. It was back before her parents split up. They used to wake her up together and bring hot chocolate and fluffy beignets powdered with sugar on a tray.

Then they'd get ready for church.

It was the primary peaceful memory of her childhood, one she hadn't thought about in such a long time.

"Stacey?"

That was her father's voice. She sat up on the bed, disoriented, tossing off an afghan she didn't remember pulling over herself. And then the events of last night flooded her mind and she cast a wild, despairing glance around the room.

Michael.

He'd left without saying good night, good morning, good-bye.

Her shoulders sagged. Loss snaked through her. She hugged her arms around her body, surprised at how desolate she felt.

"Stacey?"

Oddly enough, that was her mother's voice.

Could the two of them be outside her door at the same time?

Of course he'd had to go home, Stacey told herself sharply. He had his daughters to consider. But all the same, she ached for him and wished she'd been awake to tell him . . .

To tell him what?

"Wait a minute," she called. She rose from the bed, wondering just what she would have told him. That she had fallen for him, and fallen badly, and that she was just plain scared that she couldn't handle that sort of emotional attachment?

She hadn't even told him the truth about her parents.

Part of her argued that none of that mattered. But the rest of her was ruled by her own fears. She brushed her hair back from her face, then dragged on the shorts and shirt Michael had stripped from her body before whipping her into a frenzy of sensual desire and then satisfying her every possible wish, including some she hadn't known she had.

Stacey sighed and wrapped her arms across her chest

again. Don't run away, she told herself. But she knew she would. She'd been running away from herself for at least the past year, since Robert's defection. And if she considered the question honestly enough, she'd have to admit she'd been avoiding a lot of life even before she'd flung herself into the intensely long hours of work she'd racked up since her wedding day that had never happened.

If she couldn't even face herself, how could she make room for Michael—or any man—in her life? But who was to say she needed to worry about such a question? After all, Michael hadn't even stayed the night. He was a guy and he'd gotten what guys wanted. Boy, was she an idiot, worrying about relationships when what they had had was sex.

Sex.

Incredible sex.

Couldn't that be enough? That she even asked the question was answer enough for Stacey.

She caught sight of the wastebasket beside the bed and blushed. "Oh, my," she said aloud, "exactly what I want my parents to see first thing in the morning."

Parents. She'd thought of them together, not as her mother versus her father. She wondered if she'd ever outgrow wanting to see the two of them back together. That would be the day.

"Get a grip," she muttered as she crossed the room and opened the door.

To her amazement, her parents stood there, her dad holding a tray, and on the tray were four mugs, a pot, and a plate of Miss Abbie's heart-shaped muffins. She wondered at the fourth mug as she breathed in the aroma of hot chocolate. Her eyes misted. "Gosh," she said, "what a surprise."

They nodded. "May we come in?" That was her mother, always polite.

"Sure." Stacey opened the door and led the way to the table in front of the windows. Her dad settled the tray, glancing around the room.

"I guess we only need three cups," he said.

Stacy's cheeks warmed. Well, the two of them had obviously assumed Michael had spent the night. "Uh, yes, that's correct," she said.

"Your young man," her mother said, taking the same chair where Michael had sat the morning before, "what's his specialty?"

Exquisite pleasure. "Animals."

"Research?" her dad said, pouring out the hot chocolate. "Up here?"

"He's a veterinarian." Stacey studied her dad. He looked different this morning. Less edgy, younger, happy the way he was when he'd just played eighteen holes at English Turn and come in six under par. Her mother, on the other hand, kept twisting a large amethyst ring on her right hand, a sign that, for that normally self-assured parent, some level of tension was afoot.

"Oh," her mother said. "Well, animals need doctors, too. Is he from Arkansas or somewhere else?"

"Can't be from here," her dad said. "Doesn't talk like the others. He has a touch of Bostonian in his voice."

"I didn't detect that," her mother said.

"Then you apparently didn't listen," her dad answered as he always did. Always right.

Recognition stirred within her. Michael was like that,

too, only much nicer about it. Perhaps that was the difference between veterinarians and orthopedic surgeons, Stacey mused. They were equally dominating, but one expressed it in gentler disguise.

"Tufts," Stacey said. "He was an assistant professor."

"Aha," her dad said.

"So how'd he end up here?" Her mother sipped her chocolate. Miracle of miracles, she let the debate over the Boston accent go without escalating it.

"His ex-wife remarried and he followed to be with his daughters."

"Ah," Joanne said.

Stacey wasn't sure what else to say.

"When is he going back to Boston?" That was her father, who'd risen and walked to the window.

"Oh, I don't think he is." That idea had never occurred to Stacey.

Her father shrugged. "How old are the kids? Once he's got them to a decent age, he can take up where he left off. A man has to think of his career."

"And a woman doesn't?" Her mother plunked her mug down on the tray. "Honestly, Louis, that comment is ridiculous on two counts. One, unless his children are in college, he can't even think of leaving them. And two, well, I won't even dignify that with a response."

"What do you call a decent age?" Stacey was getting that old sick feeling in her gut. Normally she stayed out of her parents' arguments, but she had a decided stake in this discussion.

"Junior high or high school. Kids are resilient. By the time you were thirteen, Stacey Suellen, you wanted nothing to do with your parents," her father said. "If you remember, you spent all your time with your friends. Parents are simply an impediment to be gotten around so one can pursue one's social life."

"Right," Stacey said, feeling thirteen again. "You weren't ever there to notice who I spent time with. You were always off with the bimbo of the day or night."

Her dad started to huff and puff.

"Louis, you know she's right," Joanne said.

Stacey swung toward her mother. "You weren't any better. All you taught me was that if a woman was good enough at her profession she didn't need a man." She shrunk against her chair, both hands cradling her untouched mug of hot chocolate.

"You never knew this, Stacey," her mother said, "but I passed up several excellent positions to stay in New Orleans. I may have failed as a mother in your estimation, and goodness knows I've never had much concept of the whole parenting process, but I did make a few decisions along the way with your best interests in mind."

"I didn't know that," her dad said, regaining his seat at the table.

Her mother shrugged, an elegant lift of her shoulders. "There are many things you don't know."

Stacey stared from her mother to her father. He was gazing at her with a look she'd never seen in his eyes before. Puzzled, Stacey tried to identify it, but the closest word she could think of was admiration.

"And there are many things I should probably apologize for," he said. Then he jumped up and rubbed his hands together. "Well, ladies, as long as we're here, shall we go exploring? We forgot to mention there's a Mrs.

Clark out front chomping at the bit to drive us around some lake."

"You never were comfortable with emotional exchanges," Joanne said.

Stacey stared at her mother. "Are you describing me?"

"Your father," she said, but studying Stacey, she added, "though the DNA doesn't run far from home."

Stacey nodded. She was like her father. Any emotional content drove him away. She'd always thought her mother the unemotional one, the one with every flyaway feeling tamped neatly in place, but perhaps underneath that contained surface she was a maelstrom. Yet at least she experienced the feelings, unlike her father, who retreated. Rather like Kristen, who ran away from the clinic.

And you, Stacey, who run away from relationships.

She stared into her cup.

"Coming with us?" her father asked.

"Where?" she asked.

"This realtor who tracked me down says there's some property we just have to see. Your mother and I discussed it this morning and decided we might as well take a look as long as we're here."

Stacey quit studying her cup. When was the last time the two of them had discussed and agreed on any issue? And why would they bother carrying through with the charade she'd invented? "You guys don't have to do that," she said. "I never should have started the whole train in process."

"Well, you did," her mother said, "so I expect you to follow through with it."

"Go look at retirement property?" Stacey's voice rose. "In Doolittle, Arkansas?" She stared from one parent to the other. "It's sweet of you to carry out my stupid story, but it's not necessary. I'm going home today."

Her mother stared at her, clearly surprised.

"We weren't even supposed to be here until Tuesday. This is Monday. Why are you leaving?"

Stacey shrugged. She felt twelve again, scuffing a toe against the carpet, unable to come up with a decent excuse for why she'd not gotten a book report done on time.

"She's leaving because she's afraid of Michael Halliday."

Stacey glanced in surprise at her father. "That's not true."

"Then stay and prove it," he said. He reached for her mother's hand, a move that shocked Stacey as equally as his insightful challenge.

"Before we go, there's something your mother and I want to say." Her father cleared his throat and looked down at where his hand joined with her mother's.

Anxious, Stacey glanced from one to the other. "You guys are acting pretty funny."

"You mean because we're actually making an effort to be civil to one another, don't you?" That was Joanne, her tone tinged with regret. She slipped her hand free. "Stacey, I shared something with your father earlier today that you should know as well. Several months ago I went through the scare of my life." She toyed with the handle of her teacup. "Breast cancer."

"Mom!" Stacey stared. "And you never said a word."

"I didn't want to worry you. I knew how unhappy you were, after Robert did what he did."

"Forget Robert. What about you? Are you okay?"

Her mother lay a hand across her breast. Stacey wondered whether the gesture was a conscious one. "As it turned out, the surgical biopsy came back benign, despite the very suspicious clustering pattern of the microcalcifications."

"That's doctor talk," Stacey said. "Is everything all right?"

Her mother nodded. "But I did a lot of thinking in the time I waited for the pathology results."

Her dad shook his head. "You should have called us."

Her mother folded her hands in her lap. "We had far too many walls erected around us for that to have been an option for me, Louis." She took a deep breath and looked around the room, then smiled. "Stacey, I am glad you dragged us up here on this wild goose chase, because your father and I have talked, really talked, for the first time in years."

"Or maybe ever?" Her dad had the grace to look a little sheepish as he asked the question.

"Perhaps," Joanne said. "And that brings us to our apology, Stacey."

"Apology?"

Her dad cleared his throat. "We never should have used you the way we did, like a bone between two angry dogs."

"I'm sorry," Joanne said, "and I'm asking your forgiveness."

Stacey stared from one parent to the other. She had

no words. All those years of tension, all those times they'd yanked and pulled and fought over her.

"Me, too," her dad said.

"Thank you for asking," Stacey said slowly, "but all that behavior, well, it's part of me. It's my reality. You can't just wave your hand and make it go away."

Joanne rose and put one hand on Stacey's shoulder. "I know that, but don't let it stand in the way of your happiness. Life is too short for that."

Her dad stood, too. He'd shoved his hands in his pockets and looked none too comfortable.

"Listen to what your father said earlier," Joanne said. "Don't run away from Michael. You liked him enough on sight to concoct this plot to involve us, which means you'll probably explain it to him, too. Follow your heart, not your fears. If he's not right for you, that's another matter."

Her dad had edged toward the door. "We'll wait for you in the parlor. But don't be slow about it. That woman can talk one's ear off."

"I'll be with Louis," her mother said, and the two of them left her room.

Stacey was left sitting there, staring at her parents, wondering when the two of them had ganged up against her. One thing she'd always been able to depend on was that she could play one against the other.

Now, if she weren't to lose face with them, she'd have to stay at least another day.

Maybe she wouldn't run into Michael. Maybe she'd be spared the inevitable embarrassment of being polite the morning after. Perhaps that was why he'd slipped out during the night.

Right.

She showered quickly and changed, at first reaching for the suit she'd worn on Friday, but after holding it against her skin, decided against it. When she closed her eyes, she could feel Michael's kisses on her flesh, his hot lips searing her as he'd lapped the heat from between her thighs. No, the Stacey who'd writhed against Michael like a wanton woman didn't belong in a stuffy navy blue suit.

Instead she donned a skirt and blouse. She hooked her laptop into the phone line and at last e-mailed the work on Key Financial to Donna. She was still amazed her business partner hadn't called yet. But then, she didn't like to roll into the office too early and it was still before ten.

Michael hadn't called, either.

It was just as well.

Stacey stared at the phone line. Well, he couldn't get her as long as she had her computer hooked to the connection. And she'd never given him her cell phone number.

Maybe he'd realized in the warm light of morning that what the two of them had shared, though incredible and intimate and as close to perfection as Stacey had ever dreamed, could exist only in the most fleeting of moments. Real life put such a damper on the flame of passion. Stacey knew she was a chicken, but she couldn't help it. She'd rather live without the heights of passion than risk the depths of suffering she'd experienced before, especially when Michael had already affected her to such a degree.

No matter. She'd go with her parents to see whatever it was Mrs. Clark wanted to show them, and then before she drove home, she intended to sketch out a marketing plan for the animal shelter fund-raiser and leave the disk for Kristen when she picked up True.

And once she was home again, she'd have even more work to keep her busy. She'd make sure of that.

Chapter 21

It had been Joanne who insisted they spend the day with the real estate agent, Stacey figured out as the four of them drove around various golf course vistas and lakefront home lots. She'd evidently concluded that Stacey's future lay north of New Orleans and that she should educate herself as to the locale.

How she'd gotten that impression so swiftly, Stacey couldn't figure out. She would have liked to ask her, but she kept quiet.

But doing so only gave her more time to think about Michael, and to relive every glorious moment of their night together.

She could still feel his sweet touch on her breasts, his greedy and knowing kisses on the most intimate parts of her body. She sighed and realized Mrs. Clark had asked her a question, probably at least three times.

Stacey turned her attention to the realtor, who was backing her tub of a Cadillac out of the parking lot of the visitors' reception building at Lake Doolittle's retirement haven.

"Yes?"

"Oops," Mrs. Clark said with a titter as one tire scraped the curb. "I was saying, which view did you like the best?"

The view when I'm wrapped inside Michael's arms and I can see only him. "Umm, I'm not sure," she answered.

The realtor craned her head to the backseat. "What about you two lovebirds?"

Lovebirds? Stacey glanced at her parents, sitting properly fastened into their seat belts on opposite sides of the wide seat. That was certainly a term she'd never apply to Louis and Joanne St. Cyr. Of course, she'd often thought it odd that her mother hadn't taken back her maiden name of Kelly, but the one time Stacey had asked her, she'd simply said it had been due to professional reasons.

Maybe, Stacey thought wistfully, she had always wanted to be back with her husband.

The way Stacey wished she could go to Michael.

Don't be silly.

But maybe she should. It was too late for her parents, but perhaps it wasn't for her.

"Those brand-new homes," her father was saying, "just aren't what we're used to in New Orleans. I like a sense of history in a house."

"Even my condominium is in a turn-of-the-century building," her mother said, "and I don't mean this past one."

Mrs. Clark laughed gaily. "Oh, you two," she said, "do I have just the treat for you."

"I don't think my parents are actually to the point of purchasing," Stacey said, realizing she should have made this information clear from the beginning, but then how could she, when she'd told such a tangled tale?

Mrs. Clark took one hand off the wheel and patted Stacey on the arm. As she did, the car swerved over the middle white line and then whipped back with a jerk. "Don't you worry about that," she said in a conspiratorial whisper. "I didn't win the Realtor of the Year Award for three years running by sitting home and knitting doilies."

A truck pulled out from a side road and she gunned the gas and sped around it. "I do love a challenge," she said gaily. "Now, Louis and Joanne, we'll take a little drive over to the Horace House."

They headed back toward the town of Doolittle. The five miles raced by as Mrs. Clark described the historic house that had served as the town founder's home a century ago. Sad to say, it had been taken over from its last owner by the First Bank of Doolittle and for the past six years it had sat, boarded up and neglected.

"Just waiting for the right people to come along and take care of it," she said.

Stacey was surprised Michael hadn't adopted the house. He rescued so many other people and things in Doolittle.

As if reading her mind, Mrs. Clark said, "I did try to interest Dr. Mike in it when he first moved here, but he'd have none of it. Said he was all thumbs."

"No doctor is all thumbs," her father said. "The

house probably cost too much. He's a young guy with a family. This sounds like a project for someone with plenty of money and nothing but time on their hands."

"That is true," Mrs. Clark said, peeking in the rearview mirror.

She should save her breath, Stacey thought. Her parents were being unusually nice to this batty lady, but in doing so, they were wasting her time.

"Ooh, someone's had an accident," Mrs. Clark said, screeching to a halt at the Doolittle city limits and pulling over behind a van and a pickup truck.

The back tire had blown on the van. The van was facing them, backward to the direction it had obviously been traveling. A crying woman stood on the side of the road, being comforted by a man—a tall man with dark hair and broad shoulders.

"Why, that looks like Penelope Winston's van. And there's Dr. Mike to the rescue," she said. "My, my, some women will stop at nothing."

Stacey stared. Sure enough. He had his arms around the woman and was patting her on the back. She swallowed the lump in her throat as she pictured those same hands on her back, her breasts, her thighs. "What do you mean?" Stacey hoped she'd made it sound like a casual question as the woman outside clung to Michael, arms wrapping around his neck.

"Oh, she's been after him since the day he set foot in town, along with the other single ladies," the realtor said. "Not that I blame her. If Mr. Clark were to take to his grave, I might do the same."

"I see," Stacey said. Well, who wouldn't pursue a successful, intelligent, caring, sexy guy? There couldn't be anyone else like him in Doolittle.

Even in New Orleans, she'd never met anyone who held a candle to him. But, watching him now, she asked herself how well she knew him.

Mrs. Clark rolled down the window. "Yoo-hoo," she called. "Do you want me to call Ricky's Garage for a tow truck?"

Michael turned and peered at the car and the familiar voice of Mrs. Clark. When he did, he managed to free himself from Penelope's rather soggy grasp. Any man would have stopped to assist her in this predicament, but he'd wished it were anyone other than the widow who'd chased him despite his having made it as clear as possible that he wasn't interested in her.

He started to wave her on, say he'd take care of the tire himself, and then he realized who her passengers were.

He stepped to the car, Penelope trailing beside him, still sniffling. Ever so slowly the passenger window of the Cadillac lowered. He came face-to-face with Stacey, but only Mrs. Clark's voice pierced the silence, joined by Penelope as she began to detail the trauma of her blown tire in a high-pitched tone of hysteria that did nothing to calm Michael's irritation at being caught in such an awkward situation.

He could tell by Stacey's shuttered glance that all sorts of terrible thoughts were rushing through her mind. Why had he left last night without saying goodbye? Why had he given in to his desires in the first place?

But he couldn't be blamed for that.

Michael placed one hand on the car door. Penelope rattled on. Michael said, "Are you okay?"

"Of course I'm not okay," Penelope said.

Stacey nodded. "Sure," she said. "Why wouldn't I be?"

Ice couldn't have been any colder. Michael turned to Penelope, who'd snaked an arm through his. "I'm going to my truck to call Ricky."

"Oh, I'll do it," Mrs. Clark said, reaching for her cell phone.

"I'm just so lucky you came along when you did," Penelope said, resting her head on his shoulder.

He said nothing.

Stacey said nothing.

From the backseat came not a word, but Stacey's mother was looking at him in a way that made him squirm.

"All set," Mrs. Clark said, ringing off. "Well, we'll just run along. I'm taking the St. Cyrs to see Horace House."

"You are?" Now, that was interesting news. Why would two New Orleanians let themselves be dragged to that money sink? Mrs. Clark had tried to persuade him it was the best investment in town, but one look at the rambling old Victorian that had also served as a boardinghouse had sent him running to the comfortable and modern house he'd purchased.

"They like old houses," Mrs. Clark said, glancing in her side mirror. "You two be good out here." And then she pulled out onto the road, spitting gravel.

Michael stood there, staring after her car, wondering how long it would take before he could get to Stacey and talk to her. Even though he knew he should leave her alone and let her get on with her life, he couldn't let her think he'd had sex with her last night and had something going on the side with Penelope Winston.

"Michael, you are so good to help me," Penelope said. "How can I ever thank you?"

He disengaged her arm from him. "You can purchase a pound puppy poster from my daughter," he said, staring down the road. Mrs. Clark's Cadillac was a blur on the horizon.

As he watched it disappear around a curve, Michael realized something he should have known last night, that morning, certainly sooner than that very instant.

He wanted Stacey.

No matter the price he had to pay, he wanted her in his life.

"I don't think you've listened to a word I've said," Penelope said.

Michael nodded. She'd finally gotten one thing right—and so had he.

Pleading a headache, Stacey asked Mrs. Clark to drop her off at the inn. Once there, she loitered outside, hoping neither Abbie nor Martha would spot her. She'd had enough chatty conversation to last her for a solid week, if not month. As soon as the Caddy rounded the corner, she fished her keys from her purse and drove away in her own car.

With Michael rescuing the winsome Ms. Winston, the coast was clear for her to visit True.

She longed to bury her face in True's fluffy fur and give her cheek over for a happy doggie tongue-licking. For pure, unconditional love and comfort, no one matched True.

She found Michael's house without mishap. A small blue Ford was pulling away from the driveway when she arrived. Hoping she'd find Mrs. Beebe at home, Stacey let herself in through the front gate. From the side yard the shepherd, poodle, and Lab set up a bark fest.

Stacey couldn't blame them, they were doing their job, but she was thankful Michael had the front yard safely fenced off from the back.

Before she could ring the doorbell, Mrs. Beebe appeared and swung the door wide. With all the racket made by the dogs, that wasn't too surprising. "Well, a-sure and look who it is," the housekeeper said with a welcoming smile.

True pushed around the housekeeper and bounded up to Stacey, flinging her doggie self against her legs. Stacey knelt down and wrapped her arms around her dog. In the back of her mind, she wished she could do the same to Michael.

"I think she knew it was you at the door," Mrs. Beebe said, guiding Stacey inside and closing the front door behind her. Outside, the dogs calmed down.

"You're looking especially pretty today," Stacey said, noting the eye shadow and lipstick that livened Mrs. Beebe's face and took a few years off her age. She hadn't worn any makeup Saturday evening.

Mrs. Beebe blushed. "Why, thank you, dear. Come on in the kitchen with me, if you don't a-mind. It's the ironing I've been doing."

True leapt alongside Stacey as they crossed the length of the hall, obviously overjoyed at their reunion. Stacey followed Mrs. Beebe to the spacious kitchen with the first real smile of the day lighting her face.

There she hugged True again and laughed as her dog tickled her neck with her tongue. A pang of guilt struck at Stacey, as she thought of how many hours she left True alone day after day and how she'd foisted even the daily dog-walking duties off on the girl next door. Leaning down, she ran a hand lightly over True's belly, which felt heavier, fuller.

Mrs. Beebe bustled between the refrigerator and the cupboards, pouring iced tea and setting out a plate of cookies. Stacey looked up from True. Oddly enough, no clothes sat out on the ironing board and the iron wasn't even plugged in. Beside the board sat a hamper full of clothes. Maybe she hadn't said she'd been doing the ironing. Well, that was none of Stacey's business. She had trouble enough just minding her own.

"Can you believe I didn't know my dog was pregnant?" Stacey regarded her dog, the canine tongue lolling, head cocked to one side, studying her in return.

"Well, if the dear dog could speak, I'm sure she'd be a-saying she forgives you. Have a glass of tea, dear, and sit a spell." Mrs. Beebe set her glass down on a counter near the ironing board and, with a quick glance toward Stacey, bent down and plugged in the iron.

Stacey sat on a kitchen chair. She wasn't too comfortable loafing while the older woman worked, but it was homey there in the kitchen, and unlike the nonstop noise of Mrs. Clark's chatter, Stacey enjoyed Mrs. Beebe's conversation. True settled beside her feet, her nose wet and cold against her bare ankle.

"It's a sweet-natured dog she is," Mrs. Beebe said, shaking out a shirt she lifted from the top of the basket.

Stacey recognized it as one of Michael's. Like a sentimental fool, she gazed at the shirt, picturing it on his solid chest and shoulders. She must have sighed, because Mrs. Beebe glanced at her, rather sympathetically, Stacey realized.

"You and Dr. Mike seem like two people who have a-been knowing each other for a time longer than you have," she said.

"We do, don't we?" Stacey was grateful to be able to talk to someone who knew Michael, though of course, she cautioned herself, Mrs. Beebe was not at all impartial. She regarded Michael as her savior, which by every account he had indeed been.

"It's like that with some people," Mrs. Beebe said, briskly reducing the wrinkles in the body of the shirt to sleek cotton. "Take me and Sam, for instance."

"Who's Sam?" Stacey perked up. It was nice to be able to consider someone else's situation. Her own life simply sent her mind whirling in circles of desire, battling responsibility, fighting off fear of what might be and what might then be lost to her.

"He is my friend, but it would seem he'd like to be a-more than my friend."

On impulse, Stacey said, "Does he drive a blue Ford?"

"How did you be a-knowing that?" Mrs. Beebe tugged the shirt off the board and slipped it onto a hanger.

"I saw it leaving as I drove up," Stacey said.

Mrs. Beebe sipped her tea. Stacey did the same. True let out a satisfied doggie sigh and settled her nose lower on her paws.

"Once a woman's been hurt, and hurt bad," Mrs. Beebe said, spreading the next garment out on the board, "it's real hard to trust again."

Stacey nodded vigorously. She couldn't agree more.

"It's Sam who owns the feed store near the highway," she said. "He's a good man. His wife died more than twelve months ago and he's been a-hankering after me for the last oh-number of weeks."

"Do you like him?"

Mrs. Beebe shrugged and chased away a few more wrinkles from what looked like it might be one of Jessica's dresses. "What's not to like? He goes to church, he pays his taxes, he owns his company and does right well by himself."

"But there's more to a man than those factors, isn't there?" Stacey slipped her hand up and down the moist exterior of her iced tea glass. Robert had met all those criteria and he'd turned out to be a schmuck.

"Aye, to be sure," Mrs. Beebe said. She turned her blue eyes on Stacey and said, "Now, Michael, he's a man you can trust. And I'm a-thinking Sam is, too, but my heart is wary."

Stacey remembered her tale of the abuse she suffered at the hands of her ex-husband until Michael stepped in to put a stop to it. She also saw vividly in her mind the sight of Michael with his arms around that Winston woman. "Of course you're cautious," she said, reaching out a hand to the sweet woman who'd taken her into her confidence. "Nobody likes to be hurt."

Mrs. Beebe was shaking her head. "And that's to be sure." A shudder seemed to run across her shoulders and she said, "But I knew Sam's wife and she was a woman who seemed happy for her husband to come home at night."

"Why don't you spend some time with him and get to know what he's like?" Well, gosh, Stacey, should you take your own advice?

The housekeeper glanced rather shyly at Stacey and said, "That's what Sam said this afternoon when he was here. He asked me to go to the spaghetti dinner at the church with him this Friday night."

"Well, why don't you do it?"

Mrs. Beebe applied the iron vigorously to a pair of denim shorts. "Oh, I'm not sure it makes good sense. I'm happy here. Dr. Mike takes good care of me and it's his children I'm coming to love like they were my own. I don't know that I could up and leave him if things were to move forward the way I am a-knowing Sam intends them to."

"If you would be happy with Sam, Michael would never stand in your way," Stacey said, knowing she was right in that conclusion.

"But who's going to take care of him? He goes out all times of the night to take care of other people's problems. Someone has to stay with those little girls, and the Lord knows that mama of theirs is useless. How any woman on this God's green earth could want Cecil over Michael, I'll never be knowing."

"Is that the only reason you're reluctant to go to the dinner with Sam?" Stacey asked the question in a gentle voice, fairly certain she knew the answer.

Mrs. Beebe folded the denim shorts and held them

against her waist. "It's a fearful thing to trust one's heart."

"Oh, Mrs. Beebe, you're right," Stacey said, wishing she could trust her own.

A long moment of silence passed. The two women gazed at each other, then Mrs. Beebe said, "Well, if you and Michael would be willing to go there with me and Sam, I wouldn't be quite so likely to hold back."

"Me . . . and Michael?" Stacey heard the squeak in her own voice. "But you said the dinner isn't until Friday night. Today is only Monday. I really have got to be getting home."

"Oh," Mrs. Beebe said, dejection plain in her voice. "And here I was a-thinking you had taken a vacation."

"Well, yes I did," Stacey said, "but some problems have come up at work." Yeah, but Key Financial was simple to deal with, unlike the attraction she felt toward Michael.

Mrs. Beebe said nothing. She sipped her iced tea and stared at True. "Your precious dog is awfully happy here. And it's a shame you have to rush off. Life is too short to be working all the time."

Stacey reached down and stroked True's ears. Her mother had said the same words to her. What harm would it do her to stay? As long as she kept in touch with Donna, she didn't have to be back at work until a week from today. Mrs. Beebe was a sweetheart and if Stacey could help someone else find happiness and love, maybe it would make her own situation more satisfying. But she'd rather bury herself in work than experience the heights of passion and the depths of pain.

Michael had the power to bring both extremes to her life. For now, all she said to Mrs. Beebe was, "I'll think about it."

Mrs. Beebe nodded. If she was disappointed, she kept it to herself.

Stacey sipped her tea and listened as Mrs. Beebe described life in Doolittle and then turned to what appeared to be one of her favorite topics, the life and times of Dr. Michael Halliday.

Of course, that might have been simply because she was as keen on matchmaking as Donna had been on forcing Stacey to take a vacation.

She stopped ironing long enough to disappear into another room and then return carrying a photo of Michael, resplendent in an Air Force uniform, an alert dog also sporting a jaunty flight cap at his heels.

Stacey was surprised. "I didn't know Michael was in the military," she said.

Mrs. Beebe handed her the photograph and returned to her ironing. "That's how he paid for his vet school. Six kids in his family, and college is expensive. He told me he'd always had a way with animals. He gave a few years to the Air Force and they paid for him to go to school." She said it proudly, as if Michael had been her own son, and in many ways, Stacey supposed, Mrs. Beebe regarded Michael in exactly that light.

All in all, Stacey was impressed. She gazed down at the photograph of him, smiling into the dark eyes of the serious-faced man. She'd taken it for granted that if she'd followed in her parents' footsteps and gone to medical school, they would have written a check for it, the same way they'd paid for her undergraduate education.

"Oh, yes," Mrs. Beebe said, "he's a fine man who doesn't let anything stop him when it's a goal he's got fixed in his mind."

She hung a shirt on a hanger. "It's a good thing I only let Jessica work the dryer that one week," she said.

Stacey remembered the tantalizing glimpse she'd gotten of Michael's abdomen the night they'd met. "Jessica helps with the laundry?"

"Oh, yes. And Kristen sets and clears the table for dinner. They both take care of the dogs and cats, too, and straighten their rooms. Michael, he's a rare one for a-teaching his girls responsibility. It's a shame not all children have a father as good as he is."

"So with Michael as their dad they don't miss their mother too much?" It was a bold and nosy statement, but Stacey had to admit to herself she was curious as to Mrs. Beebe's take on the subject.

Mrs. Beebe shook out a pair of slacks. "I'm not one to gossip, but Ms. Pauline's not the mothering sort. Some women should be taken care of the way animals are, if you take my meaning." She smiled down at True. "Though it's a good thing not all are." She made a scissoring motion with two fingers.

Fixed, she had to mean. Stacey reflected on how her own mother would have fared with such a rule in place and said, "Well, usually even the worst mothers mean well at some level."

Mrs. Beebe sniffed, then said, "Well, Kristen and Jessica are blessings, to be sure."

Stacey said, "And they are lucky to have a most wonderful father."

Mrs. Beebe regarded her indulgently. "Oh, and that

they are." She paused, and then said, "So you think I should be a-going to that dinner Friday night?"

"Oh, of course," Stacey said, thinking she'd already made that clear. She glanced at her watch, and gasped as she realized how much time had passed. She really should be leaving, before the girls arrived home from school and Michael returned from work—or from rescuing the latest woman in distress.

"And you'll consider helping me out?"

"Well, I said I'd think it over. Does Michael know about this plan for him and me to go along to the spaghetti dinner Friday night so you'll feel safe with Sam?"

Mrs. Beebe smiled. "He does now," she said, inclining her head toward the doorway, where Michael stood, filling the room with his presence.

Chapter 22

Michael couldn't have asked for a more welcome sight than Stacey sitting in his kitchen. She looked adorable. But something more than that added to the picture. She belonged there.

Oh, he knew she'd only come to visit her dog, but his heart leapt at the fanciful idea despite the reality. She hadn't come to the house in search of Michael. If looks could kill, both he and Penelope Winston would be lying along the side of Highway 8 at that moment.

"Hello, Stacey," he said, stepping into the room. "Mrs. Beebe, as always you are a marvel of efficiency."

Then he sniffed the air. "Is something burning?" Yeah, something besides his body. Just being in Stacey's presence got him going.

Mrs. Beebe jerked her hand upward. The odor of scorched fabric wafted from the surface of the ironing board. "Oh, well, would you be looking at what I've done," she said. "Me with my mind running off in all sorts of circles instead of keeping it here on what it is I'm doing."

Michael smiled. "We all do that, Mrs. Beebe. Besides, if you had to pick one shirt to ruin, it was that one. I look ghastly in brown."

She looked doubtfully at him. He stayed where he was, as always the picture of Mrs. Beebe as she'd been when she first came to live with his family vivid in his mind. She'd flinched at any sudden approach by him or any other man. Stuffing his hands in his trouser pockets, he said, "Yep, I positively hated that shirt."

Stacey smiled up at him. "Blue does suit you better."

"See, Mrs. Beebe, you've done me a favor."

The housekeeper's lips were puckered up and her brow was clouded, but slowly she relaxed. "Maybe I shouldn't be saying yes to dinner with Sam if one little thing makes my mind that fuzzy."

"But that's a sign that you should go," Stacey said, then clamped her mouth closed.

Michael grinned. "And I take it we're to be your double date?" He lay one hand on the back of the chair where Stacey sat. She craned her neck to glance up at him. He would have given a lot to be able to decipher her expression. "Sam's a good man. He's crazy about that American Eskimo dog of his. Anyone who loves a dog that much can't have a bad bone in his body."

"Yes, he is a good man," Mrs. Beebe agreed, "but I would still be wanting you to be there, too. That is, if you would be willing," she said, digging in a drawer, then returning to the ironing board with a tube of cleaner and a cloth.

"And it's not until Friday night?"

Mrs. Beebe nodded.

Michael couldn't swear, but he thought Stacey was holding her breath. Had she agreed? Mentally, he ticked off Tuesday, Wednesday, Thursday, Friday. Four more days to convince her, using his newly conceived approach, that she was meant to spend the rest of her life with him.

"Well, I don't know," Michael said. "I don't much care for spaghetti."

Mrs. Beebe stared at him. "But you always say you like it. If I'd a-known that, I wouldn't have cooked it so much."

"Oh, no," he corrected hastily, "I like yours. It's what they're likely to pass off at the church for five bucks a plate that makes me hesitate."

"Well, then, I'll volunteer to cook and you can get some of what it is you're used to," Mrs. Beebe said, swiping the iron with the cleaner.

Some of the residual odor from the scorched shirt drifted through the room. Michael ignored it. It wouldn't do to tease Mrs. Beebe too much. She was still a fragile sort. And sure enough, Sam would be the perfect husband for her.

"As long as I don't have to eat Pauline's," Michael said.

"Is she going?" That was Stacey. Mrs. Beebe knew full well that Pauline considered herself one of the ruling troika of her church's women's group. She did it to help Cecil in politics, she said, but Michael knew she only wanted to be in charge.

She was so damn bossy.

He gazed down at Stacey's glossy hair and wished he could run his hands through it. No wonder he'd taken such an exception to Stacey that first night. She'd appeared just as much of a control freak as his ex-wife. But watching her in his kitchen, her dog curled at her feet, her concern for Mrs. Beebe's welfare evident, he could scarcely recall that image of her.

"Oh, yes," Michael said. "She and Cecil are involved in the church."

Mrs. Beebe smiled. "And that's a nice way for you to be saying that."

"I can be a nice guy," Michael said, crossing the room and pouring a glass of iced tea for himself. He leaned against the counter and studied Stacey openly.

She tilted her chin upward, obviously aware of his scrutiny, almost challenging him to look his fill.

He smiled, a slow curving of his lips, as he did exactly that. Ever since he'd turned the pesky Penelope over to Ricky and his tow truck, he'd been considering the best way to get Stacey to overcome her fears of intimacy. The one thing he knew was that chasing her would only drive her away. So, hands off had to be his policy. But admiring the curve of her calves and following the line of her legs where her short, flippy skirt covered them warned him he'd have a tough time sticking to his plan. And the swell of her breasts . . . He turned and dumped his ice cubes into the sink, thinking if he had an ounce of sense he'd slip one or two of them into his pants. Even from across the room, she had the power to beckon him.

But some things were worth waiting for. And Stacey had to feel safe with him or she'd be unable to give the two of them a chance.

"Are you planning to be in town on Friday, Stacey?" He forced a casual tone to his question, knowing full well Mrs. Beebe didn't need a double date or a chaperone.

"I'd like to help, Mrs. Beebe, but I'm afraid I have to get back to my office."

Mrs. Beebe, looking from Michael to Stacey and back again, turned her iron off and said, "I'll be going upstairs to put these things away." Loaded with a stack of pressed laundry, she scurried from the room.

Silence reigned.

Michael broke the quiet with a small chuckle. "Subtle she's not."

Stacey squared her shoulders. Clearly she wasn't in a laughing mood. "I'm sure she needed to put the clothes where they belong."

"And I'm sure you have to rush back to New Orleans this very day."

"That's right."

He lifted his brows. "Your parents arrived only last night."

Her chin took on an even more stubborn stance. "They're adults. They'll manage without me."

"So will your company."

"You don't know anything about my business," she said primly, reminding him of the night they'd met.

He ran a hand through his hair, then advanced on her. True remained calm, obviously sensing Michael meant no harm. But it was more than Michael could stand for Stacey to run away so soon. Of course, she had to leave at the end of her vacation. But not today. Not now, when he'd met a woman who delighted his mind, set his blood on fire, and, to top it off, got along with his kids. Michael stopped in front of her, close, near enough to kiss her.

"Wh-what are you doing?"

Instead of answering, he pulled her into his arms and crushed her mouth to his. She gasped and struggled briefly.

He loosened his grip. "I'm not going to hurt you," he said, his voice low in his throat. "But I am going to talk some sense into you." He smoothed her hair with one hand and spoke soft and low, his lips near her ear. "You're afraid to stay here, afraid to see if what you feel for me is worth the risk of hurt."

"No!" Stacey pushed against his chest with one fist. Then she met his gaze and said, "Why do you care? You can take whatever her name is with the flat tire to the dinner dance." Then she clapped one hand over her mouth.

Michael wrinkled his brow. "You mean Penelope Winston?"

She nodded.

"Forget about her."

"It's beneath my dignity to feel jealous," Stacey said slowly, "so I shouldn't have mentioned it, but I can't forget about her. You were standing there with your arms around her. I know we just met, but if there's something I can't handle—"

"Shh." Michael caught her close and hugged her to his body. "She clung to me. We went out for dinner one time. Over soup she confessed she can't stand dogs." He grimaced. "Too bad we had to finish the meal."

Stacey smiled, somewhat weakly.

Michael grinned and added, "If she ever stopped by the house, the girls would no doubt find a way to trap her in the back yard with our entire menagerie. They sure wouldn't like her the way they like you."

Stacey uncurled her fists and considered Michael's words. "They like me?"

He brushed a lock of hair from her cheek and nodded.

She sighed. It was nice to hear, but that information shouldn't affect her decision. The sooner she left Doolittle, the sooner she'd get her life back to normal. She started to shake her head.

"You don't strike me as a coward," Michael said.

"I am no such thing!"

"Are, too."

"Am not." Stacey was embarrassed to realize she stamped her foot to prove the truth of her words.

"Prove it." He pinned her against the wall, his gaze roving her as intimately as if he were using his hungry fingers to explore every inch of her flesh.

Her traitorous lips parted. She was breathing hard and fast. The one thing she should be doing was running out the door. Instead, she whispered, "Okay, I will."

"Stay till Friday, then?"

She swallowed. What strange power was it Michael held over her? With her pinky finger, she traced the line of his mouth. "I never can refuse a challenge."

He caught her finger between his lips and sucked it gently.

Her tummy flip-flopped in a most pleasant way. He

lifted his other hand and guided her finger in and out, in and out between his warm lips.

Stacey was finding it pretty darn hard to breathe. Her breasts rose and fell rapidly with the racing of her heart. "I must be insane," she murmured, placing her other hand around Michael's waist and pulling him tight against her body.

He groaned, dropped his hand from hers, and cupped her derriere against his groin. Then, abruptly, with a warning shake of his head, he released her and stepped back. The dogs started barking. True sat up and looked all around and then the front door banged open and shut, twice, and footsteps came running toward the kitchen.

Kristen and Jessica burst into the room.

"I'm starved," Kristen said.

"Me, too," Jessica said.

Mrs. Beebe entered the room in their wake.

"Hey, it's Stacey-o," Kristen said, flipping her a wave as she headed straight to the refrigerator. She turned back around, a Pepsi in her hand, and was just about to pop the top when Michael, now a few steps from Stacey, shot her a warning look.

She stuck it behind her back. "Dad, you're home early."

Jessica sidled over to her dad. He gave her a hug and she danced away, circling her sister's back and pointing.

"Jessica," Michael said, "come here."

She did, a grin on her face, an expression of triumph that quickly faded as Michael said, "Nobody likes a tattletale."

Kristen stuck her tongue out at her little sister.

"And to think I was about to ask you two if you'd like to visit the new puppies and take some pictures for the posters," Michael said, shaking his head.

You two. Stacey reached down and stroked True's head, the better to cover her disappointment. This man would drive her crazy, one minute kissing her, the next making her wonder if she'd imagined his actions. Perhaps she should excuse herself and return to the inn. Her parents might be back.

"Dad, we want to see them. We saved them," Kristen said.

"You can start by putting that soda back in the fridge and pouring yourself a glass of milk, and one for your sister," Michael said. "Then homework. If you've managed to behave yourselves, we'll go to the clinic after dinner."

Maybe Stacey could take her parents to dinner. Surely the town had dining accommodations other than Sonic, DQ, and Steak 'n Shake. She'd ask the Schoolhouse Sisters for a recommendation. Stacey forced her body to rise from the chair. "I was on my way out," she said.

"You were?" Kristen wailed. "But you can't be. I need your help for the project."

"What would you do if Stacey hadn't happened to be here?" Michael asked.

Kristen danced across the room toward her father. "Get you to go pick her up." She winked. "I know you would have said yes."

"Stacey's a professional marketing consultant," Michael said. "Have you and the others figured out how you're going to pay her for her services?"

Kristen's mouth dropped open. "Pay her? Dad, we don't have any money. Other than our allowance, and we need that. CDs aren't cheap, you know." She giggled.

"I already said I'd volunteer my services," Stacey said.

"You don't really want to do that," Michael said. "It will be a lot of work."

"I wouldn't have said it if I didn't mean it," Stacey said, surprised at Michael's comment. One minute he wanted her to stay in town, and now he appeared to be discouraging her participation.

And then she got it.

His mind and his heart were as equally at war as her own.

Somehow, that realization comforted her, and made her feel a lot less like arguing the point with him. After all, the issue wasn't the issue. She gave him one of her sweetest smiles and wasn't at all surprised at the puzzled look he shot back in return.

Jessica, who had moved over and was helping Mrs. Beebe fold some of the laundry, said, "Yeah, I thought Stacey was helping because she loves animals."

"I love animals, too," Michael said, "but I still charge for my professional services. And realizing the cost will be a good lesson for Kristen and her teammates."

"Nobody paid for you to fix the dog's leg and deliver the puppies," Jessica said.

"She's got you there," Kristen said.

"But I can't afford to do that for every animal, or who would pay for your Barbies and CDs and MP3 players?"

"Dad, if she said it's free, leave it alone," Kristen said. "Stacey-o knows her own mind."

"Out of the mouths of babes," Stacey murmured.

Michael shot her a rueful look. "You win this point."

Stacey smiled, doubly pleased she'd seen through his objections. Wanting to drive him a little bit crazy, the way he'd been doing to her, she said, "I'll do most of my consulting work on the project from New Orleans. It won't disrupt my schedule much at all." There, let him mull over that statement. No doubt he thought she'd have to be running up to Doolittle every other weekend.

"Won't you need to be here to help?" Jessica said.

"Oh, give me a laptop, a cell phone, and a fax line and I'm downright dangerous," Stacey said.

"But you could come visit, right?" Jessica said, those dark eyes that saw too much pinned on Stacey.

"Would you like that?" Michael asked the question Stacey couldn't.

Jessica tipped her head to the side and looked from her dad over to Stacey. She even studied True. She picked up the next piece of laundry, a bright pink pair of her shorts. "As long as she brings me one of True's puppies, that would be okay."

Stacey glanced quickly at Michael. She caught the almost imperceptible nod he gave her. "It's a deal," she said.

"Cool," Kristen proclaimed.

Michael poured himself a glass of milk. Staring into the glass, he said, "You have your laptop and your cell phone with you now, right?"

"Uh-yes." Stacey wasn't sure why he was asking when he knew the answer already.

"Given that, and considering I have a fax at my office, you just proved that you didn't need to rush back to New Orleans today in order to work."

His expression was far too triumphant for Stacey to

accept meekly. She fell back on the technique that worked so well for Jessica and Kristen and stuck her tongue out at Michael.

He grinned and saluted her with his glass of milk.

Mrs. Beebe moved from the ironing board to the oven. Stacey decided it was safer to focus on food rather than the far-too-appealing Michael. She watched as Mrs. Beebe pulled open the oven door and peeked at its contents. The delicious aroma of roast beef filled the air. Her mouth watered. True's ears perked up. Stacey had noticed the fragrant smell earlier but hadn't asked about it, not wanting Mrs. Beebe to think she was angling for a dinner invitation.

"Yuck, not pot roast," Kristen said.

"That's it," Michael said, pointing to the door to the hall. "Upstairs and to your homework now."

"But what about Stacey?" She dragged her feet out of the kitchen. "Is she staying for dinner?"

"We'll let Stacey decide," Michael said.

He stood there looking at her, a half smile in his eyes, his mouth a straight line. He wanted her to say yes, Stacey was positive. Yet, would it not be better if she left? Why make the pain of parting harder than it was already going to be?

It wasn't just about her and Michael, though. Jessica was watching her with those big dark eyes of hers. Trust shone in them. If she walked out, Jessica would have less faith in adults being willing to help for the sake of helping.

Stacey didn't want to burn that lesson in her generous mind.

It was only dinner, and then she could excuse herself when they drove to the clinic. She had her own car.

Kristen was almost to the doorway. "Once you've done the rest of your homework," Stacey said, "I'll brainstorm your marketing plan with you. If the others want to come over, that's okay by me, as long as it's all right with your dad."

"Yes!" Kristen waved her casted arm. "I knew you were okay, Stacey-o."

Jessica, unbidden, followed her sister from the room. Michael nodded, apparently satisfied with the outcome, but then said, "Mrs. Beebe, go ahead with dinner, and Stacey, you are definitely staying as our guest, but I need to get back to the clinic and check on some of the day's surgery cases. I'll be back to pick up the girls at seven." He paused and then said, "And Stacey, too, if you'd like to see what day-old pups look like. And considering you and True are going to be doggie moms, that might be a good idea."

Practical reasons.

Not, *Please come, I want to spend every waking, and sleeping moment with you.*

What did she expect?

But if he was trying to drive her nuts, wouldn't that be exactly the right approach to take?

What if he weren't, though? What if he'd had his pleasure and he truly wasn't interested in her?

Michael walked toward her, smiled down at her, and said gently, "It's not that complicated."

She broke into a smile. "Oh, it is, but I can handle complicated."

He grinned and strode from the room, singing a tune under his breath Stacey couldn't quite make out.

*   *   *

By the time Stacey made it through a meeting with the five twelve-year-olds and dinner with Kristen and Jessica absent the calming influence of their father, she was thankful she hadn't opted for a career as a teacher. She wouldn't have lasted a day.

The kids were bright and enthusiastic about the project. In exchange for her services, they offered to give her program credit on the dog show brochure. That was Bobby's solution. He'd seen "provided by" credits on various television shows and figured there had to be some worth to Stacey if the people who came to the dog show knew her company had helped out.

Kristen had liked that Bobby was so smart. That hadn't been hard for Stacey to figure out, because while she bossed the other three around, she hung back slightly with Bobby.

Ah, puppy love, Stacey reflected.

But did it ever get any less complicated, this crazy thing men and women did, trying to find happiness, seeking the opposite of themselves in order to complete the internal circle of self? She'd grown unusually philosophical, but the situation lent itself to such ponderings. Here she was, surrounded by Michael's family, and no Michael. At the same time, she was still determined to keep her feelings buttoned up. There was no point in letting him know how much he'd affected her when she felt paralyzed to act on those feelings.

Stacey sighed and True, who'd settled in the living room with them, nudged her knee.

All the kids had permission to visit the puppies. The more children involved, she reasoned, the more likely all their friends and relatives were to spring for purchasing posters. Stacey had volunteered to go after her camera, locked safely in the trunk of her car, and shoot photos to be turned into posters.

Leaving the house ahead of the others also meant she'd be gone before Michael returned.

"I'll see you all at the clinic," Stacey said. She hugged True and told her to stay. After saying good-bye to Mrs. Beebe and thanking her for dinner and her company, Stacey slipped out the front door. Behind her, the kids were debating whether they should be in a group photo or have separate pictures taken with the puppies.

"Darn it," she said, fumbling with the catch on the front gate as Michael drove up.

He lowered the window of his truck. "Stacey, I hate to put you out," he called, "but it occurs to me that we're not all going to fit in my truck."

"That's true," she said slowly.

"Would you mind taking the others with you?"

"Oh, of course not," she said, forcing a cheeriness she didn't feel. What she'd hoped to avoid was any—yet longed-for—one-on-one time with Michael. Left alone together, the two of them were dangerous. Even when she argued with him, she wanted his mouth taking hers, his hands exploring her body.

"I'll run in and round them up," he said, climbing from the truck. As he came even with her, he reached out and opened the gate for her. His hand brushed hers and she jumped from the heat that flashed between them.

"Stacey," he said.

"Yes, Michael?" She held her breath.

He gazed at her, then said rather matter-of-factly, "You're a real trouper to help the kids."

That was it? No, he'd been about to say something else, she was sure of it.

"It's no problem," she finally managed to say, standing there inhaling the nearness of him, wishing she could fling her arms around him and beg him not to let her run away from what might be the best chance at happiness she'd ever know.

He flicked a strand of hair away from her eyes, and for a second she thought he was going to kiss her. His mouth practically formed the shape of her own, and then he turned on his heel and headed for the porch. "Be right back," he said. "Don't go anywhere."

Chapter 23

Twenty-four hours earlier, Louis wouldn't have cred-
ited such a possibility, but he was starting to appreciate
the front porch of the Schoolhouse Inn.

Even though porch-sitting, as it was known in his
own hometown of New Orleans, was a fine art, it was
one he'd never practiced.

He was always too busy. You didn't get to be top dog
in the busiest orthopedic medical group in the city by
kicking back and watching the elephant ears grow.

Maybe it was the swing with room for two that ap-
pealed to him. Right now he was there alone, Joanne
having gone to her room to check in with her own staff
and return any necessary patient calls.

Doctors never left their work in the office, Louis reflected, pushing against the wide beams of the porch
surface with one foot.

He'd never intended to retire. Everyone told him he
was the youngest sixty-year-old around. But something
had clicked in his head during the day. Oh, it wasn't the

canned environment of that dotty retirement community. He'd slit his wrists before he did anything like that. Still, all in all, he had gathered food for thought.

He patted the front pocket of his shirt for the cigar he'd placed in waiting, lifted it out, and then decided against indulging. Joanie had been positively charming all day, not even complaining when the heel of her shoe broke off in the moldering flooring of the Horace House.

She'd limped lopsided through the rest of the eyesore, posture perfect, her composure unruffled.

Joanie was one hell of a woman.

Problem was, she deserved one hell of a man, something she'd gone her entire life without.

Louis gazed across the flower beds that marched down toward the street and wondered if he'd learned enough in his travels to be the man for his ex-wife.

The door opened and he knew without turning his head that it was Joanie. Rather than joining him on the swing, she crossed to the porch railing and leaned against it, hands on the railings on either side of her. Her lush dark hair was pulled into her favorite French knot and she'd changed from the suit she'd worn earlier to a black knit dress that clung to her curves. The way she was standing thrust out her breasts in the most alluring way.

What a babe, Louis thought, his body warming rapidly. He'd spent the last twenty-some years chasing every bimbo who fluttered her lashes at him. Jeez, it was as if he'd shopped at Kmart when he held the keys to Harrod's in his hands.

"Stacey hasn't been back since we dropped her off hours ago," Joanne said.

"What?" Louis pulled himself back from his dream world. He might be awash in lustful thoughts, but clearly Joanne was her usual pragmatic self.

"The proprietress said she didn't come inside. She happened to be watching out the window," Joanne said with a hint of a smile, "and saw her hop in her car and drive away."

"No doubt she had an assignation with that doctor of hers," Louis said.

"On a Monday afternoon?" Joanne shook her head. "He'd be at work."

"We're not," Louis said.

"But we're out of town."

"Let's not argue, Joanie," he said.

"I am not arguing. I am stating the facts." Then she started to laugh. "You know how many times I've said that in my life?"

He ventured a smile. He'd heard it more times than he could count. "It does sound familiar."

"They must put something in the air up here. Some sort of truth serum," she said musingly.

The front door opened and the rounder of the two ladies popped her head out. "Would you two lovebirds like some sherry?"

He started to ask for a martini with the vermouth bottle waved over the glass, but caught himself. He had a feeling that sherry was as far as the bar went at the Schoolhouse Inn.

"That would be lovely," Joanne said, obviously answering for both of them.

The woman returned so quickly, Louis suspected

she'd had the tray positioned inside the door. Fortunately, she brought out only two glasses. Louis didn't feel like sharing Joanne with any additional company.

"I phoned over to Dr. Mike's house," she said, handing around the drinks, "and learned from his housekeeper that your little girl was there most of the afternoon but they've all gone over to the clinic now."

"My, but aren't you thoughtful," Joanne murmured.

"I know you wouldn't want to be worrying about her," the woman said. "Now I'll just leave you two alone." And with that, she did indeed go back into the inn.

"She must not be feeling well," Louis said.

"Why do you say that?"

"Not as talkative as usual."

"She seemed extremely chatty to me, with all that information about Stacey laid out there like a detective making a report." Joanne made a small face. "How do people live in places like this?"

Louis glanced around him. Birds sang in the trees, squirrels chattered. A fat cat was skulking across the grass toward the flower beds, intent on some prey. An occasional car passed by.

"Rather peacefully, I'd suspect."

"Louis!" Joanne crossed the porch and sat down on the swing, half facing him. "You're not falling for the small-town mystique, are you?"

He shrugged. "I could see getting away from the rat race once in a while."

"One can do that by driving across the lake to Covington," she said, "or hopping the Concorde."

"It reminds me of our island," he said softly, hoping

against hope she wouldn't make him feel like the old fool he just might be turning out to be.

A parade of emotions chased across her face. She cradled the small sherry glass in her hands and gazed down into the liquid. "That was a long time ago, Louie."

He touched her arm, then dropped his hand. He had no right, no reason, to think she'd come back to him, even for an hour, for an evening, and certainly not for the rest of their lifetimes.

At least she didn't get up and go inside. Instead, silent, she sat back against the swing, the side of her body brushing his. She sipped her sherry and Louis felt sure she was waiting for him to say more.

He kept silent. A man didn't take an entire army in one assault. Besides, Joanie never could sit still for long.

Counting off the minutes in his head, he reached three hundred and three when she said, "I did find that old house interesting."

So had Louis, but it was the last thing he was about to admit. "What was so interesting about that ramshackle disaster?"

"It had a sense of history," she said slowly, "and the lines of the roof and porch were charming, not that one could see that too easily with the way they've let the trees overrun the place."

"Mrs. Clark insists she's correct that it's on the National Historic Register but someone stole the plaque."

"If you want to redo an old house," Joanne said, "you can pick almost any block of New Orleans and find yourself a hobby."

"True," he said, "but where's the challenge in that?"

She glanced at him then, her gaze hitting his full-on. "You want to come up here and buy that old wreck, don't you?"

"Nah," he said. "But if our daughter's going to be living here, it might be—"

"What do you mean?"

"She's ga-ga over the guy."

"I told you she hasn't known him long enough to know whether he puts his pants on one leg at a time."

Then he took her hand. "I knew within two minutes of meeting you that you were the one for me."

Surprisingly, she didn't shake him off immediately. She pressed his hand, and then returned it to her lap. "Me, too, Louis, for all the good it did me."

Stacey's car, followed by a pickup truck, pulled into the driveway at that moment.

"Don't be sad, Joanie," Louis said. "We can make things good again."

She shook her head, her expression shuttered. "I think we've found our missing daughter."

Climbing out of her car, Stacey stared at the porch. That couldn't be her mother and father sitting there, apparently still fairly peaceable; if so, it had to be some sort of a record. But then, her mother had shared how much her brush with cancer had changed her attitude toward so many things.

"I'll wait here with the kids," Michael called from the truck.

Stacey nodded, but the next thing she knew, all five of the rug rats bounded from the truck and from her car. To be fair, they were much older and well behaved than the cartoon characters of that name, but she was fairly exhausted from their nonstop energy.

They chased onto the yard and she heard Michael corralling them as she walked toward her parents. She'd stopped to pick up more film from her suitcase on the way to the clinic.

And walked into what she hoped was the prelude to the scene she'd been praying for most of her life.

And then she saw it, the subtle motion of her mother's body language, the merest turning of her shoulder away from her father, and Stacey knew she hadn't witnessed what she had so wanted to see.

"Hey," she said, her own self-generated disappointment so strong she was unable to form any other words.

Her mother rose from the swing. "I assume that would be a greeting?"

Stacey nodded. "I've got to get some film," she said, and walked on into the house.

"I'd say things aren't going too well on the doctor front." Joanne's comment to her father reached Stacey's ears.

For a moment, she felt as if she were Kristen's age again and no matter what she did, her mom or dad would never understand her. Her feelings had nothing to do with Michael; they had everything to do with Joanne and Louis St. Cyr and the pain they inflicted, certainly without meaning to, but nevertheless, it was all too real. Apologies were well and good, but the words did not erase the wounds.

"Grow up," she muttered to herself. She had her own life to live. And it wasn't as if she were alone with that particular cross to bear. So many children and adults lived through the same litany of what-if. She wondered about Kristen and Jessica. They didn't appear to dwell on the possibility, perhaps due to Pauline having re-married Cecil so quickly, but Stacey knew that the de-sire might operate on an unconscious level. Her dad had remarried in less than a year, but then, her first stepmother had been such a bimbette, Stacey had con-tinued to hope against hope.

Stacey paused with her hand on the door of her room, attempting to chase the gloomy thoughts from her mind. Then she heard strong, confident footsteps behind her and knew Michael had followed her inside.

She didn't turn the knob.

He moved behind her and reached his arms around her, cupping one strong hand over her own. His breath warmed her neck. "Allow me?"

Speechless, she nodded.

It was all too much like the night before.

They moved into the room in tandem and before she knew what had happened, Michael had turned her around and swept her into his arms. His hands were on her hair, her back, her derriere. His lips heated her own and she kissed him back, wildly, craving, needing him.

And suddenly he stopped. He didn't push her away, but he lifted his head and said, "I swore I wasn't going to do that." And then he laughed and ruffled her hair. "I guess I could argue temporary insanity."

"That's not very complimentary," Stacey said, sud-denly feeling cold despite being held in his arms.

A rueful look crossed his face. "I've never been too good with words."

And finally she asked the question that had been eating at her. "Is that why you left last night without waking me up?"

He trailed one finger along the line of her chin and down her throat. "To properly answer that question," he said, "would take more time than we have right now."

"But—"

"Shh," he said, cutting off her objections with a swift, hard kiss. "Just know that I didn't want to leave. Now where's that film?"

Frustrated, Stacey dug in her suitcase. Normally she could locate at the drop of a hat any item she packed. Her usual routine was to unload her belongings when she arrived in a hotel room, but somehow she'd never gotten around to doing that here, no doubt because she hadn't intended to stay as long as she had.

She tossed items out onto the bed until she heard Michael chuckling.

"What's so funny?" She turned around, hands on her hips.

"We could have picked up some more film at the market as I suggested, and it would have taken less time, but then I wouldn't have gotten to kiss you."

Stacey put a finger to her lips. "You are the most annoying man," she said.

He gazed toward the bed. She knew what he was thinking and it didn't help that she, too, was picturing them as they'd been last night. Oh, no, she hadn't found him annoying last night. Not at all! Stacey was getting all hot and wet inside just remembering. Her pulse speeded up and she moistened her lips with the tip of her tongue.

"I think," Michael said, in a voice that sounded a little bit as if he were starting to strangle, "I'd better wait on the porch."

He walked swiftly from the room. Stacey, feeling naughty, couldn't help but peek at the front of his jeans. Oh, yeah, he was as hot and bothered as she was.

Without his presence sucking all the air out of the room, she found the film quickly. One good thing about the frustrating Michael Halliday, she reflected, as she locked her room and headed back outside, was that he took her mind off the disappointment of her parents' behavior.

Michael took his time strolling through the inn. He couldn't very well walk out on that porch and face Stacey's parents with his breathing and body out of control.

He never should have followed her inside. Damn, but she got under his skin. It was like some magnetic field, the way he was drawn to her. "Idiot," he muttered, but smiled as he said it. He had to back off and give her time to get comfortable with him. If he remembered correctly, she'd spent six years growing accustomed to her ex-fiancé. Of course, that in itself should have told her she was making a mistake.

Seven days ought to do it.

He paused at the front door. At least Stacey had agreed to stay through Friday night. For that clever plotting, Mrs. Beebe deserved a bonus, or at the very least a most extravagant wedding present. He had a feeling he'd soon be giving her away at her wedding.

Why was it love was such a smooth path for some and so rocky for others? What were seven days when Stacey would soon be back in New Orleans? And as stubborn and afraid of her feelings as she was, Stacey was likely to limit her communication to talk of the shelter project.

Michael stepped outside. The kids were regaling Stacey's mom with tales of their pound poster project. Her dad was examining Kristen's cast.

"Looks like they did a good job on it," he was saying. "That should be coming off very soon, though."

Michael was relieved to hear that. Kristen had insisted she was fine and didn't need to see old Dr. Heller.

"Would you like to sign it?"

"I'd be honored." Dr. St. Cyr retrieved a pen from his shirt pocket and scrawled an unreadable signature on the cast.

"Michael," the older man said, "I was wondering if you and Stacey would like to have dinner tomorrow night with Joanne and me."

Michael was pretty sure by the astonished expression on Joanne's face that this was the first she'd heard of the idea.

"There must be some decent restaurant in town." Her dad returned the pen to his pocket. "It's the least we can do to thank you for taking care of our little Stacey."

Jessica giggled. "She's not little. Stacey's big."

"Who's calling me big?" Stacey moved out onto the porch.

"Your parents were asking us to have dinner tomorrow night," Michael said.

"I thought you guys had to go back first thing tomorrow," Stacey said, trying to catch her parents' attention without resorting to an out-and-out protest.

Her mother smiled. "A little more time away won't hurt."

Her dad clapped his hands together. "Good. Now, where do we make a reservation?"

"Doolittle's one claim to decent dining is the Verandah," Michael said, remembering how he'd wanted to take Stacey there the other night. But as things had turned out, he was glad she'd come to his house instead.

Her mother said, "Louis, aren't you in clinic on Tuesdays?"

"That's what partners are for," he said.

Michael, picking up on some tension between Stacey and her parents, studied them. The kids had abandoned the porch for an impromptu game of tag on the lawn. It would appear that things weren't as they seemed on the surface with the St. Cyrs.

Well, what couple enjoyed a completely smooth ride through life? Maybe that's what Stacey sought, some reassurance that she'd never know any bumps and bruises. But no one avoided them all. He'd have to think of some way to convince her that hitting all the potholes of life couldn't shake him from her side.

"I think we should get to the puppies before the kids' parents come looking for them," Stacey said, interrupting his daydreams with her practical reminder.

He flashed her an appreciative smile, but she didn't return the gesture. "Let's talk about dinner tomorrow," she said to her parents, and then headed for her car.

Michael shook her father's hand and said, "Seven o'clock. I'll make a reservation for a window table."

Her dad clapped him on the shoulder. "I like a man who makes decisions," he said.

"Kindred spirits," Stacey's mother said, and then

added, "I do think it's a nice idea. Will you be able to get a babysitter?"

He nodded.

"And," she said, a hint of fire in her eyes that reminded him of her daughter, "will you be able to persuade Stacey to join us?"

Michael gazed toward the car. The children had followed her out and were obediently climbing back into the vehicles under her instructions. "Ah," he said, "what's life without a challenge?"

Her father looked over at his wife with an adoring expression that reminded Michael of his own parents. He'd gotten the vague impression from Stacey that her parents didn't get along too well, but nothing Michael had seen had argued for that conclusion. "Too damn boring," her dad said, a twinkle in his eye.

Stacey's mother studied him for a long moment, and as she did, her expression softened. "You may be the most stubborn and annoying man I know," she said, "but I have to admit you have never been boring."

"Go on and catch up with Stacey," her dad said. "We've got some talking to do here."

Michael smiled and strode toward his truck. He'd bet talking was the last thing those two were going to be doing. Oh, yeah, it was nice to see a man and a woman still in love after so many years.

Chapter 24

The Verandah did Doolittle proud. Stacey admired the view of the lake from a prime booth beside the floor-to-ceiling windows. Candles flickered on both the indoor tables and the ones scattered around the deck outside. She'd attempted to do justice to the nicely prepared food, but she'd managed to do little more than push her trout almondine around on her plate.

"Well, they wouldn't win a Beard award," her father said, "but it's quite decent. And the bartender makes a remarkably fine martini."

"After the sherry, you'd welcome a poor martini," her mother said, though her smile took the bite off her words.

Her mother sure was more mellow than normal.

Which was just one of the reasons Stacey was so tense.

Michael had been the perfect date, solicitous to her, charming to her parents. The three of them had regaled one another with medical and veterinary war stories. Stacey had listened and smiled as seemed necessary.

She'd spent the day in her room working on some projects she'd brought along, unbeknownst to the vigilant Donna Bell. She'd also done some more work on the material she planned to leave with Kristen to guide her and her classmates on their Talk to the Animals campaign, as they'd decided, after much debate punctuated with many giggles, to name their fund-raiser.

She'd made clear the night before that for purposes of their class grade the four youngsters were responsible for the poster project. She would be retained as a consultant for the dog show and overall campaign. The last thing she wanted was for them to get in trouble at school for too much overeager assistance with their homework.

She'd designed an informational flyer. Anxious to get started, Kristen had pronounced they'd distribute it for the first time at Friday night's spaghetti dinner. As she'd informed Stacey, while stroking the newborn puppies, everyone who was anyone in Doolittle went to that church and they'd show up Friday night, if for nothing else to see what their neighbors were wearing.

The waiter removed their dinner plates. In a low voice, Michael said, "You're awfully quiet, Stacey."

Her dad chimed in. "That's right, princess. That's not like you."

She shook her head. "No, I guess I'm a little tired tonight." Michael hadn't called her all day. She'd almost decided to tell her parents she wasn't going to dinner when he'd sent a message via Miss Martha that he'd pick her up at six forty-five. Talk about bossy! But she'd been sick of her own company by that time and had decided to present herself on the porch at the appointed hour.

The waiter passed around dessert menus. A general discussion arose and saved Stacey further discussion of her temperament. To keep them from commenting, she ordered the first thing on the menu, blueberry cheesecake.

Her mother fixed her with that look that only she could do, the one Stacey had dreaded whenever she'd fallen into the categories of naughty child or errant teen. "If you'd come with us to the lake rather than spending the day holed up in your room working, you'd feel quite refreshed. Your father and I had quite a lovely time."

"What did you do?" Michael asked, looking completely charming and at-ease. Stacey wished she could be the same, but what with her tummy in tumult over whether or not Michael cared about her one way or the other and what in the world was going on with her parents, she just couldn't settle down.

Joanne laughed gaily. "We went water-skiing."

Stacey's jaw dropped. "You did? Daddy, too?"

He grinned, and when he did, Stacey thought he looked ten years younger. "I gave it my best shot. But I think I should stick to golf."

Her mother patted him on the arm. "But you tried. That's the important thing." She dropped her hand in her lap and said, "You know, Stacey, I owe you another apology."

"What for?" She knew she'd ended her sentence in a preposition, but for once she didn't care about her favorite rules. Watching her mother being so un-Joanne-like rattled her.

"For teaching you work matters more than anything else. For showing you a life way out of balance as a role model. Not that your father didn't do the same, but a mother's example to a young girl—well, that's a critical influence."

Stacey wasn't sure she liked the way this conversation was going. It was far too personal, especially in front of Michael, a man for whom she'd told a whopping fib so he wouldn't think she was the crazy workaholic she clearly was. "That's okay, Mom. It isn't as if I don't like my work."

Maybe her mother would drop the topic. A part of her knew her mother was absolutely right, and as a result, she sensed a reaction welling within her she was completely unprepared to handle. She couldn't cope with the emotions breaking through her fragile wall of self-control. Unable to stop herself, Stacey said, "You never needed anything besides your work."

Her mother sighed and shook her head. "I put up a good front," she said. "And I did such a good job that I came to believe it."

Her dad nodded, a sad smile on his face.

The waiter arrived.

Stacey stared at the cheesecake, not bothering to lift her fork. Michael was looking from her to her parents, definitely confused by the exchange. And then Stacey realized she'd never once corrected her stupid story about scouting retirement property for her parents. She'd not told him they were divorced, and based on the friendly way the two of them had been acting toward each other, how could he guess that missing piece of the puzzle?

"We both enjoy our careers," her dad said. "But your mother is right, there's more to life than working."

Her mother leaned across the table and touched Stacey's cheek. "Embrace your life, sweetheart. You don't want to look back years from now and realize you were so busy working you never hiked the Grand Canyon or walked the grounds at Gettysburg or watched the sun rise over Haleakala."

"Have you done those things?" Stacey asked the question in a whisper. She'd never done them as a child. Vacations had always been squeezed between her parents' hectic hospital schedules and, like most other decisions, been hotbeds of dissension between her parents.

"No, but I'm going to," her mother said.

Stacey nodded. She hated to admit it, even to herself, but she was guilty as charged. Rather than face the challenges and discover the joys, she'd retreated from a balanced life. She'd allowed fears of "what if the worst happened" to prevent her from venturing away from the work she buried herself in.

Her dad said, "Joanie, if you ask me along and hike slowly enough so an old guy like me can keep up with you, I'd like to join you when you do tackle the Grand Canyon."

Her mother smiled. "You'll do just fine. And Stacey, you will, too, in anything you decide you want badly enough."

Stacey studied her mother, watching how much sweeter she was acting toward her dad, amazed at the way they were discussing actually doing something as a joint venture. She took a deep breath and said, "Are you two getting back together?"

Her dad looked as interested in the answer as Stacey was. They both looked at Joanne.

Michael, his spoon stalled midway to his mouth, appeared puzzled. Naturally, since he thought Joanne and Louis were married.

"I'm sorry, sweetie," her mother said, "but the answer is no."

"And why not?" That was her dad, as usual unable to restrain himself. "Dammit, I've changed. I've mellowed. We haven't even argued once the whole damn day."

Joanne shook her head.

"Give me one good reason," he said.

Stacey held her breath. Without realizing she did so, she slipped one hand atop Michael's knee.

Her mother gazed out the windows, staring far across the lake, then turned to Stacey's father. She brushed her hand over his and said, "A wise Greek philosopher once said, 'You can't step into the same stream twice.'"

Michael stayed quiet till the two of them were in his truck and headed out of the Verandah's parking lot. Stacey hadn't said a word, but she was clearly laboring under an emotional burden.

"Want to tell me what just happened in there?" He spoke softly, as he would do with an injured animal.

She dashed a hand across her eyes and huddled against the door of the cab. Instead of answering, she shrugged.

He drove, and waited. He was a patient man.

The Verandah, situated on the far shore of Lake Doolittle, sat about five miles out of town. They'd reached the city limits sign when Stacey gave him a brief smile and said, "I'm sorry for being such bad company tonight. I'm feeling confused inside." She took a deep breath and turned sideways in the seat to face him. "I should start by apologizing for telling you what is politely known as a fib."

That statement caught him off guard. "I thought something was going on between you and your parents," he said. "Not us."

And she burst into tears.

Michael stared in shock and, as soon as he was safely able to, pulled the truck to the side of the road. He started to reach for her, then stopped. "What's wrong?"

She was boo-hooing pretty loudly and he wasn't even sure she heard him. So he forgot about caution and restraint and cast off his seat belt and slid over and took her in his arms. "Shh," he whispered. "It's okay. I'm not sure what's wrong, but whatever it is, it can be fixed."

She shook her head, her tears dampening his jacket. "That's not the point," she said, her words muffled against his chest. "It's already fixed, but it's too late."

He had to admit he couldn't follow what she was saying. "Let's take this one step at a time," he said, applying logic to what was fast getting out of hand emotionally.

She cried even harder. Finally, he heard her say, "But it makes no sense."

He nodded. He'd damn sure agree with that.

"It's my parents," Stacey said, "and—and it's you, too. I'm all confused." She started to sit up, but he held her close and when she didn't object, he kept his arms around her.

"Tell me about your parents." He'd rather she calmed down before she advanced to the topic of him and her.

"Okay," she said, the sobs pretty much dissipating. "I lied to you the other night, about looking for retirement property for them." She cast a look up at him, tears sparkling on her lashes, and it was all he could do to keep from kissing them dry. "My parents have been divorced for ages, since I was very young, probably the same age Jessica was when you and your wife separated." Her breath shuddered and Michael almost did the same as he began to process the ramifications of what Stacey hadn't told him before, and was about to share with him.

"They fought constantly. Every decision was a crisis point. I don't know if you noticed, but they are two very strong-willed people."

"Rather like you and me," Michael said slowly.

She nodded. "Anyway, like any child of divorced parents, I dreamed of the day the two of them would get back together. I think it must be hard-wired in the brain, this pathetic need to have things back to the way they were when you felt safe."

"Oh, sweetheart," he said, stroking her back. "There's so much pain in your voice."

"Yeah, well, I learned to get over it," she said, some of her bravado back in her tone. "But damn it, I lived without that dream being realized for so many years and now tonight my mother had the chance to make it happen and she said no." Her voice caught on a sob. "And I can't fairly blame her, because my dad may think he wants her back, but only last week he thought his latest bimbette was the answer to his dreams. And my mother knows how he is."

"So you actually agree with her decision?"

"Yes, but it still upsets me."

She started to cry again, but cut it off abruptly. "Stupid, isn't it?" She almost managed to laugh, but it ended in a hiccup.

"No, it's not stupid at all." He didn't know what to say, but the information filled in a lot of gaps for him concerning Stacey. "No wonder you seemed to understand Kristen and Jessica's situation."

"I've had three stepmothers," Stacey said. Then, far too hastily for Michael's comfort, she added, "Not that I'm thinking of myself in terms of that relationship, but having been through the whole custody tug-of-war, believe me, the last thing I will ever do is torture a child the way I was tormented."

"What makes you think you'd do that?"

"It's the situation," Stacey said, "not necessarily the person."

"I can't agree."

"What do you mean?"

He was shaking his head, adamant now that he realized the conclusion she had drawn. "You're saying that no matter what, I can't live my life with a woman I care about."

"I'm not saying that at all," Stacey said, her voice rising. "I'm saying that I won't put myself in a situation fraught with the kind of pain I went through."

"But your parents caused that, by their poor behavior."

"What's your point?"

"You're not being logical," Michael said. "If Pauline and I behave in a civilized fashion, then any woman who enters my life has a chance of being a fair stepparent to my daughters."

Stacey shifted away from him. "But there's still the question in their minds of whether the two of you will ever get back together again. Another woman in the equation muddies that."

Michael realized he shouldn't react so strongly, but he honestly couldn't help himself. "So you're saying that I should live the rest of my life as a monk?" He grabbed her hand and held it against him. "What about the man inside me? What about my wants and needs? What about me expressing my feelings for the most special woman in the world?"

And damn if she didn't start crying again.

And despite his frustration, he pulled her back against her chest. "Now what is it?"

She sniffled. "Do you really think I'm the most special woman in the world?"

He laughed out loud. "Was that the other thing on your mind?"

She nodded.

"Yes, you nut."

"Man, I need a vacation," she said, and then started laughing, too.

He held her, and kissed her, and then said, "So why did you tell that fib about your parents?"

"Oh," she said, "I was hoping you'd forgotten all about that."

He tapped a finger against the side of his head. "Memory like an elephant."

"It was the middle of the night and there I was alone in a strange town with a really cute doctor and, well, I didn't want to confess I was such a workaholic that my business partner forced me to take a vacation and I had no idea my dog was pregnant."

He smoothed the hair away from her face. "So why drag your parents into it?"

She smiled. "It was the calendar in your office with the picture of Lake Doolittle, retirement haven. Add that to my subconscious, and presto, the fib just rolled off my tongue."

"Well, it would seem that all's well that ends well," Michael said, putting an end to their conversation for a very long moment.

Stacey clung to Michael, feeling safe and drained and happy and excited all at once. But at least she didn't feel scared anymore. When he lifted his lips from hers, she whispered, "At this moment I feel as if I could go water-skiing without being afraid."

"I'm glad," he said. "I think your mother said some very wise things at dinner, lessons I can stand to learn for myself."

"You don't seem like you're afraid of anything," Stacey said, tracing the line of his lips with the tip of her pinky.

He grinned. "Oh, don't be fooled by that macho stuff. I fear plenty of things."

"Like what?"

He pursed his lips. "My kids being hurt, first and foremost."

"That makes sense. We worry about those we love. Only yesterday my mother told Daddy and me she'd had a breast cancer scare and never told us about it."

Michael nodded. "I can see you doing that, carrying everything wrapped up inside you."

"Not me," Stacey said.

He lifted a brow. "Right. You wouldn't even confess to a stranger you were on a forced vacation."

"Oh, well, that's different," she said, trying for an airy sort of attitude in her response.

"Kiss me," he said, "and I'll accept the argument. For the moment."

"Hey, who gave you the final say?" she said, but her words were swallowed up as his tongue claimed hers.

Chapter 25

The community center of the local church had been decorated with red and green balloons and crepe paper. It left something to be desired in terms of high concept, Stacey concluded, but the hearts of the volunteers had been in the right place.

And as someone involved in launching the town's latest charitable effort, she wasn't going to disparage any group's energies. The rather plain setting of the rectangular hall was a far cry from the Audubon Zoo done up for the Zoo To-Do or Gallier Hall decked out for the city's annual Pro Bono Ball, but as far as fund-raisers went in Doolittle, evidently the annual spaghetti dinner was top drawer.

There was a prize, Mrs. Beebe had informed her, for the best pasta dish.

And Mrs. Beebe, not to be outdone by Pauline or the other ladies of her social ilk, intended to win the blue ribbon.

Her secret, she'd confided in Stacey earlier that afternoon when she'd gone to visit with True and hoped to prolong her visit until Michael came home from work, was the meatballs.

Marinara sauce alone didn't cut it with the judges, according to Mrs. Beebe.

Stacey, reared in New Orleans, could believe that.

Michael hadn't come home early and she'd had to depart, very much like True slinking off with her tail between her legs when she hadn't gotten what she'd wanted.

Since the dinner with her parents, he'd been attentive, but hadn't ventured physically beyond kissing her. They'd spent hours together each day, Michael slipping out of the clinic during the afternoon. In the evening she shared dinner and homework with him and the girls. Stacey had even braved another swimming lesson, though her attempt at a dog paddle was pretty much an insult to any self-respecting canine.

But each evening he'd driven her to the Schoolhouse Inn, kissed her good night, and zoomed off.

Great kisses, but only kisses all the same.

Surely, if he'd been serious, he would have made love to her again?

Concluding she was an extremely horny young woman, Stacey had gotten dressed for the spaghetti dinner and been waiting on the porch when Michael arrived with Kristen and Jessica to pick her up. Kristen, brimming with excitement, had made three hundred copies of the flyer Stacey had designed heralding the upcoming Talk to the Animals campaign.

Now, standing by Michael's side, Stacey gazed around. The kids had scooted off immediately, each to find her own circle of friends. Michael smiled indulgently and said to Stacey, "The last thing they want is to be seen with their parents."

When he said it, her heart stood still.

She wasn't their parent.

She wasn't even sure if she qualified as Michael's lover.

The ambiguity was driving her nuts.

Before she could say anything coherent, several people descended on Michael, or rather "Dr. Mike," as they all called him.

Stacey spotted Mrs. Beebe and a stocky man with a shock of red hair approaching. As it had turned out, Mrs. Beebe and her man had decided to meet Michael and Stacey at the church hall. That turn of events had amused Stacey, as it had only confirmed Mrs. Beebe's suspected attempts at matchmaking.

Well, she'd stayed till Friday night.

But tomorrow she was going home.

That thought should have cheered her, but it didn't. She smiled at Mrs. Beebe and her companion. Michael finished his discussion with the cluster who'd gathered around him, shook hands with Sam, and kissed Mrs. Beebe on the cheek.

What a wonderful man he was, Stacey thought, her eyes showing a hint of sentimental dampness. What was wrong with her? Normally she was nothing of a crybaby, but this last week her emotions had been all over the place.

"And it's a-looking fine you are tonight, Stacey," Mrs. Beebe said. "This is Sam." She smiled shyly at the man by her side.

He shook hands with a pleasantly firm grip. "My

Eleanor's told me so many good things about you, I feel as if we've already met."

"My Eleanor," was it? Stacey watched, somewhat enviously, as Mrs. Beebe blushed at the possessive endearment. Michael grinned and said, "And there are many more to tell."

She smiled gratefully at him, then could have kicked herself. What was she doing, constantly seeking signs that he wanted her to stick around Doolittle? Not that she could. Her life was in New Orleans. Everyone knew that. She'd made that clear to him only yesterday, when the two of them had strolled around the courthouse square and he'd pointed out an empty storefront, commenting that it would make a great office for a small company. Stacey was torn from wanting that to be a hint, to wanting him to quit hinting and ask outright. Yet, fearful of what her response would be if he cut to the point, Stacey had responded by rattling on about how much money and effort she and Donna had spent designing the brand-new quarters of St. Cyr & Bell Advertising and Public Relations in New Orleans.

Yeah, she'd made her point. Darn her stubbornness.

Belatedly, she said, "Pleased to meet you, Sam."

"We have some news we'd like to share," Sam said.

She'd have to be blind not to know what he was about to say.

"I've asked Eleanor to be my wife." He beamed.

"Oh, that's wonderful," Stacey said, hugging Mrs. Beebe.

"Well, there's only one problem," she said.

Michael was looking very concerned. Stacey's feelings echoed his expression.

"And that's," Sam said, "she won't give me an answer until she makes sure you'll be okay without her living at your place."

"I would be honored to stay on a-keeping your darling girls for you, and the house as it needs it," Mrs. Beebe said, then she blushed daintily. "But I'd be living with Sam. As his wife, and all."

Michael leaned over and hugged them both. "With my blessing," he said. "I'll figure out some way to cope. I can always find someone else to stay over with the girls when I have to go out on a call at night." And then he winked.

Stacey added her congratulations, all the while wondering if he'd call that pesky Penelope woman to help out. She sighed. What did it matter? She'd be far away, tending to her own troubles.

After all, she was going to be a puppy mother very, very soon. There would be plenty to keep her occupied.

Out of the corner of her eye, Stacey saw Kristen talking to Cecil and Pauline. The girl's face did justice to a storm cloud. Cecil had his arms crossed over his chest and he was shaking his head.

Stacey tapped Michael on the arm and tipped her head in their direction. In one swift glance, he took in the situation and excused them from Sam and Mrs. Beebe.

"Come with me," he said, taking her by the hand.

Warmth stole across her as he walked through the rapidly growing crowd toward Kristen. And despite the impending confrontation, all Stacey could register was how much she wanted to be with Michael.

By his side, holding his hand, sharing his trials, savoring the sweetness of life's good moments. She tightened her clasp and he smiled down at her, tenderness and fire both flashing in his eyes.

"You have to learn to listen to Cecil," Pauline was saying as they approached.

Stacey could feel the bristles rising on Michael's neck as his ex-wife held out her hand to Kristen.

"Now give me those flyers. If Cecil says you're not to pass them out, I agree with him."

Kristen shook her head, the thick stack of papers protected by the cast on her forearm.

"Pauline, Cecil," Michael said. "Good evening."

How he managed to be so calm, Stacey didn't know, because she had a pretty good sense that what he wanted to do was storm up, punch Cecil in his pudgy nose, and snatch the Talk to the Animals flyers safely away.

"Hello, Michael," Pauline said.

Cecil nodded curtly, then perhaps he remembered he was a politician running for state office, because he summoned a smile and extended his hand to both of them.

"So, Kristen, have you been sharing the news of your school project with your mother?" Michael had taken Cecil's hand ever so briefly and Stacey had naturally followed suit. She was the last person to escalate tension between parents, stepparents, and kids.

Kristen's mouth trembled. Still holding Stacey's hand, Michael put his other arm around his daughter's shoulder.

"Cecil's an idiot," she said in a rush.

Pauline glared at her ex-husband. Between clenched teeth, she said to her daughter, "If I have told you once,

I have told you a thousand times not to treat Cecil with disrespect."

"Yeah, well, if he wants my respect, he can try earning it." Kristen matched her mother glare for glare.

Stacey's stomach flipped. She stared down at the floor, a wave of memories flooding her. She wanted to fold Kristen into her arms and comfort her, as well as comfort the child huddled within her self.

"Steady, Kristen," Michael said. "What's the issue here?"

Cecil puffed his chest out. "I was explaining to this young lady that a church supper is not the place to advertise another charitable event. Tonight the people are here to raise money for the church's building fund. We don't want them distracted from this good cause."

Michael glanced around the room. "Didn't we all pay at the door?"

"That's not the point," Pauline said. "There are raffle tickets for sale inside, so the church stands to make additional monies."

"Why do you even go to church if you don't want to help do good?" Kristen stared up at the adults. "These animals can't help themselves the way people can."

Michael simply gazed at Cecil.

And it was Cecil who looked away first.

"I don't see that it will hurt the church's efforts to share in another good work," Michael said. "And furthermore, it might assist you politically to be known as a sponsor of an innovative, kid-driven campaign to build a new animal shelter for the county."

Cecil rubbed his chin. "You really think you can get a lot of support for this?"

"Duh," Kristen said. "The kids in my class don't vote, but their parents do."

Cecil exchanged glances with Pauline. She said, "Most politicians do have a pet. Think of Checkers and Molly and Socks the Cat."

He nodded. "Good point."

Stacey watched as the tiny muscle in Michael's jaw wiggled. She squeezed his hand and he gave her a brief but grateful smile.

"Get behind it enough, Cecil," Michael said, "make it a major point in your own campaign, and the kids might want to talk to you about emceeing the Best of Doolittle Dog Show in September."

Kristen looked a little doubtful, but she kept silent. She was smart enough, Stacey figured, to let her dad work his angles on her stepfather.

"That's less than two months before the election," Pauline said.

"We'll take it under consideration," Cecil added.

"Great." Michael nodded. "See you around."

With that, the three of them moved off. Once out of earshot of Pauline and Cecil, he said, "Lord save me from small-minded people."

Kristen giggled. "I guess that means I don't have to r-e-s-p-e-c-t Cecil."

Michael shook his head. "We'll talk about that later. Go pass out your flyers and have some fun."

Kristen scooted off. At the front of the hall, a four-piece band was tuning up. The PA system shrieked and the rumble of voices in the room had mounted. Michael grabbed Stacey's hand and suggested, "Let's get some fresh air."

He led her across the room, deftly waving at but managing to avoid stopping to talk to Martha and Abbie standing duty behind the punch bowl table. "I hope you're not too thirsty," he said, grinning as he pushed open a side door.

"I'm fine," she said, and meant it.

A small rose garden sat in the center of the side yard. Michael led them toward the single bench alongside the flower bushes. The sun was just slipping beneath the surrounding hills and the sky had turned a pale blue-gray shade. Streaks of vivid pink lashed in lazy bolts across the horizon.

Stacey inhaled the sweet-scented air. "It's beautiful out here," she said, surprised at how peaceful she felt in the setting.

Michael put an arm around her shoulder. "Yes, it is."

She warmed to his touch and to his words. "You're a terrific father."

"Thanks. I do my best, but there are times that . . . what's the expression? Times that try men's souls?" He nestled the side of his head briefly against the top of hers and then straightened.

He cleared his throat.

Stacey held her breath. Was he going to ask her to stay?

"Mrs. Beebe tells me you're picking up True in the morning to head back to New Orleans."

She nodded. Lightly, she said, "Vacation's over."

"I see."

"And I have a lot of work piled up, things I'm sure Donna has saved for my review. Plus some new pitch meetings for clients we're trying to sign." She was babbling.

Again, he said, "I see."

"There's always so much to do," Stacey said.

"Both your mother and your father called me before they left," he said.

She was surprised, but then again, why should she be? The three of them had definitely hit it off. "Oh?"

He stroked the side of her arm in a slow, lazy circle. "They each invited me to visit once school is out in May."

"Shouldn't I be the one to do that?" She blurted out her reaction, then stopped in embarrassment.

Michael only laughed. "I'd love it if you would."

She looked up at him. "I'm kind of confused," she said.

"Don't be." He kissed her, a brief brushing of his mouth against hers, but that tiny contact alone set her blood thrumming. "Go home and think about what you want out of life. Work your butt off making other people successful. Go home alone after a twelve-hour day."

"I'm beginning to feel manipulated," Stacey said, hating his description of what pretty much was her schedule.

He grinned. And then he kissed her as if his life depended on tasting her, delving his tongue into her mouth and drinking her into his being.

Stacey was breathless, clinging to him, matching his insatiable thirst.

Dimly, she was aware of an impatient child's voice repeating, "Hey, you guys, pay attention."

Michael broke away and they both turned toward the door of the church hall. Jessica stood there.

And Stacey couldn't help but notice that Jessica didn't appear upset at all to find her kissing her dad. A boy about her age walked with her as she approached.

"Is it true that you used to train police dogs?" the boy asked.

Michael nodded. "I did that in the Air Force."

"Cool. Jessica says if I adopt one of the puppies she found that you'll teach me all about training my dog and that we'll have the smartest hound in Doolittle."

Stacey could feel Michael suppressing a laugh. "Jessica said that, did she?"

Jessica smiled up at him, all angel. "He'll take good care of it, and that only leaves two other puppies, and I was thinking we could give one to Mrs. Beebe and Sam, and take the other one home. With the mother dog," she added in a rush under her breath.

"We'll see about that," Michael said, herding them all inside.

Walking back inside the church hall, Michael didn't think he could be much prouder of his children than he was at that moment. Jessica had slipped a hand into Stacey's and one into his, and Kristen, along with her four teammates, was walking to the microphone in front of the band.

Her voice strong and confident, she described the Talk to the Animals campaign as her classmates passed out flyers and order forms for the pound puppy posters. She ended with a dramatic buildup to the competition to be held in September for the Best of Doolittle Dog Show.

The crowd applauded, Michael and Stacey more loudly than all the rest.

And then Kristen took the microphone again and said, "One more thing. I'd like to say thanks, Stacey-o."

Stacey gasped. Jessica smiled up at her. Michael

pulled her close and said, "I have to thank you, too. You made this possible."

And darn if Stacey didn't start crying.

So of course he had to kiss her again.

Chapter 26

Stacey stared at the enormous bouquet the Harkins Florist delivery person had deposited on the reception table of St. Cyr & Bell Advertising and Public Relations. That could not be from Michael. Yet her heart skipped as she reached for the card. Face it, she told herself sternly, you want it to be, and that makes you a fool.

"Key Financial, more than likely," she said aloud, and ripped open the card.

"My, my, my," Donna said, walking up on stealthy feet and then circling the floral tribute. "Have we made someone very happy?"

Stacey shrugged. Then her eyes focused on the printed message on the card. "'I promise not to let anyone pull the plug on you,'" she read.

"Now, what does that mean?" Donna buried her face in the blossoms and inhaled. "I love roses," she said, "and jasmine. You've got to admit it, the man has taste."

"What man?" Stacey thrust the card into the pocket of her skirt.

Donna gave her one of her "don't mess with me" looks. "You know, the one with the good sense and intelligence to track me down via Information and discover your office address."

"Oh, all right. These are from Michael."

"Just like last Friday," Donna said. "He has a thing about Fridays, doesn't he?"

"Three weeks in a row does not a pattern make," Stacey said, realizing how weak her statement sounded even as she made it.

"Uh-huh." Donna leaned against the back of one of the reception area couches. "So what are you going to do about this man? Hey, and why Fridays? And what's the reference to pulling the plug?"

"You ask a lot of questions," Stacey said.

"Just doing my job." She smiled as she said it, and Stacey walked over and gave her an impulsive hug. "Thank you for everything," she said, settling on the arm of the couch. "You've been very supportive these last few weeks. I know I haven't been at my best."

"Are you kidding? You knocked yourself out on that Key situation, and then turned right around and landed the MovieCo account. I stand in awe of you."

Stacey shrugged. "It's just work. Work is easy." She gave a shaky laugh. "It's the rest of life that's hard to handle."

"You simply need to practice. If you spent as many man-hours, or I guess I should say woman-hours, on the rest of your life as you do on this agency, you'd be a pro." Her voice softened. "And you'd be a heck of a lot happier."

Stacey sighed. "About your questions—I think Michael sends flowers on Fridays because we met on a Friday."

"Now, that is doggone romantic," Donna said. "Will you please give him Travis's phone number for me?"

Stacey giggled. "It is, isn't it? And the plug, well, that's a reference to a dream I told him about."

"He remembers your dreams?" Donna asked the question in a thoughtful voice.

"Yes," Stacey said, remembering how well he'd interpreted her dolphin dream.

"Then, honey, you ought to get your butt back to Arkansas and hold on tight to this one. He's not Robert. You can't spend the rest of your life judging every man by the one loser you made the mistake of throwing your lot in with."

"It's not about Robert," Stacey said, somewhat defensively.

"Yeah, well, since Drs. Louis and Joanne St. Cyr have buried the hatchet and agreed to be friends, you've kind of lost the excuse of your parents and their miserable relationship, haven't you?" Donna reached out a hand and placed it briefly on Stacey's shoulder. "I'm not trying to give you a hard time, really. But you know I had a lousy childhood. If anyone has a reason not to trust in love, it's me. But if you go through life letting your baggage weigh you down, you'll never live. And you'll certainly never love."

"Oh, Donna, I'm sorry." Stacey clasped her friend's hand. She knew what a terribly rough childhood Donna had endured, bounced from foster home to foster home. Yet she'd been happily married for years and was surrounded by a wonderful family. "I'm really selfish sometimes."

Donna patted her hand. "You're still young," she said. "But if you screw up what you could have with this Michael guy, I'm going to lose faith in you."

"I'll try not to let that happen," Stacey said, hugging her arms around her chest and gazing at the riotous display of blossoms.

Michael drove south toward New Orleans with an expectant heart. Kristen and Jessica were arguing a little less than usual. They each had an inducement to behave. For Jessica, it was the promised treat of a visit to Audubon Zoo and for the intrepid Kristen, an afternoon at Jazzland Amusement Park.

Michael's treat came in the shape of the dark-haired, brown-eyed woman who'd captivated his mind and body when she'd stumbled into Doolittle. She'd been responding to his e-mails, and he could tell she missed both him and his daughters. She asked a lot of questions about them and wrote little about work. And according to the helpful and wonderfully cooperative Donna Bell, with whom Michael had developed a partnership in wooing Stacey, she knew her mind.

She just hadn't admitted to it.

It was in a buoyant mood he drove toward the city that sprawled at the end of the delta. There was so much he wanted to share with Stacey. Some of it he'd put in e-mail, but he wanted to sit beside her and watch her expressive face as he described the progress Kristen had made via her class project on the puppy posters. He wanted to share the news that Cecil Gardner had agreed to appear as master of ceremonies at the Best of Doolittle Dog Show. With Cecil's support, as much as Michael hated to acknowledge it, the show was destined to be a financial and social success.

" 'New Orleans corporate limit,' " Jessica read, pointing to a green road sign. "Why does it say that? Isn't it a city?"

"I'm not sure," Michael said.

"You can ask Stacey-o," Kristen said. "She's pretty smart."

Michael smiled. The consulting relationship Stacey had built with Kristen and Jessica had eased them into contact with her in a way that no cycle of carefully constructed dating and family interaction could have accomplished. Stacey was their hero.

And Stacey was his heroine.

After a few wrong turns, Michael located their hotel on St. Charles Avenue, got them checked in, spent time swimming, and managed to have them all showered and changed in time to present themselves at Stacey's door at the appointed dinner hour.

He hoped she hadn't gone to too much trouble over the meal.

He was too nervous to do justice to even the most tempting of cuisine.

"Steady," Stacey said, talking to herself as she surveyed the mess she'd made in her kitchen. Normally she was a fastidious cook. She prepared food as competently as she performed most other tasks.

But today she'd been all thumbs.

She grabbed a dishcloth and dabbed at the coating of flour that still powdered her appliances. An hour ago, she'd been lifting the flour canister when the phone rang. She'd dropped the whole shebang on the floor.

She shouldn't be so nervous. She was having a few people over for dinner. No big deal.

Stacey shook her head. "Yeah, right," she said. "It's only Michael, Kristen, and Jessica." Plus Donna and her husband Travis and their brood of kids. But they weren't the ones making her anxious.

And giddy with anticipation.

The first week he'd sent flowers, the only message on the card was his e-mail address.

Had she ignored it, she'd not be making dinner on a bright May evening. No, she'd probably still be at the office, futzing over one account or another.

But Stacey had responded, sending a politely worded message of appreciation for the flowers.

And then, admitting reluctantly how much she missed him, she haunted her e-mail service, awaiting his reply.

In one weekend, she must have logged on a couple of dozen times. She fretted she'd been too restrained, too distant. She worried that something had happened to him.

Finally, Monday came and she went back to work, determined not to look one more time for a message that wasn't coming.

And of course, on Monday night, he'd written, including a photo of Kristen and Jessica with the rescued mother dog and puppies, along with an update on the Talk to the Animals campaign.

Thus began their electronic, long-distance dance of courtship.

There was a certain freedom to the exchanges that Stacey found exhilarating. She was by profession a creative writer; she took to composing long passages, sharing news of her projects, funny characters she met during the day, even venturing into dreams and hopes and fears.

Michael was the opposite. He didn't chat. He did pose questions she relished answering, though.

Stacey smiled despite the pile of dishes in her sink. Sometimes his messages were as simple as, "What did you have for breakfast?" Once he wrote, "Where were you the day Elvis died?"

She'd learned how old he was when he learned to ride without training wheels, when he'd "lost" his virginity, and that he'd been named "Most likely to join the Peace Corps" in his senior year of high school. Funny, because he'd gone into the Air Force instead.

She looked forward to his messages more than any other event of her day. Soon she came to feel that a day without an e-mail from Michael was like a day without sunshine.

And then he'd written with the date he would be bringing the girls to New Orleans.

Stacey had panicked. Conversation by electronic long distance was safe. It was intimacy without vulnerability.

Michael in person set off alarms she didn't know how to answer.

Donna, bless her heart, had taken Stacey to task and then wisely said, "Invite him to dinner. Us, too. There's safety in numbers. If it gets awkward, kick me under the table and I'll spill some wine and cause a distraction." Stacey laughed and agreed.

So here she was, a smudge of flour on her nose, an apron tucked around a brand-new deep coral body-hugging cotton jersey dress that skimmed her legs a few inches above her knees.

She could have made a New Orleans–style dinner, but she wanted everyone to feel at home. And of course she realized she was duplicating their first dinner together. She had coleslaw in the refrigerator and chicken roasting in the oven. Earlier she'd called Mrs. Beebe for directions on how to produce her mouthwatering biscuits. They were baking alongside the chicken now.

The housekeeper had been only too happy to share her recipe.

She was surrounded by matchmakers, Stacey reflected. Even her parents asked frequently about Michael. It was just one of the interests they'd finally discovered they had in common.

True padded into the kitchen, waddling as she'd been doing recently. She sat down, obviously trying to get comfortable. The paunch of her pregnancy seemed to be causing her more discomfort than usual. Stacey frowned, wondering if she'd been so busy getting ready for Michael's visit that she'd missed some important cues as to True's readiness to deliver.

Then True yawned and shook her head and bent her attention to her food bowl, and Stacey decided she was worrying too much. Her vet had estimated the pups to be near birth the coming week and Stacey had prepared a birthing bed for her beardie in her spare bedroom.

The doorbell rang. At least this time she didn't drop the crystal platter she'd dragged out from her cupboard.

She whipped the apron off and headed from the back where the kitchen was to the front of her shotgun house. The bell rang again as she neared the front door and to her mixed relief and disappointment, she recognized Donna's voice.

"Silly goose," Stacey said aloud. She was more anxious to see Michael again than she cared to admit—even to herself.

And to the romance-minded Donna, she'd confess it not at all.

She was ushering Donna and Travis and their kids onto the porch when Michael pulled up. She didn't recognize the car, a new Buick. She'd been picturing the pickup truck, even though he'd mentioned in a message he'd bought a car and planned to use the truck for clinic-related needs.

Then he climbed out and stood, stretching his arms over his head and then turning around to open the back door.

She paused in the middle of greeting her friends.

"I guess that's Michael," Donna said, dry humor in her tone. "He looks just like the hunk you described him as."

Her husband patted his protruding belly and said with a smile, "He's no more of a cover model than I am." And then, tactful soul that he was, he led his wife and children into the house and left Stacey alone to greet Michael.

He walked toward her, Jessica and Kristen by his side, and Stacey caught her breath. She wanted to run to him; she wanted to stand right where she was outside her door and savor the sight of him striding toward her. Shifting from foot to foot, she watched as he broke into a wide smile, and her anxiety melted in the warmth of his expression.

She stepped forward on the porch.

As she did, she realized she still clutched her apron in one hand.

"Stacey-o," Kristen cried, bounding up the stairs, "look, I've got my cast off."

"So I see," Stacey said. "Nice repair job."

Kristen grinned. "Where's True?"

Stacey pointed her thumb toward the front door and Kristen, never bashful, said, "I'll find my own way."

Jessica came up the stairs next, in front of her dad. With those wide, dark eyes of hers, she regarded Stacey. Stacey returned the look steadily. Then Jessica said, "What's a corporate limit?"

Michael patted her on the shoulder. "I'm sure we can look that up later."

"You said Stacey would know."

Stacey glanced from daughter to father. Somewhere in this discussion she sensed a test. Well, she didn't always have to be right about things. She'd make mistakes, that was a truth she'd come to grips with over the past several weeks.

But she was willing to do her best.

Even in small things.

"A corporate limit," she said, "is the same thing as a

city limit. In Louisiana a county is called a parish and a city is called a corporation." She hoped that was halfway accurate. She'd have to check her answer later.

"Oh," Jessica said, wrinkling her nose. Then, turning to her dad, she gave him a light punch on the thigh. "Stacey's pretty smart."

"Hey, who are you?" Donna's son Petey had stuck his head out of the front door and was gazing at Jessica with the wide-eyed interest of a child who hadn't yet learned to despise or fear the opposite sex. With four sisters, he was pretty much used to girls.

"Jessica," she said, studying him. "Do you know what a corporate limit is?"

"Nah," he said, "but want to hear the noises I can make with my mouth?"

"Cool," Jessica said, following him into the house after a swift glance toward her dad for permission.

And then the two of them were left alone on her porch. A truck rumbled by, followed by a child on a skateboard.

A bird whistled and a squirrel chattered back.

Stacey gazed at Michael, very much aware that her heart was in her throat.

"Hey," he said, holding out his arms. "Come here."

Stacey told her feet to move, but they were locked on the floorboards of the porch. She opened her mouth, but no words came out. She reached one finger toward her hair and twisted a strand as she stood there looking at the man she'd been longing to see ever since she'd loaded True in her car and left Doolittle almost six weeks ago.

"Stacey, everything's going to be okay," he said, and in one swift move wrapped her in his arms.

She clung to him then, her arms easing around his back. He didn't kiss her, only held her tight and close and warm.

She inhaled the scent of him, feeling foolish for not moving into his arms when he'd opened them to her. Slowly, she pulled back an inch or two, looked up at him, and said, "It's good to see you."

He smiled and said, "More than good."

Jessica bounded onto the porch, Petey shadowing her. "True is going into labor," she said.

Stacey whipped around. To her pleased surprise, Michael kept one arm wrapped around her waist. Jessica didn't even blink. "Her water broke on the kitchen floor."

Petey made a gagging sound. "I think I'll go play Nintendo," he said.

"What's the matter, aren't you tough enough to watch a simple delivery?" Jessica stood with her hands on her hips and Stacey stifled a laugh.

He shrugged. "I've never seen a dog have pups before. I guess it might be interesting."

"Maybe I should take a look," Michael said.

"My biscuits!" Stacey clapped a hand to her mouth. "I forgot all about them!"

She rushed into the house, relieved to find Donna had not only saved the biscuits from burning, but had located the drinks and appetizers and made herself and the others at home. Good friends were the best kind to have, she thought, scurrying to join the others where she'd told them they'd probably find True, in the spare room.

Her precious beardie was lying on her side in the birthing box, panting heavily. Jessica knelt beside the box, explaining in an authoritative voice to Petey the process of a dog giving birth. "If too much time passes between pups," she was saying, "that's not a good sign. If it's more than forty-five minutes, she might need a C-section."

"What's that?" Petey said, glancing over his handheld video game toward the box. Evidently he'd decided he could do two things at once.

Jessica made a scornful face. "Where do you go to school? That stands for caesarian section. It means the doctor has to deliver the babies surgically."

Michael put an arm around Stacey. She glanced at him and smiled. He stroked her arm. "You look even prettier than I remembered."

She blushed. "So do you. Well, I don't mean pretty, but handsome—" she broke off, somewhat breathlessly. "I'm never this silly," she said.

He nodded. "I believe you. And I take that as a compliment."

She smiled. "E-mail is useful, but it only goes so far."

He hugged her close. To Jessica, he said, "How are the contractions?"

The child studied the dog and then said, "Even. Soon, I think."

"We may have to have cold biscuits," Michael said, letting go of Stacey and hunkering down beside True. "But that's life with a vet."

Stacey hugged her arms to her chest. Life with a vet. Could she go through with it? She'd promised herself she wouldn't run away this time. She just hoped she could live up to that vow.

Michael didn't want to let go of Stacey. Since the moment he'd parked at the curb in front of her house and spotted her in the doorway, his heart had been beating double-time. But his training took over and he reluctantly eased his arm from around her waist and stepped over to observe the bearded collie's condition.

As he gently examined the dog, he felt Stacey move close behind him. This time apart had been good for them, he reflected. And sending her his e-mail address had been a stroke of genius. He'd like to think he was responsible, but Kristen was the one who'd mentioned she'd been getting advice and guidance on the Talk to the Animals project via e-mail from Stacey.

"Good True," Stacey murmured, her soft fingertips on the back of Michael's neck above the collar of his shirt. They felt cool and warm all at the same time.

True shuddered and stirred against the lining of her bed and then lifted one leg and arced it outward. She whimpered and Michael soothed her with his voice. At this stage there wasn't much to do. As long as nature and the instincts of the dog functioned, a doctor wasn't needed. But he'd stand by just in case.

"Did you ever have an ultrasound?"

"No," Stacey said. "Should I have done that?"

"It's not necessary, but it would have given you an indication of how many pups she's going to whelp."

"I think four," Jessica said.

"How can you know that?" Petey looked up from his game.

She gave him a very superior smile. "Wait and see."

Michael said to the youngster, "It's a safe guess, given average litter size."

"Dad," Jessica said, "don't give away my secrets."

Donna and Travis entered the room bearing a tray and glasses. "We're bringing the party in here," Donna said, handing out glasses of wine.

"True's having her babies," Petey informed his parents. "And I'm helping."

"Not exactly," Jessica said, giggling.

He shrugged. "Helping more than my goofy sisters. You don't see them in here, do you?"

"Where are they?" Stacey asked. And where was Kristen?

"They're outside playing soccer," Donna said. "Let them run off some excess energy."

Petey made a face. "Soccer is for girls. I like baseball."

"I hate baseball," Jessica said. "It's boring."

The boy rolled his eyes.

Michael smiled. Those two reminded him of Stacey's father and mother.

True whimpered and heaved. Stacey knelt beside Michael and clutched his hand. He took it in his and said, "She's okay."

Stacey was watching with a fascinated expression, then she said, "Do you think she minds us in here?"

"Well, she might be happier with a calmer environment," Michael said.

"I can take a hint," Donna said. "But you're not getting away from here tonight till I get to know all about you."

He grinned at her, acknowledging her as a stalwart ally in his pursuit of Stacey. "You got it," he said, then turned to True as she began pushing out the first pup.

After that, his attention was focused on the dog as

she quickly delivered that one and three more puppies. Jessica, assisting, reminded Petey of her prediction. He stopped playing his video game long enough to inform her it was too bad she hadn't thought to bet on the outcome.

She stuck her tongue out and then pulled out the worst of the soiled cloths. Stacey took them from her and disappeared, and then returned, followed by Kristen and four other girls.

They oohed and ahhed over the puppies and the exhausted but proud True leaned back in the box, showing off the glistening offspring already licked clean by her and now nursing on her teats.

Michael rose at last and guided Stacey and the kids from the room. "Let's let her rest," he said. He'd delivered dozens of puppies, not to mention calves and foals and kittens, but somehow sharing the experience with Stacey had made this even more special.

She'd whispered sweet nothings to her pet all through the process, at the same time clinging to Michael's arm.

Her touch had been driving him crazy. What he was going to do, he had no idea, because he knew that after dinner he had to leave with the girls and spend the night back at the hotel. Knowing Stacey was here in the same city and not being able to make love to her was driving him nuts.

That was the first reason he decided Donna was the best friend anyone could ever have. They'd just finished dessert when he heard her call Petey and the older of the other girls over and whisper something to them.

A short moment later, Petey looked around the dining table and said, "Hey, why don't Jessica and Kristen come spend the night with us?" He looked straight at his mom and she gave him a pleased nod.

Michael could have kissed her.

Donna's second gold star came when she said, with only a gentle thump against her husband's leg under the table, "We'd be happy to take Kristen and Jessica with us all day tomorrow. We're going to Jazzland."

"You are?" Kristen's face lit up. "Dad said I could go, but he hates those rides."

"You're too good," Michael said to Donna, watching as a flurry of emotions crossed Stacey's face.

He could tell she was pleased to be left alone with him—but also frightened.

He wanted to ease her fears. Time, he realized, would chase them away. Time and the joy of being together.

"So would you like that?" he said to his kids, holding his breath. You never could tell. They could be getting along famously and then decide they'd had enough of the company they found themselves in, especially Kristen.

"Do you have MTV?"

The oldest girl nodded. "Of course," she said.

"Okay," Kristen said. "But you and Stacey-o have to behave yourselves." And then she winked at him.

Stacey looked horrified. Michael only shook his head. Kristen was twelve going on thirteen going on twenty-one right now. The kids didn't live in a societal vacuum, and they certainly knew how animals were conceived.

"Maybe we can go on-line," Jessica said, "and figure

out why they have corporations in Louisiana."

Michael grinned at his younger daughter. "I think you're going to go into research," he said.

She shrugged. "As long as it's with animals, that's okay by me."

Donna and Travis offered to help with the cleanup, but to his relief, Stacey thanked them and said, "Certainly not. You all have done more than enough."

Taking his girls overnight did qualify as a major contribution to the evening, Michael concurred. He'd spoken with Donna over the phone several times. He liked both her and her husband and Stacey had known them both for years. Normally he'd be a lot more hesitant to let Kristen and Jessica go off for a sleepover, especially in a strange city, but in this situation, he had nothing to fret over.

Just in case of any untoward emergency, he gave Donna his cell phone number. She took it, gave him a quick peck on the cheek, and whispered, "Don't worry, we won't call."

And at last the two of them were alone again.

Chapter 27

"Gosh," Stacey said, "we'd better straighten up the kitchen."

Michael studied her, then gave a slow nod. They headed to the back of the house, Stacey incredibly aware of his shoulder brushing hers, of his scent, his warmth. She wished she could retract her words, turn and lock her arms around his.

But she was unaccountably tense. The evening had been wonderful. Stacey opened the dishwasher and began piling plates and glasses into it. Inside her head she chattered, but none of the words sounded right so she said nothing.

Finally, when he kept silent, also, and she couldn't stand it anymore, she turned from the dishwasher. He was leaning against the refrigerator, his arms crossed across his chest, a dishcloth in one hand. Then he tossed the cloth on the counter and said, "Stacey, come here."

And this time she didn't freeze. She flung herself

against him, threw her arms around his neck, and offered her mouth for his kiss.

His lips moved tenderly against hers. He stroked her back and whispered, "It's okay. It's me, Michael. You don't have to worry. I'll even leave if you tell me that's what you want."

She squeezed him tight. "Don't you dare."

"Ever?"

She stood stock-still. Had she heard him correctly? Tilting her face and gazing into his eyes, she started to ask him what he meant. And the words caught in her throat.

He was wearing his heart in his eyes.

"Stacey," Michael said, "I want you to marry me."

She said nothing.

"I know I'm supposed to have a ring and a romantic setting and get down on my knees and make a speech, but"—he pointed around the messy kitchen—"I can't think of a more perfect day and time and place."

She wasn't sure she was still breathing.

"I don't know how long it's supposed to take to know someone is the right—no, the perfect—person to spend the rest of your life with." He lifted one hand from her back and brushed a whisper of hair from her cheek. "But I know you're it for me."

Stacey willed her voice to work. "The rest of your life?" Those words should cause her to panic, but somehow they sounded reassuring as they tripped off her tongue.

"I know that concept makes you nervous," he said softly, "but it's like anything, Stacey. We'll take it a day at a time." His voice deepened. "One beautiful, joyous day at a time."

Say yes, her brain screamed. Say you'll take the risk. Her lips moved.

"There may be pain," he said. "Life always metes out its bumps and bruises. Relationships remind me of Kristen not wanting to work in the clinic because she can't stand the sad things that happen to the animals. But for every sad thing that takes place, there are five, six, seven beautiful moments."

Stacy nodded. "And I would be a fool to miss out on the good things because I'm afraid there might be pain lurking around some corner, wouldn't I?"

He kissed her, not quite so gently this time. "You would indeed," he said. "How about I remind you of what you'd be missing and then you can answer the question?"

She curled her fingers around the opening of his shirt and gazed into his loving eyes. "I'd love that reminder," she said, "but you don't have to wait for my answer."

Michael held his breath. She couldn't say no. Could she? He tightened his hold around her waist, wanting to pull her close and kiss her senseless, literally cutting off any objections she might have. "Stacey?"

"Yes, I'll marry you," she said. And then she broke into the biggest smile he'd ever seen on her sweet face. "Gosh, that felt great to say!"

Laughing with relief, he hugged her. He kissed her, and groaned as she deepened the kiss, delving her tongue into this mouth and sending blood pulsing through his body, heating his desire to a fever pitch.

"Michael, wait." Her voice had turned very, very serious.

He could have sworn his heart stopped beating. "You didn't change your mind, did you?"

"No, but we're not being very practical here."

He didn't let go of her. If he did, she might let whatever was bothering her grow and fill the space between them.

"Are we going to have one of those ultra-modern long-distance relationships?"

"Forget that," Michael said. "But I see your point. Well, you know I'm no traditionalist. I'm the one who followed Pauline from Boston to Doolittle. I can't assume you'll drop your life here and head to Doolittle."

"You can't?"

If he wasn't mistaken, she sounded slightly disappointed. Not one to miss an opportunity, and knowing Stacey well enough to know she hated to be told what to do, he said, "We can have a commuter marriage. See each other, say, once a month."

"No way."

"Yes way."

"Are you nuts?" She was clinging to his belt, frustration simmering in her gorgeous dark eyes.

"Do you want to move to Doolittle?"

"I thought you'd never ask me," she said. "As long as it's okay with Donna, I can still carry a lot of the same consulting duties from there."

"I think Donna will be so happy for you she'll insist on it." He kissed the tip of her nose. "See how easy it is for two strong-minded people to work things out?"

She smiled and said, "Especially when the reward is so special."

He cupped her derriere and pulled her up against

him. "Now that we have that settled, let's celebrate," he said.

She smiled and nodded, and before he realized what she was doing, she had his pants unzipped and her warm, devilishly clever hands cradling his arousal. He pushed against her and took her mouth with his. "I'm gonna love being married to you," he said.

Her hands stopped their sweet stroking. "Michael, we didn't . . ."

"Didn't what?" With her hands wrapped around him, he couldn't think. Was she referring to protection? Of course he had that, safely tucked in his back pocket. He slipped one hand around her breast. The nipple puckered through the clingy fabric when he brushed his thumb over it.

"We didn't say . . ."

"Whatever it was we didn't say," Michael said, "don't stop doing what you're doing."

Stacey sighed, and he realized he'd made a mistake.

A big one.

He placed a hand gently on the side of her cheek. "Sweetheart, what is it?"

"We just agreed to get married and we haven't even told each other the . . ." She trailed off.

Michael eased her hands from his pants, zipped them, and bent and cradled Stacey in his arms. What a goofus he was when it came to romance. He'd handled this all wrong. He should have gone the ring, proposal, flowers, champagne route. But more importantly, like an idiot, he hadn't told her he loved her. The words themselves didn't matter one bit to him, but he had to remember, always, that his was only one-half of the perspective.

He carried her to the sofa, sat down, and, holding her on his lap, smiled into her eyes. She was watching him, wide-eyed, expectant, her lips rosy from their kisses.

"You mean the *L*-word, don't you?"

She nodded.

"It's scary for you to say it, isn't it?" Michael tucked one of her fingers around a long strand of her hair and she laughed.

"There, that's better," he said. "Yes, I love you. And what does that mean?" He held up one hand and ticked off on his fingers. "That I understand your fears of commitment. That I want you not only to be my wife, but my best friend and lover. That I trust and respect you. And I think you're tough enough, loving enough, and smart enough to take on the challenging job of being stepmom to my daughters." He paused when he reached his thumb. "And you're the sexiest, most desirable woman in the world."

When Michael finished his recitation, Stacey brushed a hand across her eyes. She'd never heard a more precious description of love. "Thank you," she said. She wanted so badly to say the same words to him, but they made her anxious all over again.

He must have sensed that, because he pulled her close and said, "Stacey, listen to your heart. Forget about your mind. Words aren't the only way to show me what you're feeling."

"How did I get so lucky?" But the words were muffled as Stacey kissed his throat, then popped the buttons open and kissed her way down the hard plane of his chest.

This time, when she unzipped his pants, she tugged them down and off. He opened his arms and she sat on his chest, her dress pushing up to reveal the naughty panties and lacy thigh-high stockings she'd donned, hoping for this moment of reunion.

"Nice," Michael said, flicking a finger across the skin above the tops of the stockings. "Very nice."

Stacey smiled and slipped her dress over her head. She didn't need words right now. She knew she'd find them in time, in her own way. But now she wanted to share her body with the man gazing up at her, his desire for her hard and hot and pressing against her thighs.

She lifted off him enough to scoop off his briefs. He kicked them free and tugged her down against him, his mouth seeking hers. She returned the kiss, but she had other ideas.

Wiggling down his body, she kissed his arousal, lightly at first, and then, as a greediness overtook her, she slipped her mouth wide around him and tasted the length of him. He moaned and ran his hands through her hair.

Stacey loved the way he pushed against her, the incredible combination of the softest skin in the hardest mold. Silk and steel. She took him deeper and felt the heat and need driving her onward. Michael slipped a hand between her thighs and she thrilled to the excitement pleasing him set off inside her own body.

She added a hand along with her mouth and he gasped. She smiled and lifted her eyes to his face. He had his head thrown back against the pillows of the couch, a look of indescribable ecstasy etched on his face.

Oh, yes, she loved this man, and she loved pleasuring him.

Just then, he put his hands on her shoulders and said in a tortured voice, "Come here."

Reluctantly, she lifted her mouth from his hot shaft and slid her body lengthwise against his. "You taste so good," she murmured.

"How did I ever get so lucky?" Michael smiled, and then, as she assumed he was going to enter her, he scooted her up and over his chest and positioned her thighs around his face.

"What are you . . ." Stacey didn't finish her sentence. He was tasting, he was teasing, he was driving into her with his tongue, one hand thrusting aside her panties, not even bothering to strip them from her body. She rocked over him, poised on her feet, struggling to catch her breath as he stroked her inner lips with his tongue. He gazed up at her, adoration and mischief all mixed into one hot glance.

She threw her head back and gave herself up to the sensations he was calling from deep within her. Heat flowed into a throbbing, wanton wave of pleasure. She was on edge, she was going to explode. He paused and she clutched his head. "Don't stop," she said.

He grinned and sucked her explosion into his mouth.

Stacey fell onto his chest, gasping. He rolled her over, grabbed for the condom, yanked it on, and dove into her. His thrusts were wild and primitive. She answered them with her own incredible need, whispering crazy lovemaking words with a voice she didn't even recognize as her own, and as he built another crashing wave of passion within her, she clung to him and rode his own release with him.

And only when they were still at last, sated, exhausted, tangled in one another's arms, did she realize she'd been saying, "I love you," over and over again.

So Stacey said it again, tasting the words on her tongue. "I love you, Michael."

He smiled and held her tight. "And I love a happy ending," he whispered.

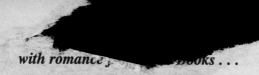
with romance ſ... ...Books . . .

ONE NIGHT OF PASSION by Elizabeth Boyle
An Avon Romantic Treasure
Georgiana Escott attends London's notorious Cyprian's Ball, determined to find the perfect man to ruin her. She feels like a princess, looks like a siren . . . and tumbles into the arms of disgraced, yet dashing, Lord Danvers. Could this one night of passion turn into a blissful future?

MAN AT WORK by Elaine Fox
An Avon Contemporary Romance
Lady lawyer Marcy Paglinowski rescues a terrified puppy—and in the process is swept off her feet by Truman Fleming. He's a working man, who's got biceps and triceps galore, and is so wonderfully different from the stuffed shirts she's used to. But Marcy wants security, and Truman's not the man to give it to her . . . or is he?

LONE ARROW'S PRIDE by Karen Kay
An Avon Romance
Be swept back to the thrilling American West in Karen Kay's newest Avon Romance. Carolyn White was a child in danger when a young Crow Indian rescued her. Now, years later, she and Lone Arrow are together again, and though their cultures collide there is one thing that both share—passion for the other.

A GAME OF SCANDAL by Kathryn Smith
An Avon Romance
Lady Lilith Mallory is the most scandalous woman in London, but that doesn't stop the gentlemen of the *ton* from drinking her wine and gambling at her tables. Then, suddenly and shockingly Gabriel Warren, the Earl of Angelwood, comes back into her life. He had once broken his vow to make her his bride . . . and destroyed her reputation. Now, however, the tables are turned . . .

REL 0602